*Dr. Kay Scarpetta returns in a terrifying novel
that demonstrates once more why
Patricia Cornwell has few peers . . .*

Scarpetta, now freelancing with the National Forensic
Academy in Florida, digs into a case more bizarre than any
she has ever faced, one that has produced not only unusual
physical evidence, but also tantalizing clues about the inner
workings of an extremely cunning and criminal mind.

She and her team—Pete Marino, Benton Wesley, and her
niece, Lucy—track the odd connections between several
horrific crimes and the people who are the likely suspects.
As one psychopath, safely behind bars and the subject of a
classified scientific study at a Harvard-affiliated psychiatric hospital, teases Scarpetta with tips that could be
fact—or fantasy—the number of killers on the loose seems
to multiply. Are these events related or merely random?
And what can the study of one man's brain tell them about
the methods of a psychopath still lurking in the shadows?

Praise for the novels of Patricia Cornwell

Trace

"Dr. Kay Scarpetta . . . is back with a vengeance."
—*The New York Times Book Review*

"Cornwell gets her Hitchcock on . . . [She] can generate
willies with subtle poetic turns." —*People*

"Fun [and] flamboyant." —*Entertainment Weekly*

continued . . .

"*Trace* is rich and satisfying, with Cornwell sprinkling a trail of tantalizing bread crumbs for the Scarpetta faithful, who are always hungry for the next installment."
—The Associated Press

"Cornwell's latest is hard to put down . . . *Trace* is solid and tightly paced, which should appeal to her legions of fans." —*BookPage*

"Will cheer fans . . . the old Scarpetta comes through."
—*Publishers Weekly*

"The mystery is intriguing, there's plenty of forensic detail, and the ending . . . opens the way for Scarpetta and her associates to proceed in any direction that calls to them."
—*Booklist*

Blow Fly

"[A] grisly fast-paced thriller . . . utterly chilling."
—*Entertainment Weekly*

"Patricia Cornwell is on target—and spectacularly so—with her latest Kay Scarpetta thriller, a story so compelling that even longtime readers will be stunned by its twists and turns." —*Chicago Tribune*

"Gruesome and suspenseful." —*New York Daily News*

The Last Precinct

"Ignites on the first page . . . Cornwell has created a character so real, so compelling, so driven that this reader has to remind herself regularly that Scarpetta is just a product of an author's imagination."
—*USA Today*

"Plots within plots, fraught atmosphere and unrelenting suspense keep readers on tenterhooks while one trap after another springs under unwary feet. Cunningly designed, ingeniously laid out, composed with Cornwellian skill, this far-from-the-*Last Precinct* is a model of the art."
—*Los Angeles Times*

"The most unexpected of the Kay Scarpetta novels so far . . . Compelling . . . Terrific."
—*The Miami Herald*

Black Notice

"Brainteasing . . . one of the most savage killers of her career . . . [a] hair-raising tale with a French twist."—*People*

"The author's darkest and perhaps best . . . a fast-paced, first-rate thriller."
—*The San Francisco Examiner*

Point of Origin

"Cornwell lights a fire under familiar characters—and sparks her hottest adventure in years."
—*People*

"Packed with action and suspense."
—*Rocky Mountain News*

Titles by Patricia Cornwell

PREDATOR

PATRICIA CORNWELL

BERKLEY BOOKS, NEW YORK

THE BERKLEY PUBLISHING GROUP
Published by the Penguin Group
Penguin Group (USA) Inc.
375 Hudson Street, New York, New York 10014, USA

Penguin Group (Canada), 90 Eglinton Avenue East, Suite 700, Toronto, Ontario M4P 2Y3, Canada
(a division of Pearson Penguin Canada Inc.)
Penguin Books Ltd., 80 Strand, London WC2R 0RL, England
Penguin Group Ireland, 25 St. Stephen's Green, Dublin 2, Ireland (a division of Penguin Books Ltd.)
Penguin Group (Australia), 250 Camberwell Road, Camberwell, Victoria 3124, Australia
(a division of Pearson Australia Group Pty. Ltd.)
Penguin Books India Pvt. Ltd., 11 Community Centre, Panchsheel Park, New Delhi—110 017, India
Penguin Group (NZ), Cnr. Airborne and Rosedale Roads, Albany, Auckland 1310, New Zealand
(a division of Pearson New Zealand Ltd.)
Penguin Books (South Africa) (Pty.) Ltd., 24 Sturdee Avenue, Rosebank, Johannesburg 2196,
South Africa

Penguin Books Ltd., Registered Offices: 80 Strand, London WC2R 0RL, England

This is a work of fiction. Names, characters, places, and incidents either are the product of the author's imagination or are used fictitiously, and any resemblance to actual persons, living or dead, business establishments, events, or locales is entirely coincidental. The publisher does not have any control over and does not assume any responsibility for author or third-party websites or their content.

PREDATOR

A Berkley Book / published by arrangement with Cornwell Enterprises, Inc.

PRINTING HISTORY
G. P. Putnam's Sons hardcover edition / October 2005
Berkley international edition / April 2006

Copyright © 2005 by Cornwell Enterprises, Inc.
Cover design by Lisa Amoroso.
Cover lettering © 2005 by Walter Harper.

ISBN: 0-425-21088-X

BERKLEY®
Berkley Books are published by The Berkley Publishing Group,
a division of Penguin Group (USA) Inc.,
375 Hudson Street, New York, New York 10014.
BERKLEY is a registered trademark of Penguin Group (USA) Inc.
The "B" design is a trademark belonging to Penguin Group (USA) Inc.

PRINTED IN THE UNITED STATES OF AMERICA

10 9 8 7 6 5 4 3 2 1

To Staci

SPECIAL THANKS

Harvard Medical School–affiliated McLean Hospital is the nation's top psychiatric hospital and is world renowned for its research programs, especially in the field of neuroscience. The most challenging and significant frontier isn't outer space. It is the human brain and its biological role in mental illness. McLean not only sets the standard for psychiatric research, but offers a compassionate alternative to debilitating suffering.

I am extremely grateful to the extraordinary doctors and scientists who so kindly shared their remarkable world with me:

Especially
DR. BRUCE M. COHEN,
President and Psychiatrist in Chief

and also
DR. DAVID P. OLSON,
Clinical Director, Brain Imaging Center

and most of all
DR. STACI A. GRUBER,
Associate Director, Cognitive Neuroimaging Laboratory

1

It is **Sunday** afternoon and Dr. Kay Scarpetta is in her office at the National Forensic Academy in Hollywood, Florida, where clouds are building, promising another thunderstorm. It's not supposed to be this rainy and hot in February.

Gunfire pops, and voices yell things she can't make out. Simulated combat is popular on the weekends. Special Ops agents can run around in black fatigues, shooting up the place, and nobody hears them, only Scarpetta, and she barely notices. She continues reviewing an emergency certificate issued by a coroner in Louisiana, an examination of a patient, a woman who later went on to murder five people and claims to have no memory of it.

The case probably isn't a candidate for the Prefrontal Determinants of Aggressive-Type Overt Responsivity research study known as PREDATOR, Scarpetta decides, vaguely aware of a motorcycle getting louder on the Academy grounds.

She writes forensic psychologist Benton Wesley an e-mail:

```
A woman in the study would be interesting, but
wouldn't the data be irrelevant? I thought you
were restricting PREDATOR to males.
```

The motorcycle blasts up to the building and stops right below her window. Pete Marino harassing her again, she thinks irritably as Benton sends her an Instant Message:

```
Louisiana probably wouldn't let us have her any-
way. They like to execute people too much down
there. Food's good, though.
```

She looks out the window as Marino kills the engine, gets off his bike, looks around in his macho way, always wondering who's watching. She is locking PREDATOR case files in her desk drawer when he walks into her office without knocking and helps himself to a chair.

"You know anything about the Johnny Swift case?" he asks, his huge, tattooed arms bulging from a sleeveless denim vest with the Harley logo on the back.

Marino is the Academy's head of investigations and a part-time death investigator at the Broward County Medical Examiner's Office. Of late, he looks like a parody of a biker thug. He sets his helmet on her desk, a scuffed black brain bucket with bullet-hole decals all over it.

"Refresh my memory. And that thing's a hood ornament." She indicates the helmet. "For show, and worthless if you have an accident on that donorcycle of yours."

He tosses a file onto her desk. "A San Francisco doctor with an office here in Miami. Had a place in Hollywood on the beach, he and his brother. Not far from the Renaissance, you know, those twin high-rise condo buildings near John Lloyd State Park? About three months ago at Thanksgiving while he was at his place down here, his brother found him on the couch, dead from a shotgun wound to the chest. By the way, he'd just had wrist surgery and it didn't go well. At a glance, a straightforward suicide."

"I wasn't at the ME's office yet," she reminds him.

She was already the Academy's director of forensic science and medicine then. But she didn't accept the position of consulting forensic pathologist at the Broward County Medical Examiner's Office until this past December when Dr. Bronson, the chief, started cutting back his hours, talking about retiring.

"I remember hearing something about it," she says, uncomfortable in Marino's presence, rarely happy to see him anymore.

"Dr. Bronson did the autopsy," he says, looking at what's on her desk, looking everywhere but at her.

"Were you involved?"

"Nope. Wasn't in town. The case is still pending, because

the Hollywood PD was worried at the time there might be more to it, suspicious of Laurel."

"Laurel?"

"Johnny Swift's brother, identical twins. There was nothing to prove anything, and it all went away. Then I got a phone call Friday morning about three a.m., a weird-ass phone call at my house that we've traced to a pay phone in Boston."

"Massachusetts?"

"As in the Tea Party."

"I thought your number's unlisted."

"It is."

Marino slides a folded piece of torn brown paper from the back pocket of his jeans and opens it.

"I'm going to read you what the guy said, since I wrote it down word for word. He called himself Hog."

"As in pig? That kind of hog?" She studies him, halfway wondering if he's leading her on, setting her up for ridicule.

He's been doing that a lot these days.

"He just said, *I am Hog. Thou didst send a judgment to mock them.* Whatever the hell that means. Then he said, *There's a reason certain items were missing from the Johnny Swift scene, and if you have half a brain, you'll take a good look at what happened to Christian Christian. Nothing is co-incidence. You'd better ask Scarpetta, because the hand of God will crush all perverts, including her dyke bitch niece.*"

Scarpetta doesn't let what she feels register in her voice when she replies. "Are you sure that's exactly what he said?"

"Do I look like a fiction writer?"

"Christian Christian?"

"Who the hell knows. The guy wasn't exactly interested in me asking questions like how to spell something. He talked in a soft voice, like someone who feels nothing, kind of flat, then hung up."

"Did he actually mention Lucy by name or just—?"

"I told you exactly what he said," he cuts her off. "She's your only niece, right? So obviously he meant Lucy. And HOG could stand for Hand of God, in case you haven't connected those dots. Long story short, I contacted the Hollywood police and they've asked us to take a look at the Johnny Swift case ASAP. Apparently, there's some other shit about the evidence showing he was shot from a distance and from close range. Well, it's one or the other, right?"

"If there was only one shot, yes. Something must be skewed with the interpretation. Do we have any idea who Christian Christian is? Are we even talking about a person?"

"So far nothing in our computer searches that's helpful."

"Why are you just telling me now? I've been around all weekend."

"Been busy."

"You get information about a case like this, you shouldn't wait days to tell me," she says as calmly as she can.

"Maybe you're not one to talk about withholding information."

"What information?" she asks, baffled.

"You should be more careful. That's all I got to say."

"It's not helpful when you're cryptic, Marino."

"I almost forgot. Hollywood's curious about what Benton's professional opinion might be," he adds as if it is an afterthought, as if he doesn't care.

He typically does a poor job hiding how he feels about Benton Wesley.

"Certainly they can ask him to evaluate the case," she replies. "I can't speak for him."

"They want him to figure out if the call I got from this wacko Hog was a crank, and I said that would be kind of hard when it's not recorded, when all he'd get is my own version of shorthand scribbled on a paper bag."

He gets up from his chair, and his big presence seems even bigger, and he makes her feel even smaller than he used to make her feel. He picks up his useless helmet and puts on his sunglasses. He hasn't looked at her throughout their entire conversation, and now she can't see his eyes at all. She can't see what's in them.

"I'll give it my complete attention. Immediately," she says as he walks to the door. "If you'd like to go over it later, we can."

"Huh."
"Why don't you come to the house?"
"Huh," he says again. "What time?"
"Seven," she says.

2

Inside the MRI suite, Benton Wesley watches his patient through a partition of Plexiglas. The lights are low, multiple video screens illuminated along the wraparound counter, his wristwatch on top of his briefcase. He is cold. After several hours inside the cognitive neuroimaging laboratory, even his bones are cold, or at least that's how it feels.

Tonight's patient goes by an identification number, but he has a name. Basil Jenrette. He is a mildly anxious and intelligent thirty-three-year-old compulsive murderer. Benton avoids the term *serial killer*. It has been so overused, it means nothing helpful and never did except to loosely imply that a perpetrator has murdered three or more people over a certain period of time. The word *serial* suggests something that occurs in succession. It suggests nothing about a violent offender's motives or state of mind, and when Basil Jenrette was busy killing, he was compulsive. He couldn't stop.

The reason he is getting his brain scanned in a 3-Tesla MRI machine that has a magnetic field sixty thousand times more powerful than the earth's is to see if there is anything about his gray and white matter and how it functions that might hint at why. Benton has asked him why numerous times during their clinical interviews.

I would see her and that was it. I had to do it.

Had to do it right that minute?

Not right there on the street. I might follow her until I figured it out, came up with a plan. To be honest, the more I calculated, the better it felt.

And how long would this take? The following, the calculating. Can you approximate? Days, hours, minutes?

Minutes. Maybe hours. Sometimes days. Depends. Stupid bitches. I mean, if it was you and you realized you were be-

ing abducted, would you just sit there in the car and not even try to get away?

Is that what they did, Basil? They sat in the car and didn't try to get away?

Except for the last two. You know about them because that's why I'm here. They wouldn't have resisted, but my car broke down. Stupid. If it was you, would you rather be killed right there in the car or wait to see what I'm going to do to you when I get you to my special spot?

Where was your special spot? Always the same place?

All because my damn car broke down.

So far, the structure of Basil Jenrette's brain is unremarkable except for the incidental finding of a posterior cerebellar abnormality, an approximately six-millimeter cyst that might affect his balance a little, but nothing else. It is the way his brain functions that isn't quite right. It can't be right. If it were, he wouldn't have been a candidate for the PREDATOR research study, and he probably wouldn't have agreed to it. Everything is a game to Basil, and he is smarter than Einstein, thinks he is the most gifted person on earth. He has never suffered one moment of remorse for what he's done and is quite candid in saying that he would kill more women given the opportunity. Unfortunately, Basil is likeable.

The two prison guards inside the MRI suite vacillate from confused to curious as they stare through the glass at the seven-foot-long tube, the bore of the magnet, on the other side. The guards wear uniforms but no guns. Weapons aren't allowed in here. Nothing ferrous, including handcuffs and shackles, is permitted, and only plastic flex-cuffs restrain Basil's ankles and wrists as he lies on the table inside the magnet, listening to the jarring knocks and wonks of radio-frequency pulses that sound like infernal music played on high-voltage power lines—or that's what Benton imagines.

"Remember, this next one is color blocks. All I want you to do is name the color," Dr. Susan Lane, the neuropsychologist, says into the intercom. "No, Mr. Jenrette, please don't nod your head. Remember, the tape is on your chin to remind you not to move."

"Ten-four," Basil's voice sounds through the intercom.

It is half past eight at night and Benton is uneasy. He has been uneasy for months, not so much worried that the Basil Jenrettes of the world are going to suddenly explode into violence inside the gracious old brick walls of McLean Hospital and slaughter everything in sight, but that the research study is doomed to failure, that it is a waste of grant money and a foolish expenditure of precious time. McLean is an affiliate of Harvard Medical School, and neither the hospital nor the university is forgiving about failure.

"Don't worry about getting all of them right," Dr. Lane is saying over the intercom. "We don't expect you to get all of them right."

"Green, red, blue, red, blue, green," Basil's confident voice fills the room.

A researcher marks down results on a data-entry sheet while the MRI technician checks images on his video screen.

Dr. Lane pushes the talk button again. "Mr. Jenrette? You're doing an excellent job. Can you see everything okay?"

"Ten-four."

"Very good. Every time you see that black screen, you are nice and still. No talking, just look at the white dot on the screen."

"Ten-four."

She releases the talk button and says to Benton, "What's with the cop jargon?"

"He was a cop. That's probably how he was able to get his victims into his car."

"Dr. Wesley?" the researcher says, turning around in her chair. "It's for you. Detective Thrush."

Benton takes the phone.

"What's up," he asks Thrush, a homicide detective with the Massachusetts State Police.

"I hope you weren't planning on an early bedtime," Thrush says. "You hear about the body found this morning out by Walden Pond?"

"No. I've been locked up in this place all day."

"White female, unidentified, hard to tell her age. Maybe in her late thirties, early forties, shot in the head, the shotgun shell shoved up her ass."

"News to me."

"She's been autopsied already, but I thought you might want to take a look. This one ain't the average bear."

"I'll be finished up in less than an hour," Benton says.

"Meet me at the morgue."

The house is quiet and Kay Scarpetta walks from room to room, turning on every light, unsettled. She listens for the sound of a car or a motorcycle, listens for Marino. He is late and hasn't returned her phone calls.

Unsettled and anxious, she checks to make sure that the burglar alarm is armed and the floodlights are on. She pauses at the video display on the kitchen phone to make sure the cameras monitoring the front, back and sides of her house are operating properly. Her property is shadowy in the video display, and dark images of citrus trees, palms and hibiscus move in the wind. The dock behind her swimming pool and the waterway beyond are a black plain dabbed with blurred lights from lamps along the seawall. She stirs tomato sauce and mushrooms in copper pots on the stove. She checks dough rising and fresh mozzarella soaking in covered bowls by the sink.

It is almost nine, and Marino was supposed to be here two hours ago. Tomorrow she is tied up with cases and teaching, and she doesn't have time for his rudeness. She feels set up. She has had it with him. She has worked nonstop on the Johnny Swift alleged suicide for the past three hours, and now Marino can't bother to show up. She is hurt, then angry. It is easier to be angry.

She is very angry as she walks into her living room, still listening for a motorcycle or a car, still listening for him. She picks up a twelve-gauge Remington Marine Magnum from her couch and sits down. The nickel-plated shotgun is heavy in her lap, and she inserts a small key in the lock. She turns the key to the right and pulls the lock free from the trigger guard. She racks the pump back to make sure there are no cartridges in the magazine.

3

W e're going to do word reading now," Dr. Lane is telling Basil over the intercom. "Just read the words from left to right. Okay? And remember, don't move. You're doing great."

"Ten-four."

"Hey, want to see what he really looks like?" the MRI technician says to the guards.

His name is Josh. He majored in physics at MIT, is working as a tech while working on his next degree, is bright but eccentric with a twisted sense of humor.

"I already know what he looks like. I got to escort him to the showers earlier today," one of the guards says.

"Then what?" Dr. Lane asks Benton. "What would he do to them after he got them into his car?"

"Red, blue, blue, red . . ."

The guards wander closer to Josh's video screen.

"Take them someplace, stab them in the eyes, keep them alive a couple days, rape them repeatedly, cut their throats, dump their bodies, pose them to shock people," Benton is telling Dr. Lane matter-of-factly, in his clinical way. "The cases we know about. I'm suspicious he killed others. A number of women vanished in Florida during the same time frame. Presumed dead, bodies never found."

"Take them where? A motel, his house?"

"Hold on a second," Josh says to the guards as he selects the menu option 3D, then SSD, or Surface Shading Display. "This is really cool. We never show it to patients."

"How come?"

"Totally freak them out."

"We don't know where," Benton is telling Dr. Lane as he keeps a check on Josh, ready to intervene if he gets too carried away. "But it's interesting. The bodies he dumped. They all had microscopic particles of copper on them."

"What on earth?"

"Mixed in with dirt and whatever else was adhering to blood, their skin, in their hair."

"Blue, green, blue, red . . ."

"That's very strange."

She pushes the talk button. "Mr. Jenrette? How are we doing in there? You okay?"

"Ten-four."

"Next, you're going to see words printed in a different color from what they spell. I want you to name the color of the ink. Just name the color."

"Ten-four."

"Isn't this awesome?" Josh says as what looks like a death mask fills his screen, a reconstruction of one-millimeter-thick high-resolution slices that make up the MRI scan of Basil Jenrette's head, the image pale, hairless and eyeless, ending raggedly just below the jaw as if he has been decapitated.

Josh rotates the image so the guards can see it from different angles.

"Why's his head look cut off?" one of them asks.

"That's where the signal from the coil stopped."

"His skin doesn't look real."

"Red uh green, blue I mean red, green . . ." Basil's voice enters the room.

"It's not really skin. How to explain . . . well, what the computer's doing is volume reconstruction, a surface rendering."

"Red, blue uh green, blue I mean green . . ."

"Only thing we really use it for is PowerPoints, mainly, to overlay structural with functional. Just an fMRI analysis package where you can put data together and look at it any way you want, have fun with it."

"Man, he's ugly."

Benton has heard enough. The color naming has stopped. He gives Josh a sharp look.

"Josh? You ready?"

"Four, three, two, one, ready," Josh says, and Dr. Lane begins the interference test.

"Blue, red I mean . . . shit, uh red I mean blue, green, red . . ." Basil's voice violates the room as he gets all of them wrong.

"He ever tell you why?" Dr. Lane asks Benton.

"I'm sorry," he says, distracted. "Why what?"

"Red, blue shit! Uh red, blue-green . . ."

"Why he gouged their eyes out."

"He said he didn't want them to see how small his penis is."

"Blue, blue-red, red, green . . ."

"He didn't do so well on this one," she says. "In fact, he missed most of them. What police department did he work for, so I remember not to get pulled for speeding in that part of the world?" She pushes the talk button. "You okay in there?"

"Ten-four."

"Dade County PD."

"Too bad. I've always liked Miami. So that's how you managed to conjure this one up. Because of your South Florida connections," she replies, pushing the talk button again.

"Not exactly." Benton stares through the glass at Basil's head in the far end of the magnet, imagining the rest of him dressed like a normal person in jeans and a button-up white shirt.

The inmates are not allowed to wear prison fatigues on the hospital campus. It's bad public relations.

"When we began querying state penitentiaries for study subjects, Florida thought he was just the guy for the job. He was bored. They were happy to get rid of him," Benton says.

"Very good, Mr. Jenrette," Dr. Lane says into the intercom. "Now, Dr. Wesley is going to come in and give you the mouse. You're going to see some faces next."

"Ten-four."

Ordinarily, Dr. Lane would go into the MRI room and deal with the patient herself. But women doctors and scientists are not allowed physical contact with the subjects of

PREDATOR. Male doctors and scientists have to be cautious, too, while inside the MRI suite. Outside of it, restraining research study subjects during interviews is up to the clinician. Benton is accompanied by the two prison guards as he turns on the lights inside the MRI room and shuts the door. The guards hover near the magnet and pay attention as he plugs in the mouse and places it in Basil's restrained hands.

He is nothing much to look at, a short, slight man with thinning blond hair and small gray eyes closely spaced. In the animal kingdom, lions, tigers and bears—the predators—have closely spaced eyes. Giraffes, rabbits, doves—the preyed upon—have eyes more widely spaced and oriented toward the sides of their heads, because they need their peripheral vision to survive. Benton has always wondered if the same evolutionary phenomenon applies to humans. That's a research study nobody's going to fund.

"You doing all right, Basil?" Benton asks him.

"What kind of faces?" Basil's head talks from the end of the magnet, bringing to mind an iron lung.

"Dr. Lane will explain it to you."

"I've got a surprise," Basil says. "I'll tell you when we're done."

He has an odd gaze, as if a malignant creature is looking out through his eyes.

"Great. I love surprises. Just a few more minutes and you're done," Benton says with a smile. "Then we'll have a follow-up chat."

The guards accompany Benton back outside the MRI room and return to the suite as Dr. Lane begins to explain over the intercom that all she wants Basil to do is click the left side of the mouse if the face is male and right if it is female.

"Nothing for you to do or say, just press the button," she reiterates.

There are three tests, and the point of them is not the patient's ability to distinguish between the two genders. What is actually measured in this series of functional scanning is affective processing. The male and female faces appearing on the screen are behind other faces that flash too quickly for the eye to detect, but the brain sees all. Jenrette's brain sees the faces behind the masks, faces that are happy, angry or afraid, faces that are provocative.

After each set, Dr. Lane asks him what he saw, and if he had to attach an emotion to the faces, what was it. The male faces are more serious than the female, he answers. He says basically the same thing for each set. It means nothing yet. None of what has gone on in these rooms will mean anything until the thousands of neuroimages are analyzed. Then the scientists can visualize which areas of his brain were most active during the tests. The point is to see if his brain works differently from someone who supposedly is normal, and to learn something besides the fact that he has an incidental cyst that is completely unrelated to his predatory proclivities.

"Anything jump out at you?" Benton asks Dr. Lane. "And by the way, thanks, as always, Susan. You're a good sport."

They try to schedule inmate scans late in the day or on the weekend, when few people are around.

"Just from the localizers, he looks okay—I don't see any gross abnormalities. Except for his incessant chatting. His hyperfluency. He ever been diagnosed as bipolar?"

"His evaluations and history make me wonder. But no. Never diagnosed. Unmedicated for any psychiatric disorders, in prison only a year. A dream subject."

"Well, your dream subject didn't do well suppressing interfering stimuli, made a huge number of errors by commission on the interference test. My bet is he doesn't stay in set, which is certainly consistent with bipolar disorder. We'll know more later."

She pushes the talk button again and says, "Mr. Jenrette? We're all done. You did an excellent job. Dr. Wesley's coming back in to get you out. I want you to sit up very slowly, okay? Very slowly so you don't get dizzy. Okay?"

"That's all? Just these stupid tests? Show me the pictures."

She gives Benton a look and releases the talk button.

"You said you'd look at my brain when I'm looking at the pictures."

"Autopsy pictures of his victims," Benton explains to Dr. Lane.

"You promised me pictures! You promised I'd get my mail!"

"All righty," she says to Benton. "He's all yours."

The shotgun is heavy and cumbersome, and she has trouble lying on the couch and pointing the barrel at her chest while trying to pull the trigger with her left toe.

Scarpetta lowers the shotgun and imagines attempting the same thing after wrist surgery. Her shotgun weighs about seven and a half pounds and starts to shake in her hands when she holds it up by its eighteen-inch barrel. She lowers her feet to the floor and takes off her right running shoe and sock. Her left foot is dominant, but she will have to try her right, and she wonders what Johnny Swift was, right-foot-dominant or left. It would make a difference, but not necessarily a significant one, especially if he was depressed and determined, but she's not sure he was either, not sure of much.

She thinks about Marino, and the more her thoughts shift back to him, the more upset she gets. He has no right to treat her this way, no right to disrespect her the same way he did when they first met, and that was many years ago, so many years ago she is surprised he can even remember how to treat her the way he once did. The aroma of her homemade pizza sauce is in the living room. It fills the house, and resentment speeds up her heart and makes her chest tight. She lies back down on her left side, props the stock of the shotgun on the back of the couch, positions the barrel at the center of her chest and pulls the trigger with her right big toe.

4

Basil Jenrette is not going to hurt him.

Unrestrained, he sits across the table from Benton inside the small examination room, the door shut. Basil is quiet and polite in his chair. His outburst inside the magnet lasted maybe two minutes, and when he calmed down, Dr. Lane was already gone. He didn't see her when he was escorted out, and Benton will make sure he never does.

"You're sure you're not lightheaded or dizzy," Benton says in his calm, understanding way.

"I feel great. The tests were cool. I've always loved tests. I knew I'd get everything right. Where are the pictures? You promised."

"We never discussed anything like that, Basil."

"I got everything right, straight A's."

"So you enjoyed the experience."

"Next time show me the pictures like you promised."

"I never promised you that, Basil. Did you find the experience exciting?"

"I guess I can't smoke in here."

"I'm afraid not."

"What did my brain look like? Did it look good? Did you see anything? Can you tell how smart someone is by looking at their brain? If you showed me the pictures you'd see they match the ones I have in my brain."

He is talking quietly and rapidly now, his eyes bright, almost glassy, as he goes on and on about what the scientists might expect to find in his brain, assuming they are able to decipher what is there, and there is definitely a there there, he keeps saying.

"A there there?" Benton inquires. "Can you explain what you mean, Basil?"

"My memory. If you can see into it, see what's in there, see my memories."

"I'm afraid not."

"Really. I'll bet all kinds of pictures came up when you were doing the beep-beep, bang-bang, knock-knock. Bet you saw the pictures and don't want to tell me. There were ten of them, and you saw them. Saw their pictures, ten of them, not four. I always say ten-four as a joke, a real big ha-ha. You think it's four and I know it's ten, and you would know if you showed me the pictures, because you'd see they matched the pictures in my brain. You'd see my pictures when you're inside my brain. Ten-four."

"Tell me which pictures you mean, Basil."

"I'm just messing with you," he says with a wink. "I want my mail."

"What pictures might we see inside your brain?"

"Those foolish women. They won't give me my mail."

"You're saying you killed ten women?" Benton asks this without shock or judgment. Basil smiles as if something has occurred to him.

"Oh. I can move my head now, can't I. No more tape on my chin. Will they tape my chin down when they give me the needle?"

"You won't be getting the needle, Basil. That's part of the deal. Your sentence has been commuted to life. You remember us talking about that?"

"Because I'm crazy," he says with a smile. "That's why I'm here."

"No. We'll go over this again, because it is important you understand. You're here because you've agreed to participate in our study, Basil. The governor of Florida allowed you to be transferred to our state hospital, Butler, but Massachusetts wouldn't agree to it unless he commuted your sentence to life. We don't have the death penalty in Massachusetts."

"I know you want to see the ten ladies. See them as I remember them. They're in my brain."

He knows it isn't possible to scan someone and see his thoughts and memories. He is being his usual clever self. He wants the autopsy photographs so he can fuel his violent fantasies, and as is true of narcissistic sociopaths, he thinks he is quite entertaining.

"Is that the surprise, Basil?" he asks. "That you committed ten murders instead of the four you were charged with?"

He shakes his head and says, "There's one you want to know about. That's the surprise. Something special just for you because you've been so nice to me. But I want my mail. That's the deal."

"I'm very interested in hearing about your surprise."

"The lady in The Christmas Shop," he says. "Remember that one?"

"Why don't you tell me about it," Benton replies, and he doesn't know what Basil means. He isn't familiar with a murder that occurred in a Christmas shop.

"What about my mail?"

"I'll see what I can do."

"Cross your heart and hope to die?"

"I'll look into it."

"I can't remember the exact date. Let me see." He stares at the ceiling, his unrestrained hands restless in his lap. "About three years ago in Las Olas, I think it was around July. So maybe two and a half years ago. Why would anyone want to buy Christmas shit in July in South Florida? She sold little Santas and his elves and nutcrackers and baby Jesuses. I went in on this particular morning after staying up all night."

"Do you remember her name?"

"I never knew her name. Well, I might have. But I forgot it. If you showed me the pictures, it might jog my memory, you might see her in my brain. Let me see if I can describe her. Let me see. Oh, yes. She was a white woman with long, dyed hair the color of *I Love Lucy*. Sort of fat. Maybe thirty-five or forty. I went in and locked the door and pulled a knife on her. I raped her in the back, in the storage area, cut her throat from here to here in one cut."

He makes a slicing motion across his neck.

"It was funny because there was one of those oscillating fans in there and I turned it on because it was hot and stuffy and it blew blood all the fuck over the place. Quite a mess to clean up. Then, let's see"—he looks up at the ceiling again, the way he often does when he's lying—"I wasn't in my cop car that day, had taken my bike and parked it in a pay lot behind the Riverside Hotel."

"Your motorcycle or a bicycle?"

"My Honda Shadow. Like I would ride a bicycle when I was going to kill someone."

"So you planned on killing someone that morning?"

"It seemed like a good idea."

"You planned on killing her or just planned on killing someone?"

"I remember there were all these ducks in the parking lot hanging out around the puddles because it had been raining for days. Mommy ducks and little baby ducks everywhere. That's always bothered me. Poor little ducks. They get run over a lot. You see little babies squashed in the road and mommy walking round and around her dead little baby, looking so sad."

"Did you ever run over the ducks, Basil?"

"I would never hurt an animal, Dr. Wesley."

"You said you killed birds and rabbits when you were a child."

"That was a long time ago. You know, boys and their BB guns. Anyway, to go on with my story, all I got was twenty-six dollars and ninety-one cents. You have to do something about my mail."

"So you've said repeatedly, Basil. I told you I'll do my best."

"Sort of disappointing after all that. Twenty-six dollars and ninety-one cents."

"From the cash drawer."

"Ten-four."

"You must have had a lot of blood on you, Basil."

"She had a bathroom in the back of the shop." He looks up at the ceiling again. "I poured Clorox on her, just now remembered it. To kill my DNA. Now you owe me. I want my fucking mail. Get me out of the suicide cell. I want a normal cell where they don't spy on me."

"We're making sure you're safe."

"Get me a new cell and the pictures and my mail, and I'll tell you more about The Christmas Shop," he says and his eyes are very glassy now and he is very restless in the chair, clenching his fists, tapping his foot. "I deserve to be rewarded."

5

Lucy sits where she can see the front door, where she can see who is coming in or leaving. She watches people without them knowing. She watches and calculates even when she is supposed to be relaxing.

The last few nights, she has wandered into Lorraine's and talked to the bartenders, Buddy and Tonia. Neither knows Lucy's real name, but both remember Johnny Swift, remember him as that hot-looking doctor who was straight. A *brain doctor* who liked Provincetown and unfortunately was straight, Buddy says. What a shame, Buddy says. Always alone, too, except for the last time he was here, Tonia says. She was working that night and remembers that Johnny had splints on his wrists. When she asked him about it, he said he'd just had surgery and it hadn't gone very well.

Johnny and a woman sat at the bar and were very friendly with each other, talking as if no one else was there. Her name was Jan and she seemed really smart, was pretty and polite, very shy, not the least bit stuck on herself, young, dressed casually in jeans and a sweatshirt, Tonia recalls. It was obvious Johnny hadn't known her long, maybe had just met her, found her interesting, obviously liked her, Tonia says.

Liked her as in sexually? Lucy asked Tonia.

I didn't get that impression. He was more, well, it's like she had some sort of problem and he was helping her out. He was a doctor, you know.

That doesn't surprise Lucy. Johnny was unselfish. He was extraordinarily kind.

She sits at the bar in Lorraine's and thinks about Johnny walking in the same way she just did and sitting at the same bar, maybe on the same stool. She imagines him with Jan, someone he may have just met. It wasn't like him to pick up women, to have casual encounters. He wasn't into one-night stands and may very well have been helping her, counseling her. But about what? Some medical problem? Some psychological problem? The story about the shy young woman named Jan is puzzling and disconcerting. Lucy isn't quite sure why.

Maybe he wasn't feeling good about himself. Maybe he was scared because the carpal tunnel surgery wasn't as successful as he had hoped. Maybe counseling and befriending a shy, pretty young woman made him forget his fears, feel powerful and important. Lucy drinks tequila and thinks about what he said to her in San Francisco when she was with him last September, the last time she saw him.

Biology is cruel, he said. *Physical liabilities are unforgiving. Nobody wants you if you're scarred and crippled, useless and maimed.*

My God, Johnny. It's just carpal tunnel surgery. Not amputation.

I apologize, he said. *We're not here to talk about me.*

She thinks about him as she sits at the bar in Lorraine's, watching people, mostly men, enter and leave the restaurant as snow gusts in.

It has begun to snow in Boston as Benton drives his Porsche Turbo S past the Victorian brick buildings of the university medical campus and remembers the early days when Scarpetta used to summon him to the morgue at night. He always knew the case was bad.

Most forensic psychologists have never been to a morgue. They have never seen an autopsy and don't even want to look at the photographs. They are more interested in the details of the offender than in what he did to his victim, because the offender is the patient and the victim is nothing more than the medium he used to express his violence. This is the excuse many forensic psychologists and psychiatrists give. A more likely explanation is they don't have the courage or the inclination to interview victims or, worse, spend time with their mauled dead bodies.

Benton is different. After more than a decade of Scarpetta, there is no way he couldn't be different.

You have no right to work any case if you won't listen to what the dead have to say, she told him some fifteen years ago when they were working their first homicide together. *If you can't be bothered with them, then, frankly, I can't be bothered with you, Special Agent Wesley.*

Fair enough, Dr. Scarpetta. I'll trust you to make introductions.

All right then, she said. *Come with me.*

That was the first time he had ever been inside a morgue refrigerator, and he can still hear the loud clack of the handle pulling back and the whoosh of cold, foul air. He would know that smell anywhere, that dark, dead stench, foul and flat. It hangs heavy in the air, and he has always imagined that if he could see it, it would look like filthy ground fog slowly spreading out from whatever has died.

He replays his conversation with Basil, analyzes every word, every twitch, every facial expression. Violent offenders promise all sorts of things. They manipulate the hell out of everybody to get what they want, promise to reveal the locations of bodies, admit to crimes that were never solved, confess the details of what they did, offer insights into their motivation and psychological state. In most cases, it is lies. In this case, Benton is concerned. Something about at least some of what Basil confessed strikes him as true.

He tries Scarpetta on his cell phone. She doesn't answer. Several minutes later, he tries again and still can't get her.

He leaves a message: "Please call me when you get this," he says.

The door opens again and a woman comes in with the snow, as if blown in by the blizzard.

She wears a long, black coat and is brushing it off as she pushes back her hood, and her fair skin is rosy from the cold, her eyes quite bright. She is pretty, remarkably pretty, with dark blond hair and dark eyes and a body that she flaunts. Lucy watches her glide to the back of the restaurant, glide between tables like a sexy pilgrim or a sensuous witch in her long, black coat, and it swirls around her black boots as she heads straight back to the bar where there are plenty of empty stools. She chooses one next to Lucy's and takes off her coat and folds it and sits on it without a word or a glance.

Lucy drinks tequila and stares at the TV over the bar as if the latest celebrity romance is interesting. Buddy makes the woman a drink as if he knows what she likes.

"I'll have another," Lucy tells him soon enough.

"Coming up."

The woman with the black hooded coat gets interested in the colorful tequila bottle that Buddy lifts from a shelf. She keenly watches the pale amber liquor pour in a delicate stream, filling the bottom of the brandy snifter. Lucy slowly swirls the tequila, and the smell of it fills her nose all the way up to her brain.

"That stuff will give you the headache from Hades," the woman with the black hooded coat says in a husky voice that is seductive and full of secrets.

"It's much purer than regular liquor," Lucy says. "Haven't heard the word Hades in a while. Most people I know say hell."

"The worst headaches I ever got were from margaritas," the woman offers, sipping a Cosmopolitan that is pink and lethal-looking in a champagne glass. "And I don't believe in hell."

"You'll believe in it if you keep drinking that shit," Lucy replies, and in the mirror behind the bar, she watches the front door open again and more snow blow into Lorraine's.

Wind gusting in from the bay sounds like silk whipping, reminding her of silk stockings whipping on a clothesline, although she has never seen silk stockings on a clothesline or heard what they sound like in the wind. She is aware of the woman's black stockings because tall stools and short, slitted skirts are not a safe combination unless a woman is in a bar where the men are interested only in one another, and in Provincetown, this is usually the case.

"Another Cosmo, Stevie?" Buddy asks, and now Lucy knows her name.

"No," Lucy answers for her. "Let Stevie try what I'm having."

"I'll try anything," Stevie says. "I think I've seen you at the Pied and the Vixen, dancing with different people."

"I don't dance."

"I've seen you. You're hard to miss."

"You come here a lot?" Lucy asks, and she has never seen Stevie before, not at the Pied or the Vixen or any other club or restaurant in Ptown.

Stevie watches Buddy pour more tequila. He leaves the bottle on the bar, steps away and busies himself with another customer.

"This is my first time," Stevie says to Lucy. "A Valentine's Day present to myself, a week in Ptown."

"In the dead of winter?"

"Last I checked, Valentine's Day was always in the winter. It happens to be my favorite holiday."

"It's not a holiday. I've been here every night this week and never seen you."

"What are you? The bar police?" Stevie smiles and looks into Lucy's eyes so intensely it has an effect.

Lucy feels something. *No*, she thinks. *Not again*.

"Maybe I don't come in here only at night like you do," Stevie says, reaching for the tequila bottle, brushing Lucy's arm.

The feeling gets stronger. Stevie studies the colorful label, sets the bottle back on the bar, taking her time, her body touching Lucy. The feeling intensifies.

"Cuervo? What's so special about Cuervo?" Stevie asks.

"How would you know what I do?" Lucy says.

She tries to make the feeling go away.

"Just guessing. You look like a night person," Stevie says. "Your hair is naturally red, isn't it. Maybe mahogany mixed with deep red. Dyed hair can't look like that. You haven't always worn it long, as long as it is now."

"Are you some kind of psychic?"

The feeling is awful now. It won't go away.

"Just guessing," Stevie's seductive voice says. "So, you haven't told me. What's so special about Cuervo?"

"Cuervo Reserva de la Familia. It's special enough."

"Well, that's something. It looks like this is my night for first times," Stevie says, touching Lucy's arm, her hand resting on it for a minute. "First time in Ptown. First time for one hundred percent agave tequila that costs thirty dollars a shot."

Lucy wonders how Stevie can know it costs thirty dollars a shot. For someone unfamiliar with tequila, she seems to know a lot.

"I believe I'll have another," Stevie calls out to Buddy, "and you really could pour a little more in the glass. Be sweet to me."

Buddy smiles as he pours her another, and two shots later, Stevie leans against Lucy and whispers in her ear, "You got anything?"

"Like what?" Lucy asks, and she gives herself up to it.

The feeling is fueled by tequila and plans to stay for the night.

"You know what," Stevie's voice says quietly, her breath touching Lucy's ear, her breast pressed against her arm. "Something to smoke. Something that's worth it."

"What makes you think I'd have something?"

"Just guessing."

"You're remarkably good at it."

"You can get it anywhere here. I've seen you."

Lucy made a transaction last night, knows just where to do it, at the Vixen, where she doesn't dance. She doesn't remember seeing Stevie. There weren't that many people, never are this time of year. She would have noticed Stevie. She would notice her in a huge crowd, on a busy street, anywhere.

"Maybe you're the one who's the bar police," Lucy says.

"You have no idea how funny that is," Stevie's seductive voice says. "Where you staying?"

"Not far from here."

6

The state Medical Examiner's Office is located where most are, on the fringe of a nicer part of town, usually at the outer limits of a medical school. The red-brick-and-concrete complex backs up to the Massachusetts Turnpike, and on the other side of it is the Suffolk County House of Corrections. There is no view and the noise of traffic never stops.

Benton parks at the back door and notes only two other cars in the lot. The dark-blue Crown Victoria belongs to Detective Thrush. The Honda SUV probably belongs to a forensic pathologist who doesn't get paid enough and probably wasn't happy when Thrush persuaded him to come in at this hour. Benton rings the bell and scans the empty back parking lot, never assuming he is safe or alone, and then the door opens and Thrush is motioning him inside.

"Jeez, I hate this place at night," Thrush says.

"There's not much to like about it any time of day," Benton remarks.

"I'm glad you came. Can't believe you're out in that," he says, looking out at the black Porsche as he shuts the door behind them. "In this weather? You crazy?"

"All-wheel drive. It wasn't snowing when I went to work this morning."

"These other psychologists I've worked with, they never come out, snow, rain or shine," Thrush says. "Not the profilers, either. Most FBI I've met have never seen a dead body."

"Except for the ones at headquarters."

"No shit. We got plenty of them at state police headquarters, too. Here."

He hands Benton an envelope as they follow a corridor.

"Got everything on a disk for you. All the scene and autopsy pictures, whatever's written up so far. It's all there. It's supposed to snow like a bitch."

Benton thinks of Scarpetta again. Tomorrow is Valentine's Day, and they're supposed to spend the evening together, have a romantic dinner on the harbor. She's supposed to stay through Presidents' Day weekend. They haven't seen each other in almost a month. She may not be able to get here.

"I heard light snow showers are predicted," Benton says.

"A storm's moving in from the Cape. Hope you got something to drive other than that million-dollar sports car."

Thrush is a big man who has spent his life in Massachusetts and talks like it. There isn't a single R in his vocabulary. In his fifties, he has military-short gray hair and is dressed in a rumpled brown suit, has probably worked nonstop all day. He and Benton follow the well-lit corridor. It is spotless and scented with air deodorizer and lined with storage and evidence rooms, all of them requiring electronic passes. There is even a crash cart—Benton can't imagine why—and a scanning electron microscope, the facility the most spacious and best equipped of any morgue he has ever seen. Staffing is another story.

The office has suffered crippling personnel problems for years because of low salaries that fail to attract competent forensic pathologists and other staff. Added to this are alleged mistakes and misdeeds resulting in scathing controversies and public-relations problems that make life and death difficult for everyone involved. The office isn't open to the media or to outsiders, and hostility and distrust are pervasive. Benton would rather come here late at night. To visit during business hours is to feel unwelcome and resented.

He and Thrush pause outside the closed door of an autopsy room that is used in high-profile cases or those that are considered a biohazard or bizarre. His cell phone vibrates. He looks at the display. No ID is usually her.

"Hi," Scarpetta says. "I hope your night's been better than mine."

"I'm at the morgue." Then, to Thrush, "One minute."

"That can't be good," Scarpetta says.

"I'll fill you in later. Got a question. You ever heard of something that happened at a Christmas shop in Las Olas maybe two and a half years ago?"

"By *something* I assume you mean a homicide."

"Right."

"Not offhand. Maybe Lucy can try to track it down. I hear it's snowing up there."

"I'll get you here if I have to hire Santa's reindeer."

"I love you."

"Me, too," he says.

He ends the call and asks Thrush, "Who are we dealing with?"

"Well, Dr. Lonsdale was nice enough to help me out. You'll like him. But he didn't do the autopsy. *She* did."

She is the chief. *She* got where she is because she's a *she*.

"You ask me," Thrush says, "women got no business doing this anyway. What kind of woman would want to do this?"

"There are good ones," Benton says. "Very good ones. Not all of them get where they are because of their gender. More likely, in spite of it."

Thrush is unfamiliar with Scarpetta. Benton never mentions her, not even to people he knows rather well.

"Women shouldn't see shit like this," Thrush says.

The night air is penetrating and milky-white up and down Commercial Street. Snow swarms in lamplight and lights the night until the world glows and seems surreal as the two of them walk in the middle of the deserted silent street east along the water to the cottage Lucy began renting several days ago after Marino got the strange phone call from the man named Hog.

She builds a fire, and she and Stevie sit in front of it on quilts and roll a joint with very good stuff from British Columbia, and they share it. They smoke and talk and laugh, and then Stevie wants more.

"Just one more," she begs as Lucy undresses her.

"That's different," Lucy says, staring at Stevie's slender nude body, at the red handprints on it, maybe tattoos.

There are four of them. Two on her breasts as if someone is grabbing them, two on her upper inner thighs as if someone is forcing her legs apart. There are none on her back, none where Stevie couldn't reach and apply them herself, assuming they are fake. Lucy stares. She touches one of the handprints, places her hand over one of them, fondling Stevie's breast.

"Just checking to see if it's the right fit," Lucy says. "Fake?"

"Why don't you take off your clothes."

Lucy does what she wants, but she won't take off her clothes. For hours, she does what she wants in the firelight, on the quilts, and Stevie lets her, is more alive than anyone Lucy has ever touched, smooth with soft contours, lean in a way Lucy isn't anymore, and when Stevie tries to undress her, almost fights her, Lucy won't allow it, then Stevie gets tired and gives up and Lucy helps her to bed. After she is asleep, Lucy lies awake listening to the eerie whining of the wind, trying to figure out exactly what it sounds like, deciding it doesn't sound like silk stockings after all, but like something distressed and in pain.

7

The autopsy room is small with a tile floor and the usual surgical cart, digital scale, evidence cabinet, autopsy saws and various blades, dissecting boards and a transportable autopsy table latched to the front of a wall-mounted dissecting sink. The walk-in refrigerator is built into a wall, the door partially open.

Thrush hands Benton a pair of blue nitrile gloves, asks him, "You want booties or a mask or anything?"

"No thanks," Benton says as Dr. Lonsdale emerges from the refrigerator, pushing a stainless-steel cadaver carrier bearing the pouched body.

"We need to make this quick," he says as he parks near the sink and locks two of the swivel casters. "I'm already in deep shit with my wife. It's her birthday."

He unzips the pouch and spreads it open. The victim has raggedly cut short, black hair that is damp and still gory with bits of brain and other tissue. There is almost nothing left of her face. It looks as if a small bomb blew up inside her head, which is rather much what happened.

"Shot in the mouth," Dr. Lonsdale says, and he is young with an intensity that borders on impatience. "Massive skull fractures, brain pulpifaction, which of course we usually associate with suicides, but nothing else about this case is consistent with suicide. It appears to me that her head was tilted pretty far back when the trigger was pulled, explaining why her face is basically shot off, some of her teeth blown out. Again, not uncommon in suicides."

He switches on a magnifying lamp and positions it close to the head.

"No need to pry open her mouth," he comments. "Since she has no face left. Thank God for small favors."

Benton leans close and smells the sweet, putrid stench of decomposing blood.

"Soot on the palate, the tongue," Dr. Lonsdale continues. "Superficial lacerations of the tongue, the perioral skin and nasolabial fold due to the bulging-out effect when gases from the shotgun blast expand. Not a pretty way to die."

He unzips the pouch the rest of the way.

"Saved the best for last," Thrush says. "What do you make of it? Reminds me of Crazy Horse."

"You mean the Indian?" Dr. Lonsdale gives him a quizzical look as he unscrews the lid from a small glass jar filled with a clear liquid.

"Yeah. I think he put red handprints on his horse's ass."

There are red handprints on the woman, on her breasts, abdomen and upper inner thighs, and Benton positions the magnifying lamp closer.

Dr. Lonsdale swabs the edge of a handprint and says, "Isopropyl alcohol, a solvent like that will get it off. Obviously, it's not water-soluble and brings to mind the sort of stuff people use for temporary tattooing. Some type of paint or dye. Could also have been done in permanent Magic Marker, I suppose."

"I'm assuming you haven't seen this in any other cases around here," Benton says.

"Not at all."

The magnified handprints are well defined with clean margins, as if made with a stencil, and Benton looks for feathering strokes of a brush, for anything that might indicate how the paint, ink or dye was applied. He can't tell, but based on the density of color, he suspects the body art is recent.

"I suppose she could have gotten this at some point earlier. In other words, it's unrelated to her death," Dr. Lonsdale adds.

"That's what I'm thinking," Thrush agrees. "There's a lot of witchcraft around here with Salem and all."

"What I'm wondering is how quickly something like this begins to fade," Benton says. "Have you measured them to see if they're the same size as her hand?" He indicates the body.

"They look bigger to me," Thrush says, holding out his own hand.

"What about her back?" Benton asks.

"One on each buttock, one between her shoulder blades," Dr. Lonsdale replies. "Look like a man's size, the hands do."

"Yeah," Thrush says.

Dr. Lonsdale pulls the body partially on its side, and Benton studies the handprints on the back.

"Looks like she has some sort of abrasion here," he says, noting a scraped area on the handprint between the shoulder blades. "Some inflammation."

"I'm not clear on all the details," Dr. Lonsdale replies. "It's not my case."

"Looks as if it was painted after she got the scrape," Benton says. "Am I seeing welts, too?"

"Maybe some localized swelling. Histology should answer that. It's not my case," he reminds them. "I didn't participate in her autopsy," he is sure to remind them. "I glanced at her. That was it before I just now rolled her out. I did look over the autopsy report."

Should the chief's work be negligent or incompetent, he's not about to take the blame.

"Any idea how long she's been dead?" Benton asks.

"Well, the cold temperatures would have slowed rigor."

"Frozen when she was found?"

"Not yet. Apparently, her body temperature when she got here was thirty-eight degrees. Fahrenheit. I didn't go to the scene. I can't give you those details."

"The temperature at ten o'clock this morning was twenty-one degrees," Thrush tells Benton. "The weather conditions are on the disk I gave you."

"So the autopsy report has already been dictated," Benton says.

"It's on the disk," Thrush answers.

"Trace evidence?"

"Some soil, fibers, other debris adhering to blood," Thrush replies. "I'll get them run in the labs as quick as I can."

"Tell me about the shotgun shell you recovered," Benton says to him.

"Inside her rectum. You couldn't see it from the outside, but it showed up on x-ray. Damnedest thing. When they first showed me the film, I thought maybe the shell was under her body on the x-ray tray. Had no idea the damn thing was inside her."

"What kind?"

"Remington Express Magnum, twelve-gauge."

"Well, if she shot herself, she's certainly not the one who shoved the shell up her rectum after the fact," Benton says. "You running it through NIBIN?"

"Already in the works," Thrush says. "The firing pin left a nice drag mark. Maybe we'll get lucky."

8

Early the next morning, snow blows sideways over Cape Cod Bay and melts when it touches the water. The snow barely dusts the tawny sliver of beach beyond Lucy's windows but is deep on nearby rooftops and the balcony beyond her bedroom. She pulls the comforter up to her chin and looks out at the water and the snow, unhappy that she has to get up and deal with the woman sleeping next to her, Stevie.

Lucy shouldn't have gone to Lorraine's last night. She wishes she hadn't and can't stop wishing it. She is disgusted with herself and in a hurry to leave the tiny cottage with its wraparound porch and shingled roof, the furniture dingy from endless rounds of renters, the kitchen small and musty with outdated appliances. She watches the early morning play with the horizon, turning it various shades of gray, and the snow is falling almost as hard as it was last night. She thinks of Johnny. He came here to Provincetown a week before he died and met someone. Lucy should have found that out a long time ago, but she couldn't. She couldn't face it. She watches Stevie's regular breathing.

"Are you awake?" Lucy asks. "You need to get up."

She stares at the snow, at sea ducks bobbing on the ruffled gray bay, and wonders why they aren't frozen. Despite what she knows about the insulating qualities of down, she still can't believe that any warm-blooded creature can comfortably float on frigid water in the middle of a blizzard. She feels cold beneath the comforter, chilled and repulsed and uncomfortable in her bra and panties and button-down shirt.

"Stevie, wake up. I've got to get going," she says loudly.

Stevie doesn't stir, her back gently rising and falling with each slow breath, and Lucy is sick with regret and is annoyed and disgusted because she can't seem to stop herself from doing this thing, this thing she hates. For the better part of a year, she has told herself *no more,* and then nights like last night happen and it isn't smart or logical and she is always sorry, always, because it is degrading and then she has to extricate herself and tell more lies. She has no choice. Her life is no longer a choice. She is too deeply into it to choose anything different, and some choices have been made for her. She still can't believe it. She touches her tender breasts and distended belly to make sure it's true and still can't comprehend it. How could this happen to her?

How could Johnny be dead?

She never looked into what happened to him. She walked away and took her secrets with her.

I'm sorry, she thinks, hoping wherever he is, he knows her mind the way he used to, only differently. Maybe he can know her thoughts now. Maybe he understands why she kept away, just accepted he did it to himself. Maybe he was depressed. Maybe he felt ruined. She never believed his brother killed him. She didn't entertain the possibility that someone else did. Then Marino got the phone call, the ominous one from Hog.

"You've got to get up," she says to Stevie.

Lucy reaches for the Colt Mustang .380 pistol on the table by the bed.

"Come on, wake up."

Inside Basil Jenrette's cell, he lies on his steel bed, a thin blanket pulled over him, the kind that doesn't give off poisonous gases like cyanide if there's a fire. The mattress is thin and hard and won't give off deadly gases if there's a fire. The needle would have been unpleasant, the chair worse, but the gas chamber, no. Choking, not breathing, suffocating. *God no.*

When he looks at his mattress when he is making the bed, he thinks about fires and not being able to breathe. He's not so bad. At least he's never done that to anybody, that thing that his piano teacher did until Basil quit his lessons, didn't

care how hard his mother whipped him with the belt. He quit
and wouldn't go back for one more episode of almost gagging, choking, almost suffocating. He didn't think about it
much until the subject of the gas chamber came up. No matter what he knew about the way they execute people down
there in Gainesville, with the needle, the guards threatened
him with the gas chamber, laughed and hooted when he'd
curl up on the bed and start to shake.

Now he doesn't have to worry about the gas chamber or
any other means of execution. He's a science project.

He listens for the drawer at the bottom of the steel door,
listens for it to open, listens for his breakfast tray.

He can't see that it is light outside because there is no window, but he knows it is dawn by the sounds of guards making
their rounds and drawers sliding open and slamming shut as
other inmates get eggs and bacon and biscuits, sometimes
fried eggs, sometimes scrambled. He can smell the food as he
lies on the bed under his nonpoisonous blanket on his nonpoisonous mattress and thinks about his mail. He has to have it.
He feels as furious and anxious as he's ever been. He listens to
footsteps and then Uncle Remus's fat, black face appears behind the mesh opening high up on the door.

That's what Basil calls him. Uncle Remus. Calling him
Uncle Remus is why Basil's not getting his mail anymore.
He hasn't gotten it for a month.

"I want my mail," he says to Uncle Remus's face behind
the mesh. "It's my constitutional right to get my mail."

"What makes you think anybody would write your sorry
ass," the face behind the mesh asks.

Basil can't make out much, just the dark shape of the face
and the wetness of eyes peering in at him. Basil knows what
to do about eyes, how to put them out so they don't shine at
him, so they don't see places they shouldn't before they turn
dark and crazed and he almost suffocates. He can't do much
in here, in his suicide cell, and rage and anxiety twist his
stomach like a dishrag.

"I know I have mail," Basil says. "I want it."

The face vanishes and then the drawer opens. Basil gets

off the bed, takes his tray and the drawer loudly clangs shut
at the bottom of the thick, gray, steel door.

"Hope nobody spit on your food," Uncle Remus says
through the mesh. "Enjoy your breakfast," he says.

The wide plank floor is cold beneath Lucy's bare feet as
she returns to the bedroom. Stevie is asleep under the covers, and Lucy sets two coffees on the bedside table and
slides her hand under the mattress, feeling for the pistol's
magazines. She may have been reckless last night, but not so
reckless that she would leave her pistol loaded with a
stranger in the house.

"Stevie?" she says. "Come on. Wake up. Hey!"

Stevie opens her eyes and stares at Lucy standing by the
bed inserting a magazine into the pistol.

"What a sight," Stevie says, yawning.

"I've got to go." Lucy hands her a coffee.

Stevie stares at the gun. "You must trust me, leaving it
right there on the table all night."

"Why wouldn't I trust you?"

"I guess you lawyers have to worry about all those people
whose lives you've ruined," Stevie says. "You never know
about people these days."

Lucy told her she is a Boston attorney. Stevie probably
thinks a lot of things that aren't true.

"How did you know I like my coffee black?"

"I didn't," Lucy says. "There's no milk or cream in the
house. I've really got to go."

"I think you should stay. Bet I can make it worth your
while. We never finished, now did we? Got me so liquored
up and stoned, I never got your clothes off. That's a first."

"Seems like a lot of things were your first."

"You didn't take your clothes off," Stevie reminds her,
sipping coffee. "That's a first, all right."

"You weren't exactly with it."

"I was with it enough to try. It's not too late to try again."

She sits up and settles into the pillows, and the covers slip

below her breasts, and her nipples are erect in the chilled air.
She knows exactly what she has and what to do with it, and
Lucy doesn't believe what happened last night was a first,
that any of it was.

"God, my head hurts," Stevie says, watching Lucy look at
her. "I thought you told me good tequila wouldn't do that."

"You mixed it with vodka."

Stevie plumps the pillows behind her and the covers settle
low around her hips. She pushes her dark-blond hair out of
her eyes, and she is quite something to look at in the morning light, but Lucy wants nothing more with her and is put
off by the red handprints again.

"Remember I asked you about those last night?" Lucy
says, looking at them.

"You asked me a lot of things last night."

"I asked you where you got them done."

"Why don't you climb back in." Stevie pats the bed, and
her eyes seem to burn Lucy's skin.

"It must have hurt getting them. Unless they're fake and I
happen to think they are."

"I can clean them off with nail polish remover or baby oil.
I'm sure you don't have nail polish remover or baby oil."

"What's the point?" Lucy stares at the handprints.

"It wasn't my idea."

"Then whose?"

"Someone annoying. She does it to me and I have to
clean them off."

Lucy frowns, staring at her. "You let someone paint them
on you. Well, kind of kinky," and she feels a pinch of jealousy as she imagines someone painting Stevie's naked
body. "You don't have to tell me who," Lucy says as if
it's unimportant.

"Much better to be the one who does it to someone else,"
Stevie says, and Lucy feels jealous again. "Come here," Stevie says in her soothing voice, patting the bed again.

"We need to head out of here. I've got things to do,"
Lucy replies, carrying black cargo pants, a bulky black
sweater and the pistol into the tiny bathroom that adjoins
the bedroom.

She shuts the door and locks it. She undresses without looking at herself in the mirror, wishing what has happened to her body is imagined or a nightmare. She touches herself in the shower to see if anything has changed and avoids the mirror as she towels herself dry.

"Look at you," Stevie says when Lucy emerges from the bathroom, dressed and distracted, her mood much worse than it was moments before. "You look like some kind of secret agent. You're really something. I want to be just like you."

"You don't know me."

"After last night, I know enough," she says, staring Lucy up and down. "Who wouldn't want to be just like you? You don't seem afraid of anything. Are you afraid of anything?"

Lucy leans over and rearranges the bed linens around Stevie, covering her up to her chin, and Stevie's face changes. She stiffens, stares down at the bed.

"I'm sorry. I didn't mean to offend you," Stevie says meekly, her cheeks turning red.

"It's cold in here. I was just covering you because . . ."

"It's okay. It's happened before." She looks up, her eyes bottomless pits filled with fear and sadness. "You think I'm ugly, don't you. Ugly and fat. You don't like me. In the daylight, you don't."

"You're anything but ugly or fat," Lucy says. "And I do like you. It's just . . . Shit, I'm sorry. I didn't mean to . . ."

"I'm not surprised. Why would someone like you like someone like me?" Stevie says, pulling the blanket around her and off the bed, covering herself completely as she gets up. "You could have anybody. I'm grateful. Thank you. I won't tell anyone."

Lucy is speechless, watching Stevie retrieve her clothes from the living room, getting dressed, shaking, her mouth contorting in peculiar ways.

"God, please don't cry, Stevie."

"At least call me the right thing!"

"What is that supposed to mean?"

Her eyes huge and dark and scared, Stevie says, "I'd like to go now, please. I won't tell anyone. Thank you, I'm very grateful."

"Why are you talking like this?" Lucy says.

Stevie retrieves her long, black, hooded coat and puts it on. Through the window, Lucy watches her walk off in a swirl of snow, her long, black coat flapping around her tall, black boots.

9

Half an hour later, Lucy zips up her ski jacket and tucks the pistol and two extra magazines in a pocket.

She locks the cottage and climbs down the snow-covered wooden steps to the street as she thinks about Stevie and her inexplicable behavior, feeling guilty. She thinks about Johnny and feels guilty, remembering San Francisco, when he took her to dinner and reassured her that everything would be all right.

You're going to be fine, he promised.

I can't live like this, she said.

It was women's night at Mecca on Market Street, and the restaurant was crowded with women, attractive women who looked happy and confident and pleased with themselves. Lucy felt stared at, and it bothered her in a way it never had before.

I want to do something about it now, she said. *Look at me.*

Lucy, you look great.

I haven't been this fat since I was ten.

You stop taking your medicine and . . .

It makes me sick and exhausted.

I'm not going to let you do anything rash. You have to trust me.

He held her gaze in the candlelight, and his face will always be in her mind, looking at her the way he did that night. He was handsome, with fine features and unusual eyes the color of tiger eyes, and she could keep nothing from him. He knew all there was to know in every way imaginable.

Loneliness and guilt follow her as she follows the snowy sidewalk west along the Cape Cod Bay. She ran away. She remembers when she heard about his death. She heard about it the way no one should, on the radio.

A prominent doctor was found shot to death in a Hollywood apartment in what sources close to the investigation say is a possible suicide. . . .

She had no one to ask. She wasn't supposed to know Johnny and had never met his brother, Laurel, or any of their friends, so who could she ask?

Her cell phone vibrates, and she tucks the earpiece in her ear and answers.

"Where are you?" Benton says.

"Walking through a blizzard in Ptown. Well, not literally a blizzard. It's starting to taper off." She is dazed, a little hung-over.

"Anything interesting come up?"

She thinks of last night and feels bewildered and ashamed. What she says is, "Only that he wasn't alone when he was here last, the week before he died. Apparently, he came here right after his surgery, then went down to Florida."

"Laurel with him?"

"No."

"How did he manage alone?"

"As I said, it appears he wasn't alone."

"Who told you?"

"A bartender. Apparently, he met someone."

"We know who?"

"A woman. Someone a lot younger."

"A name?"

"Jan, don't know the rest of it. Johnny was upset about the surgery, which wasn't all that successful, as you know. People do a lot of things when they're scared and don't feel good about themselves."

"How are you feeling?"

"Okay," she lies.

She was a coward. She was selfish.

"You don't sound okay," Benton says to her. "What happened to Johnny isn't your fault."

"I ran away from it. I didn't do a damn thing."

"Why don't you spend some time with us. Kay's going to be up here for a week. We'd love to see you. You and I will find some private time to talk," Benton the psychologist says.

"I don't want to see her. Somehow make her understand."

"Lucy, you can't keep doing this to her."

"I'm not trying to hurt anyone," she says, thinking of Stevie again.

"Then tell her the truth. It's that simple."

"You called me." She abruptly changes the subject.

"I need you to do something for me as soon as possible," he replies. "I'm on a secured phone."

"Unless there's anyone around here with an intercept system, I am too. Go ahead."

He tells her about a murder that supposedly occurred at some sort of Christmas shop, supposedly in the Las Olas area about two and a half years ago. He tells her everything Basil Jenrette told him. He says Scarpetta is unfamiliar with any case that sounds similar, but she wasn't working in South Florida back then.

"The information came from a sociopath," he reminds her, "so I'm not holding my breath that there's anything to it."

"The alleged victim in the Christmas shop have her eyes gouged out?"

"He didn't tell me that. I didn't want to ask him too many questions until I check out his story. Can you run it in HIT, see what you can find?"

"I'll get started on the plane," she says.

10

The clock on the wall above the bookcase reads half past noon, and the attorney representing a kid who probably murdered his baby brother is taking his time going through paperwork on the other side of Kay Scarpetta's desk.

Dave is young, dark, nicely built, one of those men whose irregular features somehow fit together in a very appealing way. He is known for his flamboyance in the malpractice arena, and whenever he comes to the Academy, the secretaries and female students suddenly find reasons to walk past Scarpetta's door, except Rose, of course. She has been Scarpetta's secretary for fifteen years, is well past retirement age and isn't particularly vulnerable to male charm unless it is Marino's. He is probably the only man whose flirtations she welcomes, and Scarpetta picks up the phone to ask her where he is. He is supposed to be here for this meeting.

"I tried him last night," Scarpetta says over the phone to Rose. "Several times."

"Let me see if I can find him," Rose says. "He's been acting rather odd lately."

"Not just lately."

Dave studies an autopsy report, his head tilted back as he reads through the horn-rimmed glasses low on his nose.

"The last few weeks have been worse. I have a funny feeling it's about a woman."

"See if you can find him."

She hangs up and looks across her desk to see if Dave is ready to get on with his prejudicial questions about another difficult death that he is convinced can be resolved for a substantial fee. Unlike most police departments that invite the assistance of the Academy's scientific and medical experts, lawyers usually pay, and, as a rule, most clients who can pay are representing people who are as guilty as hell.

"Marino not coming?" he asks.

"We're trying to find him."

"I've got a deposition in less than an hour." He turns a page of the report. "Seems to me when all is said and done, the findings are in favor of an impact and nothing more."

"I'm not going to say that in court," she replies, looking at the report, at the details of an autopsy she didn't perform. "What I can say is that while a subdural hematoma can be caused by an impact—in this case, the alleged fall off the couch onto the tile floor—it is highly unlikely, was more likely caused by violent shaking that causes shearing forces in the cranial cavity and subdural bleeding and injury to the spinal cord."

"As for the retinal hemorrhages, aren't we in agreement those can also be caused by trauma, such as his head striking the tile floor, resulting in a subdural?"

"Not at all in a short fall like this. Again, was more likely caused by the head whipping back and forth. Just as the report makes clear."

"I don't think you're helping me out much here, Kay."

"If you don't want an unbiased opinion, you should find another expert."

"There is no other expert. You're unrivaled." He smiles. "What about a vitamin K deficiency?"

"If you have antemortem blood that revealed protein-induced vitamin K deficiency," she replies. "If you're looking for leprechauns."

"Problem is, we don't have antemortem blood. He didn't survive long enough to get to the hospital."

"That's a problem."

"Well, shaken baby syndrome can't be proved. It's definitely unclear and improbable. You can at least say that."

"What's clear is you don't have mama's fourteen-year-old son babysit his newborn brother when the son has already been to juvenile court twice for assault on other children and is legendary for his explosive temper."

"And you won't say that."

"No."

"Look, all I ask is you point out there's no definitive evidence that this baby was shaken."

"I will also point out there's no definitive evidence that he wasn't, that I can find no fault with the autopsy report in question."

"The Academy's great," Dave says, getting up from his chair. "But you guys are roughing me up. Marino's a no-show. Now you're leaving me hanging out to dry."

"I'm sorry about Marino," she says.

"Maybe you need to control him better."

"That's not exactly possible."

Dave tucks in his bold striped shirt, straightens his bold silk tie, puts on his tailored silk jacket. He arranges his paperwork inside his crocodile briefcase.

"Rumor has it you're looking into the Johnny Swift case," he then says, snapping shut the silver clasps.

Scarpetta is caught for a minute. She can't imagine how Dave could know this.

What she says is, "It's been my practice to pay little attention to rumors, Dave."

"His brother owns one of my favorite restaurants in South Beach. Called Rumors, ironically," he says. "You know, Laurel's had some problems."

"I don't know anything about him."

"Someone who works there is passing around the story that Laurel killed Johnny for money, for whatever Johnny might have left him in his will. Says Laurel's got habits he can't afford."

"Sounds like hearsay. Or maybe someone who has a grudge."

Dave walks to the door.

"I haven't talked to her. Every time I try, she's not there. I personally think Laurel's a really nice guy, by the way. I just find it a bit coincidental that I start hearing stories and then Johnny's case is reopened."

"I'm not aware it was ever closed," Scarpetta says.

Snowflakes are icy and sharp, the sidewalks and streets frosted white. Few people are out.

Lucy walks briskly, sipping from a steaming hot latte, heading to the Anchor Inn, where she checked in several days ago under a fictitious name so she could hide her rented Hummer. She hasn't parked it at the cottage once, never interested in strangers knowing what she drives. She veers off on a narrow drive that winds around to the small parking lot on the water where the Hummer is covered with snow. She unlocks the doors, starts the engine and turns on the defrost, and the white-blanketed windows give her the cool, shady sensation of being inside an igloo.

She is calling one of her pilots when a gloved hand suddenly begins wiping snow off her side window and a black-hooded face fills the glass. Lucy aborts the call and drops the phone on the seat.

She stares at Stevie for a long moment, then lowers the window as her mind races through possibilities. It isn't a good thing that she was followed here. It is a very bad thing that she didn't notice she was being followed.

"What are you doing?" Lucy asks.

"I just wanted to tell you something."

Stevie's face has an expression that is hard to read. Maybe she is near tears and extremely upset and hurt, or it could be the cold, sharp wind blowing in from the bay that is making her eyes so bright.

"You're the most awesome person I've ever met," Stevie says. "I think you're my hero. My new hero."

Lucy isn't sure if Stevie is mocking her. Maybe she isn't.

"Stevie, I've got to get to the airport."

"They haven't started canceling flights yet. But it's supposed to be terrible the rest of the week."

"Thanks for the weather update," Lucy says, and the look in Stevie's eyes is fierce and unnerving. "Look, I'm sorry. I never meant to hurt your feelings."

"You didn't," Stevie says, as if this is the first she's heard of it. "Not at all. I didn't think I'd like you so much. I wanted to find you to tell you that. Tuck it away in some part of that clever head of yours, maybe remember it on a rainy day. I just never thought I would like you so much."

"You keep saying that."

"It's intriguing. You come across so sure of yourself, arrogant really. Hard and distant. But I realize it's not who you are inside. Funny how things turn out so differently from what you expect."

Snow is blowing inside the Hummer, dusting the interior.

"How did you find me?" Lucy asks.

"I went back to your place but you were gone. I followed your footprints in the snow. They led right here. You wear what? Size eight? It wasn't hard."

"Well, I'm sorry for . . ."

"Please," Stevie says intensely, strongly. "I know I'm not just another notch on your belt, as they say."

"I'm not into that," Lucy says, but she is.

She knows it, even if she would never describe it like that. She feels bad for Stevie. She feels bad for her aunt, for Johnny, for everyone she has failed.

"Some might argue you're a notch on mine," Stevie says playfully, seductively, and Lucy doesn't want to have the feeling again.

Stevie is sure of herself again, full of secrets again, amazingly attractive again.

Lucy shoves the Hummer into reverse as snow blows in and her face stings from the snow and the wind blowing off the water.

Stevie digs in her coat pocket, pulls out a slip of paper, hands it to her through the open window.

"My phone number," she says.

The area code is 617, the Boston area. She never told Lucy where she lived. Lucy never asked.

"That's all I wanted to say to you," Stevie says. "And happy Valentine's Day."

They look at each other through the open window, the engine rumbling, snow coming down and clinging to Stevie's black coat. She's beautiful and Lucy feels what she felt at Lorraine's. She thought it was gone. She is feeling it.

"I'm not like all the rest," Stevie says, looking into Lucy's eyes.

"You're not."

"My cell phone number," Stevie says. "I actually live in Florida. After I left Harvard, I never bothered to change my cell phone number. It doesn't matter. Free minutes, you know."

"You went to Harvard?"

"I usually don't mention it. It can be rather off-putting."

"Where in Florida?"

"Gainesville," she says. "Happy Valentine's Day," she says again. "I hope it turns out to be the most special one you've ever had."

11

The smart board inside classroom 1A is filled with a colorful photograph of a man's torso. His shirt is unbuttoned, a large knife plunged into his hairy chest.

"Suicide," one of the students volunteers from his desk.

"Here's another fact. Although you can't tell from this picture," Scarpetta says to the sixteen students who make up this session's Academy class, "he has multiple stab wounds."

"Homicide." The student quickly changes his answer and everybody laughs.

Scarpetta flashes up the next slide, this one of multiple wounds clustered near the fatal one.

"They look shallow," another student says.

"What about the angle? They should be angled up if he did it to himself?"

"Not necessarily, but here's a question," Scarpetta says from the podium in the front of the classroom. "What might his unbuttoned shirt tell you?"

Silence.

"If you were going to stab yourself, would you do it through your clothing?" she asks. "And, by the way, you're right." She directs this to the student who made the comment about shallow stab wounds. "Most of these"—she points them out on the smart board—"barely broke the skin. What we call *hesitation marks*."

The students take notes. They are a bright, eager bunch, different ages, different backgrounds, from different areas of the country, two of them from England. Several are detectives who want intensive forensic training in crime-scene investigation. Others are death investigators who want the same thing. Some are college graduates working on master's degrees in psychology, nuclear biology and microscopy. One is an assistant district attorney who wants more convictions in court.

She displays another slide on the smart board, this one an especially gruesome photograph of a man with his intestines spilling out of a gaping incision to his abdomen. Several students groan. One says "ouch."

"Who's familiar with seppuku?" Scarpetta asks.

"Hari-kari," a voice sounds from the doorway.

Dr. Joe Amos, this year's forensic pathology fellow, walks in as if it is his class. He is tall and gangly, with an unruly shock of black hair, a long, pointed chin and dark, glittering eyes. He reminds Scarpetta of a black bird, a crow.

"I don't mean to interrupt," he says, then he does it anyway. "This guy"—he nods at the gruesome image on the smart board—"took a big hunting knife, stabbed it into one side of his abdomen and slashed across to the other. That's called motivation."

"Was it your case, Dr. Amos?" a student asks, this one female and pretty.

Dr. Amos moves closer to her, looks very serious and important. "No. What you need to remember, though, is this: The way you can tell suicide versus homicide is if it's a suicide, the person will slash the knife across his abdomen and then cut upwards, making the classic L shape that you see in hari-kari. Which is not what you see here."

He directs the students' attention to the smart board.

Scarpetta holds in her temper.

"Be kind of hard to do that in a homicide," he adds.

"This one's not L-shaped."

"Precisely," he says. "Who wants to vote for homicide?"

A few students raise their hands.

"My vote, too," he says with confidence.

"Dr. Amos? How quickly would he have died?"

"You might survive a few minutes. You're going to bleed out really fast. Dr. Scarpetta, I wonder if I could see you for a minute. I'm sorry to interrupt," he says to the students.

She and Joe walk into the hallway.

"What is it?" she asks.

"The hell scene we have scheduled for later this afternoon," he says. "I'd like to spice it up a little."

"This couldn't wait until after class?"

"Well, I thought you could get one of the students to volunteer. They'll do anything you ask."

She ignores the flattery.

"Ask if one of them will help out with this afternoon's hell scene, but you can't tell the details in front of everyone."

"And what are the details, exactly?"

"I was thinking of Jenny. Maybe you'll let her skip your three o'clock class so she can help me." He refers to the pretty student who asked him if the evisceration was his case.

Scarpetta has seen them together on more than one occasion. Joe is engaged, but that doesn't seem to stop him from being quite friendly with attractive female students, no matter how much the Academy discourages it. So far, he hasn't been caught committing an unredeemable infraction, and, in a way, she wishes he had been. She'd love to get rid of him.

"We get her to play the perp," he explains quietly, excitedly. "She looks so innocent, so sweet. So we take two students at a time, have them work a homicide, the victim shot multiple times while on the toilet. This is in one of the motel rooms, of course, and Jenny comes in acting all broken up, hysterical. The dead guy's daughter. We'll see if the students let their guard down."

Scarpetta is silent.

"Of course, there'll be a few cops at the scene. Let's say they're looking around, assuming the perp's fled. Point is, we'll see if anybody's smart enough to make sure this pretty young thing isn't the person who just blew the guy away, her father, while he was taking a dump. And guess what? She is. They let their guard down, she pulls a gun and starts shooting, gets taken out. And voilà. A classic suicide by police."

"You can ask Jenny yourself after class," Scarpetta says as she tries to figure out why the scenario seems familiar.

Joe is obsessed with hell scenes, an innovation of Marino's, extreme mock crime scenes that are supposed to mirror the real risks and unpleasantries of real death. She sometimes thinks Joe should give up forensic pathology and sell his soul to Hollywood. If he has a soul. The scenario he has just proposed reminds her of something.

"Pretty good, huh?" he says. "It could happen in real life."

Then she remembers. It did happen in real life.

"We had a case in Virginia like that," she recalls. "When I was chief."

"Really?" he says, amazed. "Guess there's nothing new under the sun."

"And by the way, Joe," she says. "In most cases of seppuku, of hari-kari, the cause of death is cardiac arrest due to sudden cardiac collapse due to a sudden drop in intra-abdominal pressure due to sudden evisceration. Not exsanguination."

"Your case? The one in there?" He indicates the classroom.

"Marino's and mine. From years back. And one other thing," she adds. "It's a suicide, not a homicide."

12

The Citation X flies south at just under mach one as Lucy uploads files on a virtual private network that is so firewall-protected not even Homeland Security can break in.

At least, she believes her information infrastructure is secure. She believes that no hacker, including the government, can monitor the transmissions of classified data generated by the Heterogenous Image Transaction database management system that goes by the acronym HIT. She developed and programmed HIT herself. The government doesn't know about it, she is sure of it. Few people do, she is sure of it. HIT is proprietary, and she could sell the software easily, but she doesn't need the money, having made her fortune years ago from other software development, mostly from some of the same search engines she is conducting through cyberspace this minute, looking for any violent deaths that might have occurred in a South Florida business of any description.

Other than homicides in the expected convenience and liquor stores, massage parlors and topless clubs, she has found no violent crime, unsolved or otherwise, that might verify what Basil Jenrette told Benton. However, there once was a business called The Christmas Shop. It was located at the intersection of A1A and East Las Olas Boulevard, along a strip of tacky touristy boutiques and cafés and ice-cream joints on the beach. Two years ago, The Christmas Shop was sold to a chain called Beach Bums that specializes in T-shirts, swimwear and souvenirs.

It is hard for Joe to believe how many cases Scarpetta has worked in what is a relatively brief career. Forensic patholo-gists rarely land their first job until they are thirty, assuming their arduous educational track is continuous. Added to her six years of postgraduate medical training were three more for law school. By the time she was thirty-five, she was the chief of the most prominent medical examiner system in the United States. Unlike most chiefs, she wasn't just an administrator. She did autopsies, thousands of them.

Most of them are in a database that is supposed to be accessible to her only, and she's even gotten federal grants to conduct various research studies on violence—sexual violence, drug-related violence, domestic violence—all kinds of violence. In quite a number of her old cases, Marino, a local homicide detective when she was chief, was the lead investigator. So she has his reports in the database as well. It's a candy store. It's a fountain spewing fine champagne. It's orgasmic.

Joe scrolls through case C328-93, the police suicide that is the model for this afternoon's hell scene. He clicks on the scene photographs again, thinking about Jenny. In the real case, the trigger-happy daughter is facedown in a pool of blood on the living-room floor. She was shot three times, once in the abdomen, twice in the chest, and he thinks about the way she was dressed when she killed her daddy while he was on the toilet and then put on an act in front of the police before pulling out her pistol again. She died barefoot, in a pair of cutoff blue jeans and a T-shirt. She wasn't wearing panties or a bra. He clicks to her autopsy photographs, not as interested in what she looked like with a Y incision as in how she looked naked on the cold, steel table. She was only fifteen when the police shot her dead, and he thinks of Jenny.

He looks up, smiles at her from the other side of his desk. She has been sitting patiently, waiting for instructions. He opens a desk drawer and gets out a Glock nine-millimeter, drops out the magazine, pulls back the slide to make sure the chamber is clear, and pushes the pistol across the desk to her.

"You ever shot a gun before?" he asks his newest teacher's pet.

She has the cutest turned-up nose and huge eyes the color of milk chocolate, and he imagines her naked and dead like the girl in the scene photograph on his screen.

"I grew up with guns," she says. "What's that you're looking at, if you don't mind my asking."

"E-mail," he says, and not telling the truth has never bothered him.

He rather likes not telling the truth, likes it far more than dislikes it. Truth isn't always truth. What is true? What is true is what he decides is true. It's all a matter of interpretation. Jenny cranes her head to get a better look at what's on his screen.

"Cool. People e-mail entire case files to you."

"Sometimes," he says, clicking to a different photograph, and the color printer behind his desk starts up. "What we're doing is classified," he then says. "Can I trust you?"

"Of course, Dr. Amos. I completely understand classified. If I didn't, I'm training for the wrong profession."

A color photograph of the dead girl in a pool of blood on the living-room floor slides into the printer tray. Joe turns around to get it, looks it over, hands it to her.

"That's going to be you this afternoon," he says.

"I hope not literally," she teases.

"And this is your gun." He looks at the Glock in front of her on the desk. "Where do you propose you hide it?"

She looks at the photograph, not fazed by it, and asks, "Where did she hide it?"

"You can't see it in the photograph," he replies. "A pocketbook, which, by the way, should have cued somebody. She finds her father dead, supposedly, calls nine-one-one, opens the door when the cops get there and has her pocketbook. She's hysterical, never left the house, so why's she walking around with her pocketbook?"

"That's what you want me to do."

"The pistol goes in your pocketbook. At some point, you reach in for tissues because you're boo-hooing, and you pull the gun and start shooting."

"Anything else?"

"Then you're going to get killed. Try to look pretty."

She smiles. "Anything else?"

"The way she's dressed." He looks at her, tries to show it in his eyes, what he wants.

She knows.

"I don't have the exact same thing," she replies, playing him a little, acting naïve.

She's anything but, probably been fucking since kindergarten.

"Well, Jenny, see if you can approximate. Shorts, T-shirt, no shoes or socks."

"She doesn't have on underwear, looks to me."

"Then there's that."

"She looks like a slut."

"Okay. Then look like a slut," he says.

Jenny thinks this is very funny.

"I mean, you are a slut, aren't you?" he asks, his small, dark eyes looking at her. "If not, I'll ask somebody else. This hell scene requires a slut."

"You don't need someone else."

"Oh, really."

"Really," she says.

She turns around, glancing at the shut door as if worried that someone might walk in. He doesn't say anything.

"We could get in trouble," she says.

"We won't."

"I don't want to get kicked out," she says.

"You want to be a death investigator when you grow up."

She nods, looking at him, coolly playing with the top button of her Academy polo shirt. She looks good in it. He likes the way she fills it.

"I'm a grown-up," she says.

"You're from Texas," he then says, looking at the way she fills her polo shirt, the way she fills her snug-fitting khaki cargo pants. "They grow things big in Texas, don't they."

"Why, are you talking dirty to me, Dr. Amos?" she drawls.

He imagines her dead. He imagines her in a pool of blood, shot dead on the floor. He imagines her naked on the steel table. One of life's fables is that dead bodies can't be sexy. Naked is naked if the person looks good and hasn't been dead long. To say a man has never had a thought about a beautiful woman who happens to be dead is a joke. Cops pin photographs on their corkboards, pictures of female victims who are exceptionally fine. Male medical examiners give lectures to cops and show them certain pictures, deliberately pick the ones they'll like. Joe has seen it. He knows what guys do.

"You do a good job getting killed in the hell scene," he says to Jenny, "and I'll cook dinner for you. I'm a wine connoisseur."

"You're also engaged."

"She's at a conference in Chicago. Maybe she'll get snowed in."

Jenny gets up. She looks at her watch, then looks at him.

"Who was your teacher's pet before me?" she asks.

"You're special," he says.

13

An hour out from Signature Aviation in Fort Lauderdale, Lucy gets up for another coffee and a bathroom break. The sky beyond the jet's small oval windows is overcast with mounting storm clouds.

She settles back into her leather seat and executes more queries of Broward County tax assessment and real-estate records, news stories and anything else she can think of to see what she can find out about the former Christmas shop. From the mid-seventies to the early nineties, it was a diner called Rum Runner's. For two years after that, it was a fudge and ice-cream parlor called Coco Nuts. Then, in 2000, the building was rented to a Mrs. Florrie Anna Quincy, the widow of a wealthy landscaper from West Palm Beach.

Lucy's fingers rest lightly on the keyboard as she scans a feature article that ran in the *Miami Herald* not long after The Christmas Shop opened. It says that Mrs. Quincy grew up in Chicago, where her father was a commodities broker, and every Christmas he volunteered as a Santa at Macy's department store.

"Christmas was just the most magical time in our lives," Mrs. Quincy said. "My father's love was lumber futures, and maybe because he grew up in the logging country of Alberta, Canada, we had Christmas trees in the house all year round, big potted spruces decorated with white lights and little carved figures. I guess that's why I like to have Christmas all year round."

Her shop is an astonishing collection of ornaments, music boxes, Santas of every description, winter wonderlands and tiny electric trains running on tiny tracks. One has to be careful moving down the aisles of her fragile, fanciful world, and it is easy to forget there are sunshine, palm trees and the ocean right outside her door. Since opening The Christmas Shop last month, Mrs. Quincy says there has been quite a lot of traffic, but far more customers come to browse than to buy . . .

Lucy sips her coffee and eyes the cream-cheese bagel on the burlwood tray. She is hungry but afraid to eat. She thinks about food constantly, obsessed with her weight, knowing that dieting won't help. She can starve herself all she wants and it won't change the way she looks and feels. Her body was her most finely tuned machine, and it has betrayed her.

She executes another search and tries Marino on the phone built into the armrest of her seat as she scans more results from her queries. He answers but the reception is bad.

"I'm in the air," she says, reading what is on her screen.

"When you going to learn to fly that thing?"

"Probably never. Don't have time to get all the ratings. I barely have time for helicopters these days."

She doesn't want to have time. The more she flies, the more she loves it, and she doesn't want to love it anymore. Medication has to be explained to the FAA unless it is some innocuous over-the-counter remedy, and the next time she goes to the flight surgeon to renew her medical certificate, she will have to list Dostinex. Questions will be raised. Government bureaucrats will rip apart her privacy and probably find some excuse to revoke her license. The only way around it is to never take the medicine again, and she has tried to do without it for a while. Or she can give up flying completely.

"I'll stick to Harleys," Marino is saying.

"I just got a tip. Not about that case. A different one, maybe."

"From who?" he says suspiciously.

"Benton. Apparently, some patient passed along a story about some unsolved murder in Las Olas."

She is careful how she words it. Marino hasn't been told about PREDATOR. Benton doesn't want him involved, fearing Marino wouldn't understand or be helpful. Marino's philosophy about violent offenders is to rough them up, to lock them up, to put them to death as cruelly as possible. He is probably the last person on the planet to care if a murderous psychopath is really mentally ill as opposed to evil, or if a pedophile can no more help his proclivities than a psychotic individual can help his delusions. Marino thinks psychological insights and explorations in structural and functional brain imaging are a crock of shit.

"Apparently, this patient claims that maybe two and a half years ago, a woman was raped and murdered in The Christmas Shop," Lucy is explaining to Marino, worried that one of these days she will let it slip that Benton is evaluating inmates.

Marino knows that McLean, the teaching hospital for Harvard, the model psychiatric hospital with its self-pay Pavillion that caters to the rich and famous, is certainly not a forensic psychiatric institution. If prisoners are being transported there for evaluations, something unusual and clandestine is going on.

"The what?" Marino asks.

She repeats what she just said, adding, "Owned by a Florrie Anna Quincy, white woman, thirty-eight, husband had a bunch of nurseries in West Palm . . ."

"Trees or kids?"

"Trees. Mostly citrus. The Christmas Shop was around for only two years, from 2000 to 2002."

Lucy types in more commands and converts data files to text files that she will e-mail to Benton.

"Ever heard of a place called Beach Bums?"

"You're breaking up on me," Marino says.

"Hello? Is this better? Marino?"

"I can hear you."

"That's the name of the business there now. Mrs. Quincy and her seventeen-year-old daughter, Helen, vanished in July of 2002. I found an article about it in the newspaper. Not much in the way of follow-up, just a small article here and there and nothing at all in the past year."

"So maybe they turned up and the media didn't cover it," Marino replies.

"Nothing I can find would indicate they're alive and well. In fact, the son tried to have them declared legally dead last spring with no success. Maybe you can check with the Fort Lauderdale police, see if anybody remembers anything about Mrs. Quincy's and her daughter's disappearance. I plan to drop by Beach Bums at some point tomorrow."

"The Fort Lauderdale cops wouldn't let it go like that without a damn good reason."

"Let's find out what it is," she says.

At the USAir ticket counter, Scarpetta continues to argue.

"It's impossible," she says again, about to lose her temper, she's so frustrated. "Here's my record location number, my printed receipt. Right here. First class, departure time six-twenty. How can my reservation have been cancelled?"

"Ma'am, it's right here in the computer. Your reservation was cancelled at two-fifteen."

"Today?" Scarpetta refuses to believe it.

There must be a mistake.

"Yes, today."

"That's impossible. I certainly didn't call to cancel."

"Well, someone did."

"Then rebook it," Scarpetta says, reaching in her bag for her wallet.

"The flight's full. I can waitlist you for coach, but there's seven other people ahead of you."

Scarpetta reschedules her flight for tomorrow and calls Rose.

"I'm afraid you're going to have to come back and get me," Scarpetta says.

"Oh, no. What happened. Weathered out?"

"Somehow my reservation got cancelled. The plane's overbooked. Rose, did you call for a confirmation earlier?"

"I most certainly did. Around lunchtime."

"I don't know what happened," Scarpetta says, thinking about Benton, about their Valentine's Day together. "Shit!" she says.

14

The yellow moon is misshapen like an overripe mango, hanging heavy over scrubby trees and weeds and dense shadows. In the uneven light of the moon, Hog can see well enough to make out the thing.

He sees it coming because he knows where to look. For several minutes, he has detected its infrared energy in the Heat Stalker he moves horizontally in the dark in a slow scan, like a wand, like a magic wand. A line of bright-red hatch marks marches across the rear LED window of the lightweight olive-green PVC tube as it detects differences in the surface temperatures of the warm-blooded thing and the earth.

He is Hog, and his body is a thing, and he can leave it on demand and no one can see him. No one can see him now in the middle of the empty night holding the Heat Stalker like a leveler while it detects warmth radiating from living flesh and alerts him with small bright-red marks that flow in single file across the dark glass.

Probably the thing is a raccoon.

Stupid thing. Hog silently talks to it as he sits cross-legged on sandy soil and scans. He glances down at the bright red marks moving across the lens at the rear end of the tube, the front end pointed at the thing. He searches the shadowy berm and feels the ruined old house behind him, feels its pull. His head is thick because of the earplugs, his breathing loud, the way it sounds when you breathe through a snorkel, submerged and silent, nothing but the sound of your own rapid, shallow breaths. He doesn't like earplugs, but it is important to wear them.

You know what happens now, he silently says to the thing. *I guess you don't know.*

He watches the dark, fat shape creep along, low to the ground. It moves like a thick, furry cat, and maybe it is a cat. Slowly, it moves through ragged Bermuda and torpedo grass and sedge, moving in and out of thick shadows beneath the spiny silhouettes of spindly pines and the brittle litter of dead trees. He scans, watching the thing, watching the red marks flow across the lens. The thing is stupid, the breeze blowing the wrong way for it to pick up his scent and be anything but stupid.

He turns off the Heat Stalker and rests it in his lap. He picks up the camouflage finished Mossberg 835 Ulti-Mag pump, the stock hard and cool against his jaw as he lines up the tritium ghost ring with the thing.

Where you think you're going? he mocks it.

The thing doesn't run. Stupid thing.

Go on. Run. See what happens.

It continues its oblivious lumbering pace, low to the ground.

He feels his own heart thud hard and slow, and hears his own rapid breathing as he follows the thing with the glowing green post and squeezes the trigger and the shotgun blast cracks open the quiet night. The thing jerks and goes still in the dirt. He removes the earplugs and listens for a cry or grunt but hears nothing, just distant traffic on South 27 and the gritty sound of his own feet as he gets up and shakes out the cramps in his legs. He slowly ejects the shell, catches it, stuffs it in a pocket and walks through the berm. He pushes the pressure pad on the shotgun's slide and the SureFire WeaponLight shines down on the thing.

It is a cat, furry and striped with a swollen belly. He nudges it over. It is pregnant, and he considers shooting it again as he listens. There is nothing, not a movement, not a sound, not a sign of any life left. The thing was probably slinking toward the ruined house, looking for food. He thinks about it smelling food. If it thought there was food in the house, then recent occupation is detectable. He ponders this possibility as he presses in the safety and shoulders the shotgun, draping his forearm over the stock like a lumberjack shouldering an ax. He stares at the dead thing and thinks of the carved wooden lumberjack in The Christmas Shop, the big one by the door.

"Stupid thing," he says, and there is no one to hear him, only the dead thing.

"No, you're the stupid thing," God's voice sounds from behind him.

He takes out the earplugs and turns around. She is there in black, a black, flowing shape in the moonlit night.

"I told you not to do that," she says.

"No one can hear it out here," he replies, shifting the shotgun to his other shoulder and seeing the wooden lumberjack as if it is right in front of him.

"I'm not telling you again."

"I didn't know you were here."

"You know where I am if I choose for you to know."

"I got you the *Field & Stream*s. Two of them. And the paper, the glossy laser paper."

"I told you to get me six in all, including two *Fly Fishing*, two *Angling Journals*."

"I stole them. It was too hard to get six at once."

"Then go back. Why are you so stupid?"

She is God. She has an IQ of a hundred and fifty.

"You will do what I say," she says.

God is a woman, and she is it, and there is no other. She became God after he did the bad thing and was sent away, sent very far away where it was cold and kept snowing, and then he came back and by then, she had somehow become God and she told him he is her Hand. The Hand of God. Hog.

He watches God go away, dissolving in the night. He hears the loud engine as she flies away, flying down the highway. And he wonders if she'll ever have sex with him again. All the time he thinks about it. When she became God, she wouldn't have sex with him. Theirs is a holy union, she explains it. She has sex with other people but not with him, because he is her Hand. She laughs at him, says she can't exactly have sex with her own Hand. It would be the same thing as having sex with herself. And she laughs.

"You were stupid, now weren't you?" Hog says to the dead pregnant thing in the dirt.

He wants to have sex. He wants it right now as he stares at the dead thing and nudges it with his boot again and thinks about God and what she looks like naked with hands all over her.

I know you want it, Hog.

I do, he says. *I want it.*

I know where you want to put your hands. I'm right, aren't I?

Yes.

You want to put them where I let other people put them, don't you?

I wish you wouldn't let anybody. Yes, I want it.

She makes him paint the red handprints in places he doesn't want other people to touch, places where he put his hands when he did the bad thing and was sent away, sent to the cold place where it snows, the place where they put him in the machine and rearranged his molecules.

15

The next morning, Tuesday, clouds pile up from the distant sea and the pregnant dead thing is stiff on the ground and flies have found it.

"Now look what you did. Killed all your children, didn't you? Stupid thing."

Hog nudges it with his boot. Flies scatter like sparks. He watches as they buzz back to the gory, coagulated head. He stares at the stiff, dead thing and the flies crawling on it. He stares at it, not bothered by it. He squats beside it, getting close enough to craze the flies again and now he smells it. He gets a whiff of death, a stench that in several days will be overpowering and noticeable an acre away, depending on the wind. Flies will lay their eggs in orifices and the wounds, and soon the carcass will team with maggots, but it won't bother him. He likes to watch what death does.

He walks off toward the ruined house, the shotgun cradled in his arms. He listens to the distant rumble of traffic on South 27, but there is no reason for anybody to come out here. Eventually, there will be. But now there isn't. He steps up on the rotting porch and a curling plank gives under his boots, and he shoves open the door, entering a dark, airless space thick with dust. Even on a clear day, it is dark and suffocating inside the house, and this morning it is worse because a thunderstorm is on the way. It is eight o'clock and almost as dark as night inside the house, and he begins to sweat.

"Is that you?" The voice sounds from the darkness, from the rear of the house, where the voice ought to be.

Against a wall is a makeshift table of plywood and cinder blocks, and on top is a small glass fish tank. He points the shotgun at the tank and pushes the pressure pad on the slide, and the xenon light flashes brilliantly on glass and illuminates the black shape of the tarantula inside. It is motionless on sandy dirt and wood chips, poised like a dark hand next to its water sponge and favorite rock. In a corner of the tank, small crickets stir in the light, disturbed by it.

"Come talk to me," the voice calls out, demanding but weaker than it was not even a day ago.

He isn't sure if he is glad the voice is alive, but he probably is. He takes the lid off the tank and talks quietly, sweetly, to the spider. Its abdomen is balding and crusty with dried glue and pale yellow blood, and hatred wraps around him as he thinks about why it is bald and what caused it to almost bleed to death. The spider's hair won't grow back until he molts, and maybe he will heal and maybe he won't.

"You know whose fault it is, don't you?" he says to the spider. "And I did something about it, didn't I?"

"Come here," the voice calls out. "Do you hear me?"

The spider doesn't move. He might die. There's a good chance he will.

"I'm sorry I've been gone so much. I know you must be lonely," he says to the spider. "I couldn't take you with me because of your condition. It was a very long drive. Cold, too."

He reaches inside the glass tank and gently strokes the spider. It barely moves.

"Is that you?" The voice is weaker and hoarse but demanding.

He tries to imagine what it will be like when the voice is gone, and he thinks about the dead thing, stiff and fly-infested on the dirt.

"Is that you?"

He keeps his finger pressed against the pressure pad, and the light points where the shotgun points, illuminating wooden flooring filthy with dirt and the hulls of dried-out insect eggs. His boots move behind the moving light.

"Hello? Who's there?"

16

Inside the firearms and tool marks lab, Joe Amos zips a Harley-Davidson black leather jacket around an eighty-pound block of ordnance gelatin. On top is a smaller block weighing twenty pounds, and it wears a pair of Ray-Ban sunglasses and a black do-rag with a skull-and-bones pattern.

Joe steps back to admire his work. He is pleased but a little tired. He stayed up late with his newest teacher's pet. He drank too much wine.

"It's funny, isn't it," he says to Jenny.

"Funny but disgusting. You'd better not let him know. I hear he's not somebody to tangle with," she says, sitting on a countertop.

"The person not to tangle with is me. I'm thinking of putting red food coloring in a batch. To look more like blood."

"Cool."

"Add a little brown, and maybe it will look like it's de-composing. Maybe find a way to make it stink."

"You and your hell scenes."

"My mind never stops. My back hurts," he says, admiring his work. "I hurt my damn back and I'm suing her."

The gelatin, an elastic transparent material comprised of denatured animal bone and connective-tissue collagen, isn't easy to handle, and the blocks he has dressed up were hard as hell to transfer from the ice chests to the back padded wall of the indoor firing range. The lab door is locked. The red light on the wall outside is on, warning that the range is hot.

"All dressed up with no place to go," he says to the unappetizing mass.

More properly known as gelatin hydrolysate, it is also

used in shampoos and conditioners, lipsticks, protein drinks, arthritis relief formulas and many other products that Joe will never touch the rest of his life. He won't even kiss his fiancée if she is wearing lipstick, not anymore. Last time he did, he closed his eyes as her lips pressed against his and suddenly he imagined cow, pig and fish shit boiling in a huge pot. He reads labels now. If hydrolyzed animal protein is listed in the ingredients, the item goes into the trash or back on the shelf.

Properly prepared, ordnance gelatin simulates human flesh. It is almost as good a medium as swine tissue, which Joe would prefer. He's heard of firearms labs that shoot up dead swine to test bullet penetration and expansion in a multitude of different situations. He would rather shoot up a hog. He would rather dress up a big hog carcass to look like a person and let the students riddle it with bullets from different distances and with different weapons and ammunition. That would be a good hell scene. A more hellish one would be to shoot a live hog, but Scarpetta would never allow it. She wouldn't even hear of the students shooting a dead one.

"It won't do any good to try to sue her," Jenny is saying. "She's also a lawyer."

"Big shit."

"Well, from what you tell me, you tried that before and didn't get anywhere. Anyway, Lucy's the one with all the money. I hear she thinks she's something. I've never met her. None of us have."

"You're not missing anything. One of these days, someone will put her in her place."

"Like you?"

"Maybe I already am." He smiles. "I'll tell you one thing, I'm not leaving here without my share. I deserve something after all the shit she's put me through." And now he's thinking about Scarpetta again. "She treats me like shit."

"Maybe I'll meet Lucy before I graduate," Jenny says thoughtfully, sitting on the counter, staring at him and the gelatin man he has dressed up like Marino.

"They're all crap," he says. "The fucking trinity. Well, I've got a little surprise for them."

"What?"

"You'll see. Maybe I'll share it with you."

"What is it?"

"Put it this way," he says. "I'm getting something out of this. She underestimates me, and that's a huge mistake. At the end of the day, it's going to be a lot of laughs."

Part of his fellowship entails his assisting Scarpetta in the Broward County morgue, where she treats him like a common laborer, forcing him to suture up the bodies after autopsies and count the pills in bottles of prescription drugs that come in with the dead and catalogue personal effects as if he is a lowly morgue assistant and not a doctor. She has made it his responsibility to weigh, measure, photograph and undress the bodies, and to sift through any disgusting mess that might linger in the bottom of a body bag, especially if it is putrid, maggot-infested slop from a floater, or rancid flesh and bones from partially skeletonized remains. Most insulting is the chore of mixing up ten percent ordnance gelatin for the ballistic gelatin blocks used by the scientists and students.

Why? Give me one good reason, he said to Scarpetta when she gave him the assignment last summer.

It's part of your training, Joe, she replied in her typically unflappable way.

I'm training to be a forensic pathologist, not a lab tech or a cook, he complained.

My method is to train forensic fellows from the ground up, she said. *There isn't anything you shouldn't be able or willing to do.*

Oh. And I suppose you're going to tell me you've made ordnance jelly blocks, that you used to do that when you were getting started, he said.

I still do it and am happy to pass along my favorite recipe, she replied. *I prefer Vyse but Kind & Knox Type two-fifty-A will do just fine. Always start with cold water, between seven and ten degrees centigrade, and add the gelatin to the water and not the other way around. Keep stirring, but not vigorously, because you don't want to introduce air. Add two-point-five milliliters of Foam Eater per twenty-pound block and make sure the mold pan is whistle-clean.*

For the pièce de résistance, add point-five milliliters of cin-namon oil.

That's cute.

Cinnamon oil prevents fungus growth, she said.

She wrote out her personal recipe and then an equipment list that included a triple-beam balance, graduated pitcher, paint stirrer, 12cc hypodermic syringe, propionic acid, aquarium hose, aluminum foil, large spoon and so on, and next gave him a Martha Stewart demonstration in the lab kitchen, as if that makes it all fine and dandy when he's scooping animal-pieces-and-parts powder out of twenty-five-pound drums and weighing and curing and lifting or dragging huge, heavy pans and placing them inside ice chests or the walk-in refrigerator and then making sure the students gather at the indoor range or outdoor rifle deck before the damn things start deteriorating, because they do. They melt like Jell-O and are best when served no longer than twenty minutes after removal from refrigeration, depending on the ambient temperature of the test environment.

He retrieves a window screen from a storage closet and props it flush against the Harley-outfitted blocks of ordnance gelatin, then puts on hearing protectors and protective glasses. He nods for Jenny to do the same. He picks up a stainless-steel Beretta 92, a top-of-the-line double-action pistol with a tritium front post sight. He loads a magazine with 147-grain Speer Gold Dot ammunition, which has six serrations around the rim of the hollowpoint so the projectile will expand or blossom even after passing through clothing as heavy as four layers of denim or a thick leather motorcycle jacket.

What will be different in this test-fire is the mesh pattern produced when the bullet passes through the window screen before ripping through the Harley jacket and buzz-sawing a swath through the chest of Mr. Jell-O, as he calls his ordnance-gelatin test dummies.

He racks back the slide and fires fifteen rounds, imagining Mr. Jell-O is Marino.

17

Palm trees thrash in the wind beyond the conference-room windows. *It will rain,* Scarpetta thinks. It looks like a bad thunderstorm is headed her way, and Marino is late again and still hasn't returned her phone calls.

"Good morning and let's get going," she says to her staff. "We've got a lot to go over, and it's already quarter of nine."

She hates being late. She hates it when someone else causes her to be late, and in this instance, it's Marino. Again, it's Marino. He is ruining her routines. He is ruining everything.

"This evening, hopefully, I'll be on a plane, heading to Boston," she says. "Providing my reservation isn't magically cancelled again."

"The airlines are so screwed up," Joe says. "No wonder they're all going bankrupt."

"We've been asked to take a look at a Hollywood case, a possible suicide that has some disturbing circumstances associated with it," she begins.

"There's one thing I'd like to bring up first," says Vince, the firearms examiner.

"Go ahead." Scarpetta slides eight-by-ten photographs out of an envelope and begins passing them around the table.

"Someone was test-firing in the indoor range about an hour ago." He looks pointedly at Joe. "It wasn't on the schedule."

"I meant to reserve the indoor range last night but forgot," Joe says. "No one was waiting for it."

"You've got to reserve it. It's the only way we can keep track of . . ."

"I was trying out a new batch of ballistic gelatin, where I used hot water instead of cold to see if it made any difference in the calibration test. A difference of one centimeter. Good news. It passed."

"There's probably a difference of plus or minus one centimeter every time you mix up the damn stuff," Vince says irritably.

"We aren't supposed to use any block that isn't valid. So I'm constantly checking the calibration and trying to perfect it. That requires me to spend a lot of time in the firearms lab. It's not my choice."

Joe looks at Scarpetta.

"Ordnance gelatin is one of my assignments."

He looks at her again.

"I hope you remembered to use stopper blocks before you started pounding the back wall with a lot of firepower," Vince says. "I've asked you before."

"You know the rules, Dr. Amos," Scarpetta says.

In front of his colleagues, she always calls him Dr. Amos instead of Joe. She shows him more respect than he deserves.

"We have to enter everything in the log," she adds. "Every firearm removed from the reference collection, every round, every test-fire. Our protocols must be followed."

"Yes, ma'am."

"There are legal implications. Most of our cases end up in court," she adds.

"Yes, ma'am."

"All right." She tells them about Johnny Swift.

She tells them that in early November he had surgery on his wrists, and soon after came to Hollywood to stay with his brother. They were identical twins. The day before Thanksgiving, the brother, Laurel, went out shopping and returned to the house at approximately four thirty p.m. After carrying in the groceries, he discovered Dr. Swift on the couch, dead from a shotgun wound to the chest.

"I sort of remember this case," Vince says. "It was in the news."

"Well, I happen to remember Dr. Swift very well," Joe says. "He used to call Dr. Self. Once when I was on her show, he called in, gave her hell about Tourette's syndrome, and I happen to agree with her, usually nothing more than an excuse for bad behavior. He rambled on about neurochemical dysfunction, about abnormalities of the brain. Quite the expert," he says sarcastically.

Nobody is interested in Joe's appearances on Dr. Self's show. Nobody is interested in his appearances on any show.

"What about an ejected shell and the weapon?" Vince asks Scarpetta.

"According to the police report, Laurel Swift noted a shotgun on the floor some three feet behind the back of the couch. No shell casing."

"Well, that's a bit unusual. He shoots himself in the chest and then somehow manages to toss the shotgun over the back of the couch?" It is Joe talking again. "I'm not seeing a scene photograph with the shotgun."

"The brother claims he saw the shotgun on the floor behind the couch. I say *claims*. We'll get to that part in a minute," Scarpetta says.

"What about gunshot residue on him?"

"I'm sorry Marino isn't here, since he's our investigator in this case and working closely with the Hollywood police," she replies, keeping her feelings about him barricaded. "All I know is that Laurel's clothing wasn't tested for GSR."

"What about his hands?"

"Positive for GSR. But he claims he touched him, shook him, got blood on him. So theoretically, that could explain it. A few more details. His wrists were in splints when he died, his blood alcohol point-one, and according to the police report, there were numerous empty wine bottles in the kitchen."

"We sure he was drinking alone?"

"We're not sure of anything."

"Sounds like holding a heavy shotgun might not have been easy for him if he'd just had surgery."

"Possibly," Scarpetta says. "And if you can't use your hands, then what?"

"Your feet."

"It can be done. I tried it with my twelve-gauge Remington. Unloaded," she adds a little humor.

She tried it herself because Marino didn't show up. He didn't call. He didn't care.

"I don't have photographs of the demonstration," she says, diplomatic enough not to add that the reason she doesn't have them is because Marino didn't show up. "Suffice it to say the blast would have kicked the gun back, or maybe his foot jerked and kicked the gun back, and the shotgun would have fallen off the back of the couch. Saying he killed himself. No abrasions on either of his big toes, by the way."

"A contact wound?" Vince asks.

"Density of soot on his shirt, the abraded margin and diameter and shape of the wound, the absence of petal marks from the wad, which was still in the body, are consistent with a contact wound. Problem is, we have a gross inconsistency, which, in my opinion, is due to the medical examiner relying on a radiologist for a distance determination."

"Who?"

"It's Dr. Bronson's case," she says, and several of the scientists groan.

"Jesus, he's as old as the damn Pope. When the hell's he going to retire?"

"The Pope died," Joe jokes.

"Thank you, CNN news flash."

"The radiologist decided the shotgun wound is a, quote, *distant* wound," Scarpetta resumes. "A distance of at least three feet. Uh-oh. Now we have a homicide, because you couldn't possibly hold the barrel of a shotgun three feet from your own chest, now could you?"

Several clicks of the mouse, and a digital x-ray of Johnny Swift's fatal shotgun blast is sharply displayed on the smart board. Shotgun pellets look like a storm of tiny white bubbles floating through the ghostly shapes of ribs.

"The pellets are spread out," Scarpetta points out, "and to give the radiologist a little credit, the spread of the pellets inside the chest is consistent with a range of three or four feet, but what I think we're dealing with here is a perfect example of the billiard-ball effect."

She clears the x-ray off the smart board and collects several styluses, different ones for different colors.

"The leading pellets slowed when they entered the body

and were then hit by the trailing pellets, causing colliding pellets to ricochet and spread out into a pattern that simulates distant-range fire," she explains, drawing red ricocheting pellets hitting blue pellets like billiard balls. "Therefore simulating a distant gunshot wound, when in fact, it wasn't a distant shot at all but a contact wound."

"None of the neighbors heard a shotgun blast?"

"Apparently not."

"Maybe a lot of people were out on the beach or out of town for the Thanksgiving holiday."

"Maybe."

"What kind of shotgun, and whose was it?"

"All we can tell is it's a twelve-gauge, based on the pellets," Scarpetta says. "Apparently, the shotgun disappeared before the police showed up."

18

Ev Christian is awake and sitting on a mattress that is black with what she by now believes is old blood.

Scattered about the filthy floor inside the small, filthy room with its caving ceiling and water-stained wallpaper are magazines. She sees poorly without her glasses and can barely make out the pornographic covers. She barely makes out soda-pop bottles and fast-food wrappers scattered about. Between the mattress and the splintery wall is a small pink Keds tennis shoe, a girl's size. Ev has picked it up countless times and held it, wondering what it means and who it once belonged to, worried the girl is dead. Sometimes Ev tucks the shoe behind her when he comes in, fearful he will take it from her. It is all she has.

She never sleeps longer than an hour or two at a stretch and has no idea how much time has passed. There is no such thing as time. Gray light fills the broken window on the other side of the room, and she can't see the sun. She smells rain.

She doesn't know what he has done with Kristin and the boys. She doesn't know what he has done to them. She dimly remembers the first hours, those awful, unreal hours when he brought her food and water and stared at her from the darkness, and he was as dark as the darkness, dark like a dark spirit, hovering in the doorway.

How does it feel? he said to her in a soft, cold voice. *How does it feel to know you're going to die?*

It is always dark inside the room. It is so much darker when he is in it.

I'm not afraid. You can't touch my soul.

Say you're sorry.

It's not too late to repent. God will forgive even the most vile sin if you humble yourself and repent.

God is a woman. I am her Hand. Say you're sorry.

Blasphemy. Shame on you. I've done nothing to be sorry about.

I'll teach you shame. You'll say you're sorry just like she did.

Kristin?

Then he was gone, and Ev heard voices from another part of the house. She couldn't make out what they were saying, but he was talking to Kristin, must have been. He was talking to a woman. Ev really couldn't hear it, but she heard them talking. She could not make out what they said, and she remembers feet scuffing and voices on the other side of the wall, and then she heard Kristin, knew it was her. When Ev thinks about it now, she wonders if she dreamed it.

Kristin! Kristin! I'm right here! I'm right here! Don't you dare hurt her!

She hears her own voice in her head, but it might have been a dream.

Kristin? Kristin? Answer me! Don't you dare hurt her!

Then she heard talking again, so maybe it was all right. But Ev's not sure. She might have dreamed it. She might have dreamed she heard his boots moving down the hallway and the front door shutting. All this might have taken place in minutes, maybe hours. Maybe she heard a car engine. Maybe it was a dream, a delusion. Ev sat in the dark, her heart flying as she listened for Kristin and the boys and heard nothing. She called out until her throat was on fire and she could barely see or breathe.

Daylight came and went, and his dark shape would appear with paper cups of water and something to eat, and his shape would stand and watch her, and she could not see his face. She has never seen his face, not even the first time, when he came into the house. He wears a black hood with holes cut in it for his eyes, a hood like a black pillowcase, long and loose around his shoulders. His hooded shape likes to poke her with the barrel of the shotgun as if she is an animal in the zoo, as if he is curious about what she will do if he pokes her. He pokes her in her private places and watches what she will do.

Shame on you, Ev says when he pokes her. *You can harm*

*my flesh but you can't touch my soul. My soul belongs
to God.*

She isn't here. I am her Hand. Say you're sorry.

My God is a jealous God. "Thou shalt have no other gods
before me."

She isn't here, and he pokes her with the gun barrel,
sometimes pokes her so hard it leaves perfect blackish-blue
circles on her flesh.

Say you're sorry, he says.

Ev sits on the stinking, rotting mattress. It has been used
before, used horribly, stiff and stained black, and she sits on
it inside the stinking, airless, trash-strewn room, listening
and trying to think, listening and praying and screaming for
help. No one answers. No one hears her, and she wonders
where she could be. Where is she that no one can hear
her scream?

She can't escape because of the clever way he bent and
twisted coat hangers around her wrists and ankles with ropes
through them and looped over a rafter in the falling-down
ceiling, as if she is some sort of grotesque marionette,
bruised and covered with insect bites and rashes, her naked
body itching and racked with pain. With effort, she can get
to her feet. She can move off the mattress to relieve her blad-
der and bowels. When she does, the pain is so searing, she
almost faints.

He does everything in the dark. He can see in the dark.
She hears his breathing in the dark. He is a black shape. He
is Satan.

"Help me God," she says to the broken window, to the
gray sky beyond, to the God beyond the sky, somewhere in
His heaven. "Please God help me."

19

Scarpetta hears the distant roar of a motorcycle with very loud pipes.

She tries to concentrate as the motorcycle gets closer, cruising past the building toward the faculty parking lot. She thinks about Marino and wonders if she is going to have to fire him. She's not sure she could.

She is explaining that there were two phones inside Laurel Swift's house and both of them were unplugged, the cords missing. Laurel had left his cell phone in his car and says he was unable to find his brother's cell phone, so he had no way to call for help. Panicking, Laurel fled and flagged somebody down. He didn't return to the house until the police arrived, and by then the shotgun was gone.

"This is information I got from Dr. Bronson," Scarpetta says. "I've talked to him several times and I'm sorry I don't have a better grasp of the details."

"The phone cords. Have they ever shown up?"

"I don't know," Scarpetta says, because Marino hasn't briefed her.

"Johnny Swift could have removed them to make sure no one could call for help in case he didn't die right away, assuming he's a suicide," Joe offers another one of his creative scenarios.

Scarpetta doesn't answer because she knows nothing about the phone cords beyond what Dr. Bronson relayed to her in his vague, somewhat disjointed way.

"Anything else missing from the house? Anything besides the phone cords, the decedent's cell phone and the shotgun? As if that's not enough."

"You'll have to ask Marino," she says.

"I believe he's here. Unless someone else has a motorcycle as loud as the space shuttle."

"I'm surprised Laurel hasn't been charged with murder, you want my opinion," Joe says.

"You can't charge someone with murder when the manner of death hasn't been determined," Scarpetta replies. "The manner is still pending, and there isn't sufficient evidence to change it to suicide or homicide or accident, although I certainly fail to see how this is an accident. If the death isn't resolved to Dr. Bronson's satisfaction, he'll eventually change the manner to undetermined."

Heavy footsteps sound on carpet in the hallway.

"What happened to common sense?" Joe says.

"You don't determine manner of death based on common sense," Scarpetta says, and she wishes he could keep his unwelcome comments to himself.

The conference-room door opens, and Pete Marino walks in carrying a briefcase and a box of Krispy Kreme donuts, dressed in black jeans, black leather boots, a black leather vest with the Harley logo on the back, his usual garb. He ignores Scarpetta as he sits in his usual chair next to hers and scoots the box of donuts across the table.

"I sure wish we could test the brother's clothing for GSR, get our hands on whatever he was wearing when he was shot," Joe says, leaning back in his chair the way he does when he's about to pontificate, and he tends to pontificate more than usual when Marino is around. "Take a look at them on soft x-ray, the Faxitron, SEM/spectrometry."

Marino stares at Joe as if he might hit him.

"Of course, it's possible to get trace amounts on your person from sources other than a gunshot. Plumbing materials, batteries, automobile greases, paints. Just like in my lab practicum last month," Joe says as he plucks out a chocolate-iced donut that is smashed, most of its icing stuck to the box. "You know what happened to them?"

He licks his fingers as he looks across the table at Marino.

"That was quite a practicum," Marino says. "Wonder where you got the idea."

"What I asked is, do you know what happened to the brother's clothes," Joe says.

"I think you been watching too many fantasy forensic shows," Marino says, his big face staring at him. "Too much Harry Potter policing on your big flat-screen TV. Think you're a forensic pathologist, or almost one, a lawyer, a scientist, a crime-scene investigator, a cop, Captain Kirk and the Easter Bunny all rolled up in one."

"By the way, yesterday's hell scene was a screaming success," Joe says. "Too bad all of you missed it."

"Well, what is the story about the clothes, Pete?" Vince asks Marino. "We know what he had on when he found his brother's body?"

"What he had on, according to him, was nothing," Marino says. "Supposedly, he came in through the kitchen door, put the groceries on the counter, then went straight back to the bedroom to pee. Supposedly. Then he took a shower because he had to work at his restaurant that night and happened to look out the doorway and saw the shotgun on the carpet behind the couch. At this point, he was naked, so he says."

"Sounds like a lot of crap to me." Joe talks with his mouth full.

"My personal opinion is it's probably a robbery that got interrupted," Marino says. "Or something got interrupted. A rich doctor maybe gets tangled up with the wrong person. Anybody seen my Harley jacket? Black with a skull and bones on one shoulder, an American flag on the other."

"Where did you have it last?"

"I took it off in the hangar the other day when Lucy and me were doing an aerial. Came back, it was gone."

"I haven't seen it."

"Neither have I."

"Shit. That thing cost me. And the patches are custom. Goddamn it. If someone stole it . . ."

"Nobody steals around here," Joe says.

"Oh yeah? What about stealing ideas?" Marino glares at him. "And that reminds me," he says to Scarpetta, "while we're on the subject of hell scenes . . ."

"We're not on the subject," she says.

"I came here this morning with a few things to say about them."

"Another time."

"I got some good ones, left a file on your desk," Marino says to her. "Give you something interesting to think about during your vacation. Especially since you'll probably get snowed in up there, we'll probably see you again in the spring."

She controls her irritation, tries to keep it tucked into a secret place where she hopes no one can see it. He is deliberately disrupting staff meeting and treating her the same way he did some fifteen years ago when she was the new chief medical examiner of Virginia, a woman in a world where women didn't belong, a woman with an attitude, Marino decided, because she has an M.D. and a law degree.

"I think the Swift case would be a damn good hell scene," Joe says. "GSR and x-ray spectrometry and other findings tell two different stories. See if the students figure it out. Bet they've never heard of the billiard-ball effect."

"I didn't ask the peanut gallery." Marino raises his voice. "Anybody hear me ask the peanut gallery?"

"Well, you know my opinion about your creativity," Joe says to him. "Frankly, it's dangerous."

"I don't give a shit about your opinion."

"We're lucky the Academy isn't bankrupt. That would have been one hell of an expensive settlement," Joe says, as if it never has occurred to him that one of these days Marino might knock him across the room. "Real lucky after what you did."

Last summer, one of Marino's mock crime scenes traumatized a student who then quit the Academy, threatened to sue and fortunately was never heard from again. Scarpetta and her staff are paranoid about allowing Marino to participate in training, whether it is mock scenes, hellish or otherwise, or even classroom lectures.

"Don't think what happened doesn't enter my mind when I'm creating hell scenes," Joe goes on.

"Hell scenes you create?" Marino declares. "You mean all those ideas you stole from me?"

"I believe that's called sour grapes. I don't need to steal anyone's ideas, certainly not yours."

"Oh really? You think I don't recognize my own shit? You don't know enough to come up with the kind of shit I do, Dr. Almost a Forensic Pathologist."

"That's it," Scarpetta says. She raises her voice. "That's enough."

"I happen to have a great one of a body found in what appears to be a drive-by shooting," Joe says, "but when the bullet's recovered, it has an unusual waffle or mesh pattern in the lead because the victim was actually shot through a window screen, his body dumped . . ."

"That's mine!" Marino slams his fist down on the table.

20

The **Seminole belongs** to a beat-up white pickup truck filled with ears of corn, parked some distance from the gas pumps. Hog has been watching him for a while.

"Some motherfucker took my fucking wallet, my cell phone, I think maybe when I was in the fucking shower," the man is saying on the pay phone, standing with his back to the CITGO station and all the eighteen-wheelers rumbling in and out.

Hog doesn't show his amusement as he listens to the man rant and rave about overnighting again, complaining and cursing because he'll have to sleep in the cab of his truck, has no phone, no money for a motel. He doesn't even have money for a shower, and anyway, a shower has gone up to five bucks, and that's a lot to pay for a shower when nothing comes with it, not even soap. Some of the men double up and get a discount, disappearing behind an unpainted privacy fence on the west side of the CITGO food mart, piling their clothes and shoes on a bench inside the fence before stepping into a tiny concrete space dimly lit with a single showerhead and a big, rusty drain in the middle of the floor.

It is always wet inside the shower. The shower head always drips, and the water handles screech. The men carry in their own soap, shampoo, toothbrushes and toothpaste, usually in plastic bags. They bring their own towels. Hog has never showered in there, but he's looked at the men's clothes, figuring out what might be in the pockets. Money. Cell phones. Sometimes drugs. Women shower in a similar arrangement on the east side of the food mart. They never go in two at a time, no matter the discount, and are in a nervous hurry when they shower, shamed by their nakedness and terrified that someone will walk in on them, that a man will, a big, powerful man who can do what he wants.

Hog dials the 800 number on the green card he keeps folded in his back pocket, a rectangular card maybe eight inches long with a large hole and a slit in one end so it can be attached to a door handle. Printed on the card is information and a cartoon of an animated citrus fruit wearing a tropical shirt and sunglasses. He is doing God's will. He is the Hand of God doing God's work. God has an IQ of a hundred and fifty.

"Thank you for calling the Citrus Canker Eradication Program," the familiar recording says. "Your call may be monitored for quality."

The canned female voice goes on to say that if he is calling to report damage in Palm Beach, Dade or Broward Counties or Monroe to please dial the following number. He watches the Seminole climb into his pickup truck, and his red-plaid shirt reminds him of a lumberjack, the carved one by the front door of The Christmas Shop. He dials the number the recorded voice gave him.

"Department of Agriculture," a woman answers.

"I need to speak to a citrus inspector, please," he says as he stares at the Seminole and thinks about alligator wrestling.

"What may I help you with?"

"Are you an inspector?" he asks as he thinks of the alligator he saw about an hour ago on the bank of the narrow canal that runs along South 27.

He took it as a good sign. The gator was at least five feet long and very dark and dry, and not interested in the big lumber trucks rumbling by. He would have pulled over if there had been any place to do it. He would have watched the gator, studied the way it fearlessly handles life, quiet and calm but poised to flash into the water or grab its unsuspecting prey and drag it down to the bottom of the canal, where it would drown and rot and be eaten. He would have watched the gator for a long time, but he couldn't safely get off the highway, and he is on a mission.

"Do you have something to report?" the woman's voice is asking over the line.

"I work for a lawn service and happened to notice citrus canker in a yard about a block from where I was cutting the grass yesterday."

"Can you give me the address?"

He gives her an address in the West Lake Park area.

"May I have your name?"

"I'd rather report this anonymously. I could get in trouble with my boss."

"All right. I'd like to ask you a few questions. Did you actually enter this yard where you think you spotted the canker?"

"It's an open yard, so I walked in because there are a lot of really nice trees and hedges and a lot of grass, and I was thinking maybe I could do some work there if they needed anyone. Then I noticed the suspicious-looking leaves. Several of the trees have tiny lesions on their leaves."

"Did you notice a watery-looking margin around any of these lesions?"

"It's my impression these trees were recently infected, which is probably why your routine inspections have missed them. What worries me is the yards on either side. They have citrus that in my estimation are less than nineteen hundred feet from the infected ones, meaning they're probably infected, too, and the citrus in other yards beyond that in my estimation are also less than nineteen hundred feet away. And on and on throughout the neighborhood. So you can understand my concern."

"What makes you think our routine inspections have missed the properties you're mentioning?"

"Nothing to indicate you've been there. I've been working with citrus trees down here for a long time, working with professional lawn services most of my life. I've seen the worst of the worst, entire orchards that had to be burned. People wiped out."

"Did you notice any lesions on any of the fruit?"

"As I've been explaining, it looks like the canker's in the early stages, very early stages. I've seen entire orchards burned because of the canker. People's lives ruined."

"When you walked into the yard where you think you saw citrus canker, did you disinfect after you left?" she asks, and he doesn't like her tone.

He doesn't like her. She's stupid and tyrannical.

"Of course I deconned. I've been in the lawn-care business for a long time. I always spray myself and my tools with GX-1027, according to regulation. I know all about what happens. I've seen entire commercial orchards destroyed, burned up and abandoned. People ruined."

"Excuse me . . ."

"Very bad things happen."

"Excuse me . . ."

"People need to take the canker seriously," Hog says.

"What's the registration number for your vehicle, the one you use for your lawn service? I'm assuming you have a yellow-and-black regulatory sticker on the left side of the windshield? I need that number."

"My number's irrelevant," he says to the inspector, who thinks she's so much more important and powerful than he. "The vehicle belongs to my boss and I'll get in trouble if he knows I made this call. If people find out his lawn service reported citrus canker that's probably going to result in every citrus tree in the neighborhood being eradicated, what do you think will happen to our lawn-care business?"

"I understand, sir. But it's important I have your decal number for our records. And I really would like a way to contact you, if necessary."

"No," he says. "I'll get fired."

21

The **CITGO station** is getting busy with truckers who park their semis behind the food mart and off to the side of the Chickee Hut restaurant, line them up at the edge of the woods and sleep in them and probably have sex in them.

The truckers eat at the Chickee Hut, which is misspelled because the people who come here are too ignorant to know how to spell chikee and probably don't even know what it is. Chikee is a Seminole word, and even the Seminoles can't spell it.

The ignorant truckers live from mile to mile and pull over here to spend their money at the food mart, where there is plenty of diesel fuel, beer, hotdogs and cigars, and a selection of folding knives in a glass case. They can play pool in the Golden Tee game room and get their trucks repaired at the CB antenna or tire services. The CITGO is a full-service stop out in the middle of nothing, where people come and go and mind their own business. Nobody bothers Hog. They barely look at him, so many people in and out, hardly anybody to see him twice, except the guy who works in the Chickee Hut restaurant.

It is behind a chain-link fence at the edge of the parking lot. Signs posted on the fence announce that solicitors will be prosecuted and the only dogs allowed are K9s, and wildlife can enter at its own risk. There is plenty of wildlife at night, but Hog wouldn't know about it firsthand because he doesn't waste money in the game room, not on pool or the jukebox. He doesn't drink. He doesn't smoke. He doesn't want sex with any of the women at the CITGO.

They are disgusting in skimpy shorts and tight tops, their

faces made harsh by too much cheap makeup and too much sun. They sit in the open-air restaurant or at the bar, which is nothing but a roof thatched with palmetto leaves and a scarred wooden counter lined with eight stools. They eat dinner specials like BBQ ribs and meatloaf and country-fried steak, and they drink. The food is good and cooked right there on the premises. Hog likes the trucker burger, and it's only three ninety-five. A grilled cheese is three dollars and a quarter. Cheap, disgusting women, bad things happen to women like that. They deserve it.

They want it.

They tell everyone.

"I'll have a grilled cheese to go," Hog says to the man behind the bar. "And a trucker burger for here."

The man has a big belly and wears a soiled white apron. He is busy popping caps off dripping bottles of beer that he keeps on ice inside tubs. The man with the big belly has waited on him before but never seems to remember him.

"You want the grilled cheese the same time as your burger?" he asks, sliding two bottles of beer closer to a trucker and his lady who are already drunk.

"Just make sure the grilled cheese is wrapped to go."

"I asked you if you wanted them at the same time." He isn't annoyed but rather indifferent about it.

"That would be fine."

"What do you want to drink?" the man with the big belly asks as he opens another beer.

"Plain water."

"Now what the hell is plain water?" the drunk trucker asks loudly as his lady giggles and presses her breast against his big, tattooed arm. "Water you get on an *airplane*?"

"Just plain water," Hog says to the man behind the bar.

"I don't like nothing plain, do I baby?" the drunk trucker's drunk girlfriend slurs, gripping the stool with her plump legs in their tight shorts, her plump breasts bulging from her low-cut top.

"So where you heading?" the drunk girlfriend asks.

"North," he says. "Eventually."

"Well you be careful driving around down here all by your lonesome," the woman slurs. "There's a lot of crazies."

22

Do we have any idea where he is?" Scarpetta asks Rose.

"He's not in his office and he's not answering his cell phone. When I spoke to him after staff meeting and said you needed to see him, he told me he had an errand to run and would be right back," Rose reminds her. "That was an hour and a half ago."

"What time did you say we should leave for the airport?" Scarpetta looks out the window at palm trees shaking in the gusting wind and thinks again about firing him. "We're going to have a thunderstorm, a bad one. That figures. Well, I'm not going to sit around and wait for him. I should just leave."

"Your flight's not until six thirty," Rose says as she hands Scarpetta several phone messages.

"I don't know why I'm bothering. Why am I bothering to talk to him?" Scarpetta glances through the messages.

Rose looks at her in a way that only Rose can. She stands quietly, thoughtfully, in the doorway, her white hair swept up and pinned back in a French twist, her gray linen suit out of style but elegant and crisp. After ten years, her gray lizard-skin pumps still look new.

"One minute you want to talk to him, the next you don't. What is it?" Rose remarks.

"I guess I should go."

"I didn't say which is it. I asked what is it."

"I don't know what I'm going to do about him. I keep thinking about firing him, but I'd rather resign than do that."

"You could take the position of chief," Rose reminds her. "They'd force Dr. Bronson to retire if you'd agree, and maybe you should seriously consider it."

Rose knows what she's doing. She can seem very sincere when suggesting something that she secretly doesn't want Scarpetta to do, and the result is predicable.

"No thank you," Scarpetta says adamantly. "Been there, done that, and in case you've forgotten, Marino's one of their investigators, so I wouldn't exactly get away from him by resigning from the Academy and ending up at the ME's office full-time. Who's Mrs. Simister and what church?" she asks, puzzling over one of the phone messages.

"I don't know who she is, but she acted as if she knows you."

"Never heard of her."

"She called a few minutes ago and said she wanted to talk to you about some missing family in the West Lake Park area. She didn't leave her number, said she'd call back."

"What missing family? Here in Hollywood?"

"That's what she said. Let's see, you're flying out of Miami, unfortunately. Worst airport on earth. I'd say we don't need to leave . . . well, you know the traffic down here. Maybe we should leave as early as four. But we're not going anywhere until I check on your flight."

"You're sure I'm in first class? And it's not been cancelled."

"I have your printed reservation, but you're going to have to check in because it's last-minute."

"Can you believe it? They cancel me, and now it's last-minute because I had to rebook?"

"You're all set."

"No offense, but that's what you said last month, Rose. And I wasn't in the computer and ended up in coach. All the way to Los Angeles. And look what happened yesterday."

"I confirmed it first thing this morning. I'll do it again."

"Do you think this is all about Marino's hell scenes? Maybe that's what's wrong with him."

"I suspect he feels you shunned him after that, no longer trusted or respected him."

"How can I trust his judgment?"

"I'm still not sure what Marino did," Rose replies. "I typed up that particular hell scene and edited it just like I do all of his, and as I've told you before, his script didn't include a hypodermic needle in that big, old, fat dead man's pocket."

"He set up the scene. He supervised it."

"He swears someone else put that needle in the pocket. Probably she did. For money, which thankfully, she didn't get. I don't blame Marino for the way he feels. Hell scenes were his idea, and now Dr. Amos is doing them and getting all sorts of attention from the students while Marino's treated like . . ."

"He's not nice to the students. Not from day one."

"Well, now it's worse. They don't know him and think he's an ill-tempered dinosaur, a cranky old has-been. And I know just how it feels to be treated like a cranky old has-been or, worse, to feel like one."

"You're anything but cranky or a has-been."

"At least you agree that I'm old," Rose says as she steps back through the doorway, adding, "I'll try him again."

Inside room 112 of the Last Stand motel, Joe sits at the cheap desk across from the cheap bed and checks the computer for Scarpetta's plane reservation, jotting down the flight number and other information. He calls the airline.

After five minutes of dead time on hold, he gets a real person.

"I need to change a reservation," he says.

He recites the information, then changes the seating to coach, as far back in the plane as is available, preferably a middle seat, because his boss doesn't like windows or the aisle. Just like he did last time so successfully, when she was flying to Los Angeles. He could cancel her flight again. But this is more fun.

"Yes, sir."

"What about an E-ticket?"

"No sir, a change this close to departure, and you're going to have to check in at the desk."

He hangs up, exhilarated, as he imagines the Almighty Scarpetta trapped between two strangers, hopefully two enormous, smelly ones for three hours. He smiles as he plugs a digital recorder into his super hybrid system telephone handset. The window air-conditioning unit rattles loudly but is ineffective. He is getting uncomfortably warm and detects the faint, foul stench of rotting meat from a recent hell scene that included racks of raw pork ribs, beef liver and chicken skin rolled up in carpet and hidden beneath closet flooring.

He scheduled the exercise right after a special lunch he charged to the Academy that included barbecue ribs and rice and resulted in several students gagging when the foul bundle was discovered oozing with rotting fluids and teeming with maggots. In their haste to recover the simulated human remains and clear the scene, Team A neglected to notice a torn bit of fingernail that was also beneath the flooring, lost in the stinking, putrid slop, and as it turned out, that piece of evidence was the only one that could have revealed the identity of the killer.

Joe lights a cigar as he fondly remembers the success of that hell scene, a success made all the better because of Marino's outrage, his insistence that Joe once again had stolen an idea from him. The big bumpkin cop has yet to figure out that Lucy's choice of a communications-monitoring system that interfaces with the Academy's PBX means that given the appropriate security clearance, one can monitor whomever he pleases in almost any way imaginable.

Lucy was careless. The intrepid super-agent Lucy left her Treo—an ultra-high-tech palm-size communications device that is a personal digital assistant, cell phone, e-mail, camera and everything else—inside one of her helicopters. It happened almost a year ago. He'd barely started his fellowship when he had the most amazing bit of luck, was in the hangar with one of the students, an especially pretty one, showing her Lucy's helicopters when he happened to notice a Treo inside the Bell 407.

Lucy's Treo.

She was still logged on. He didn't need her password to access everything in it. He kept the Treo long enough to download all its files before returning it to the helicopter, leaving it on the floor, partially under a seat, where Lucy found it later that day, having no idea what had happened. She still has no idea.

Joe has passwords, dozens of them, including Lucy's system-administrator password, which enables her and now him to access and alter the computer and telecommunications systems of the South Florida regional headquarters, the central headquarters in Knoxville, satellite offices in New York and Los Angeles, and Benton Wesley and his *top-secret* PREDATOR research study and everything else he and Scarpetta confide in each other. Joe can redirect files and e-mail, get hold of the unlisted phone numbers of anybody who has ever had anything to do with the Academy, wreak havoc. His fellowship ends in a month, and by the time he moves on, and he will in a big way, he might just have succeeded in causing the Academy to implode and everybody, especially the big stupid thug Marino and the overbearing Scarpetta, to hate each other.

It is easy to monitor the big dope's office line, to secretly activate his speakerphone so it is like having an open mic in the room. Marino dictates everything, including his hell scenes, and Rose types them up because he can't spell, has terrible grammar, rarely reads and is practically illiterate.

Joe feels a rush of euphoria as he taps cigar ash into a Coke can and logs into the PBX system. He accesses Marino's office line, activates the speakerphone to see if he is in and up to something.

23

When Scarpetta agreed to serve as the consulting forensic pathologist for PREDATOR, she wasn't enthusiastic about it.

She warned Benton, tried to talk him out of it, repeatedly reminded him that the subjects of the research study don't care if someone is a physician or a psychologist or a Harvard professor.

They'll break your neck or smash your head against a wall just like they will anybody else, she said. *There's no such thing as sovereign immunity.*

I've been around these people most of my life, he replied. *That's what I do, Kay.*

You've never done it in this type of setting. Not at an Ivy League–affiliated psychiatric hospital that has historically never dealt with convicted murderers. You're not only staring into the abyss, you're installing lights and an elevator in it, Benton.

She hears Rose talking on the other side of the wall in her office.

"Where on earth have you been?" Rose is saying.

"So when am I taking you for that ride?" Marino replies loudly.

"I told you, I'm not getting on the back of that thing. I think there's something wrong with your phone."

"I've always had this fantasy of seeing you in black leather."

"I went looking for you, and you weren't in your office. Or, at least, you didn't answer the door . . ."

"I ain't been in there all morning."

"But your line's lit up."

"No it ain't."

"It was a few minutes ago."

"You checking on me again? I think you're sweet on me, Rose."

Marino goes on in his boisterous voice as Scarpetta reviews an e-mail she just got from Benton, another recruitment ad that is to run in *The Boston Globe* and on the Internet.

HEALTHY ADULTS MRI STUDY

HARVARD MEDICAL SCHOOL–AFFILIATED RESEARCHERS ARE CURRENTLY STUDYING BRAIN STRUCTURE AND FUNCTION IN HEALTHY ADULTS AT THE MCLEAN HOSPITAL BRAIN IMAGING CENTER IN BELMONT, MA.

"Go on now. Dr. Scarpetta's waiting and you're late again." She hears Rose chastise Marino in her firm but affectionate way. "You need to quit the disappearing acts."

YOU MAY QUALIFY FOR THE STUDY IF YOU:

* ARE A 17- TO 45-YEAR-OLD MALE
* ARE AVAILABLE TO COME TO MCLEAN HOSPITAL FOR
  FIVE VISITS
* HAVE NO HISTORY OF HEAD TRAUMA OR DRUG ABUSE
* HAVE NEVER BEEN DIAGNOSED WITH SCHIZOPHRENIA
  OR BIPOLAR DISORDER

Scarpetta scrolls through the rest of the ad, getting to the good part, a P.S. from Benton.

```
You'd be amazed how many people think they're
normal. I wish the damn snow would stop. I
love you.
```

Marino's big presence fills the doorway.

"What's up?" he asks.

"Please shut the door," Scarpetta says as she reaches for the phone.

He pulls it shut, takes a chair, not directly across from her

but at an angle so he doesn't have to look at her straight on
as she sits at her big desk in her big leather chair. She knows
about his tricks. She knows all about his gauche manipulations. He doesn't like dealing with her from the other side of
her big desk, but would prefer they were seated with nothing
between them, like equals. She knows about office psychology, knows a lot more about it than he does.

"Just give me a minute," she says.

Bong-bong-bong-bong-bong-bong,
the rapid sounds of a radio frequency pulse causing a magnetic field to excite protons.

In the MRI lab, the structure of another so-called normal's brain is being scanned.

"Just how bad is the weather up there?" Scarpetta is saying over the phone.

Dr. Lane pushes the intercom button. "Are you all right?"
she asks their latest research study subject for PREDATOR.

He claims to be normal. He probably isn't. He has no
idea the point is to compare his brain to a killer's.

"I don't know," the normal's unnerved voice answers.

"It's okay," Benton is saying to Scarpetta over the phone.
"If you don't get delayed again. But tomorrow night it's supposed to get bad . . ."

BWAWWH . . . BWAWWH . . . BWAWH . . . BWAWH . . .

"I can't hear a damn thing," he says in exasperation.

The reception is bad. Sometimes his cell phone doesn't
even ring in here, and he is distracted, frustrated, tired. The
scan isn't going well. Nothing has gone well today. Dr. Lane
is dejected. Josh sits in front of his screen, bored.

"I don't feel hopeful," Dr. Lane says to Benton, a re-
signed look on her face. "Even with earplugs."

Twice today, normal control subjects have refused to be
scanned because they're claustrophobic, a detail they failed
to mention when they were accepted into the study. Now this
control subject is complaining about the noise, says it
sounds like electric bass guitars being played in hell. At least
he's creative.

"I'll call before I take off," Scarpetta is saying over the phone. "The ad looks fine, as fine as any of them look."

"Thanks for the enthusiasm. We're going to need a big response. The casualties are mounting. Must be something phobic in the air. Add to that, about one out of three normal subjects isn't."

"I'm not sure what's normal anymore."

Benton covers his other ear, walks around, trying to hear, trying to get a better signal. "I'm afraid a big case has come in, Kay. It's going to be a lot of work."

"How are we doing in there?" Dr. Lane asks over the intercom.

"Not good," the subject's voice comes back.

"They always do when we're about to get together," Scarpetta is saying above what now sounds like a hammer rapidly striking wood. "I'll help in any way I can."

"I'm really starting to freak out," the normal subject's voice says.

"This isn't going to work." Benton looks through the Plexiglas at the normal control subject on the far side of the magnet.

He is moving his taped-down head.

"Susan?" Benton looks at her.

"I know," Dr. Lane says. "I'm going to need to reposition him."

"Good luck. I think he's done," Benton says.

"He's destroyed the landmark," Josh looks up and says.

"Okay," Dr. Lane tells the subject. "We're going to stop. I'm coming in to get you out."

"I'm sorry, man, I can't take this," his stressed voice sounds.

"Sorry. Another one bites the dust," Benton says to Scarpetta over the phone as he watches Dr. Lane open the magnet room and head in to free their latest failure. "I just spent two hours evaluating this guy and bye-bye. He's out. Josh?" Benton says. "Call someone to get him a taxi."

Black leather creaks as Marino makes himself comfortable in his Harley gear. He goes out of his way to show

how relaxed he is, slumped back in the chair, his legs spread.

"What ad?" he asks when Scarpetta hangs up.

"Just another research study he's involved in up there."

"Huh. What kind of study?" He says it as if he is suspicious of something.

"A neuropsychological study. How different types of people process different types of information, that sort of thing."

"Huh. That's a line all right. Probably the same line they use every time a reporter calls, a line that says nothing. What did you want to see me about?"

"Did you get my messages? Since Sunday night, I've left you four."

"Yeah I got them."

"It would have been nice if you'd returned them."

"You didn't say it was a nine-one-one."

That has been their code over the years when they paged each other, back when cell phones weren't so popular, then later because they were insecure. Now Lucy has scramblers and who-knows-what to protect privacy, and it's fine to leave voicemail.

"I don't leave a nine-one-one when it's a phone message," she says. "How does that work? After the beep I say 'nine-one-one'?"

"My point being, you didn't say it was an emergency. What did you want?"

"You stood me up. We were set to review the Swift case, remember?"

She fixed dinner for him, too, but she leaves out that part.

"I've been busy, on the road."

"Would you like to tell me what you've been doing and where?"

"Riding my new bike."

"For two solid days? You didn't stop for gas, maybe go to the men's room? Couldn't find time for one phone call?"

She leans back in the big chair behind her big desk and feels small as she looks at him. "You're being contraire. That's what this is about."

"Why should I tell you what I'm doing?"

"Because I'm the director of forensic science and medicine, if for no other reason."

"And I'm the head of investigations, and that really falls under training and Special Ops. So Lucy's really my supervisor, not really you."

"Lucy isn't your supervisor."

"Guess you'd really better talk to her about that."

"Investigations really falls under forensic science and medicine. You really aren't a Special Ops agent, Marino. My department pays your salary. Really." She is about to rip into him and knows she shouldn't.

He looks at her with his big, tough face, his big, thick fingers drumming the armrest. He crosses his legs and starts jiggling a big Harley-booted foot.

"Your job is to assist me in casework," she says. "You're the person I depend on most. "

"Guess you better take that up with Lucy."

He slowly drums the armrest and jiggles his foot, his flinty eyes looking past her.

"I'm supposed to tell you everything and you don't tell me shit," he says. "You do whatever the hell you want and don't think you ever owe me an explanation. I'm sitting right here, listening to you lie like I'm so stupid I don't see through it. You don't ask or tell me nothing unless it suits you."

"I don't work for you, Marino." She can't stop herself from saying it. "I believe it's the other way around."

"Oh yeah?"

He leans closer to her big desk, his face turning crimson.

"Ask Lucy," he says. "She owns this damn place. She pays everybody's salary. Ask her."

"Obviously, you weren't present for most of our discussion about the Swift case," she says, changing her tone, trying to abort what is about to turn into a battle.

"Why bother? I'm the one with the damn information."

"We were hoping you might share it. We're all in this together."

"No kidding. Everybody's into everything. Nothing of

mine's private anymore. It's open season on my old cases, my hell scenes. You just give away whatever you want and don't care how I feel."

"That's not true. I wish you'd calm down. I don't want you having a stroke."

"You hear about yesterday's hell scene? Where do you think that came from? He's getting into our files."

"That's not possible. The hard copies are locked up. Electronic copies are completely inaccessible. As for yesterday's hell scene, I agree it's very similar . . ."

"Similar my ass. It's exactly the same."

"Marino, it was also in the news. In fact, you can still pull it up on the Internet. I checked."

His big flushed face stares at her, a face so unfriendly she scarcely recognizes it anymore.

"Can we talk about Johnny Swift for a minute, please?" she says.

"Ask me anything you want," he says glumly.

"I'm confused about the possibility of robbery as a motive. Was there a robbery or not?"

"Nothing of value missing from the house except we can't figure out the credit-card shit."

"What credit-card shit?"

"The week after his death, someone withdrew a total of twenty-five hundred dollars cash. Each withdrawal was five hundred bucks from five different ATMs in the Hollywood area."

"Tracked?"

Marino shrugs and says, "Yeah. To machines in parking lots, different days, different times, everything different except the amount. Always the limit of five hundred bucks. By the time the credit-card company tried to notify Johnny Swift—who was dead by then—about an out-of-pattern behavior that might indicate someone was using his card, the withdrawals had stopped."

"What about cameras? Any chance the person was caught on video?"

"Each ATM machine that was picked didn't have one.

Somebody knew what he was doing, has probably done it before."

"Did Laurel have the PIN number?"

"Johnny wasn't able to drive yet because of the surgery. So Laurel had to do everything, including cash withdrawals."

"Anybody else have the PIN number?"

"Not as far as we know."

"It certainly doesn't look good for him," Scarpetta says.

"Well, I don't think he whacked his twin brother for his ATM card."

"People have killed for a lot less."

"I think we're talking someone else, maybe someone Johnny Swift had some kind of encounter with. Maybe the person had just killed him and heard Laurel drive up. So he ducked, explaining why the shotgun was still on the floor. Then when Laurel ran from the house, the guy grabbed it and bolted."

"Why was the shotgun on the floor to begin with?"

"Maybe he was staging the scene to look like a suicide and got interrupted."

"You're telling me you have no doubt it's a homicide."

"You telling me you don't think it is?"

"I'm just asking questions."

Marino's eyes wander around the office, over the top of her piled desk, across stacks of paperwork and case files. He looks at her with hard eyes that she might find frightening had she not seen insecurity and pain in them so often in the past. Maybe he seems different and distant only because he shaves his balding head and has taken to wearing a diamond stud earring. He works out in the gym obsessively and is the biggest she's ever seen him.

"I'd appreciate it if you'd review my hell scenes," he says. "Every one I've ever come up with is on that disk. I'd like you to look at them carefully. Since you'll be sitting on a plane with nothing better to do."

"I might have something better to do." She tries to tease him a little, get him to lighten up.

It doesn't work.

"Rose put all of them on a disk going back to the first of last year, and it's in the file there. In a sealed envelope"—he indicates files on her desk. "Maybe you can pop it in your laptop and take a look. The bullet with the mesh pattern from the screen door's in there. That lying piece of shit. I swear I came up with it first."

"You do a search on the Internet of intermediary targets in shootings and I guarantee you'll find cases and firearms tests that include bullets fired through screen doors," she says. "I'm afraid there really isn't much that's new or private anymore."

"He's nothing but a laboratory rat who lived inside a microscope until a year ago. He couldn't know the stuff he's writing about. It's impossible. It's because of what happened at the Body Farm. At least you could have been honest about it."

"You're right," she says. "I should have told you I stopped reviewing your hell scenes after that. All of us did. I should have sat you down and explained, but you were so angry and combative, none of us wanted to deal with you."

"Maybe if you got set up the way I did, you'd be angry and combative, too."

"Joe wasn't at the Body Farm or even in Knoxville when it happened," she reminds him. "So please explain how he could have slipped a hypodermic needle into a dead man's jacket pocket."

"The field exercise was supposed to expose the students to a real dead body rotting away at the Body Farm and see if they could overcome the puke factor and recover several items of evidence. A dirty needle wasn't one of them. He set that up to get me."

"Not everybody is out to get you."

"If he didn't set me up, then why did the girl not follow through with the lawsuit? Because it's bogus, that's why. The damn needle didn't have AIDS on it, now did it, had never been used. A little oversight on the asshole's part."

She gets up from her desk.

"What I'm going to do about you is the bigger issue," she says, locking her briefcase.

"I'm not the one who has secrets," he says, watching her.

"You have plenty of secrets. I never know where you are or what you're doing half the time."

She grabs her suit jacket off the back of the door. He looks steadily at her with his flinty eyes. His fingers stop drumming the armrest. Leather creaks as he gets up from his chair.

"Benton must feel like a real big shot working with all those Harvard people," he says, and it's not the first time he's said it. "All those rocket scientists with all their secrets."

She stares at him, her hand on the doorknob. Maybe she's getting paranoid, too.

"Yup. Must be exciting, what he's doing up there. But if you'd asked my opinion, I'd been happy to tell you not to waste your time."

It can't be possible he is alluding to PREDATOR.

"Not to mention a waste of money. Money that could sure as hell be better spent. Me? I just can't stomach the thought of giving all that money and attention to scumbags like that."

No one is supposed to know about PREDATOR except the study team, the hospital's president, the Internal Review Board and certain key prison officials. Even the normal subjects in the study don't know the name of it or what it is about. Marino couldn't know unless he has somehow broken into her e-mail or the hard copies she keeps locked up in file drawers. For the first time, it occurs to her that if anyone is breaching security, it might be him.

"What are you talking about?" she asks quietly.

"Maybe you should be more careful about forwarding files, make sure nothing is attached to them," he replies.

"Forwarding what files?"

"The notes you typed up after your first meeting with Darling Dave about that shaken baby case he wants everyone to think is an accident."

"I didn't forward any notes to you."

"Sure as hell did. Sent this past Friday, didn't happen to open it until after I saw you on Sunday. Notes accidentally attached to an e-mail to you from Benton. An e-mail I sure as hell wasn't supposed to see."

"I didn't," she insists with growing alarm. "I didn't send you anything."

"Maybe not on purpose. Funny how lies catch up with people," he says as a light knock sounds at the door.

"Is that why you didn't show up at my house Sunday night? Why you didn't show up for the meeting with Dave yesterday morning?"

"Excuse me," Rose says as she lets herself in. "I think one of you should handle this."

"You could have said something, given me a chance to defend myself," Scarpetta says to him. "I may not always tell you everything, but I don't lie."

"Lying by omission is still lying."

"Excuse me," Rose tries again.

"PREDATOR," Marino says to Scarpetta. "Try that lie on for size."

"Mrs. Simister," Rose interrupts them loudly. "The lady from the church who called a little while ago. I'm sorry, but it seems rather urgent."

Marino makes no move to go to the phone, as if to remind Scarpetta that he doesn't work for her, that she can take the call herself.

"Oh for God's sake," she says, walking back to her desk. "Put her through."

24

Marino digs his hands into the pockets of his jeans and leans against the doorway, watching her deal with whoever Mrs. Simister is.

In the old days, he used to enjoy sitting in Scarpetta's office for hours, listening to her while he drank coffee and smoked. He didn't mind asking her to explain what he didn't understand, didn't mind waiting when she was interrupted, which was often. He didn't mind when she was late.

Things are different now, and it's her damn fault. He doesn't intend to wait for her. He doesn't want her to explain anything and would rather remain ignorant than ask her a medical question, professional or personal, even if he was dying, and he used to ask her whatever he wanted. Then she betrayed him. She humiliated him and meant to, and is doing it again and means to, no matter what she says. She has always rationalized whatever suits her, done hurtful things in the name of logic and science, as if she thinks he is so stupid he'll never see through it.

It's no different than what happened to Doris. She came home one day crying, and he couldn't tell if she was angry or sad but he knew she was upset, maybe as upset as he had ever seen her.

What's the matter? He going to have to pull your tooth? Marino asked her as he drank beer in his favorite chair and watched the news.

Doris sat down on the sofa and sobbed.

Shit. What is it, baby?

She covered her face and cried as if someone were about to die, so Marino sat next to her and put his arm around her. He held her for a few minutes, and when no information was forthcoming, he demanded she tell him what the hell was wrong.

He touched me, she said, crying. *I knew it wasn't right and I kept asking him why, but he said to relax, that he's a doctor, and a part of me knew what he was doing but I was scared. I should have known better, should have said no but I just didn't know what to do,* and she went on to explain that the dentist or root canal specialist or whatever the hell he called himself said Doris possibly had a systemic infection because of a root fracture and he needed to check her glands. That was the word he used, according to Doris.

Glands.

"Hold on," Scarpetta is saying to whoever Mrs. Simister is. "Let me put you on speakerphone. I have an investigator sitting right here."

She gives Marino a look, indicating she is concerned about what she is hearing, and he tries to chase Doris out of his thoughts. He still thinks about her often, and it seems the older he gets, the more he remembers what went on between them and the way he felt when the dentist touched her and the way he felt when she left him for that car salesman, that fucking loser car salesman. Everybody leaves him. Everybody betrays him. Everybody wants what he has. Everybody thinks he's too stupid to figure out their plots and manipulations. The last few weeks, it has been almost more than he can stand.

Now this. Scarpetta lies about the study up there. Excludes him. Degrades him. Helps herself to whatever she wants when it suits her, treats him like he's nothing.

"I wish I had more information." Mrs. Simister's voice enters the room, and she sounds as old as Methuselah. "I certainly hope something bad hasn't happened, but I fear it. It's just awful when the police don't care."

Marino has no idea what Mrs. Simister is talking about or who she is or why she is calling the National Forensic Academy, and he can't exorcise Doris from his head. He wishes he had done more than threaten the damn dentist or root canal specialist or whatever the hell he was. He should have destroyed the asshole's face and maybe broken a few of his fingers.

"Explain to Investigator Marino what you mean by the police not caring," Scarpetta says over speakerphone.

"The last I saw any sign of life over there was this past Thursday night, and when I realized everybody was gone without a trace, I called nine-one-one right away and they sent a police officer to the house and then he called a detective. She obviously doesn't care."

"You're talking about the Hollywood police," Scarpetta says, looking at Marino.

"Yes. A Detective Wagner."

Marino rolls his eyes. This is unbelievable. With all his bad luck of late, he doesn't need this.

He asks from the doorway, "You talking about Reba Wagner?"

"What?" the querulous voice asks.

He steps closer to the phone on the desk and repeats his question.

"All I know is the initials on her card are R.T. So I suppose it could be Reba."

Marino rolls his eyes again and taps his head, indicating that Detective R. T. Wagner is as dumb as a rock.

"She looked around the yard and the house and said there was no sign of foul play. She felt they ran off on their own and said there's nothing the police can do about it."

"Do you know these people?" Marino asks.

"I live right across the water from them. And I go to their church. I just know something bad has happened."

"All right," Scarpetta says. "What is it you're asking us to do, Mrs. Simister?"

"To at least look at the house. You see, the church rents it, and they've kept it locked up since they disappeared. But the lease is up in three months, and the landlord says he'll let the church out of it without a penalty because he's got someone else to rent it. Some of the ladies at the church plan to go over there first thing in the morning and start packing up. Then what happens to any clues?"

"All right," Scarpetta says again. "I tell you what we'll do. We're going to call Detective Wagner. We can't go in the house without permission from the police. We don't have jurisdiction unless they ask for our help."

"I understand. Thank you very much. Please do something."

"All right, Mrs. Simister. We'll get back to you. We need your phone number."

"Huh," Marino says when Scarpetta hangs up. "Probably some mental case."

"How about you call Detective Wagner, since it seems you're familiar with her," Scarpetta says.

"She used to be a motorcycle cop. Dumb as dirt but handled her Road King pretty good. I can't believe they made her a detective."

He gets out his Treo and dreads hearing Reba's voice and wishes Doris would get out of his mind. He tells Hollywood police dispatch to have Detective Wagner contact him immediately. He ends the call and looks around Scarpetta's office, looks everywhere but at her as he thinks about Doris and the dentist, or whatever the hell he was, and the car salesman. He thinks about how satisfying it would have been to beat the dentist, or whatever the hell he was, senseless instead of getting drunk and barging into his office and demanding he step out of an examination room and in front of a lobby full of patients asking why he thought it was necessary to examine his wife's tits and to please explain how tits might be relevant in a root canal case.

"Marino?"

Why that incident should still bother him all over again after all these years is a mystery. He doesn't understand why a lot of things have started bothering him again. The last few weeks have been hell.

"Marino?"

He comes to and looks at Scarpetta at the same time he realizes his cell phone is buzzing.

"Yeah," he answers.

"Detective Wagner here."

"Investigator Pete Marino," he says, as if he doesn't know her.

"What do you need, Investigator Pete Marino." She sounds as if she doesn't know him, either.

"I understand you got a family that's disappeared from the West Lake area. Apparently last Thursday night."

"How did you hear about that?"

"Apparently there's some concern foul play might be involved. And the word is you aren't being very helpful."

"We'd be investigating the hell out of it if we thought there was anything to it. What's the source of your information?"

"A lady from their church. You got the names of these people who supposedly have vanished?"

"Let me think. They're kind of odd names, Eva Christian and Crystal or Christine Christian. Something like that. I can't think of the boys' names."

"Could you mean Christian Christian?"

Scarpetta and Marino look at each other.

"Something a whole lot like that. I don't have my notes in front of me. You want to look into it, be my guest. My department's not going to devote a lot of resources to something when there's absolutely no evidence . . ."

"I got that part," Marino says rudely. "Supposedly the church is going to start packing up that house tomorrow and if we're gonna take a look, now's the time."

"They've not even been gone for a week and the church is already packing up the house? Sounds to me they know they've skipped town and aren't coming back. What's it sound like to you?"

"Sounds like we ought to make sure," Marino says.

The man behind the counter is older and more distinguished than Lucy imagined. She expected someone who looks like a has-been surfer, someone leathery and covered in tattoos. That's the sort of person who ought to be working in a shop called Beach Bums.

She sets down a camera case, and her fingers flutter

through big, loud shirts printed with sharks, flowers, palm trees and other tropical designs. She peruses stacks of straw hats and bins of flip-flops and displays of sunglasses and lotions, not interested in buying any of it but wishing she were. For a moment she browses, waiting for two other customers to leave. She wonders how it would feel to be like everybody else, to care about souvenirs and gaudy things to wear and days in the sun, to feel good about the way she looks half-naked in a swimsuit.

"You got any of that stuff with zinc oxide in it?" one of the customers is asking Larry, who is seated behind the counter.

He has thick, white hair and a neatly trimmed beard, is sixty-two, was born in Alaska, drives a Jeep, has never owned a home, didn't go to college and in 1957 was arrested for drunk and disorderly. Larry has managed Beach Bums for about two years.

"Nobody likes that anymore," he is telling the customer.

"I do. It doesn't break out my skin like all these other lotions. I think I'm allergic to aloe."

"These sunblocks don't have aloe."

"You carry Maui Jim's?"

"Too expensive, my dear. The only sunglasses we got are the ones you're looking at."

This goes on for a while, both customers making minor purchases, finally leaving. Lucy wanders up to the counter.

"Can I help you with something?" Larry asks, looking at the way she is dressed. "Where'd you just come from, a *Mission Impossible* movie?"

"I rode my motorcycle here."

"Well, you're one of the few with any sense. Look out the window. Every one of them in shorts and T-shirts, no helmet. Some of them in flip-flops."

"You must be Larry."

He looks surprised and says, "You been in here before? I don't remember you, and I'm pretty good with faces."

"I'd like to talk to you about Florrie and Helen Quincy," she says. "But I need you to lock the door."

The **Harley-Davidson** Screamin' Eagle Deuce with its flames over blue paint and chrome is parked in a far corner of the faculty lot, and as Marino gets closer to it, he picks up his pace.

"Goddamn son of a bitch." He starts to run.

He yells his obscenities loudly enough for Link the maintenance man, who is weeding a flower bed, to stop what he is doing and jump to his feet. "You all right over there?"

"Fucking motherfucker!" Marino yells.

The front tire of his new bike is flat. Flat all the way down to the shiny chrome rim. Marino gets down to look at the tire, upset and furious, looks for a nail or a screw, anything sharp he might have picked up on his ride in to work this morning. He rolls the bike backward and forward and discovers the puncture. It is about an eighth of an inch cut that appears to have been made with something sharp and strong, possibly a knife.

Possibly a stainless-steel surgical knife, and his eyes dart around, looking for Joe Amos.

"Yeah, I was noticing that," Link says, walking toward him, wiping his dirty hands on his blue coveralls.

"Nice of you to let me know," Marino says angrily as he angrily digs through a saddlebag for his tire-plug kit as he angrily thinks of Joe Amos, getting angrier with each thought.

"Must have picked up a nail somewhere," Link supposes, getting down for a closer inspection. "That looks bad."

"You see anybody around here looking at my bike? Where the hell's my tire-plug kit?"

"I've been right here all day and haven't seen anyone anywhere near your bike. It's quite a bike. What? About fourteen hundred CCs? I used to have a Springer until some no-nuts pulled in front of me and I ended up flying over his hood. I started working on the flower beds around ten this morning. The tire was already flat by then."

Marino thinks back. He got here between nine fifteen and nine thirty.

"A puncture like this and the tire would have gone flat so fast I'd never have gotten it into the damn lot and it sure as hell wasn't flat when I stopped to get donuts," he says. "It had to have happened after I parked in here."

"Well, I don't like the sound of it."

Marino looks around, thinking about Joe Amos. He'll kill him. If he touched his bike, he's dead.

"I hate to think it," Link is saying. "Awfully bold to come right into this lot in the middle of the morning and do something like that. If that's what happened."

"Goddamn it, where is it?" Marino says, going through the other saddlebag. "You got anything to plug this thing? Shit! What the hell." He quits rummaging. "Probably not going to work anyway, not with a hole this big, damn it!"

He's going to have to change the tire. There are extra ones in the hangar.

"What about Joe Amos? You seen him? You seen his ugly ass anywhere within a mile of here?"

"No."

"None of the students?"

The students hate him. Every one of them does.

"No," Link says. "I would have noticed if someone went into this lot and started fooling with your bike or any of the cars."

"Nobody?" Marino keeps pushing, then entertains the suspicion that maybe Link had something to do with it.

Probably nobody at the Academy likes Marino. Probably half the world is jealous of his tricked-out Harley. He certainly gets enough people staring at it, following him into gas stations and rest stops to get a better look.

"You're going to have to roll it to the garage down there by the hangar," Link says, "unless we want to get it on one of those trailers Lucy uses for all those new V-Rods of hers."

Marino thinks about the gates at both the back and front entrances of the Academy grounds. No one can get in without a code. It had to be an inside job. He thinks about Joe Amos again and realizes an important fact. Joe was in staff meeting. He was already sitting in there, shooting off his big mouth, when Marino showed up.

25

The orange-colored house with its white roof was built in the same decade that Scarpetta was born, the fifties. She imagines the people who live here and feels their absence as she walks around the backyard.

She can't stop thinking about the person who said his name is Hog, about his cryptic reference to Johnny Swift and what Marino thought was Christian Christian. Scarpetta feels certain what Hog actually said was Kristin Christian. Johnny is dead. Kristin is missing. It has often occurred to Scarpetta that there are plenty of places to dispose of dead bodies in South Florida, plenty of wetlands, canals, lakes and vast pine forests. Flesh decomposes quickly in the sub-tropics, and insects gorge themselves, and animals gnaw on bones and scatter them like sticks and stones. Flesh doesn't last long in the water, and salt in the sea leaches the minerals from skeletons, dissolving them completely.

The waterway behind the house is the color of putrid blood. Dead leaves float in the brown, stagnant water like debris from an explosion. Green and brown coconuts bob like decapitated heads. The sun slips in and out of mounting storm clouds, the warm air heavy and humid, the wind gusting.

Detective Wagner prefers to be called Reba. She is attractive and rather sexy in an overblown, sun-weathered way, her shaggy hair dyed platinum, her eyes bright blue. She doesn't have the brains of a maggot. She isn't as dumb as a cow and has yet to come across as a bitch on ten-spoke custom wheels, to quote Marino, who also called her a cock stalker, although Scarpetta isn't clear on what that means. Most assuredly, Reba is inexperienced, but she seems to be trying. Scarpetta debates whether to tell her about the anonymous phone call that referenced Kristin Christian.

"They've lived here for a while but aren't citizens," Reba is saying of the two sisters who live in this house with two boys, a foster situation. "They're originally from South Africa. The two boys are too, which is probably why they took them in to begin with. You ask me, the four of them are back over there somewhere."

"And they would have decided to disappear, perhaps flee to South Africa, for what reason?" Scarpetta asks, staring across the narrow, dark waterway as humidity presses down on her like a warm, sticky hand.

"I understand they wanted to adopt the boys. And it's unlikely they were going to get to."

"Why not?"

"Seems like relatives of the boys back there in South Africa want them but just couldn't take them at first, not until they move into a bigger house. And the sisters are religious kooks, which might have weighed against them."

Scarpetta is aware of the houses on the other side of the water, aware of patches of bright green grass and small, pale-blue swimming pools. She's not certain which house is Mrs. Simister's, and wonders if Marino is talking with her yet.

"The boys are how old?" she asks.

"Seven and twelve."

Scarpetta glances at her notebook and flips back several pages. "Eva and Kristin Christian. I'm not clear on why they are taking care of them."

She is careful to speak of the missing people in the present tense.

"No, not Eva. There's no 'a,'" Reba says.

"Ev or Eve?"

"It's Ev as in Evelyn only her name is just Ev. No 'e' or 'a.' Just Ev."

Scarpetta writes down "Ev" in her black notebook and thinks, *What a name.* She stares at the waterway, and sunlight on the water has turned it the color of strong tea. Ev and Kristin Christian. What names for religious women who have vanished like ghosts. Then the sun slips behind clouds again and the water is dark.

"Ev and Kristin Christian are their real names?" Scarpetta asks. "We're sure they're not aliases? We're sure they didn't change their names at some point, perhaps to give them religious connotations?" she asks, staring across the waterway at houses that look sketched in pastel chalk.

She watches a figure in dark pants and a white shirt walking into someone's backyard, possibly Mrs. Simister's backyard.

"As far as we know, it's their real names," Reba replies, looking where Scarpetta is looking. "Damn canker inspectors are all over the map. Politics. It's all about preventing people from growing their own citrus fruit so they have to buy it."

"Actually, it's not. Citrus canker is a terrible blight. If it's not controlled, nobody will be growing citrus fruit in their yards."

"It's a conspiracy. I've been listening to what all these commentators are saying on the radio. You ever listen to Dr. Self on the radio? You should hear what she has to say about it."

Scarpetta never listens to Dr. Self if she can avoid it. She watches the figure across the waterway squat in the grass and dig inside what appears to be some sort of dark bag. He pulls out something.

"Ev Christian's a reverend or priest or whatever you want to call it in some offbeat little church. . . . Okay, I'm gonna have to read this to you. It's too much to remember," Reba says, flipping through her notepad. "The True Daughters of the Seal of God."

"Never heard of that denomination," Scarpetta comments rather ironically as she writes it down. "And Kristin? What does she do?"

The inspector stands up, screwing together what looks like a fruit picker. He raises it high up in a tree, pulling down a grapefruit that lands on the grass.

"Kristin also works at the church. An assistant who does readings and meditations during the services. The kids' parents got killed in a scooter accident about a year ago. You know, one of those Vespas."

"Where?"

"South Africa."

"And this information came from?" Scarpetta asks.

"Someone at the church."

"You have a report on the accident?"

"Like I said, it happened in South Africa," Detective Wagner replies. "We're trying to track it down."

Scarpetta continues to deliberate over when she should tell her about the disturbing phone call from Hog.

"What are the boys' names?" Scarpetta asks.

"David and Tony Luck. Kind of funny, when you think about it. Luck."

"You're not getting cooperation from the South African authorities? Where in South Africa?"

"Capetown."

"Where the sisters are also from?"

"That's what I'm told. After the parents got killed, the sisters took the kids in. Their church is maybe twenty minutes from here on Davie Boulevard, right next to one of these alternative pet stores, kind of figures."

"Have you checked with the medical examiner's office in Capetown?"

"Not yet."

"I can help you with that."

"That would be great. Kind of figures, doesn't it? Spiders, scorpions, poisonous frogs, all these little white rat pups you can buy to feed to your snakes," Reba says. "Sounds like some sort of cultville over there."

I've never let anybody come in and photograph a business of mine unless it's a genuine police matter. I was robbed once. That was a while back," Larry explains from the stool behind the counter.

Through the window is the constant traffic along A1A, then the ocean beyond. A light rain has begun to fall, a storm moving in, heading south. Lucy thinks about what Marino told her a few minutes ago, about the house and the missing people, and of course his flat tire, which was his bigger complaint. She thinks of what her aunt must be doing right now, of the storm heading her way.

"Of course I've heard quite a lot about it." Larry gets back to the subject of Florrie and Helen Quincy after a long digression about how much South Florida has changed, how much he has been seriously considering moving back to Alaska. "It's like everything else. The details get more exaggerated with time. But I don't think I want you videotaping," he says again.

"This is a police matter," Lucy reiterates. "I've been asked to privately investigate the case."

"How do I know you aren't a reporter or something?"

"I'm former FBI, former ATF. You ever heard of the National Forensic Academy?"

"That big training camp out there in the Everglades?"

"It's not exactly in the Everglades. We have private labs and experts and an agreement with most of the police departments in Florida. We help them out as needed."

"Sounds expensive. Let me guess, taxpayers like me."

"Indirectly. Grants, quid pro quo—services for services. They help us, we train them. All sorts of things."

She reaches into a back pocket and works out a black wallet and hands it to him. He studies her credentials, a fake ID, an investigator shield that isn't worth the brass it's made from because it's also fake.

"There's no picture on it," he says.

"It's not a driver's license."

He reads her fictitious name out loud, reads that she's Special Operations.

"That's right."

"Well, if you say so." He hands the wallet back to her.

"Tell me what you've heard," Lucy says, setting the video camera on top of the counter.

She looks at the locked front door, at a young couple in skimpy swimsuits trying to open it.

They peer through the glass and Larry shakes his head. No, he's not open.

"You're losing me business," he says to Lucy, but he doesn't seem to care very much. "When I had a chance to take over this space, I got quite an earful about the Quincys disappearing. The story I heard is she always got here at seven-thirty in the morning so she could get the little electric trains running on their tracks and light up the trees, turn on the Christmas music and do all this other stuff. It appears she never opened up that day. The closed sign was still on the door when her son finally got worried and came looking for her and the daughter."

Lucy reaches inside a pocket of her cargo pants and removes a black ballpoint pen from the holder of a concealed tape recorder. She slips out a small notebook.

"Mind if I take a few notes?" she asks.

"Don't take everything I say as gospel. I wasn't here when it happened, just passing along what I've been told."

"I understand Mrs. Quincy called in a take-out order," Lucy says. "There was something in the paper about it."

"At the Floridian, that old diner on the other side of the drawbridge. A pretty nifty place, if you've never eaten there. It's my understanding she didn't call it in, didn't need to. They always had the same thing ready for her. A tuna plate."

"Something for the daughter, too? Helen?"

"I don't remember that."

"Mrs. Quincy usually pick it up herself?"

"Unless her son was in the area. He's one of the reasons I know a few things about what happened."

"I'd like to talk to him."

"I haven't seen him in a year. For a while early on, I did. He would drop by, look around, chat. I guess you could say he was obsessed for maybe the first year after they disappeared. Then, it's my opinion, he couldn't bear to think about it. He lives in a real nice house in Hollywood."

Lucy looks around the store.

"There's no Christmas stuff here," Larry says, in case that's what she is wondering.

She doesn't ask anything about Mrs. Quincy's son, Fred. She already knows from HIT that Fred Anderson Quincy is twenty-six years old. She knows his address and that he's self-employed, into computer graphics, a Web designer. Larry goes on to say that on the day Mrs. Quincy and Helen disappeared, Fred tried numerous times to reach them and finally drove to the shop and found it closed, his mother's Audi still parked in back.

"We're sure they actually had unlocked the shop that morning?" Lucy asks. "Any possibility something happened to them after they got out of the car?"

"I suppose anything's possible."

"Were Mrs. Quincy's pocketbook, her car keys, inside the shop? Had she made coffee, used the phone, done anything at all that might indicate she and Helen had been there? For example, were the trees lit up, the toy trains running? Was there Christmas music playing? Were the shop lights on?"

"I heard they never did find her pocketbook and car keys. I've heard different stories about things being turned on inside the shop. Some say they were. Others say they weren't."

Lucy's attention wanders to the doorway in the back of the store. She thinks about what Basil Jenrette told Benton. She doesn't see how it's possible that Basil raped and murdered anybody in the storage area. It's hard to believe he could clean up and remove the body from the shop, place it in a car and drive off without being seen. It was daylight. It is a populated area, even during the off-season of July, and such a scenario certainly wouldn't explain what happened to the daughter unless he abducted her, perhaps killed her elsewhere, as he did to his other victims. A gruesome thought. A seventeen-year-old girl.

"What happened to this place after they disappeared?" Lucy asks. "Did it reopen?"

"Nope. Wasn't much of a market for Christmas stuff anyway. You ask me, it was more an eccentric hobby of hers than anything else. Her shop never reopened, and her son cleared out the merchandise a month or two after they disappeared. Beach Bums moved in that September and hired me."

"I'd like to take a look in back," Lucy says. "Then I'll get out of your hair."

Hog **pulls** down two more oranges, then grabs at grapefruits with the clawlike basket on the end of the long-handled picker. He looks across the waterway, watching Scarpetta and Detective Wagner walk around the pool.

The detective gestures a lot. Scarpetta takes notes, looking at everything. It gives Hog extreme pleasure to watch the show. Fools. None of them are as smart as they think. He can outsmart all of them, and he smiles as he imagines Marino running a little late, delayed by an unexpected flat tire that could have been remedied easily and quickly by driving here in an Academy vehicle. But not him. He couldn't stand it, would have to fix it right then. Big, stupid redneck. Hog squats in the grass, breaks down the picker by unscrewing its aluminum segments, tucks them back into the big black nylon bag. The bag is heavy, and he props it on his shoulder like a lumberjack shouldering an ax, like the lumberjack in The Christmas Shop.

He takes his time walking through the yard, toward the tiny white stucco house next door. He sees her rocking on her sunporch, looking through binoculars at the pale orange house on the other side of the waterway. She's been watching the house for days. How entertaining is that. Hog has been in and out of the pale orange house three times now, and no one has noticed. In and out to remember what happened, to relive it, to take all the time he wants in there. No one can see him. He can make himself disappear.

He enters Mrs. Simister's yard and begins to examine one of her lime trees. She trains the binoculars on him. In a moment, she opens the slider but doesn't walk out into the yard. He's never once seen her in her yard. The yard man comes and goes, but she never leaves the house or speaks to him. Her groceries are delivered, the same man each time. It might be a relative, maybe a son. All he does is carry in the bags. He never stays long. Nobody bothers with her. She should be grateful to Hog. Pretty soon she'll get plenty of attention. A lot of people will hear about her when she ends up on Dr. Self's show.

"Leave my trees alone," Mrs. Simister says loudly with a thick accent. "You people have been out here two times this week and it's harassment."

"Sorry, ma'am. I'm almost finished up here," Hog says politely as he pulls a leaf off the lime tree, looks at it.

"Get off my property or I'm calling the police." Her voice gets more shrill.

She is frightened. She's angry because she is terrified that she will lose her precious trees, and she will, but by then, it won't matter. Her trees are infected. They are old trees, at least twenty years old, and they're ruined. It was easy. Wherever the big orange trucks roll in to cut down canker-infected trees and grind them up, there are leaves on the road. He picks them up, tears them, puts them in water and watches the bacteria stream up like tiny bubbles. He fills a syringe, the one God gave him.

Hog unzips his black bag and pulls out a can of red spray paint. He sprays a red stripe around the trunk of the lime tree. Blood painted over the door, like the angel of death, but no one will be spared. Hog hears preaching in a dark place somewhere in his head, like a box hidden way out of reach somewhere in his head.

A false witness shall not be unpunished.

I won't say anything.

Liars are punished.

I didn't say anything. I didn't.

Punishment from my hand is endless.

I didn't. I didn't!

"What are you doing? Leave my trees alone, you hear me!"

"I'm happy to explain it to you, ma'am," Hog says politely, sympathetically.

Mrs. Simister shakes her head. She angrily closes the sliding glass door and locks it.

26

It has been unseasonably hot and raining a lot lately, and the grass is spongy and coarse beneath Scarpetta's shoes, and when the sun emerges from the dark clouds again, the sunlight feels flat and hot against her head and shoulders as she walks around the backyard.

She notices the pink-and-red hibiscus bushes, the palm trees, notices several citrus trees with red-painted stripes around their trunks, and she stares across the waterway at the inspector zipping up his bag after the old woman just yelled at him. She wonders if the old woman is Mrs. Simister and assumes Marino hasn't gotten to her house yet. He is always late, never in a hurry to do what Scarpetta asks if he bothers to do it at all. She walks closer to a concrete wall that drops precipitously to the waterway. This one probably doesn't have alligators, but it has no fence, and any child or dog could easily fall over the edge and drown.

Ev and Kristin took custody of two children and didn't bother putting up a fence along the backyard. Scarpetta imagines the property after dark and how easy it would be to forget where the dark yard ends and the dark waterway begins. It runs east–west and is narrow behind the house but gets wider farther off. In the distance, handsome sailboats and motorboats are docked behind much finer homes than the one where Ev, Kristin, David and Tony lived.

According to Reba, the sisters and the boys were last seen on Thursday night, February 10. Early the next morning, Marino got the phone call from the man who said his name was Hog. By then, the people had disappeared.

"Was there anything in the news about their disappearance?" Scarpetta asks Reba, wondering if the anonymous caller might have gotten Kristin's name that way.

"Not that I know of."

"And you filled out a police report."

"Not something that would have gone into the press basket. I'm afraid people disappear down here all the time, Dr. Scarpetta. Welcome to South Florida."

"Tell me what else you know about the last time they were allegedly seen, last Thursday night."

Reba replies that Ev preached at her church and Kristin gave several readings from the Bible. When the two women didn't show up at the church the following day for a prayer meeting, an associate tried to call them and got no answer, so this associate, a woman, drove to the house. She had a key and let herself in. Nothing seemed out of the ordinary except Ev, Kristin and the boys were gone and the stove had been left on low, an empty skillet on top of it. The detail about the stove is important, and Scarpetta will turn her attention to it when she goes inside the house, but she isn't ready yet, her approach to a scene similar to a predator's. She moves from the outer edge to the inside, saving the worst for last.

Lucy asks Larry if the storeroom is different from how it was when he moved in approximately two years ago.

"Didn't do a thing to it," he says.

She scans big cardboard boxes and shelves of T-shirts, lotions, beach towels, sunglasses, cleaning equipment and other inventory in the glare of a single naked lightbulb overhead.

"No point in caring what it looks like back here," Larry says. "What exactly are you interested in?"

She makes her way into the bathroom, a cramped, windowless space with a sink and a toilet. The walls are cinderblock with a light coat of pale green paint, the floor brown asphalt tile. Overhead is another bare lightbulb.

"You didn't repaint, retile?" she asks.

"It was exactly like this when I took over the place. You're not thinking something happened in here?"

"I'd like to come back and bring somebody with me," she says.

On the other side of the waterway, Mrs. Simister watches.

She rocks on her glass-enclosed sunporch, pushing the glider with her feet, rocking back and forth, her slippers barely touching the tile floor as she makes a quiet sliding sound. She looks for the blonde woman in the dark suit who was walking around the yard of the pale orange house. She looks for the inspector who was trespassing, daring to bother Mrs. Simister's trees again, daring to spray red paint on them. He's gone. The blonde woman's gone.

At first, Mrs. Simister thought the blonde woman was a religious nut. There have been plenty of those visiting that house. Then she looked through binoculars and wasn't so sure. The blonde woman was taking notes and had a black bag slung over her shoulder. She's a banker or a lawyer, Mrs. Simister was about to decide when the other woman appeared, this one quite tan, with white hair and wearing khaki pants and a gun in a shoulder holster. Maybe she's the same one who was over there the other day. Friday. She was tan with white hair. Mrs. Simister isn't sure.

The two women talked and then walked out of sight along the side of the house, toward the front. Maybe they'll be back. Mrs. Simister watches for the inspector, that same one who was so nice the first time, asking her all about her trees and when they were planted and what they mean to her. Then he comes back and paints them. It made her think about her gun for the first time in years. When her son gave it to her, she said all that would happen is the bad person would get hold of it and use it against her. She keeps the gun under the bed, out of sight.

She wouldn't have shot the inspector. She wouldn't have minded scaring him, though. All these citrus inspectors getting paid to rip out trees that people have had for half their lives. She hears talk about it on the radio. Her trees will probably be next. She loves her trees. The yard man takes care of them, picks fruit and leaves it on the stoop. Jake planted a yard full of trees for her when he bought the house right after they got married. She is lost in her past when the phone on the table by her glider rings.

"Hello?" she answers.

"Mrs. Simister?"

"Who is this?"

"Investigator Pete Marino. We talked earlier."

"We did? You're who?"

"You called the National Forensic Academy a few hours ago."

"I most certainly did not. Are you selling something?"

"No, ma'am. I'd like to stop by and talk to you, if that's all right."

"It's not all right," she says, hanging up.

She grips the cool metal armrests so tightly that her big knuckles blanch beneath the loose, sun-spotted skin of her useless old hands. People call all the time and they don't even know her. Machines call and she can't imagine why people sit there and listen to tape recordings made by solicitors after money. The phone rings again, and she ignores it as she picks up the binoculars to peer at the pale orange house where the two ladies live with the two little hoodlums.

She sweeps the binoculars over the waterway, then over the property on the other side of it. The yard and pool are suddenly big and bright green and blue. They are sharply defined, but the blonde woman in the dark suit and the tan lady with the gun are nowhere to be seen. What are they looking for over there? Where are the two ladies who live there? Where are the hoodlums? All children are hoodlums these days.

The doorbell rings and she stops rocking as her heart begins to pound. The older she gets, the more easily she is startled by sudden movements and sounds, the more she fears death and what it means, if it means anything. Several minutes pass, and the bell rings again and she sits still and waits. It rings again and someone knocks loudly. Finally, she gets up.

"Hold on, I'm coming," she mutters, annoyed and anxious. "You'd better not be someone selling something."

She walks into the living room, her slow feet brushing over the carpet. She can't pick up her feet the way she once could, can hardly walk.

"Hold on, I'm coming as fast as I can," she says impatiently when the bell rings again.

Maybe it's UPS. Sometimes her son orders things for her on the Internet. She looks through the peephole in the front door. The person on her porch certainly isn't wearing a brown or blue uniform or carrying mail or a package. It's him again.

"What is it this time?" she says angrily, her eye against the peephole.

"Mrs. Simister? I've got some forms for you to fill out."

27

The gate leads to the front yard, where Scarpetta pays attention to thick hibiscus barricading the property from the sidewalk that dead-ends at the waterway.

There are no broken twigs or branches, nothing to indicate that anyone has entered the property by pushing his way through the hedge. Reaching inside the black nylon shoulder bag she routinely carries to scenes, she pulls out a pair of white cotton examination gloves as she looks at the car on the cracked concrete driveway, an old, gray station wagon parked haphazardly, one tire partially on the lawn, where it has gouged the grass. She works her hands into the gloves and wonders why Ev or Kristin parked the car like that, assuming one or the other was driving.

She looks through the car windows at gray vinyl bench seats and the SunPass transponder neatly affixed to the inside of the windshield. She makes more notes. Already a pattern is becoming apparent. The backyard and pool are meticulous. The screened-in patio and lawn furniture are meticulous. She sees no trash or clutter inside the car, nothing but a black umbrella on the mat in back. Yet the car is parked sloppily, carelessly, as if someone couldn't see well or was in a hurry. She bends down to take a closer look at dirt and bits of dead vegetation caked in the tire tread. She looks at thick dust that has turned the undercarriage the grayish tan of old bones.

"It appears this was driven off-road somewhere," Scarpetta says, getting up as she continues to study the dirty tires, walking from one to the other.

Reba follows her around the car, looking, a curious expression on her lined, tan face.

"The dirt in the tread makes me think the ground was

damp or wet when the car was driven over it," Scarpetta says. "Is the church parking lot paved?"

"Well, it dug up the grass here," Reba says, looking at the gouged yard beneath a back tire.

"That wouldn't explain it. All four tires are caked with dirt."

"The strip mall where the church is has a big parking lot. Nothing unpaved in the area that I noticed."

"Was the car here when the lady from the church showed up looking for Kristin and Ev?"

Reba walks around, interested in the dirty tires. "They said so, and I can tell you for sure it was here when I arrived that afternoon."

"It wouldn't be a bad idea to check the SunPass, see what tollbooths it's gone through and when. Have you opened the doors?"

"Yes. They were unlocked. I didn't see anything significant."

"So it's never been processed."

"I can't ask the crime-scene techs to process something when there's no evidence a crime's been committed."

"I understand the problem."

Reba's dark, tanned face watches her peer through the windows again. They are covered with a fine film of dust. Scarpetta steps back and walks around the station wagon, taking in every inch.

"Who owns it?" Scarpetta says.

"The church."

"Who owns the house?"

"Same thing."

"I was told the church leases the house."

"No, the church definitely owns the house."

"Do you know someone named Simister?" Scarpetta says as she begins to get a strange feeling, the sort that starts in her stomach and works its way up her throat, the same feeling she got when Reba mentioned the name Christian Christian to Marino.

"Who?" Reba frowns as a muffled explosion sounds from the other side of the waterway.

She and Scarpetta stop talking. They step closer to the gate, looking at the houses on the other side of the water. There is no one in sight.

"Car backfire," Reba decides. "People drive a lot of junkers around here. Most of them shouldn't be driving at all. Old as the Grim Reaper and blind as bats."

Scarpetta repeats the name *Simister*.

"Never heard of her," Reba says.

"She said she's talked to you several times. I believe she said three times, to be exact."

"I never heard of her, and she's never talked to me. I guess she's the one who bad-mouthed me, said I didn't care about the case."

"Excuse me," Scarpetta then says, and she tries Marino on his cell phone and gets his voicemail.

She tells him to call her immediately.

"When you find out who this Mrs. Simister is," Reba says, "I'd like to know about it. There's something weird about all this. Maybe we should at least dust the inside of the car for prints. If nothing else, for exclusionary purposes."

"Unfortunately, you probably won't get the boys' prints from inside the car," Scarpetta says. "Not after four days. You probably won't get them from inside the house, either. Certainly not the young boy's prints, the seven-year-old boy's prints."

"I don't get why you would say that."

"The prints of prepubescent children don't survive long. Hours, maybe a few days at most. We're not entirely sure why, but it probably has to do with the oils people secrete when they reach puberty. David is twelve? You might get his prints. I emphasize *might*."

"Well, that sure is news to me."

"I suggest you get this station wagon into the lab, process it for trace evidence and fume the inside of it ASAP with superglue for possible fingerprints. We can do it at the Academy, if you want. We have a bay for processing vehicles and can take care of it."

"Maybe that's not a bad idea," Reba says.

"We should find Ev's and Kristin's prints inside the

house. And DNA, including the boys' DNA. Their tooth-brushes, hairbrushes, shoes, clothing," and then she tells Reba about the anonymous caller who mentioned Kristin Christian's name.

Mrs. Simister lives alone in a small white rancher built of stucco that by South Florida standards is a tear-down.

She has an aluminum carport that is empty, which doesn't mean she isn't home, since she no longer owns a car or has a valid driver's license. Marino also notices that the curtains are drawn in the windows to the right of the front door and there are no newspapers on the sidewalk. She has daily delivery of *The Miami Herald,* implying she can see well enough to read as long as she is wearing her glasses.

Her phone has been busy for the past half-hour. Marino cuts the engine of his motorcycle and climbs off as a white Chevy Blazer with tinted windows drives past on the street. It is a quiet street. Probably a lot of the people who live in this neighborhood are elderly and have been here a long time and can no longer afford the property taxes. It angers him to think of living in the same place for twenty or thirty years, to have your house finally paid for, only to discover you can't pay the taxes because of rich people who want places on the water. Mrs. Simister's tear-down house is assessed at almost three quarters of a million dollars, and she will have to sell it, probably soon, if she doesn't end up in an assisted-living facility first. She has only three thousand dollars in savings.

Marino learned quite a lot about Dagmara Schudrich Simister. After talking to who he now suspects was someone claiming to be her, on speakerphone in Scarpetta's office, he ran a search in HIT. Mrs. Simister goes by the name Daggie and is eighty-seven years old. She is Jewish and a member of a local synagogue that she hasn't attended in years. She has never been a member of the same church as the missing people across the waterway, so what she said on the phone isn't true, assuming it was Daggie Simister on the phone, and Marino doesn't believe it was.

She was born in Lublin, Poland, and survived the Holocaust, remaining in Poland until she was almost thirty, explaining the strong accent Marino heard when he tried to call her a few minutes ago. The woman he talked to on speakerphone had no accent he could discern. She simply sounded old. Mrs. Simister's only child, a son, lives in Fort Lauderdale and has been charged with two DUIs and three moving violations over the past ten years. Ironically, he is a contractor and developer, one of the very sorts of people responsible for causing his mother's mounting property taxes.

Mrs. Simister is under the care of four physicians for arthritis, cardiac and foot problems, and her eyesight. She doesn't travel, at least not on commercial airlines. It appears she stays home most of the time and possibly is aware of what goes on around her. Often in neighborhoods like this one, many homebound people are snoops and he hopes she is one them. He hopes she has noticed whatever has gone on across the waterway in the pale orange house. He hopes she might have some idea who called Scarpetta's office claiming to be her, assuming that is what happened.

He rings the bell, his wallet ready to display his badge, which isn't exactly honest because he is retired from policing, was never a cop in Florida and was supposed to turn in his credentials and pistol when he left the last police department he worked for, a modest-sized one in Richmond, Virginia, where he always felt the outsider, unappreciated and underestimated. He rings the bell again and tries again to reach Mrs. Simister by phone.

It's still busy.

"Police! Anybody home?" he calls out loudly as he knocks on the door.

28

Scarpetta is hot in her dark suit but doesn't consider doing anything about it. If she takes off her jacket, she will have to drape or hang it somewhere, and she doesn't make herself at home at crime scenes, not even ones the police don't believe are crime scenes.

Now that she is inside the house, she is about to decide that one of the sisters suffers from an obsessive-compulsive disorder. The windows, tile floors and furniture are spotless and immaculately arranged. A rug is perfectly centered, and the fringe border is so neat it looks combed. She checks a thermostat on the wall and jots in her notebook that the air-conditioning is on, the temperature in the living room seventy-two degrees.

"Has the thermostat been adjusted?" she asks. "Was it like this?"

"Everything's been left the way it was," Reba says, in the kitchen with Academy crime-scene investigator Lex. "Except the stove. It was turned off. The lady who came over here when Ev and Kristin didn't show up at the church. She turned it off."

Scarpetta makes a note that there is no alarm system.

Reba opens the refrigerator. "I'd go ahead and dust the cabinet doors," she tells Lex. "May as well dust the heck out of everything while you're at it. There's not much food in here for two growing boys." She directs this to Scarpetta. "Not much to eat at all. I think they're vegetarians."

She shuts the refrigerator door.

"The powder will ruin the wood," Lex says.

"That's up to you."

"Do we know what time they got home from church last Thursday night? Allegedly got home?" Scarpetta asks.

"It ended at seven, and Ev and Kristin stayed over for a while, talking to people. Then they went back to Ev's office and had a meeting. It's just a small office. It's a very small church. The room where they have the services can't hold more than fifty people, looked like to me."

Reba leaves the kitchen and walks into the living room.

"A meeting with whom, and where were the boys?" Scarpetta asks as she lifts up a cushion from the floral-printed couch.

"Some of the women met. I don't know what you call them. They're the women who run things in the church, and as I understand it, the boys weren't in the meeting, were doing whatever, horsing around. Then they left with Ev and Kristin at around eight p.m."

"Are there always meetings after church on Thursday nights?"

"I believe so. Their regular services are Friday night, so they meet the night before. Something about Good Friday being when God died for our sins. They don't talk about Jesus, just God, and are sure into sin and going to hell. It's an oddball church. Like a cult, you ask me. Probably into snake-handling and the likes."

Lex taps a small amount of Silk Black oxide powder onto a sheet of paper. The white countertop is chipped but clean and completely bare, and she dabs a fiberglass brush into the powder on the paper and begins to gently swirl the brush over the Corian, turning it an uneven, sooty black wherever the powder adheres to oils or other latent residues.

"I didn't find a wallet, a pocketbook, anything like that," Reba tells Scarpetta. "Which just adds to my suspicion they ran off."

"You can be abducted and bring your pocketbook," Scarpetta says. "People are abducted with their wallets, their keys, their cars, their children. A few years ago, I worked an abduction-homicide in which the victim was allowed to pack a suitcase."

"I know about cases, too, ones where the whole thing is faked to look like a crime, when all that really happened is the people ran off. Maybe that weird phone call you told me about was some crank caller from the church."

Scarpetta walks into the kitchen to look at the stove. On a back burner is a copper pan covered with a lid, and the metal is dark gray and streaked.

"This is the burner that was on?" she asks, removing the lid.

The stainless-steel lining inside the pan is discolored dark gray.

Lex tears off a segment of lifting tape with a loud snap.

"When the church lady got here, that left back burner was on simmer, and the pot was hot as hell with nothing in it," Reba says. "So I was told."

Scarpetta notices a sprinkling of fine, whitish-gray ash inside the pan.

"There might have been something in it. Perhaps cooking oil. Not food. No food was out on the counter?" she asks.

"What you see is the way things looked when I got here. And the lady from the church said she didn't find any food out."

"A little ridge detail, but mostly smudges," Lex says, peeling the tape off several inches of countertop. "I'm not going to bother with the cabinets. The wood's not a great surface. No point in ruining it for no reason."

Scarpetta pulls open the refrigerator door and cold air touches her face as she takes in one shelf at a time. What is left of a turkey breast suggests someone at least isn't a vegetarian. There is lettuce, fresh broccoli, spinach, celery and carrots, plenty of carrots, nineteen bags of the small, peeled kind that are an easy, low-calorie snack.

The sliding glass door to Mrs. Simister's sunporch is unlocked, and Marino waits outside it, standing in the grass, looking around.

He stares across the waterway at the pale orange house and wonders if Scarpetta is finding anything. Maybe she's cleared the scene. He's late. Getting his motorcycle onto a trailer, then to the hangar, then changing the tire took a while. Then it took a little longer for him to talk to other maintenance people and a few students in the area and the faculty members whose cars were in the same lot, hoping somebody saw something. Nobody did. Or at least that's what they said.

He opens Mrs. Simister's slider a little and calls out to her.

No one answers, and he knocks loudly on the glass.

"Anybody home?" he yells. "Hello?"

He tries her phone again, and it's still busy. He sees that Scarpetta tried to call him a little while ago, probably when he was on his motorcycle, heading this way. He calls her back.

"What's going on over there?" he asks right off.

"Reba says she's never heard of Mrs. Simister."

"Someone's fucking with us," he replies. "She's not a member of the church, either. The missing people's church. And she's not answering her door. I'm going inside."

He looks back across the waterway at the pale orange house. He opens the slider and steps inside the sunporch.

"Mrs. Simister?" he calls out loudly. "Anybody home? Police!"

A second set of sliders is also unlocked, and he steps inside the dining room, pauses, then calls out again. In a back area of the house a television is on, the volume turned up high, and he heads toward the sound as he continues to announce himself loudly, and now he has his gun out. He follows a hallway and can make out a talk show and a lot of laughter.

"Mrs. Simister? Anybody here?"

The television is inside a back room, probably a bedroom, and the door is shut. He hesitates, calls out again. He knocks, then bangs on the door, then goes inside and sees blood, a small body on the bed and what is left of the head.

29

Inside a desk drawer are pencils, ballpoint pens and Magic Markers. Two of the pencils and one pen are chewed, and Scarpetta looks at the indentations made by teeth in wood and plastic, wondering which of the boys nervously chews things.

She places the pencils, pens and markers in separate evidence bags. Shutting the drawer, she looks around, thinking about the lives of these orphaned South African boys. There are no toys in the room, no posters on the walls, no hint that the brothers like girls, cars, movies, music or sports, or have heroes or simply have fun.

Their bathroom is one door down, and it is an old bathroom with unattractive green tile and a white toilet and tub. Her face appears in the mirrored medicine cabinet as she opens the door. She scans narrow metal shelves lined with dental floss, aspirin and small bars of wrapped soap, the type found in motel bathrooms. She picks up an orange plastic prescription bottle by its white cap, looks at the label and is surprised by the name Marilyn Self, M.D.

The celebrity psychiatrist Dr. Self prescribed Ritalin hydrochloride to David Luck. He is supposed to take ten milligrams three times daily, and one hundred tablets were refilled last month, exactly three weeks ago to the day. Scarpetta removes the cap and pours the scored green tablets into her hand. She counts forty-nine of them. Three weeks at the prescribed dosage and there should be thirty-seven left, she calculates. He supposedly disappeared Thursday night. That's five days ago, fifteen tablets ago. Fifteen plus thirty-seven is fifty-two. Close enough. If David's disappearance was voluntary, why was his Ritalin left behind? Why was the stove left on?

She returns the tablets to their bottle and seals it inside an evidence bag. She walks down the hallway and at the end is the only other bedroom, one the sisters obviously shared. There are two beds, both covered with emerald-green spreads. The wallpaper and carpet are green. The furniture is lacquered green. The lamps and ceiling fan are green, and green draperies are drawn, blocking the daylight completely. The bedside lamp is on, and its low light and the light from the hall are the only light in the room.

There is no mirror, no artwork and only two photographs, framed and on the dresser, one of the sun setting over the ocean and two boys on the beach, in swim trunks and smiling, both of them towheads. They look like brothers, one older than the other. The other photograph is of two women with walking sticks, squinting in the sun, surrounded by a huge, blue sky. Behind them is an odd-shaped mountain that hulks over the horizon, the top of it obscured by an unusual layer of clouds that rise from the rocks like thick, white steam. One woman is short and full-figured with long, graying hair pulled back, while the other is taller and thinner with very long, wavy black hair she is pushing out of her face because of the wind.

Scarpetta gets a lens out of her shoulder bag and studies the photographs more closely, looking carefully at the boys' exposed skin, their faces. She studies the women's faces and their exposed skin, looking for scars, tattoos, physical anomalies, jewelry. She moves the lens over the thinner woman with the long black hair, noting that her complexion is unhealthy. Maybe it is the lighting or an artificial tanning product that has given her skin a slight yellowish tint, but she looks almost jaundiced.

She opens the closet. Inside it are inexpensive casual clothes and shoes, and dressier suits in sizes eight and twelve. Scarpetta pulls out everything white or off-white and checks the fabric for yellowish sweat stains, finding them under the arms of several blouses that are size eight. She returns her attention to the photograph of the woman with long dark hair and jaundiced-looking skin and thinks of the raw vegetables inside the refrigerator, the carrots, and she thinks of Dr. Marilyn Self.

There are no books inside the bedroom except a brown leather Bible on a bedside table. It is old and open to the Apocrypha, and light from the lamp falls on fragile pages that are dry and browned by the passing of many years. She puts on her reading glasses and leans closer, writing in her notebook that the Bible is open to the Wisdom of Solomon, and verse twenty-five of chapter twelve is marked with three small X's in pencil.

Therefore unto them, as to children without the use of reason, thou dids't send a judgment to mock them.

She tries Marino's cell phone and it goes directly to voicemail. She opens the draperies to see if the sliders behind them are locked as she tries Marino again and leaves another urgent message. It has begun to rain, and raindrops pockmark the pool and the waterway, and thunderclouds are piled up like anvils. Palms flutter in fits, and low hedges of hibiscus on either side of the sliders are thick with pink and red blossoms that shake in the wind. She notices two smudges on the glass. They have a distinctive shape that she recognizes, and she finds Reba and Lex in the laundry room, checking to see what's inside the washer and dryer.

"There's a Bible in the master bedroom," Scarpetta says. "It's open to the Apocrypha and a lamp is on, a lamp by the bed."

Reba seems confused.

"My question is, was the bedroom exactly like that when the lady from the church came into the house? Was the bedroom exactly like that the first time you saw it?"

"When I went into the bedroom, it looked undisturbed. I remember the curtains were shut. I didn't see a Bible or anything like that, and I don't remember a lamp on," Reba says.

"There's a photograph of two women. Ev and Kristin?"

"The lady from the church said so."

"The other one Tony and David?"

"I think so."

"Does one of the women have some sort of eating disorder? Is she sick? Do we know if one or both of them is under the care of a physician? And do we know which woman is which in the photograph?"

Reba is at a loss for answers. Before now, answers didn't seem very important. No one thought there might be questions like the ones Scarpetta is asking now.

"Did you or anyone open the sliding glass doors in their bedroom, the green one?"

"No."

"They aren't locked, and I noticed smudges on the outside of the glass. Earprints. I'm wondering if they were there when you looked around the property last Friday."

"Earprints?"

"Two of them made by someone's right ear," Scarpetta says as her phone rings.

30

It is raining hard when she pulls up to Mrs. Simister's house, and there are three police cruisers and an ambulance parked in front.

Scarpetta gets out of her car and doesn't bother with an umbrella as she concludes a conversation with the Broward County Medical Examiner's Office, which has jurisdiction over all sudden, unexpected and violent deaths that occur between Palm Beach and Miami. She will examine the body on site because she is already here, she is saying, and as soon as possible she needs a removal service to transport the body to the morgue. She recommends the autopsy be done right away.

"You don't think it can wait until morning? I understand it might be a suicide, that she has a history of depression," the administrator points out cautiously because he doesn't want to sound as if he is questioning Scarpetta's judgment.

He doesn't want to come right out and say that he isn't sure the case is urgent. He is careful how he words it, but she knows what he is thinking.

"Marino says there's no weapon at the scene," she explains, hurrying up the steps to the front porch, getting soaked.

"Okay. Didn't know that."

"I'm not aware anyone is assuming it's a suicide."

She thinks of the so-called backfire she and Reba heard earlier. She tries to remember when.

"You coming in, then?"

"Of course," she says. "Tell Dr. Amos to come in and get everything ready."

Marino is waiting for her as she reaches the door and goes inside, pushing her wet hair out of her eyes.

"Where's Wagner?" he asks. "I assume she's coming.

Unfortunately. Shit, we don't need a moron like her handling this."

"She left a few minutes after I did. I don't know where she is."

"Probably lost. Got the worse sense of direction I've ever seen."

Scarpetta tells him about the Bible inside Ev and Kristin's bedroom, about the verse that was marked with X's.

"The same thing the caller said to me," Marino exclaims. "Jesus Christ. What the hell's going on? Damn moron," he exclaims, and he's talking about Reba again. "I'm going to have to do an end run around her and get a real detective so this doesn't get screwed up."

Scarpetta has heard enough of his disparaging comments. "Do me a favor, help her as best you can and tuck your grudges out of sight. Tell me what you know."

She looks past him through the partially opened front door. Two emergency medical technicians are carrying cases of their equipment, finished with an effort that was a waste of time.

"Shotgun wound to the mouth, blew the top of her head off," Marino says, moving out of the way as the EMTs walk out the door, heading to the ambulance. "She's on the bed in back, fully clothed, TV on. Nothing to imply forced entry, robbery or sexual assault. We found a pair of latex gloves in the bathroom sink. One of them is bloody."

"Which bathroom?"

"The one in her bedroom."

"Any other sign the killer might have cleaned up afterwards?"

"No. Just the gloves in the sink. No bloody towels, no bloody water."

"I'll need to look. We sure who she is?"

"We know whose residence it is. Daggie Simister's. I can't say for a fact who's back there on the bed."

Scarpetta digs inside her bag for a pair of gloves and steps into the foyer. She stops to look around as she thinks of the unlocked sliders in the master bedroom in the house across the waterway. She scans the terrazzo floor, the pale blue walls, then the small living room. It is crowded with furniture, photographs and porcelain birds and other figurines from an earlier era. Nothing seems disturbed. Marino leads her through the living room, past the kitchen and to the other side of the house, where the body is inside a bedroom that faces the water.

She is clothed in a pink warm-up suit and pink slippers and is lying on her back on top of the bed. Her mouth gapes open, her dull eyes staring below a massive wound that has opened the top of her head like an egg cup. Her brain is eviscerated, chunks of it and fragments of bone on a pillow soaked with blood that is a deep red, just beginning to coagulate. Bits of brain and skin adhere to the blood-spattered and streaked headboard and wall.

Scarpetta slides her hand inside the bloody warm-up jacket and feels the chest and belly, then touches the hands. The body is warm, and rigor mortis isn't apparent yet. She unzips the jacket and tucks a chemical thermometer under the right arm. While she waits for a reading on the body temperature, she looks for any injury besides the obvious one to the head.

"How long you think she's been dead?" Marino asks.

"She's still very warm. Rigor's not even present yet."

She thinks about what she and Reba assumed was a backfire, decides it was about an hour ago. She walks over to a thermostat on the wall. The air-conditioning is on, the bedroom a chilly sixty-eight degrees. She writes it down and looks around, taking her time, scanning. The small bedroom has a terrazzo floor, and a dark-blue throw rug covers almost half of it from the foot of the blue duvet–covered bed to the window that overlooks the waterway. The blinds are shut. On a bedside table is a glass of what looks like water, a large-print edition of a Dan Brown novel and a pair of glasses. At first glance, there is no sign of a struggle.

"So maybe she got killed right before I got here," Marino is saying, and he is agitated, trying not to show it. "So it could have happened minutes before I got here on my bike. I was running late. Someone punctured my front tire."

"Deliberately?" she says, wondering about the coincidence of that happening when it did.

If he had gotten here earlier, this lady might not be dead, and she tells him about what she now assumes was a gunshot while a uniformed officer emerges from the bathroom, his hands full of prescription bottles that he sets on a dresser.

"Yeah, it was deliberate all right," Marino says.

"Obviously, she hasn't been dead long. What time did you find her?"

"I'd been here maybe fifteen minutes when I called you. I wanted to make sure the house was clear before I did anything. Make sure whoever killed her wasn't hiding in a closet or something."

"The neighbors didn't hear anything?"

He says there is nobody home in the houses on either side of this one. One of the uniformed officers already checked. He is sweating profusely, his face deep red, his eyes wide, half crazy.

"I just don't know what's going on," he says again as the rain drums the roof. "I feel like we've been set up somehow. You and Wagner were right across the water. I was late because of a flat tire."

"There was an inspector," she says. "Someone inspecting citrus trees over here." She tells him about the fruit picker he disassembled and tucked inside a big black bag. "I'd check into that right away."

She withdraws the thermometer from under the dead woman's arm and writes down ninety-seven-point-two degrees. She walks into the tiled bathroom and looks inside the shower. She looks in the toilet and the waste paper basket. The sink is dry, with no blood, not the slightest residue, which makes no sense. She looks at Marino.

"The gloves were in this sink?" she asks.

"That's right."

"If he—or she, I suppose—took them off after killing her and dropped them into the sink, they should have left a bloody residue. The bloody one should have."

"Unless the blood was already dry on the glove."

"It shouldn't have been," Scarpetta says, opening the

medicine cabinet and finding the usual alchemies for aches and pains and troublesome bowels. "Not unless the killer had them on long enough for the blood to dry."

"Wouldn't take all that long."

"It might not. You got them handy?"

They walk out of the bathroom, and Marino retrieves a large brown-paper evidence envelope from a crime-scene case. He opens the envelope so she can look inside without touching the gloves. One is clean, the other partially inside out and stained with dark-brown dried blood. The gloves aren't talc-lined, and the clean glove looks as if it has never been worn.

"We'll want to do DNA on the inside, too. And prints," she says.

"He must not know you can leave prints on the inside of latex gloves," Marino says.

"Then he must not watch TV," an officer says.

"Don't talk to me about the crap on TV. It's ruining my life," another officer comments from halfway under the bed. Then, "Well, well."

He gets up holding a flashlight and a small, stainless-steel revolver with rosewood grips. He opens the cylinder, touching as little of the metal as possible.

"Unloaded. So that did her a lot of good. Doesn't look like it's been fired since it was cleaned last, if it was ever fired at all," he says.

"We'll check it for prints anyway," Marino tells him. "A weird place to hide a gun. How far under the bed?"

"Too far to reach without getting down on the floor and crawling under it like I just did. Twenty-two caliber. What the hell's a Black Widow?"

"You're kidding," Marino says, taking a look. "North American Arms, single-action. Sort of a stupid gun for a little old lady with gnarly, arthritic hands."

"Someone must have given it to her for home protection and she never bothered."

"See a box of ammo anywhere?"

"Not so far."

The officer drops the gun into an evidence bag, which he

places on a dresser where another officer begins taking an inventory of prescription bottles.

"Accuretic, Diurese and Enduron," he reads labels. "Got no idea."

"An ace inhibitor and diuretics. For hypertension," Scarpetta says.

"Verapamil, an old one. Dates back to July."

"Hypertension, angina, arrhythmia."

"Apresoline and Loniten. Try to pronounce this stuff. Over a year old."

"Vasodilators. Again, for hypertension."

"So maybe she died of a stroke. Vicodin. I know what that is. And Ultram. These are more recent prescriptions."

"Pain medications. Possibly for arthritis."

"And Zithromax. That's an antibiotic, right? Date on it's December."

"Nothing else?" Scarpetta asks.

"No, ma'am."

"Who told the Medical Examiner's Office she has a history of depression?" she asks, looking at Marino.

No one answers at first.

Then Marino says, "I sure as hell didn't."

"Who called the Medical Examiner's Office?" she asks.

The two officers and Marino look at each other.

"Shit," Marino says.

"Hold on," Scarpetta says, and she calls the Medical Examiner's Office and gets the administrator on the phone. "Who notified you about the shotgun death?"

"Hollywood police."

"But which officer?"

"Detective Wagner."

"Detective Wagner?" Scarpetta puzzles. "What time's on the call sheet?"

"Uh, let me see. Two eleven."

Scarpetta looks at Marino again and asks him, "Do you know exactly what time you called me?"

He checks his cell phone and replies, "Two twenty-one."

She glances at her watch. It is almost three thirty. She won't be on her six-thirty flight.

"Is everything all right?" the administrator asks her over the phone.

"Anything come up on caller ID when you got that call, the one supposedly from Detective Wagner?"

"Supposedly?"

"And it was a woman who called."

"Yes."

"Anything unusual about the way she sounded?"

"Not at all," he says, pausing. "She sounded credible."

"What about an accent?"

"What's going on, Kay?"

"Nothing good," she says.

"Let me scroll through. Okay, two eleven. Came in as unavailable."

"Of course it did," Scarpetta says. "See you in about an hour."

She leans closer to the bed and looks carefully at the hands, turning them gently. She is always gentle, doesn't matter that her patients can't feel anything anymore. She notices no abrasions, cuts or bruises that might suggest binding or defense injuries. She checks again with a lens and finds fibers and dirt adhering to the palms of both hands.

"She might have been on the floor at some point," she says as Reba walks into the room, pale and wet from the rain and obviously shaken.

"The streets are like a maze back here," Reba says.

"Hey," Marino says to her, "what time did you call the ME?"

"About what?"

"About the price of eggs in China."

"What?" she says, staring at the gore on the bed.

"About this case," Marino says gruffly. "What the hell do you think I meant? And why don't you get a damn GPS."

"I didn't call the ME. Why would I when she was standing right next to me?" she replies, looking at Scarpetta.

"Let's bag her hands and her feet," Scarpetta says. "And I want her wrapped in the quilt and a clean plastic sheet. The bed linens need to come in, too."

She goes to a window that overlooks the backyard and the

waterway. She looks at citrus trees pommeled by rain and thinks about the inspector she saw earlier. He was in this yard, she's pretty sure, and she tries to pinpoint the exact time she saw him. She knows it wasn't long before she heard what she now suspects was a gunshot. She looks around the bedroom again and notices two dark stains on the rug near the window that overlooks the citrus trees, the water.

The stains are very hard to see against the dark blue background, and she gets a presumptive blood kit out of her bag, gets chemicals and medicine droppers out of it. There are two stains several inches apart. Each is about the size of a quarter and oval-shaped, and she swabs one of them, then drips isopropyl alcohol, then phenolphthalein, then hydrogen peroxide on the swab and it turns bright pink. That doesn't mean the stains are human blood, but there's a very good chance they are.

"If it's her blood, what's it doing way over here?" Scarpetta talks to herself.

"Maybe back spatter," Reba volunteers.

"Not possible."

"Drips and not exactly round," Marino says. "Looks like whoever was bleeding was upright, almost."

He looks around for any other stains.

"Kind of unusual they're here and nowhere else. If someone was bleeding a lot, you'd expect more drips," he then says, as if Reba isn't in the room.

"It's hard to see them on a dark textured surface like this," Scarpetta replies. "But I don't see any others."

"Maybe we should come back with luminol." Marino talks around Reba and anger begins to flicker on her face.

"We need a sample of these carpet fibers when the techs get here," Scarpetta says to everyone.

"Vacuum the rug, check for trace," Marino adds, avoiding Reba's stare.

"I'll need to get a statement from you before you leave, seeing as how you're the one who found her," Reba says to him. "I'm not sure what you were doing just walking in her house."

He doesn't answer her. She doesn't exist.

"So how about you and me step outside for a few minutes so I can hear what you've got to say," she says to him. "Mark?" she says to one of the officers. "How about checking Investigator Marino for gunshot residue?"

"Fuck off," Marino says.

Scarpetta recognizes the low rumble in his voice. It is usually the prelude to a major eruption.

"It's just pro forma," Reba replies. "I know you wouldn't want anybody accusing you of something."

"Uh, Reba," the officer named Mark says. "We don't carry GSR stubs. The crime-scene techs got to do that."

"Where the hell are they, anyway?" Reba asks irritably, embarrassed, still so new on the job.

"Marino," Scarpetta says. "How about checking on the removal service. See where they are."

"I'm just curious," Marino says, getting so close to Reba she is forced to back up a step. "How many scenes you been the only detective at a scene where there's a dead body?"

"I'm going to need you to clear out," she replies. "You and Dr. Scarpetta both. So we can start processing."

"The answer's none." He keeps talking. "Not a single goddamn one." He gets louder. "Well, if you go back and take a look at your *Detective for Dummies* notes, you might find out that the body is the medical examiner's jurisdiction, meaning right now the Doc here's in charge, not you. And since I just so happen to be a certified death investigator in addition to all my other fancy titles and assist the Doc as needed, you can't order my ass around, either."

The uniformed officers are struggling not to laugh.

"All of which adds up to one very important fact," Marino goes on. "Me and the Doc are in charge at the moment and you don't know chicken shit and are in the goddamn way."

"You can't talk to me like that!" Reba exclaims, near tears.

"Could one of you please get a real detective here?" Marino asks the uniformed cops. "Because I'm not leaving until you do."

31

Benton sits in his office on the ground floor of the Cognitive Neuroimaging Laboratory, one of few contemporary buildings on a two-hundred-and-thirty-seven-acre campus graced with century-old brick and slate, and fruit trees and ponds. Unlike most offices at McLean, his has no view, just a handicapped-parking space directly beyond his window, then a road, then a field that is popular with Canada geese.

His office is small and cluttered with papers and books, and is located in the middle of the H-shaped lab. At each corner is an MR scanner, and collectively, their electromagnetic fields are powerful enough to pull a train off its tracks. He is the only forensic psychologist whose office is located in the lab. He has to be easily accessible to the neuroscientists because of PREDATOR.

He buzzes his study coordinator.

"Has our newest normal called back yet?" Benton stares out the window at two geese wandering along the road. "Kenny Jumper?"

"Hold on, that might be him now." Then, "Dr. Wesley? He's on the line."

"Hello," Benton says. "Good afternoon, Kenny. It's Dr. Wesley. How are you today?"

"Not too bad."

"You sound as if you have a bit of a cold."

"Maybe allergies. I petted a cat."

"I'm going to ask you some more questions, Kenny," Benton says, looking at a secondary phone screening form.

"You already asked me all those questions."

"These are different ones. Routine questions, the same ones we ask everybody who participates in our study."

"Okay."

"First of all, where are you calling from?" Benton asks.

"A pay phone. You can't call me back on it. I have to call you."

"You don't have a phone where you're staying?"

"Like I told you, I'm at a friend's house here in Waltham, and he don't have a phone."

"All right. Let me just confirm a few things you told me yesterday, Kenny. You're single."

"Yeah."

"Twenty-four years old."

"Yeah."

"White."

"Yeah."

"Kenny, are you right- or left-handed?"

"Right-handed. I don't have a driver's license, if you want an ID."

"That's all right," Benton says. "It's not required."

Not only that, but to ask for proof of identification, to photograph patients or make any effort whatsoever to verify who they really are is a violation of HIPPA's Protected Health Information Restriction. Benton goes through the questions on the form, asking Kenny about dentures or braces, medical implants, metal plates or pins, and how he supports himself. He inquires about any allergies in addition to cats, any breathing problems, any illnesses or medications, and whether he has ever suffered a head injury or had thoughts of harming himself or others or is currently in therapy or on probation. Typically, the answers are no. More than a third of the people who volunteer as normal control subjects have to be removed from the study because they're anything but normal. However, so far, Kenny seems promising.

"What is your drinking pattern over the last month?" Benton continues down the list, hating every minute of it.

Telephone screening is tedious and pedestrian. But if he doesn't do it himself, he'll end up on the phone anyway, because he doesn't trust information gathered by research assistants and other untrained personnel. It's not helpful to bring in a potential study subject off the street and find out after countless hours of valuable staff time spent in screening, diagnostic interviews, rating scales, neurocognitive testing, brain imaging and lab work that he is unsuitable or unstable or potentially dangerous.

"Well, maybe a beer or two now and then," Kenny is saying. "You know, I don't drink much. I don't smoke. When can I start? The ad says I get paid eight hundred dollars and you pay for the taxi. I don't got a car. So I don't got transportation, and I could use the money."

"Why don't you come in this Friday? At two o'clock in the afternoon. Would that work for you?"

"For the magnet thing?"

"That's right. Your scan."

"No. Thursday at five. I can do Thursday at five."

"All right, then. Okay. Thursday at five." Benton writes it down.

"And you can send a taxi."

Benton says he will send a taxi and asks for an address and is puzzled by Kenny's answer. He tells Benton to send a cab to the Alpha & Omega Funeral Home in Everett, a funeral home he has never heard of in a not-so-nice area just outside of Boston.

"Why a funeral home?" Benton inquires, tapping the pencil on the form.

"It's close to where I'm staying. It has a pay phone."

"Kenny, I'd like you to call me back tomorrow so we can confirm you're coming in the next day, Thursday at five. Okay?"

"Okay. I'll call you on this same pay phone."

Wesley hangs up and checks directory assistance to see if there is such a place as the Alpha & Omega Funeral Home in Everett. There is. He calls it and is put on hold and subjected to Hoobastank's *The Reason.*

The reason for what? he thinks impatiently. *Dying?*

"Benton?"

He looks up and sees Dr. Susan Lane in his doorway, holding a report.

"Hi," he says, hanging up.

"Have some news about your friend Basil Jenrette," she says, looking closely at him. "You look stressed."

"When don't I? The analysis already done?"

"Maybe you should go home, Benton. You look exhausted."

"Preoccupied. Staying up too late. Tell me how our boy Basil's brain works. I'm on pins and needles," Benton says.

She hands him his copy of the structural and functional imaging analysis and begins to explain, "Increased amygdalar activity in response to affective stimuli. Especially faces, overt or masked that were fearful or had any negative content."

"Continues to be an interesting point," Benton says. "May eventually tell us something about how they select their victims. An expression on someone's face that we might interpret as surprise or curiosity, they might interpret as anger or fear. And it sets them off."

"Rather unnerving to think about."

"I need to pursue that more vigorously when I talk to them. Starting with him."

He opens a drawer and takes out a bottle of aspirin.

"Let's see. During the Stroop interference task," she says, looking at the report, "he has decreased activity of the anterior cingulate in both dorsal and subgenual regions, accompanied by increased dorsolateral prefrontal activity."

"Give me the upshot, Susan. I've got a headache."

He shakes three aspirin into his palm and swallows them without water.

"How in the world do you do that?"

"Practice."

"So." She resumes the analysis of Basil's brain. "Overall, the findings certainly reflect anomalous connectivity of frontal-limbic structures, suggesting anomalous response inhibition that may be due to deficits in a number of frontally mediated processes."

"Implicating his ability to monitor and inhibit behavior," Benton says. "We're seeing a lot of that with our lovely guests from Butler. Consistent with bipolar disorder?"

"Certainly can be. That and other psychiatric disorders."

"Excuse me a minute," Benton says as he picks up his phone and dials his study coordinator's extension.

"Can you check your in-log and tell me the number Kenny Jumper called from?" he asks.

"No ID."

"Hmmm," he says. "I'm not aware that pay phones show up as No ID."

"Actually I just got off the line with Butler," she says. "Apparently, Basil isn't doing well. He wonders if you could come see him."

It is half past five p.m. and the parking lot of the Broward County Medical Examiner's Laboratory & Office is almost empty. Employees, particularly nonmedical ones, rarely linger at the morgue after hours.

This one is on Southwest 31st Avenue, in the midst of relatively undeveloped land thick with palms, live oak trees and pines, and scattered with mobile homes. Typical of South Florida architecture, the one-story building is stucco and coral stone. It backs up to a narrow brackish canal where mosquitoes are a menace and alligators sometimes wander where they don't belong. Next door to the morgue is the county Fire and Rescue service where emergency medical technicians are constantly reminded of where their less-fortunate patients end up.

The rain has almost stopped, and there are puddles everywhere as Scarpetta and Joe walk out to a silver H2 Hummer, not her choice but quite adept at handling off-road death scenes and hauling bulky equipment. Lucy is fond of Hummers. Scarpetta always worries where to park them.

"I just can't understand how someone managed to walk in with a shotgun in the middle of the day," Joe says, and he has been saying it for the past hour. "Must be a way to tell if it was sawed off."

"If the barrel wasn't smoothed after it was sawn, there could be tool marks on the wad," Scarpetta replies.

"But the absence of tool marks doesn't mean it wasn't sawn."

"Correct."

"Because he might have smoothed off the sawed-off barrel. If he did that, there's no way for us to tell without recovering the weapon. A twelve-gauge. We know that much."

They know that much from the Remington plastic four-petaled Power Piston wad that Scarpetta recovered from the inside of Daggie Simister's devastated head. Beyond that fact, there are only a few more Scarpetta can state with certainty, such as the nature of the attack on Mrs. Simister, which the autopsy revealed to be different from what everyone presumed. Had she not been shot, there is a good chance she would have died anyway. Scarpetta is fairly certain Mrs. Simister was unconscious when her killer stuck the shotgun barrel into her mouth and pulled the trigger. It wasn't an easy conclusion to determine.

Examinations of massive gaping injuries to the head can mask wounds that may have occurred before the final mutilating trauma. Sometimes forensic pathology requires plastic surgery, and in the morgue, Scarpetta did what she could to repair Mrs. Simister's head, fitting pieces of bone and scalp back together, then shaving off the hair. What she found was a laceration on the back of the head and a skull fracture. The point of impact correlated with a subdural hematoma in an underlying part of her brain that had been left relatively intact after the shotgun blast.

If the stains on the carpet by the window in Mrs. Simister's bedroom turn out to be her blood, then it's likely this was where she was first attacked and would also explain the dirt and bluish fibers on the palms of her hands. She was struck hard from behind with a blunt object and went down. Then her assailant picked her up, all eighty-six pounds of her, and placed her on the bed.

"I mean, you could easily carry a sawed-off shotgun in a knapsack," Joe is saying.

Scarpetta points the remote at the Hummer and unlocks the doors and replies wearily, "Not necessarily."

Joe makes her tired. He annoys her more each day.

"Even if you sawed twelve or even eighteen inches off the barrel and six inches off the stock," she remarks, "you're still left with an eighteen-inch-long gun, at least. Assuming we're talking about an autoloader."

She thinks of the big black bag the citrus inspector was carrying.

"If we're talking about a pump, you're likely to have a longer gun than that," she adds. "Neither scenario works with a knapsack, unless it's a big one."

"A tote bag, then."

She thinks of the citrus inspector, of the long picker that he disassembled and packed inside his black bag. She's seen citrus inspectors before and never noticed them using pickers. Usually, they look at what they can reach.

"I bet he had a tote bag," Joe says.

"I've got no idea." She's about to snap at him.

Throughout the entire autopsy, he prattled and divined and pontificated until she could scarcely think. He found it necessary to announce everything he was doing, everything he was writing on the protocol attached to his clipboard. He felt it necessary to tell her the weight of every organ and deduce when Mrs. Simister ate last based on the partially digested meat and vegetables in her stomach. He made sure Scarpetta heard the crunching sound of calcium deposits when he opened partially occluded coronaries with the scalpel and announced that maybe atherosclerosis killed her.

Ha, ha.

And, well, Mrs. Simister didn't have much to look forward to, anyway. She had a bad heart. Her lungs had adhesions, probably from old pneumonia, and her brain was somewhat atrophied, so she probably had Alzheimer's.

If you have to be murdered, Joe said, *you may as well be in bad health.*

"I'm thinking he hit her in the back of the head with the butt of the gun," now he is saying. "You know, like this."

He rams an imaginary head with the imaginary stock of a shotgun.

"She wasn't even five feet tall," he continues his scenario. "So for him to slam her head with the butt of a gun that weighs maybe six or seven pounds, assuming it wasn't sawed off, he would need to be reasonably strong and taller than her."

"We can't say that at all," Scarpetta replies, driving out of the parking lot. "So much depends on his position in relation to her. So much depends on a lot of things. And we don't know that she was struck with the gun. We don't know that the killer was a he. Be careful, Joe."

"Of what?"

"In your great enthusiasm to reconstruct exactly how and why she died, you run the risk of confusing the theoretical with the truth and turning fact into fiction. This isn't a hell scene. This is a real human being who is really dead."

"Nothing wrong with creativity," he says, staring straight ahead, his thin mouth and long, pointed chin set the way they always are when he gets petulant.

"Creativity is good," she replies. "It should suggest where to look and for what, but not necessarily choreograph the sort of reenactments you see in movies and on TV."

32

The small guesthouse is tucked behind a Spanish-tile swimming pool amid fruit trees and flowering shrubs. It is not a normal place to see patients, probably not the best place to see them, but the setting is poetic and full of symbols. When it rains, Dr. Marilyn Self feels as creative as the warm, wet earth.

She tends to interpret the weather as a manifestation of what happens when patients walk through her door. Repressed emotions, some of them torrential, are released in the safety of her therapeutic environment. Weather volatilities happen all around her and are unique to her and intended for her. They are full of meaning and instruction.

Welcome to my storm. Now let's talk about yours.

It's a good line, and she uses it often in her practice and on her radio show and now her new television show. Human emotions are internal weather systems, she explains to her patients, to her multitude of listeners. Every storm front is caused by something. Nothing comes from nothing. Talking about the weather is neither idle nor mundane.

"I see the look on your face," she says from her leather chair in her cozy living-room setting. "You got the look again when the rain stopped."

"I keep telling you I don't have a look."

"It's interesting that you get the look when the rain stops. Not when it starts or is even at its worst, but when it suddenly stops as it did just now," she says.

"I don't have a look."

"Just now the rain stopped and you got that look on your face," Dr. Self says again. "It's the same look you get when our time is up."

"No it isn't."

"I promise it is."

"I don't pay three hundred dollars a damn hour to talk about storms. I don't have a look."

"Pete, I'm telling you what I see."

"I don't have a look," Pete Marino replies from the reclining chair across from hers. "That's crap. Why would I care about a storm? I've seen storms all my life. I didn't grow up in a desert."

She studies his face. He is rather handsome in a very rough, masculine way. She probes the dusky gray eyes behind the wire-rimmed glasses. His balding head reminds her of a newborn's bottom, pale and naked in the soft lamplight. His fleshy, rounded pate is a tender buttock waiting to be spanked.

"I think we're having a trust issue," she says.

He glowers at her from his chair.

"Why don't you tell me why you care about rainstorms, about them ending, Pete. Because I believe you do. And you have the look even as we speak. I promise. You still have it," she says to him.

He touches his face as if it is a mask, as if it is something that doesn't belong to him.

"My face is normal. There's nothing about it. Nothing."

He taps his massive jaw. He taps his big forehead.

"If I had a look, I could tell. I don't have a look."

For the past few minutes they have driven in silence, heading back to the Hollywood Police Department parking lot, where Joe can retrieve his red Corvette and get out of her way for the rest of the day.

Then he suddenly says, "Did I tell you I got my scuba-diving license?"

"Good for you," Scarpetta says, not pretending to care.

"I'm buying a condo in the Cayman Islands. Well, not exactly. My girlfriend and I are buying it. She makes more money than me," he says. "How about that. I'm a doctor and she's a paralegal, not even a real lawyer, and she earns more than me."

"I never assumed you chose forensic pathology for the money."

"I didn't go into it intending to be poor."

"Then maybe you should consider doing something else, Joe."

"Doesn't look to me like you're wanting for much."

He turns toward her as they stop at a red light. She feels his stare.

"I guess it doesn't hurt to have a niece who's as rich as Bill Gates," he adds. "And a boyfriend from some rich New England family."

"What exactly is it that you're implying?" she says, and she thinks of Marino.

She thinks of his hell scenes.

"That it's easy to not care about money if you've got plenty. And maybe that you didn't exactly earn it yourself."

"Not that my finances are any of your business, but if you work as many years as I have and are smart, you can manage just fine."

"Depends on what you mean by 'manage.'"

She thinks of how impressive Joe was on paper. When he applied for the Academy's fellowship, she thought he just might be the most promising fellow she had ever had. She doesn't understand how she could have been so wrong.

"Nobody I'm watching in your camp is merely managing," he says, his voice turning more snide. "Even Marino makes more than I do."

"How would you know how much he makes?"

The Hollywood Police Department is just ahead on the left, a four-story precast building so close to a public golf course it's not uncommon for misguided balls to fly over the fence and pelt police cars. She spots Joe's precious red Corvette in a distant spot, tucked out of the path of anything that might so much as ding it.

"Everybody sort of knows what everybody makes," Joe is saying. "It's public knowledge."

"It's not."

"You can't keep secrets in a place so small."

"The Academy's not that small, and there should be plenty that's confidential. Such as salaries."

"I should be paid more. Marino's not a damn doctor. He barely finished high school and he makes more than I do. All Lucy does is run around playing secret agent in her Ferraris, helicopters, jets, motorcycles. I want to know what the hell she does to have all that. Big shot, superwoman, what arrogance, what an attitude. It's no wonder the students dislike her so much."

Scarpetta stops behind his Corvette and turns to him, her face as serious as he has probably ever seen it.

"Joe?" she says. "You have one month left. Let's get through it."

In Dr. Self's professional opinion, the cause of Marino's biggest difficulties in life is the look he has on his face just now.

It is the subtlety of this negative facial expression, as opposed to the facial expression itself, that makes matters worse for him, as if he needs anything to make matters worse. If only he weren't subtle about his secret fears, loathing, abandonments, sexual insecurities, bigotries and other repressed negativities. While she recognizes the tension in his mouth and eyes, other people probably don't, not consciously. But unconsciously, they pick up on it and react.

Marino frequently is the victim of verbal abuse, rude behavior, dishonesty, rejection and betrayal. He gets into his share of fights. He claims to have killed several people during his demanding and dangerous career. Clearly, whoever is unwise enough to go after him gets quite a lot more than he bargains for, but Marino doesn't look at it that way. People pick on him for no good reason, according to him. Some of the hostility is related to his job, according to him. Most of his problems stem from prejudice because he grew up poor in New Jersey. He doesn't understand why people have been shitty to him all of his life, he frequently says.

The last few weeks he has been much worse. This afternoon, he is worse yet.

"Let's talk about New Jersey for the few minutes we have left." Dr. Self deliberately reminds him that the session is about to end. "Last week, you mentioned New Jersey several times. Why do you think New Jersey still matters?"

"If you grew up in New Jersey, you'd know why," he says, and the look on his face intensifies.

"That's not an answer, Pete."

"My father was a drunk. We was on the wrong side of the tracks. People still look at me like I'm from New Jersey and that starts it."

"Maybe it's the look on your face, Pete, and not theirs," she says again. "Maybe you're the one who starts it."

The answering machine clicks from the table next to Dr. Self's leather chair and Marino gets the look on his face, very intense now. He doesn't like it when a call interrupts their session, even if she doesn't answer it. He doesn't understand why she still relies on old technology instead of voicemail that is silent, that doesn't click when someone leaves a message, that isn't annoying and intrusive. He reminds her of this often. Discreetly, she glances at her watch, a large, gold watch with Roman numerals that she can see without her reading glasses.

In twelve minutes, the session will end. Pete Marino has difficulties with endings, with codas, with anything that is over, finished, spent or dead. It isn't coincidental that Dr. Self schedules his appointments for late afternoons, preferably around five, when it is beginning to get dark or afternoon thundershowers stop. He is an intriguing case. She wouldn't see him if he wasn't. It is just a matter of time before she coaxes him to be a guest patient on her nationally broadcast radio show or maybe her new television show. He would be impressive in front of the camera, so much better than that unattractive and foolish Dr. Amos.

She hasn't had a cop yet. When she was the guest lecturer at the National Forensic Academy's summer session and sat next to Marino one night at a dinner in her honor, it entered her mind then that he would be a fascinating guest on her show, possibly a frequent guest. Certainly, he needed therapy. He drank too much. He did so right in front of her, had four bourbons. He smoked. She could smell it on his breath. He was a compulsive eater, helped himself to three desserts. When she met him, he was brimming with self-destructiveness and self-hate.

I can help you, she said to him that night.

With what? He reacted as if she had grabbed him under the table.

With your storms, Pete. Your internal storms. Tell me about your storms. I'll say the same thing to you I've been saying to all these bright young students. You can master your weather. You can make it what you want. You can have storms or sunshine. You can duck and hide or walk out in the open.

In my line of work, you got to be careful about walking out in the open, he said.

I don't want you to die, Pete. You're a big, smart, good-looking man. I want you around for a long time.

You don't even know me.

I know you better than you think.

He started seeing her. Within a month, he cut back on the booze and cigarettes and lost ten pounds.

"I don't have the look right now. I don't know what you're talking about," Marino says, feeling his face with his fingertips like a blind person.

"You have it. The instant the rain stopped, you got the look. Whatever you're feeling is on your face, Pete," she says with emphasis. "I'm wondering if the look doesn't trace all the way back to New Jersey. What do you think?"

"I think this is garbage. I came to see you originally because I couldn't quit smoking and was eating and drinking a little bit too much. I didn't come see you because I got some stupid look on my face. No one's ever complained about some stupid look on my face. Now my wife, Doris, she com-

"She could have called him while I wasn't there. She did it on purpose."

"It's a habit of hers, isn't it," Dr. Self says. "Introducing her lover into the mix right in front of you when she must know the way you feel about it, about your jealousy."

"Jealous? Of fucking what? He's a rich-boy has-been FBI fortune-cookie profiler."

"That's not true, now is it. He's a forensic psychologist on the faculty at Harvard, comes from a distinguished New England family. Sounds pretty impressive to me."

She hasn't met Benton. She would like to, would love to have him on her show.

"He's a has-been. People who are has-beens teach."

"I believe he does more than teach."

"He's a goddamn has-been."

"Seems like most people you know are has-beens. Including Scarpetta. You've said that about her as well."

"I call it like I see it."

"I'm wondering if you might feel like a has-been."

"Who me? You kidding? I can bench-press more than twice my body weight now and was running on the treadmill the other day. First time in twenty damn years."

"We're almost out of time," she reminds him again. "Let's talk about your anger towards Scarpetta. It's about trust, isn't it."

"It's about respect. About her treating me like shit and lying."

"You feel she doesn't trust you anymore because of what happened last summer at that place in Knoxville where they do all that research on dead bodies. What's it called? The Decay Research something or other."

"The Body Farm."

"Oh, yes."

What an intriguing topic for discussion on one of her shows: The Body Farm Isn't a Health Spa. What Is Death? *Talk It Out* with Dr. Self.

She has already composed the promo.

Marino looks at his watch, makes a big production of lift-

ing his thick wrist to see what time it is, as if it doesn't
bother him that their time is about up, as if he is looking forward to its being up.

She isn't fooled.

"Fear," Dr. Self begins her summary. "An existential fear
of not counting, of not mattering, of being left utterly alone.
When the day ends, when the storm ends. When things end.
It's scary when things end, isn't it? Money ends. Health
ends. Youthfulness ends. Love ends. Maybe your relationship with Dr. Scarpetta will end? Maybe she'll finally
reject you?"

"There's nothing to end except work and that will go on
forever because people are shits and will keep killing each
other long after I got my little angel wings. I'm not coming
here anymore and listening to this bullshit. All you do is talk
about the Doc. I think it's pretty obvious my problem
isn't her."

"We do have to stop now."

She rises from her chair and smiles at him.

"I quit taking that medicine you prescribed. A couple
weeks ago, forgot to tell you."

He gets up and his big presence seems to fill the room.

"It didn't do nothing, so why bother," he says.

When he is on his feet, she is always a bit startled by what
a big man he is. His sun-darkened hands reminded her of
baseball mitts, of baked hams. She can imagine him crush-
ing someone's skull or neck, of smashing another person's
bones like potato chips.

"We'll talk about the Effexor next week. I'm seeing
you . . ." She picks up the appointment book from her
desk. "Next Tuesday at five."

Marino stares through the open doorway, scanning the
small sunroom with its one table and two chairs and potted
plants, several of them palms that are almost as high as the
ceiling. There are no other patients waiting. There never are
this time of day.

"Huh," he says. "Good thing we hurried up and finished
on time. Hate for you to keep someone waiting."

"Would you like to pay me at our next appointment?"

It is Dr. Self's way of reminding him that he owes her three hundred dollars.

"Yeah, yeah. I forgot my checkbook," he replies.

Of course he did. He isn't about to owe her money. He will be back.

33

Benton parks his Porsche in a visitor's slot outside tall metal fencing that is curved like a breaking wave and topped with coils of razor wire. Guard towers rise starkly against the cold, overcast sky from each corner of the grounds. Parked in a side lot are unmarked white vans with steel dividers, no windows and no interior locks, mobile holding cells used to transport prisoners like Basil off-grounds.

Butler State Hospital is eight stories of precast and steel-mesh-covered windows on twenty acres amid woods and ponds less than an hour southwest of Boston. Butler is where offenders are committed by reason of insanity and is considered a model of enlightenment and civility with pods called cottages, each one housing patients requiring different levels of security and attention. D Cottage stands alone not far from the administration building, and houses approximately one hundred dangerous predatory inmates.

Segregated from the rest of the hospital population, they spend most of the day, depending on their status, in single cells, each with its own shower that can be used ten minutes per day. Toilets can be flushed twice an hour. A team of forensic psychiatrists is assigned to D Pod, and other mental health and legal professionals such as Benton are in and out regularly. Butler is supposed to be humane and constructive, a place to get well. To Benton, it is nothing more than attractive maximum-security confinement for people who can never be repaired. He has no illusions. People like Basil have no lives and never did. They ruin lives and always will, given the chance.

Inside the beige-painted lobby, Benton approaches a bulletproof window and speaks through an intercom.

"How you doing, George?"

"No better than last time you asked."

"Sorry to hear that," Benton says as a loud metallic click grants him entrance through the first set of airlocked doors. "That mean you haven't gotten around to seeing your doctor yet?"

The door shuts behind him and he places his briefcase on a small metal table. George is in his sixties and never feels well. He hates his job. He hates his wife. He hates the weather. He hates politicians and, when he can, removes the photograph of the governor from the wall in the lobby. For the past year, he has struggled with extreme fatigue, stomach problems and achiness. He also hates doctors.

"I'm not taking medicine, so what's the point? That's all doctors do anymore is throw drugs at you," George says as he searches Benton's briefcase and returns it to him. "Your pal's in the usual spot. Have fun."

Another click and Benton steps through a second steel door, and a guard in a tan-and-brown uniform, Geoff, leads him along a polished hallway, passing through another set of airlock doors into the high-security unit where lawyers and mental-health workers meet with inmates in small, windowless rooms made of cinder block.

"Basil says he's not getting his mail," Benton says.

"He says a lot of things," Geoff replies without smiling. "All he does is run his mouth."

He unlocks a gray steel door and holds it open.

"Thanks," Benton says.

"I'll be right outside." Geoff fires a look at Basil, shuts the door.

Basil sits at a small wooden table and doesn't get up. He is unrestrained and wears his usual prison garb of blue pants, white T-shirt and flip-flops with socks. His eyes are bloodshot and distracted, and he stinks.

"How are you, Basil?" Benton asks, taking a seat across from him.

"I had a bad day."

"That's what I hear. Tell me."

"I'm feeling anxious."

"How are you sleeping?"

"I was awake most of the night. I kept thinking about our talk."

"You seem fidgety," Benton says.

"I can't sit still. It's because of what I told you. I need something, Dr. Wesley. I need some Ativan or something. Have you looked at the pictures yet?"

"What pictures?"

"The ones of my brain. You must have. I know you're curious. Everybody over there is curious, right?" he says with a nervous smile.

"Is that what you wanted to see me about?"

"Pretty much. And I want my mail. They won't give it to me and I can't sleep or eat, I'm so upset and stressed. Maybe some Ativan, too. I hope you've thought about it."

"About?"

"What I told you about that lady who got killed."

"The lady in The Christmas Shop."

"Ten-four."

"Yes, I have been thinking quite a lot about what you told me, Basil," Benton says, as if he accepts that what Basil told him is true.

He can never let on when he thinks a patient is lying. In this instance, he's not sure Basil is, not at all.

"Let's go back to that day in July, two and a half years ago," Benton says.

It bothers Marino that Dr. Self shut the door behind him and wasted no time flipping the deadbolt, as if he is the one she is locking out.

He is insulted by the gesture and what it implies. He always is. She doesn't care about him. He's just an appointment. She is glad he is out of her way and she won't have to subject herself to his company for another week, and then it will be for fifty minutes and fifty minutes only, not a second more, even if he's quit his medicine.

That stuff is shit. He couldn't have sex. What good is an

easily penetrates the wooden door and flows right into the sunporch.

She talks much louder on the phone than she does in her sessions. It's a good thing. It wouldn't be good if some other patient were sitting on the sunporch and could hear every word Dr. Self says to Marino during their brief but expensive fifty minutes together. She doesn't talk this loudly when they are together behind that shut door. Of course, there is never anyone waiting on the sunporch when he has a session. He is always the last one, all the more reason she ought to cut him some slack and throw in a few extra minutes. It isn't like she would keep anyone waiting, because there isn't anyone. There never is after his appointment. One of these days, he will say something so moving and important, she will give him a few extra minutes. It might be the first time she has ever done it in her life, and she will do it with him. She will want to do it. Maybe it will be him who doesn't have the extra time on that occasion.

I've got to go, he imagines himself saying.

Please finish. I really want to hear what happened.

Can't do it. Got to be somewhere. He will get up from his chair. *Next time. I promise I'll tell you the rest of it when . . . let's see . . . Next week, whenever. Just remind me, okay?*

Marino realizes Dr. Self has gotten off the phone, and he moves across the sunporch as silently as a shadow and lets himself out the glass door. He shuts it without a sound and follows the walkway around the pool, through the garden with its fruit trees that have the red stripes around them, and along the side of the small, white, stucco house where Dr. Self lives but shouldn't live, simply has no business living. Anybody could walk right up to her front door. Anybody could walk right up to her office in back by the palm-shaded pool. It isn't safe. Millions of people listen to her every week and she lives like this. It isn't safe. He should go back and knock on her door and tell her.

His tricked-out Screamin' Eagle Deuce is parked on the street, and he walks around it once to make sure nobody has done anything to it while he was in his appointment. He thinks about his flat tire. He thinks about getting his hands on whoever did it. A light film of dust coats the flames over blue paint and the chrome, and he is more than a little irritated. He detailed the motorcycle early this morning, polished every inch of trim and then had a flat tire and now there is dust. Dr. Self should have covered parking. She should have a damn garage. Her fancy white Mercedes convertible is in the driveway and no other car will fit, so her patients park on the street. It isn't safe.

He unlocks the bike's front fork and ignition and swings his leg over the warrior seat, thinking how much he loves not living like the poor city cop he was most of his life. The Academy supplies him with an H2 Hummer, black with a turbo-diesel V8, 250-horsepower engine, four-speed overdrive transmission, a load-bearing exterior rack, winch and off-road adventure package. He bought the Deuce and tricked it out to his heart's content, and he can afford a psychiatrist. Imagine that.

He shifts the bike into neutral and presses the starter button as he stares at the attractive white house where Dr. Self lives but shouldn't live. He holds in the clutch and gives the bike some gas, the ThunderHead pipes making plenty of noise as lightning flashes in the distance and a dark army of retreating clouds wastes its artillery over the sea.

34

Basil smiles again.

"I can't find anything about a murder," Benton is saying to him, "but two and a half years ago, a woman and her daughter disappeared from a business called The Christmas Shop."

"Didn't I tell you that?" Basil says, smiling.

"You didn't say anything about people disappearing or a daughter."

"They won't give me my mail."

"I'm checking on it, Basil."

"You said you'd check on it a week ago. I want my mail. I want it today. They quit giving it to me right after I had the disagreement."

"When you got angry at Geoff and called him Uncle Remus."

"And for that I don't get my mail. I think he spits in my food. I want all of it, all the old mail that's been sitting around for a month. Then you can move me to a different cell."

"That I can't do, Basil. It's for your own good."

"I guess you don't want to know," Basil says.

"How about I promise you'll have all your mail by the end of the day."

"I better get it or that's the end of our friendly conversation about The Christmas Shop. I'm getting rather bored with your little science project."

"The only Christmas shop I could find was in Las Olas on the beach," Benton says. "July fourteenth, Florrie Quincy and her seventeen-year-old daughter, Helen, disappeared. Does that mean anything to you, Basil?"

"I'm not good with names."

"Describe for me what you remember about The Christmas Shop, Basil."

"Trees with lights, little trains and ornaments everywhere," he says, no longer smiling. "I already told you all that. I want to know what you found inside my brain. You see their pictures?" He points at his head. "You should see everything you want to know. Now you're wasting my time. I want my damn mail!"

"I promised, didn't I?"

"And there was a trunk in back, you know, a big footlocker. It was stupid as shit. I made her open it and she had these collector's ornaments made in Germany in painted wooden boxes. Stuff like Hansel and Gretel and Snoopy and Little Red Riding Hood. She kept them locked up because of how expensive they were, and I said, 'What the fuck for? All someone has to do is steal the trunk. You really think locking them up in there is going to stop someone from stealing them?' "

He falls silent, staring off at the cinder-block wall.

"What else did you talk about with her before you killed her?"

"I told her, 'You're going down, bitch.' "

"At what point did you talk to her about the trunk in the back of the store?"

"I didn't."

"I thought you said . . ."

"I never said I talked to her about it," Basil says impatiently. "I want to be put on something. Why can't you give me something. I can't sleep. I can't sit still. I feel like fucking everything and then get depressed and can't get out of bed. I want my mail."

"How many times a day are you masturbating?" Benton asks.

"Six or seven. Maybe ten."

"More than usual."

"Then you and me had our little talk last night and that's all I've done all day. Didn't get out of bed except to pee, barely ate, haven't bothered with a shower. I know where she is," he then says. "Get me my mail."

"Mrs. Quincy?"

"See, I'm in here." Basil leans back in the chair. "What do I have to lose? What incentive do I have to do the right thing? Favors, a little special treatment, maybe cooperation. I want my fucking mail."

Benton gets up and opens the door. He tells Geoff to go to the mail room, find out about Basil's mail. Benton can tell by the guard's reaction that he knows all about Basil's mail and isn't happy about doing anything that might make his life more pleasant. So it's probably true. He hasn't been getting it.

"I need you to do it," Benton tells Geoff, meeting his eyes. "It's important."

Geoff nods, walks off. Benton shuts the door again and sits back down at the table.

Fifteen minutes later, Benton and Basil are finishing their conversation, a tangled mess of misinformation and convoluted games. Benton is annoyed. He doesn't show it and is relieved to see Geoff.

"Your mail will be waiting on your bed," Geoff says from the doorway, his eyes flat and cold as they stare at Basil.

"You better not have stolen my magazines."

"Nobody's interested in your fucking fishing magazines. Excuse me, Dr. Wesley." And to Basil, "There are four of them on your bed."

Basil casts an imaginary fly rod. "The one that got away," he says. "It's always the biggest one. My father used to take me fishing when I was a little boy. When he wasn't beating my mother."

"I'm telling you," Geoff says. "I'm telling you right in front of Dr. Wesley. You mess with me again, Jenrette, and your mail and fishing magazines won't be your only problem."

"See, this is what I mean," Basil tells Benton. "This is how I'm treated around here."

35

In the storage area, Scarpetta opens a crime-scene case that she carried in from the Hummer. She removes vials of sodium perborate, sodium carbonate and luminol, mixes them with distilled water in a container, shakes it and transfers the solution into a black pump spray bottle.

"Not exactly how you thought you'd spend your week off," Lucy says as she attaches a thirty-five-millimeter camera to a tripod.

"Nothing like a little quality time," Scarpetta says. "At least we get to see each other."

Both of them are shrouded in disposable white coveralls, shoe covers, safety glasses, face masks and caps, the door to the storage room shut. It is almost eight p.m., and Beach Bums is once again locked up before closing time.

"Give me just a minute to get the context," Lucy says, screwing a cable release on the camera's power switch. "Remember the days when you had to use a sock?"

It is important that the spray bottle stay out of the photograph, and that's not possible unless the bottle and nozzle are black or covered with something black. If nothing else is available, a black sock works fine.

"Nice to have a bigger budget, isn't it," Lucy adds, the shutter opening as she presses the cable-release button. "We haven't done something together like this in a while. Anyway, money problems are no fun."

She captures an area of shelving and concrete flooring, the camera fixed in place.

"I don't know," Scarpetta says. "We always managed. In many ways, it was better, because defense attorneys didn't have an endless list of *no* questions: Did you use a Mini-Crime scope? Did you use super sticks? Did you use laser trajectory? Did you use ampules of sterile water? What? You used bottled distilled water and you bought it where? A 7-Eleven? You bought evidence-collecting items at a convenience store?"

Lucy takes another photograph.

"Did you test the DNA of the trees, birds and squirrels in the yard?" Scarpetta goes on, pulling a black rubber glove over the cotton examination glove covering her left hand. "What about vacuuming the entire neighborhood for trace evidence?"

"I think you're in a really bad mood."

"I think I'm tired of your avoiding me. The only time you call is at times like this."

"No one better."

"That's all I am to you? A member of your staff?"

"I can't believe you'd even ask that. You ready for me to cut the lights?"

"Go."

Lucy pulls a string, clicking off the overhead lightbulb, casting them into total darkness. Scarpetta starts by spraying luminol on a control sample of blood, a single dried drop on a square of cardboard, and it glows greenish-blue and fades. She begins spraying in sweeps, misting areas of the floor and they begin to glow vividly as if the entire floor is on fire, a neon greenish-blue fire.

"Good God," Lucy says, and the shutter clicks again and Scarpetta sprays. "I've never seen that."

The bright greenish-blue luminescence glows and fades to the slow, eerie rhythm of the spraying and when the spraying stops, the glow vanishes in the dark and Lucy turns on the light. She and Scarpetta look closely at the concrete floor.

"I don't see anything except dirt," Lucy says, getting frustrated.

"Let's sweep it up before we walk on it any more than we have."

"Shit!" Lucy says. "I wish we'd tried the Mini-Crime scope first."

"Not now, but we can," Scarpetta says.

With a clean paintbrush, Lucy sweeps dirt from the floor into a plastic evidence bag, then repositions the camera and tripod. She takes more context photographs, these of wooden shelving, cuts the lights and this time the luminol reacts differently. Splotchy areas light up an electric blue and dance like popping sparks, and the shutter clicks and clicks and Scarpetta sprays, and the blueness pulses rapidly, fading in and out much more quickly than is typical of blood and most other substances that react to chemiluminescence.

"Bleach," Lucy says, because a number of substances result in false positives, and bleach is a common one, and the way it looks is distinctive.

"Something with a different spectra, certainly reminiscent of bleach," Scarpetta replies. "Could be any cleanser containing a hypochlorite-based bleach. Clorox, Drano, Fantastic, The Works, Babo Cleanser, to name a few. I wouldn't be surprised to find something like that back here."

"You got it?"

"Next."

The lights go on and both of them squint in the harsh glare of the overhead bulb.

"Basil told Benton he cleaned up with bleach," Lucy says. "But luminol's not going to react to bleach after two and a half years, is it?"

"Maybe if it soaked into wood and was left alone. I say maybe because I don't know one way or the other, don't know of anyone who's ever done tests like that," Scarpetta says, reaching into her scene bag for a lighted magnifier.

She moves it over the edges of plyboard shelving stacked with snorkel equipment and T-shirts.

"If you look closely," she adds, "you can barely make out a lightening of the wood here and here. Possibly a splash pattern."

Lucy gets next to her and takes the magnifier.

"I think I see it," she says.

Today, he has been in and out and has ignored her except to bring a grilled cheese sandwich and more water. He doesn't live here. He is never here at night, or if he is, he is as quiet as the dead.

It is late, but she doesn't know how late, and the moon is trapped behind clouds on the other side of the broken window. She hears him move about the house. Her pulse quickens as his feet sound in her direction, and she tucks the small, pink tennis shoe behind her back because he will take it from her if it means anything to her, and then he is a dark shadow with a long finger of light. He has the spider with him. It covers his hand. It is the biggest spider she has ever seen.

She listens for Kristin and the boys as the light probes her raw, swollen ankles and wrists. He probes the filthy mattress and the soiled bright-green robe draped over her lower legs. She draws up her knees and arms, trying to cover herself as the light touches private parts of her body. She recoils as she feels him staring at her. She can't see his face. She has no idea what he looks like. He always wears black. During daylight, he covers his face with the hood and wears black, everything black, and at night she can't see him at all, just a shape. He took her glasses.

That was the first thing he did when he forced his way into the house.

Give me your glasses, he said. *Now.*

She stood paralyzed in the kitchen. Her terror and disbelief were numbing. She couldn't think, felt as if the blood was completely draining from her body, and then olive oil in the pan on the stove began to smoke and the boys began to cry and he pointed the shotgun at them. He pointed it at Kristin. He had on the hood, the black clothing, when Tony opened the back door and then he was inside and it happened fast.

Give me your glasses.

Give them to him, Kristin said. *Please don't hurt us. Take whatever you want.*

Shut up or I'll kill every one of you right now.

He ordered the boys to lie facedown on the living-room floor and hit them in the back of the head, hit them hard with the butt of the gun so they wouldn't try to run. He turned out all the lights and ordered Kristin and Ev to carry and drag the boys' limp bodies down the hall and out the master-bedroom slider, and blood dripped and smeared along the floor and she keeps thinking that someone should have seen the blood. By now somebody should have been to the house, trying to figure out what happened to them, and they should have seen the blood. Where are the police?

The boys didn't move on the grass by the pool, and he tied them up with phone cords and gagged them with dish towels even though they weren't moving or making a sound, and he forced Kristin and Ev to walk through the dark to the station wagon.

Ev drove.

Kristin sat in the front seat and he was in the back with the barrel of the gun pointed at her head.

His cold, quiet voice told Ev where to go.

I'm taking you somewhere, then I'll go back for them, his cold, quiet voice said as she drove.

Just call someone, Kristin begged. *They need to get to the hospital. Please don't leave them there to die. They're children.*

I said I'd go back for them.

They need help. They're just little boys. Orphans. Both their parents are dead.

Good. Nobody to miss them, then.

His voice was cold and flat and inhuman, a voice with no feeling or personality.

She remembers seeing signs for Naples. They were heading west toward the Everglades.

I can't drive without my glasses, Ev said, her heart pounding so hard she thought it might break her ribs. She couldn't catch her breath. When she ran off on the shoulder, he gave her the glasses, then took them away again when they reached the dark, hellish place where she has been since.

Scarpetta sprays the cinder-block walls inside the bathroom, and they glow in a pattern of sweeps and swipes and spatters that aren't visible when the lights are on.

"Someone cleaned up," Lucy says in the dark.

"I'm going to stop, don't want to risk destroying blood, if it is. You got it on film?"

"Right." She turns on the light.

Scarpetta gets out a presumptive blood kit and swabs areas of the wall where she saw the luminol react, working the cotton tip into the porous concrete where blood might lurk, even after washing. With medicine droppers, she drips her chemical concoction on a swab and it turns bright pink, reaffirming that what is lighting up on the wall could be blood, possibly human blood. It will have to be verified in the lab.

If it's blood, it wouldn't surprise her if it is old, two and a half years old. Luminol reacts to the hemoglobin in red blood cells, and the older the blood, the more it oxidizes and the stronger the reaction. She continues swabbing with sterile water, gathering samples and sealing them inside evidence boxes that she labels, tapes and initials.

This has been going on for an hour, and she and Lucy are hot inside their protective clothing. They can hear Larry on the other side of the door, moving about his store. Several times, his phone rings.

They return to the storage area, and Lucy opens a sturdy black carrying case and removes a Mini-Crime scope forensic light source, a portable boxy metal unit with side intakes, a high-intensity halide lamp with a flexible arm that looks like a shiny steel hose fitted with a light guide that allows her to change wavelengths. She plugs in the scope and turns on the power switch and a fan begins to whir. She adjusts the intensity knob, setting the wavelength at 455 nanometers. They put on orange-tinted goggles that improve contrast and protect their eyes.

Lights out, and Scarpetta carries the unit by its handle and slowly sweeps the blue light over walls, shelving and the floor. Blood and other substances that react to luminol don't necessarily react to an alternate light source, and the areas that luminesced earlier are dark. But several small smears on the floor pop up a bright, hot red. Lights on, and Lucy positions the tripod again and places an orange filter over the camera lens. Lights out, and she photographs the fluorescing red smears. Lights back on, and the smears are barely visible. They are nothing more than a dirty discoloration of a dirty, discolored floor, but under magnification, Scarpetta detects a very faint blush of red. Whatever the substance is, it doesn't dissolve in sterile water, and she doesn't want to use a solvent and run the risk of destroying whatever it is.

"We need to get a sample." Scarpetta studies the concrete.

"I'll be right back."

Lucy opens the door and calls out for Larry. He is behind the counter again, talking on the phone, and when he looks up and sees her from head to toe in white plasticized paper, he is visibly startled.

"Did someone just beam me to the Mir space station?" he says.

"You got any tools around this joint so I don't have to go out to the car?"

"There's a small toolbox in back. Up on the shelf against the wall." He indicates which wall. "A small, red toolbox."

"I may have to mess up your floor. Just a little."

He starts to say something but changes his mind, shrugs, and she shuts the door. She retrieves a hammer and a screwdriver from the toolbox, and with a few blows, chips out small samples of the dirty red stains and seals them inside evidence bags.

She and Scarpetta remove their white clothing and stuff it into a trash can. They pack up their equipment and leave.

Why are you doing this?" Ev asks the same question she asks every time he comes in, asks it hoarsely as he points the light and it shoots through her eyes like knives. "Please get that light out of my face."

"You're the ugliest fat pig I've ever seen," he says. "No wonder nobody likes you."

"Words can't hurt me. You can't hurt me. I belong to God."

"Look at you. Who would have you. You're thankful I pay attention to you, aren't you."

"Where are the others?"

"Say you're sorry. You know what you did. Sinners must be punished."

"What have you done with them?" She asks the same question she always does. "Let me go. God will forgive you."

"Say you're sorry."

He nudges her ankles with his boots and the pain is horrific.

"Dear God, forgive him," she prays out loud. "You don't want to go to hell," she says to him, the evil one. "It's not too late."

36

It is very dark, the moon like a shadowy shape on an x-ray, vague behind clouds. Small insects swarm in the light of streetlamps. The traffic never quits on A1A, and the night is filled with noise.

"What's bothering you?" Scarpetta asks as Lucy drives. "This is the first alone time you and I have had since I can't remember when. Please talk to me."

"I could have called Lex. I didn't mean to drag you out."

"And I could have told you to. I didn't have to be your partner in crime tonight."

Both of them are tired and in humorless moods.

"So, here we are," Lucy says. "Maybe I used this as an opportunity for us to catch up. I could have called Lex," she says again, staring straight ahead as she drives.

"I can't tell if you're making fun of me."

"I'm not." Lucy looks over at her without smiling. "I'm sorry about things."

"You should be."

"You don't have to be so quick to agree. Maybe you don't always know what my life is like."

"The problem is, I want to. You consistently shut me out."

"Aunt Kay, you really don't want to know as much as you think you do. Did it ever occur to you that maybe I'm doing you a favor? That maybe you should enjoy me as you know me and leave the rest of it alone?"

"What is the rest of it?"

"I'm not like you."

"In the important ways, you are, Lucy. We're both intelligent, decent, hard-working women. We try to make a difference. We take risks. We're honest. We try, we really try."

"I'm not as decent as you think. All I do is hurt people.

I'm good at it, getting better at it all the time. And every time I do it, I care less. Maybe I'm turning into a Basil Jenrette. Maybe Benton ought to enroll me in his study up there. I bet my brain looks like Basil's, like all the other fucking psychopaths."

"I don't know what's going on with you," Scarpetta says quietly.

"I think it's blood." Lucy makes one of her fast breaks again, changing the subject so abruptly, it's jolting. "I think Basil's telling the truth. I think he killed her in the back of the shop. I have a feeling it will turn out to be blood, what we found back there."

"Let's wait and see what the labs say."

"The entire floor lit up. That was weird."

"Why would Basil say anything about it? Why now? Why to Benton?" Scarpetta says. "That bothers me. Worries me, actually."

"There's always a reason with these people. Manipulation."

"It worries me."

"So he's talking to get something he wants, to get his rocks off. How could he make it up?"

"He could know about the missing people from The Christmas Shop. It was in the paper, he was a Miami cop. Maybe he heard about it from other cops," Scarpetta says.

The more they talk about it, the more she worries that Basil really did have something to do with what happened to Florrie and Helen Quincy. But she can't imagine how he could have raped and murdered the mother in the back of the store. How did he get her bloody, dead body out of there, or get both dead bodies out of there, assuming he killed Helen, too.

"I know," Lucy says. "I can't envision it, either. And if he did kill them, why didn't he just leave them there? Unless he didn't want anyone to know they were murdered, wanted them presumed missing, presumed missing of their own volition."

"That suggests motive to me," Scarpetta says. "Not compulsive sexual homicide."

"I forgot to ask you," Lucy says. "I'm assuming I'm taking you to your house."

"At this hour, yes."

"What are you going to do about Boston?"

"We've got to deal with the Simister scene, and I just can't do it now. I've had it for the night. Reba's probably had it."

"She agreed to let us in, I assume."

"As long as she's with us. We'll do it in the morning. I'm thinking about not going to Boston at all, but it's not fair to Benton. Not fair to either of us," she says, unable to keep the frustration and disappointment out of her voice. "Of course, it's the same thing. I suddenly have urgent cases. He suddenly has an urgent case. All we'll do is work."

"What's his case?"

"A woman dumped near Walden Pond, nude, bizarre fake tattoos on her body that I suspect were done after her murder. Red handprints."

Lucy grips the steering wheel harder.

"What do you mean, fake tattoos?"

"Painted ones. Body art, Benton says. A hood over her head, a shotgun shell inserted in her rectum, posed, degrading, all the rest. I don't know much, but I'm sure I will."

"Do they know who she is?"

"They know very little."

"Anything similar happen in the area? Similar homicides? With the red handprints?"

"You can divert the conversation all you want, Lucy, but it won't work. You're not yourself. You've gained weight, and for that to happen means something is off, very off. Not that you look bad, not at all, but I know what you're like. You're tired a lot and don't look well. I hear about it. I haven't said anything, but I know something's wrong. I've known it for a while. Are you going to tell me?"

"I need to know more about the handprints."

"I've told you what I know. Why?" Scarpetta keeps her eyes on Lucy's tense face. "What's going on with you?"

She stares straight ahead and seems to struggle with how to put the right answer together. She's good at that, so bright, so quick, she can rearrange information until her concoctions are more believable than the truth, and rarely does anybody doubt or question. What saves her is that she doesn't believe her misinformation and manipulations, doesn't for a moment forget the facts and fall headlong into her own traps. Lucy always has a rational reason for what she does, and sometimes it's a good one.

"You must be hungry," Scarpetta then says. She says it quietly, gently, the way she used to talk when Lucy was an impossible child, always acting out because she hurt so much.

"You always feed me when you can't do anything else with me," Lucy says in a subdued way.

"It used to work. When you were a little girl, I could get you to do anything in exchange for my pizza."

Lucy is silent, her face grim and unfamiliar in the red glow of a traffic light.

"Lucy? Are you going to smile or look at me even once this night?"

"I've been doing stupid things. One-night stands. I hurt people. Just the other night in Ptown, I did it again. I don't want to be close to anybody. I want to be left alone. I can't seem to help it. This time, it may have been really stupid. Because I haven't been paying attention. Because maybe I don't give a shit."

"I didn't even know you were in Ptown," Scarpetta remarks, and she isn't judgmental.

Lucy's sexual orientation isn't what bothers her.

"You used to be careful," Scarpetta says. "More careful than anyone I've ever met."

"Aunt Kay, I'm sick."

37

The black shape of the spider covers the back of his hand, floating toward her, passing through the beam of light, inches from her face. He has never moved the spider this close to her. He has placed a pair of scissors on the mattress and illuminates them briefly with the light.

"Say you're sorry," he says. "This is all your fault."

"Give up your evil ways before it's too late," Ev says, and the scissors are within reach.

Maybe he is tempting her to grab them. She can barely see them, even in the light. She listens for Kristin and the boys, the spider a blur in front of her face.

"None of this would have happened. You've brought it upon yourself. Now comes punishment."

"This can be undone," she says.

"Time for the punishment. Say you're sorry."

Her heart pounds, her fear so intense she might vomit. She won't apologize. She has committed no sin. If she says she's sorry, he will kill her. Somehow, she knows it.

"Say you're sorry!" he says.

She refuses to say it.

He orders her to say she's sorry and she won't. She preaches. She preaches her stupid, mindless garbage about her feeble god. If her god were so powerful, she wouldn't be on the mattress.

"We can pretend it never happened," she says in her hoarse, demanding voice.

He can feel her fear. He demands she say she's sorry. No matter how much she preaches at him, she's scared. The spider makes her tremble, her legs jumping on the mattress.

"You will be forgiven. You will be forgiven if you repent and let us go. I'll never tell the police."

"No, you won't. You'll never tell. People who tell get punished, punished in ways you can't imagine. His fangs can go all the way through a finger, right through the nail," he says of the spider. "Some tarantulas are repeat biters."

The spider is almost touching her face. She jerks her head back, gasping.

"They strike and strike. They won't stop until you rip them off you. If they bite you in a major artery, you die. They can shoot their hairs into your eyes and blind you. It's very painful. Say you're sorry."

Hog told her to say it, say she was sorry, and he sees the door shutting, old wood with peeling paint, the mattress on the dirty, old floor. Then the sound of the shovel digging because he told her not to tell after he did the bad thing and said that people who tell get punished by God, get punished in unthinkable ways until they learn their lesson.

"Ask forgiveness. God will forgive you."

"Say you're sorry!" He shines the light in her eyes and she clamps them shut and jerks her face away from the light, but he finds her with it.

She won't cry.

When he did the bad thing, she cried. He told her she would cry, all right, if she ever told. Then she finally did. She told, and Hog had no choice but to confess because it was true, he did the bad thing, and Hog's mother didn't believe a word of it, said Hog didn't, couldn't possibly have, that he obviously was sick and delusional.

It was cold and snowing. He didn't know there was weather like that, had seen it on TV and in the movies but he didn't know about it from his own experience. He remembers old brick buildings, seeing them through the window of the car when he was driven there, remembers the small lobby where he sat with his mother before the doctor came, a brightly lit place where a man sat in a chair moving his lips, rolling his eyes upward, having a conversation with someone who wasn't there.

His mother went in and talked to the doctor, leaving him

alone in the lobby. She told the doctor the bad thing Hog said he did, that it wasn't true and he was very sick, that it was a private matter and all she cared about was that Hog got well, that he didn't go around talking like that, ruining the family's good name with his lies.

She didn't believe he did the bad thing.

She told Hog what she intended to say to the doctor. *You're not well,* she told Hog. *You can't help it. You imagine things and lie and are easily influenced. I'll pray for you. You'd best pray for yourself, ask God to forgive you, say you're sorry for hurting people who have been nothing but kind to you. I know you're sick, but shame on you.*

"I'm going to put him on you," Hog says, moving the light closer to her. "If you hurt him like she did"—he pokes her forehead with the barrel of the shotgun—"you'll learn the true meaning of punishment."

"Shame on you."

"I told you not to say that."

He pokes her harder, the barrel of the shotgun striking bone, and she cries out. He presses the pressure light, shines it on her ugly, puffy, blotchy face. She bleeds. Blood runs down her face. When the other one brushed the spider to the floor, his abdomen ruptured and he bled his yellow blood. Hog had to glue him back together.

"Say you're sorry. She said she was sorry. Do you know how many times she said it?"

He imagines her feeling the furry legs on her bare right shoulder, imagines her feeling the spider move on her skin and stop, lightly gripping her. She sits against the wall and shakes violently, glancing at the scissors on the mattress.

"All the way to Boston. That was a long trip, and it was cold in the back, her naked and tied up. There's no seat back there, just a cold metal floor. She was cold. I gave them something to think about up there."

He remembers the old brick buildings with grayish-blue slate roofs. He remembers when his mother drove him up there after he did the bad thing, and then years later, when he went back on his own and lived in the midst of the old brick and slate and didn't last long. Because of the bad thing, he didn't last long.

"What have you done with the boys?" She tries to sound strong, tries to sound unafraid. "Let them go."

He pokes her private places and she jumps and he laughs and calls her ugly and fat and stupid, says no one would ever want her, the same thing he said when he did the bad thing.

"No wonder," he keeps on, staring at her sagging breasts, her thick, flabby body. "You're lucky I'm doing this to you. No one else would. You're too disgusting and stupid."

"I won't tell anyone. Just let me go. Where are Kristin and the boys?"

"I went back and got them, poor little orphans. Just like I said. I even returned your car. I'm so pure of heart, not a sinner like you. Don't worry. I brought them here just like I said."

"I don't hear them."

"Say you're sorry."

"Did you drive them up to Boston, too?"

"No."

"You didn't really take Kristin . . ."

"I gave them something to think about up there. I'm sure he's impressed. I hope he knows. He will soon, one way or other. There isn't much time left."

"Who? You can talk to me. I don't hate you," and now she sounds sympathetic.

He knows what she's trying to do. She thinks they'll be friends. If she talks to him enough and pretends she's not afraid, even acts as if she likes him, they'll be friends and he won't punish her.

"It won't work," Hog says. "They all tried that and it didn't work. It was quite the special delivery. He'd have been impressed if he knew. I'm keeping people busy up there. There isn't much time left. You'd better make the most of it. Say you're sorry!"

"I don't know what you're talking about," she says in the same hypocritical voice.

The spider stirs on her shoulder, and he reaches out his

hand in the dark and the spider crawls back on it. He walks across the room, leaving the scissors on the mattress.

"Cut your filthy hair," he says. "Cut all of it off. If you haven't done it by the time I get back, it will be worse for you. Don't try to cut the ropes. There's no place for you to run."

38

The snow is full of moonlight beyond Benton's up-stairs office window, and the lamps are switched off. He sits at his computer, displaying photographs on the screen until he finds the ones he wants.

There are one hundred and ninety-seven photographs—disturbing, grotesque photographs—and it has been an ordeal to find these particular ones because he is disconcerted by what is before him. He is unsettled. He feels that something beyond the obvious has happened and is happening, and he is personally upset by the case, and at this stage of his vast experience, that is hard to imagine. Distracted, he didn't jot down the sequence numbers, and it took him the better part of half an hour to find the photographs in question, numbers 62 and 74. He is impressed with Detective Thrush, with the Massachusetts State Police. In a homicide, especially a homicide like this, one can never do too much.

In violent deaths, nothing improves with time. The scene vanishes or is contaminated and one can't go back. The body changes after death, especially after the autopsy, and one can't go back, not really. So state police investigators went into high alert and were aggressive with their cameras, and now Benton is overwhelmed with photographs and video recordings and has been studying them since he got home from his visit with Basil Jenrette. During Benton's twenty-some years with the FBI, he thought he had seen it all. As a forensic psychologist, he assumed he had seen just about every permutation of bizarreness. But he has never seen anything quite like this.

Photographs 62 and 74 aren't as explicit as most, because they don't show what is left of the unidentified woman's destroyed head. They don't show her in all her faceless, gory horror. She reminds him of a spoon, a hollowed-out shell on the stalk of a neck, her black, raggedly cut hair matted with bits of brain, tissue and dried blood. Photographs 62 and 74 are close-ups of her body from the neck to the knees, and they give him a feeling he can't describe, the sensation he has when something reminds him of something disturbing he can't remember. The images are trying to tell him something he already knows but can't reach. What? What is it?

In 62, the torso is face-up on the autopsy table. In 74, it is facedown, and he clicks back and forth between the two images, studying her naked torso, trying to make sense of the bright red handprints and the angry, abraded skin between her shoulderblades, a six- by eight-inch area of flesh rubbed raw and embedded with what appears to be "wood-like splinters and dirt," according to the autopsy report.

He has been contemplating the possibility that the red handprints were painted before the woman died, that it has nothing to do with her murder. Maybe for some reason she already had gotten the bodypainting before she encountered her assailant. He has to consider it, but he doesn't believe it. More likely, it was the killer who turned her torso into a work of art, one that is degrading and suggestive of sexual violence, suggestive of hands grabbing her breasts and forcing open her legs, symbols he painted on her while he held her hostage, possibly when she was incapacitated or dead. Benton doesn't know. He can't tell. He wishes the case were Scarpetta's, that she had gone to the scene and done the autopsy. He wishes she were here. As usual, something came up.

He reviews more photographs and reports. The victim is presumed to be in her mid-thirties or early forties, and her postmortem findings reiterate what Dr. Lonsdale said in the morgue, she hadn't been dead long when her body was discovered on an easement that leads through Walden Woods, not far from Walden Pond, in the wealthy town of Lincoln. Swabs from the physical evidence recovery kit are negative for seminal fluid, and it is Benton's preliminary assessment that whoever killed her and posed her body in the woods is driven by sadistic fantasies, the sort of sexual fantasies that objectify the victim.

Whoever she is, she was nothing to him. She wasn't a person, just a symbol, just a thing for him to do with as he pleased, and what pleased him was to degrade and terrorize, to punish, to make her suffer, to force her to face her own impending violent and humiliating death, to taste the shotgun barrel in her mouth and watch him pull the trigger. He might have known her, or she might have been a stranger to him. He might have stalked her and abducted her. No one fitting her description has been reported missing from New England, say the Massachusetts State Police. No one fitting her description has been reported missing from anywhere.

Beyond the pool is the seawall. It is big enough to moor a sixty-foot boat, although Scarpetta doesn't have one and has never wanted one of any size or description.

She watches the boats, especially at night when bow and stern lights move like aircraft along the dark waterway, silent but for the rumbling of their engines. If the lights are on in the cabins, she watches people moving around or sitting and lifting glasses, laughing or serious or just there, and she doesn't want to be them or be like them or be with them.

She was never like them. She never wanted anything to do with them. When she was growing up poor and isolated, she wasn't like them and couldn't be with them, and that was their choice. Now the choice is hers. She knows what she knows, is on the outside looking into lives that are irrelevant, depressing, empty and scary. She has always feared something tragic would happen to her niece. It is natural for her to entertain morbid thoughts about anyone she loves, but the inclination has always been more extreme with Lucy. Scarpetta has always worried that Lucy would die a violent death. Never did it occur to her that she might get sick, that biology might turn on her, not because it's personal but because it isn't.

"I started having symptoms that didn't make sense," Lucy says in the dark, between two wooden pilings, where they sit in teak chairs.

There is a table, and on it are drinks and cheese and

crackers. They haven't touched the cheese and crackers. This is their second round of drinks.

"Sometimes I wish I smoke," Lucy adds, reaching for her tequila.

"That's a strange thing to say."

"You didn't think it strange when you did it all those years. You still want it."

"It doesn't matter what I want."

"That is something you would say, as if you're exempt from the same feelings other people have, " Lucy replies in the dark to the water. "Sure it matters. Whatever you want matters. Especially when you can't have it."

"Do you want her?" Scarpetta asks.

"Which her?"

"Whatever her you were with last," she reminds her. "Your most recent conquest. In Ptown."

"I don't look at them as conquests. I look at them as brief escapes. Like smoking pot. I guess that's the most disappointing part. It means nothing. Only this time it may mean something. Something I don't understand. I may have walked into something. Been really blind and stupid."

She tells Scarpetta about Stevie, about her tattoos, the red handprints. She has a difficult time talking about it but tries to sound detached, as if she is talking about what somebody else did, as if she is discussing a case.

Scarpetta is silent. She picks up her drink and tries to think about what Lucy has just said.

"Maybe it means nothing," Lucy goes on. "A coincidence. A lot of people are into weird body art, all kinds of weird stuff in acrylics and latex that they airbrush all over themselves."

"I'm getting tired of coincidences. There seem to have been a lot of them lately," Scarpetta says.

"This is pretty good tequila. I wouldn't mind a joint right now."

"Are you trying to shock me?"

"Pot's not as bad for you as you think."

"So you're the doctor now."

"Really. It's true."

"Why do you seem to hate yourself so much, Lucy?"

"You know what, Aunt Kay?" Lucy turns toward her, her face strong and sharp in the soft glow of lights along the sea-wall. "You really don't have a clue about what I do or what I've done. So don't pretend to."

"That sounds like an indictment of some sort. Most of what you've said tonight sounds like an indictment. If I've somehow failed you, I'm sorry. Sorrier than you'll ever imagine."

"I'm not you."

"Of course you're not. And you keep saying that."

"I'm not looking for something permanent, someone who really matters, someone I can't live without. I don't want a Benton. I want people I can forget. One-night stands. Do you want to know how many I've had? Because I don't."

"You've had virtually nothing to do with me this past year. Is that why?"

"It's easier."

"Are you afraid I'd judge you?"

"Maybe you should."

"It's not who you're sleeping with that bothers me. It's the rest of it. You keep to yourself at the Academy, have nothing to do with the students, are virtually never there, or when you are you're killing yourself in the gym or up in a helicopter or out on the range or testing something, prefer-ably a machine, a dangerous one."

"Maybe machines are the only thing I get along with."

"Whatever you fail begins to fail, Lucy. Just so you know."

"Including my body."

"What about your heart and soul? How about we start with that."

"That's pretty cold. So much for my health."

"I feel anything but cold. Your health means more to me than my own."

"I think she set me up, knew I was in the bar, had some-thing in mind."

She is back to that woman again, the one with the hand-prints that are similar to the ones in Benton's case.

"You need to tell Benton about Stevie. What's her last name? What do you know about her?" Scarpetta asks.

"I know very little. I'm sure it has nothing to do with anything, but it's strange, isn't it. She was up there the same time the woman was murdered and dumped. In the general area."

Scarpetta is quiet.

"Maybe there's some cult thing up there in that area," Lucy then says. "Maybe there are a lot of people painting red handprints all over themselves. Don't judge me. I don't need to hear how stupid and reckless I am."

Scarpetta looks at her and is quiet.

Lucy wipes her eyes.

"I'm not judging you. I'm trying to understand why you've turned your back on everything you care about. The Academy is yours. It's your dream. You hated organized law enforcement, the Feds in particular. So you started your own force, your own posse. Now your riderless horse wanders the parade ground. Where are you? And all of us—all of the people you have brought together in your cause—feel pretty much abandoned. Most of last year's students never met you, and some of the faculty don't know you and wouldn't recognize you on sight."

Lucy watches a sailboat with furled sails putter past in the night. She wipes her eyes.

"I have a tumor," she says. "In my brain."

39

Benton enlarges another photograph, this one taken at the scene.

The victim looks like a hideous work of violent pornography, on her back, legs and arms splayed, bloody white slacks wrapped around her hips like a diaper, a pair of fecal-stained slightly bloody white panties covering her destroyed head like a mask, with two holes cut out for her eyes. He leans back in his chair, thinking. It would be too simple to assume that whoever posed her in the Walden Woods did so only to shock. There is something else.

The case reminds him of something.

He ponders the diaper-folded slacks. They are inside out, suggesting several possibilities: At some point, she might have taken them off under duress, then put them back on. The killer might have removed them after she was dead. They are linen. Most people don't wear white linen in New England this time of year. In a photograph that shows the slacks laid out on a paper-covered autopsy table, the pattern of the bloodstains is telling. The slacks are stiff with dark brown blood in front, from the knee up. From the knee down, there are a few smears and that's all. Benton imagines her on her knees when she was shot. He envisions her kneeling. He tries Scarpetta's phone. She doesn't answer.

Humiliation. Control. Complete degradation, rendering the victim absolutely powerless, as powerless as an infant. Hooded like somebody about to be executed, possibly. Hooded like a prisoner of war, to torture, to terrorize, possibly. The killer is reenacting something from his own life, probably. His childhood, probably. Sexual abuse, probably. Sadism, possibly. So often that is the case. Do unto others as was done unto you. He tries Scarpetta again and doesn't get her.

Basil slips into his mind. He posed some of his victims, leaned them up against things, in one case a wall in a rest-stop ladies' room. Benton conjures up the scene and autopsy photographs of Basil's victims, the ones anybody knows about, and sees the gory, eyeless faces of the dead. Maybe that's the similarity. The eyeholes in the panties are sugges-tive of Basil's eyeless victims.

Then again, it might be about the hood. Somehow, it seems more about the hood. Hooding someone is to over-power that person completely, to obviate any possibility of fight or flight, to torment, to terrify, to punish. None of Basil's victims were hooded, not that anybody knows of, but there is always so much nobody knows about what really happened during a sadistic homicide. The victim isn't around to tell.

Benton worries that maybe he has been spending too much time in Basil's head.

He tries Scarpetta again.

"It's me," he says when she answers.

"I was getting ready to call you," she says tersely, coldly, in an unsteady voice.

"You sound upset."

"You go first, Benton," she says in the same voice, one that barely sounds like her.

"Have you been crying?" He doesn't understand why she is acting like this. "I wanted to talk to you about this case up here," he says.

She is the only person who can make him feel this way. Scared.

"I was hoping to talk to you about it. I'm looking at the case right now," he says.

"I'm glad you want to talk to me about something." She emphasizes *something*.

"What's wrong, Kay?"

"Lucy," she says. "That's what's wrong. You've known about it for a year. How could you do this to me."

"She told you," he says, rubbing his jaw.

"She was scanned at your damn hospital, and you never said a thing to me. Well, guess what? She's my niece, not yours. You have no right . . ."

"She made me promise."

"She had no right."

"Of course she did, Kay. No one could talk to you without her consent. Not even her doctors."

"But she told you."

"For a very good reason . . ."

"This is serious. We're going to have to deal with it. I'm not sure I can trust you anymore."

He sighs, his stomach as tight as a fist. They rarely fight. When they do, it's awful.

"I'm getting off the phone now," she says. "We've got to deal with this," she says again.

She hangs up without saying good-bye, and Benton sits in his chair, unable to move for a moment. He stares blankly at a gruesome photograph on his screen and idly starts clicking through the case again, reading reports, scanning the narrative Thrush wrote up for him, trying to divert his thoughts from what just happened.

There were drag marks in the snow leading from a parking area to where the body was found. There are no footprints in the snow that might have been the victim's, only her killer's. Approximately size nine, maybe ten, big tread, some type of hiking boot.

It's not fair that Scarpetta should blame him. He had no choice. Lucy swore him to secrecy, said she would never forgive him if he told anyone, especially her aunt, especially Marino.

There are no blood drips or smears along the trail the killer left, suggesting he wrapped her body in something, dragged her wrapped up. Police recovered some fibers from the drag marks.

Scarpetta is projecting, she's attacking him because she can't attack Lucy. She can't attack Lucy's tumor. She can't get angry at someone who is sick.

Trace evidence on the body includes fibers and microscopic debris under the fingernails and adhering to blood and to abraded skin and hair. A preliminary lab analysis indicates most of the trace is consistent with carpet and cotton fibers, and there are minerals, the fragments of insects and vegetation and pollen found in soil, or what the medical examiner so eloquently called "dirt."

When the telephone rings on Benton's desk, the call is identified as unavailable, and he assumes it is Scarpetta. He snaps up the phone.

"Hello," he says.

"This is the McLean Hospital operator."

He hesitates, disappointed deeply and hurt. Scarpetta could have called him back. He doesn't remember the last time she hung up on him.

"I'm trying to reach Dr. Wesley," the operator says.

It still sounds strange when people call him that. He has had his Ph.D. for many years, as far back as his career with the FBI, but never insisted on or wanted people to call him doctor.

"Speaking," he says.

Lucy sits up in bed in her aunt's guest room. The lights are out. She had too many tequilas to drive. She looks at the number on the illuminated display of her Treo, the one with the 617 exchange. She's a little woozy, a little drunk.

She thinks about Stevie, remembers her acting upset and insecure as she abruptly left the cottage. She thinks of Stevie following her to the Hummer in the parking lot and acting like the same seductive, mysterious and self-assured woman Lucy had met in Lorraine's, and as she thinks about that first meeting in Lorraine's, she feels what she felt then. She doesn't want to feel anything but she does and it unsettles her.

Stevie unsettles her. She might know something. She was in New England around the same time the lady was murdered and dumped at Walden Pond. Both of them had red handprints on their bodies. Stevie claims she didn't paint the handprints, someone else did.

Who?

Lucy hits send, a little bleary, a little scared. She should have traced the 617 number Stevie gave her, see who it really comes back to, see if it really is Stevie's number or if her name is Stevie.

"Hello?"

"Stevie?" So it is her number. "You remember me?"

"How could I forget you? No one could."

She sounds seductive. Her voice is soothing and rich, and Lucy feels what she felt at Lorraine's. She reminds herself why she is calling.

The handprints. Where did she get them? Who?

"I was sure I'd never hear from you again," Stevie's seductive voice is saying.

"Well, you have," Lucy says.

"Why are you talking so quietly?"

"I'm not in my own house."

"I suppose I shouldn't ask what that means. But I do quite a lot of things I shouldn't. Who are you with?"

"No one," Lucy says. "You still up in Ptown?"

"I left right after you did. Drove straight through. I'm back home."

"Gainesville?"

"Where are you?"

"You never have told me your last name," Lucy says.

"What house are you in if it's not yours? I assume you live in a house. I guess I don't know."

"You ever come south?"

"I can go anywhere I want. South of where? Are you in Boston?"

"I'm in Florida," Lucy says. "I'd like to see you. We need to talk. How about telling me your last name, you know, like maybe we're not strangers."

"You want to talk about what."

She's not going to tell Lucy her full name. There's no point in asking again. She's probably not going to tell Lucy anything, at least not over the phone.

"Let's talk in person," Lucy says.

"That's always better."

She asks Stevie to meet her in South Beach tomorrow night at ten.

"You heard of a place called Deuce?" Lucy asks.

"It's quite famous," Stevie's seductive voice says. "I know it well."

40

The round, brass head shines like a moon on the screen.

Inside the Massachusetts State Police firearms lab, Tom, a firearms examiner, sits amid computers and comparison microscopes in a low-lighted room where the National Integrated Ballistics Information Network, NIBIN, has finally answered his query.

He stares at the magnified images of fine striations and gouges transferred from the metal parts of a shotgun to the brass heads of two shells. The two images are superimposed, the two halves joined in the middle, the microscopic signatures, as Tom calls them, lining up perfectly.

"Of course, officially, I'm calling it a *possible* match until I can validate it on the comparison scope," he is explaining to Dr. Wesley over the phone, the legendary Benton Wesley.

This is cool, Tom can't help but think.

"Which means the examiner down in Broward County needs to send me his evidence, and fortunately, that's not a problem," Tom goes on. "Preliminarily, let me just say that I don't think there's going to be a question about this one being a hit in the computer. It's my opinion—again, preliminarily—that the two shells were fired by the same shotgun."

He waits for the reaction and feels charged-up, excited, as high as if he's had two whisky sours. To say there's a hit is like telling the investigator he won the lottery.

"What do you know about the Hollywood case?" Dr. Wesley says without so much as a hint of gratitude.

"For one thing, it's solved," Tom answers, insulted.

"I'm not sure I understand," Dr. Wesley says in the same ungracious tone.

He's unappreciative and high-handed, and that figures. Tom has never met him, never talked to him and had no idea what to expect. But he's heard of him, heard about his past career with the FBI, and everyone knows the FBI throws its considerable weight around, exploits the local investigators while treating them like inferiors and then takes credit for anything good that comes of a case. He's an arrogant prick. That figures. No wonder Thrush made him talk directly to the legendary Dr. Benton Wesley. Thrush doesn't want to deal with him or anyone that is or was or even knows the FBI.

"Two years ago," Tom is saying, his friendliness withdrawn.

He sounds obtuse, dull. That's what his wife tells him when his ego is bruised and he justifiably reacts. He has a right to react, but he doesn't want his affect to become obtuse and dull, as if he's been hit on the head with a wooden plank, as his wife puts it.

"Hollywood had a robbery in a convenience store," he is saying, trying not to sound obtuse and dull. "Guy comes in wearing a rubber mask and pointing a shotgun. He shoots this kid who's sweeping the floor, and then the night manager shoots him in the head with the pistol he kept under the counter."

"And they ran the shotgun shell through NIBIN?"

"Apparently, to see if this same masked guy might have been connected to some other unsolved cases."

"I don't understand," Dr. Wesley impatiently says again. "What happened to the weapon after the masked guy was killed? It should have been recovered by the police. And now it's just been used again in a homicide up here in Massachusetts?"

"I asked the Broward County examiner the same thing," he replies, trying with all his might not to sound obtuse and dull. "He said after he test-fired the gun, he returned it to Hollywood PD."

"Well, I can promise you it's not there now," Dr. Wesley says as if Tom is a simpleton.

Tom chews on a hangnail, making his cuticle bleed, an old habit that annoys the hell out of his wife.

"Thanks," Dr. Wesley says, getting off the phone, dismissing him.

Tom's attention wanders to the NIBIN microscope where the shotgun shell in question is mounted, a red, plastic twelve-gauge shell with a brass head that has an unusual drag mark made by the firing pin. He made the case a priority. He has been sitting in his chair the entire day and now into the night, using ring lighting and side lighting and proper orientations of three o'clock and six o'clock positions and saving each picture as a file, doing this repeatedly with breech marks, the firing pin impression and the ejector mark before searching the NIBIN database.

Then he had to wait four hours for the results while his family went to the movies without him. Then Thrush was out to dinner and asked him to call Dr. Wesley but forgot to give him a direct phone number, and Tom had to call the McLean Hospital answering service and be handled, at first, as if he were a patient. A little appreciation is in order, he thinks. Dr. Wesley couldn't bother to say "thanks" or "job well done" or "I can't believe you got results so fast or got them at all." Does he have any idea how hard it is to run a shotgun shell through NIBIN? Most examiners won't even try.

He stares at the shell. He's never had one that was recovered from a dead person's ass.

He glances at his watch and calls Thrush at home.

"Just tell me one thing," he says when Thrush answers. "How come you made me talk to Dr. Fuck-B-I. And a thank-you would be nice."

"You talking about Benton?"

"No, I'm talking about Bond. James Bond."

"He's a nice guy. I don't know what you're talking about except you got such a thing about the Feds, you constitute what I call a bigot. And you want to know what else, Tom?" Thrush goes on, and he sounds slightly drunk. "Let me give you a word to the wise. NIBIN belongs to the Feds, meaning you do, too. Where the hell you think you got all that pretty equipment to work on and all that training so you could sit there and do what you do every day? Well, guess who? The Feds."

"I don't need this right now," Tom says, the phone tucked under his chin as he types on the keyboard, closing out files, getting ready to go home to his empty house while his family enjoys the movies without him.

"Besides, just so you know, Benton quit the Bureau a long time ago, doesn't have anything to do with them."

"Well, he should be grateful. That's all. It's the first time we got a hit in NIBIN on a shotgun shell."

"Grateful? Are you fucking kidding me? Grateful for what? That the shell from this dead lady's ass matches up with a dead man's gun that's supposed to be in the custody of the fucking Hollywood police or sold as scrap metal by now?" Thrush says loudly, and he tends to say fuck a lot when he's been drinking. "Let me tell you, he ain't fucking grateful. Like me, all he probably wants to do right now is get shit-faced drunk."

41

It is hot inside the ruined house, and the air is heavy and doesn't move. It smells like mildew, mold and rancid food, and stinks like a latrine.

Hog moves with self-assuredness through the dark, from room to room, knowing by feel and smell exactly where he is. He can pick his way nimbly from one corner to the next, and when the moon is bright as it is tonight, his eyes hold the moonlight and he can see as clearly as if it is midday. He can see beyond the shadows, so far beyond them they may as well not exist. He can see the red welts on the woman's neck and face, see the sweat shining on her dirty, white skin, see the fear in her eyes, see her cut hair all over the mattress and the floor, and she can't see him.

He walks toward her, toward the stinking stained mattress on the rotting wooden floor where she sits up, leaning against the wall, her shiny, green-draped legs straight out in front of her. What is left of her hair stands straight up, as if she's got her finger in a wall socket, as if she's seen a ghost. She was wise enough to leave the scissors on the mattress. He picks them up and with the toe of his boot rearranges the bright-green robe, hears her breathing, feels her eyes on him, like damp spots on him.

He took the beautiful green robe that was draped over the sofa. She had just carried it into the house from the car, from the church, where she'd had it on hours earlier. He took the robe because it pleased him. Now it is wilted and wrinkled and reminds him of a slain dragon in a crumpled heap. He captured the dragon. It is his, and his disappointment in what has become of it makes him edgy and violent. The dragon has failed him. It has betrayed him. When the brilliant green dragon moved freely and beautifully through the air and people listened to it and could not take their eyes off it, he coveted it. He wanted it. He almost loved it. Now look at it.

He drifts closer to her and kicks her green-draped wire-bound ankles. She barely moves. She was more alert a while ago, but the spider seems to have worn her out. She hasn't preached the usual lowbrow drivel to him. She has said nothing. She has pissed since he was in here not even an hour ago. The ammonia smell is sharp in his nostrils.

"Why are you so disgusting?" Hog says, looking down at her.

"Are the boys asleep? I don't hear them." She sounds delirious.

"Shut up about them."

"I know you don't want to hurt them. I know you're a nice person."

"It won't do any good," he says. "You can just shut up about it. You don't know a damn thing and never will. You're so stupid and ugly. You're disgusting. No one would believe you. Say you're sorry. This is all your fault."

He kicks her ankles again, this time harder, and she cries out in pain.

"What a joke. Look at you. Who's my little pretty now? You're filth. Spoiled little brat, ungrateful little smart aleck. I'll teach you humility. Say you're sorry."

He kicks her ankles harder, and she screams and tears fill her eyes and they shine like glass in the moonlight.

"You're not so high and mighty now, are you. Think you're so much better, so much smarter than everybody else? Look at you now. Obviously, I'm going to have to find some more effective way to punish you. Put your shoes back on."

Confusion touches her eyes.

"We're going back outside. It's the only thing you listen to. Say you're sorry!"

Her glassy, wide eyes stare at him.

"You want the snorkel again? Say you're sorry!"

He pokes her with the shotgun and her legs jerk.

"You're going to tell me how much you want it, aren't you. Thank me because you're so ugly no one would ever touch you. You're honored, aren't you." He lowers his voice, knows how to make it scarier.

He pokes her again, pokes her breasts.

"Stupid and ugly. Let's get your shoes. You've left me no choice."

She doesn't say anything. He kicks her ankles, kicks them hard, and tears roll down her blood-caked face. Her nose is probably broken.

She broke Hog's nose, slapped him so hard his nose bled for hours and he knew it was broken. He can feel the bump in the bridge of his nose. She slapped him when he did the bad thing, when she struggled at first, the bad thing that happened in the room behind the paint-peeled door. Then his mother took him to that place where the buildings are old and it snows. He had never seen snow before, he had never been so cold. She took him there because he lied.

"Hurts, doesn't it?" he says. "Hurts like hell when you've got coat hangers biting into your anklebones and someone kicks them. That's what you get for disobeying me. For lying. Let's see, where's the snorkel."

He kicks her again and she moans. Her legs shake beneath the wilted green robe, beneath the dead green dragon draped over her.

"I don't hear the boys," she says, and her voice is getting weaker, her fire going out.

"Say you're sorry."

"I forgive you," she says with wide, shiny eyes.

He raises the shotgun and points it at her head. She stares straight at the barrel, stares as if she doesn't care anymore, and he seethes.

"You can say *forgive* all you want, but God is on my side," he says. "You deserve punishment. That's why you're here. Do you understand? It's your fault. You have heaped these burning coals on top of your own head. Do what I say! Tell me you're sorry!"

His big boots creak very little as he moves through the thick, hot air and stands in the doorway, staring back into the room. The slain green dragon stirs and warm air moves through the broken window. The room faces west, and in the late afternoon the low sun seeps in through the gaping broken window, and light touches the shiny green dragon and it shimmers and glows like emerald-green fire. But it doesn't move. It is nothing now. It is broken and ugly and it is her fault.

He looks at her pale flesh, her doughy, sour flesh covered with insect bites and rashes. He can smell her stench halfway down the hallway. The dead green dragon stirs when she stirs, and it incenses him when he thinks of capturing the dragon and discovering what was under it. She was under it. He was tricked. It's her fault. She wanted this to happen, tricked him. It's her fault.

"Say you're sorry!"

"I forgive you." Her wide, shiny eyes stare at him.

"I guess you know what happens now," he says.

She barely moves her mouth and no sound emerges.

"I guess you don't know."

He stares at her, ruined and disgusting in her foulness on the filthy mattress, and feels coldness in his chest, and the coldness feels quiet and indifferent like death, as if anything he has ever felt is as dead as the dragon.

"I guess you really don't know."

The shotgun's pump slides back with a loud crack in the empty house.

"Run," he says.

"I forgive you," she mouths, her wide, watery eyes fixed on him.

He steps out in the hallway, surprised by the sound of the front door shutting.

"Are you here?" he calls out.

He lowers the gun and walks toward the front of the house, his pulse picking up. He wasn't expecting her, not yet.

"I told you not to do that," God's voice greets him, but he can't see her, not yet. "You do only what I say."

She materializes in the darkness, her black, flowing self in the dark, flowing toward him. She is beautiful and so powerful and he loves her and could never be without her.

"What do you think you're doing?" she says to him.

"She still isn't sorry. She won't say it," he tries to explain.

"It isn't time. Did you think to bring the paint before you got so carried away in there?"

"It's not here. It's in the truck. Where I used it on the last one."

"Bring it in. Prepare first. Always prepare. You lose control and then what. You know what to do. Don't disappoint me."

God flows closer to him. She has an IQ of a hundred and fifty.

"We're almost out of time," Hog says.

"You are nothing without me," God says. "Don't disappoint me."

42

D r. Self sits at her desk, staring at the pool and getting anxious about the time. Every Wednesday morning, she is supposed to be at the studio by ten to get ready for her live radio show. "I absolutely can't confirm that," she says on the phone, and were she not in such a hurry, she would enjoy this conversation for all the wrong reasons.

"There's no question you prescribed Ritalin hydrochloride to David Luck," Dr. Kay Scarpetta replies.

Dr. Self can't help but think of Marino and everything he has said about Scarpetta. Dr. Self isn't intimidated. At the moment, she has the advantage over this woman she has met only once and hears about incessantly every single week.

"Ten milligrams three times daily," Dr. Scarpetta's voice comes over the line.

She sounds tired, maybe depressed. Dr. Self could help her. She told her so when they met last June at the Academy, at the dinner in honor of Dr. Self.

Highly motivated, successful professional women like us must be careful not to neglect our emotional landscapes, she said to Scarpetta when they happened to be in the ladies' room at the same time.

Thank you for your lectures. I know the students are enjoying them, Scarpetta replied, and Dr. Self saw right through her.

The Scarpettas of the world are masters at evading personal scrutiny or anything that might expose their secret vulnerability.

I'm sure the students are quite inspired, Scarpetta said, washing her hands in the sink, washing them as if she were scrubbing for surgery. *Everyone appreciates your finding time in your busy schedule to come here.*

I can tell you really don't mean that, Dr. Self replied quite candidly. *The vast majority of my colleagues in the medical profession look down on anyone who takes their practice beyond closed doors, walks out in the wide open arena of radio and television. The truth, of course, is usually jealousy. I suspect half the people who criticize me would ransom their souls to be on the air.*

You're probably right, Scarpetta replied, drying her hands.

It was a comment that lent itself to several very different interpretations: Dr. Self is right, the vast majority of people in the medical profession do look down on her; or half the people who criticize her are jealous; or it is true that she suspects half the people who criticize her are jealous, meaning they may not be jealous at all. No matter how many times she has replayed their conversation in the ladies' room and analyzed that particular remark, she can't decide what it meant and whether she was subtly and cleverly insulted.

"You sound as if something is bothering you," she says to Scarpetta over the phone.

"It is. I want to know what happened to your patient David." She dodges the personal comment. "One hundred tablets were refilled a little over three weeks ago," Scarpetta says.

"I can't verify that."

"I don't need you to verify it. I collected the prescription bottle from his house. I know you prescribed the Ritalin hydrochloride, and I know exactly when it was filled and where. The pharmacy is in the same strip mall as Ev and Kristin's church."

Dr. Self doesn't confirm this, but it's true.

What she says is, "Certainly, of all people, you understand confidentiality."

"I would hope you might understand that we're greatly concerned about the welfare of David and his brother and the two women they live with."

"Has anyone considered the possibility that the boys might have been homesick for South Africa? I'm not saying they were," she adds. "I'm simply posing a hypothetical."

"Their parents died last year in Capetown," Scarpetta says. "I spoke to the medical examiner who . . ."

"Yes, yes," she interrupts. "It's terribly tragic."

"Were both boys your patients?"

"Can you imagine how traumatizing that was? As I understand it from comments I heard outside of any sessions I might have had with either of them, their foster home was temporary. I believe it was always a given that at an appropriate time, they would return to Capetown and move in with relatives who had to move to a larger house or something like that before they could take the boys."

She probably shouldn't offer any further details but is enjoying the conversation too much to abort it.

"How were they referred to you?" Scarpetta asks.

"Ev Christian contacted me, was familiar with me, of course, because of my shows."

"That must happen quite a lot. People listen to you and want to become your patient."

"It certainly does."

"Meaning you must turn down most."

"I have no choice."

"So what made you decide to take on David and perhaps his brother?"

Dr. Self notices two people out by her pool. Two men in white shirts, black baseball caps and dark glasses are looking at her fruit trees, at the red stripes around them.

"It looks like I have trespassers," she says, annoyed.

"I beg your pardon?"

"Those damn inspectors. I'm doing a show on the very subject tomorrow, my new TV show. Well, now I really will be armed and dangerous on the air. Look at them just helping themselves to my property. I really do have to go."

"This is extremely important, Dr. Self. I wouldn't be calling you were there not reason for . . ."

"I'm in a terrible rush and now this. Now these idiots are back, probably to kill off all my beautiful trees. Well, we'll see. I'll be damned if they're coming in here with a crew of dunces and stump grinders and wood chippers. We'll see," she says in a threatening way. "If you want any further information from me, you'll have to get a court order or permission from the patient."

"Rather difficult to get permission from someone who's vanished."

Dr. Self hangs up and walks out into the bright, hot morning, heading with purpose toward the men in white shirts that on closer inspection have a logo on the front, the same logo that is on their caps. In bold black print on the back of the shirts is Florida Department of Agriculture and Consumer Services. One inspector holds a PDA, and is doing something with it while the other inspector talks on his cell phone.

"Excuse me," Dr. Self says aggressively. "May I help you?"

"Good morning. We're Department of Agriculture citrus inspectors," the man with the PDA says.

"I can see who you are," Dr. Self says, unsmiling.

Each of them wears a green badge with his photograph, but Dr. Self doesn't have her glasses on and can't read their names.

"We rang the bell and didn't think anyone was home."

"So you just walk on my property and help yourselves?" Dr. Self says.

"We're allowed to enter open yards, and, like I said, we didn't think anyone was home. We rang the bell several times."

"I can't hear the bell from my office," she says, as if it's their fault.

"We apologize. But we need to inspect your trees and didn't realize inspectors have already been here . . ."

"You've already been here. So you admit you've trespassed before."

"Not us specifically. What I mean is we've not inspected your property before, but someone has. Even if there's no record of it," the inspector with the PDA says to Dr. Self.

"Ma'am, did you paint these stripes?"

Dr. Self looks blankly at the stripes on her trees.

"Why would I do that? I assumed you put them there."

"No, ma'am. They were already here. You mean you haven't noticed them before now?"

"Of course I've noticed them."

"If you don't mind my asking, when?"

"Several days ago. I'm not sure."

"What it indicates is your trees are infected with citrus canker and will have to be removed. That they've been infected for years."

"For years?"

"They should have been removed long before now," the other inspector explains.

"What on earth are you talking about?"

"We stopped painting red stripes a couple years ago. Use orange tape now. So someone marked your trees for eradication and it looks like no one ever got around to it. I don't understand that, but in fact, these trees do show signs of canker."

"Not old canker, though."

"Ma'am, you didn't get a notice, a green notice that indicates we found symptoms and instructs you to call a one-eight-hundred number? No one showed you something like a specimen report?"

"I've got no idea what you're talking about," Dr. Self says, and she thinks of the anonymous phone call she got yesterday evening right after Marino left. "And it really does look like my trees are infected?"

She steps closer to a grapefruit tree. It is heavy with fruit and looks healthy to her. She leans close to a branch as an inspector's gloved finger points out several leaves that have pale lesions on them, scarcely noticeable ones shaped like fans.

"See these areas?" he explains. "They indicate recent infection. Maybe just a few weeks. But they're peculiar."

"I don't get it," the other inspector says. "If the red stripes are to be believed, you should be seeing dieback and fruit drop, should be able to count the rings to see how long ago. You know, there's four or five flushes a year, so you count rings . . ."

"I really don't give a damn about counting rings and fruit drop! What are you saying?" she exclaims.

"I was just thinking that. If the stripes were painted a couple years ago . . . ?"

"Man, I'm stumped."

"You trying to be funny?" Dr. Self yells at him. "Because I don't think any of this is funny." She looks at the pale, fan-shaped lesions and keeps thinking of yesterday's anonymous phone call. "Why did you come here today?"

"Well, that's what's kind of strange about this," the inspector with the PDA replies. "We've got no record of your trees already being inspected and quarantined and scheduled for eradication. I don't understand. Everything's supposed to be registered in the computer. The lesions on your leaves are peculiar. See?"

He holds one out, shows her, and she looks at the odd fan-shaped lesion again.

"They don't normally look like that. We need to get a pathologist out here."

"Why my damn yard today?" she demands to know.

"We received a phone tip that your trees might be infected, but . . ."

"A phone tip? From whom?"

"Someone doing yard work in the area."

"This is crazy. I have a yard man. He's never said anything to me about something being wrong with my trees. None of this is making any sense. No wonder the public is infuriated. You people don't know what the hell you're doing, just barge into people's private property and can't even keep it straight which damn trees to cut down."

"Ma'am, I know how you feel. But the canker's not a joke. If we don't deal with it, there won't be any citrus trees left . . ."

"I want to know who called."

"We don't know that, ma'am. We'll get it straightened out, and we certainly apologize for the inconvenience. We'd like to explain your options. When's a good time to come back? Will you be around later in the day? We'll get a pathologist to look."

"You can tell your damn pathologists and supervisors and whoever that they've not heard the last from me about this. Do you know who I am?"

"No, ma'am."

"Turn on your damn radio today at noon. *Talk It Out* with Dr. Self."

"You're kidding. That's you?" one of the inspectors, the one with the PDA, asks, impressed, as he ought to be. "I listen to you all the time."

"I also have a new TV show. ABC, tomorrow at one-thirty. Every Thursday," she says, suddenly pleased and feeling a bit more charitable toward them.

The scraping sound beyond the broken window sounds like someone digging. Ev breathes shallowly, rapidly, her arms raised above her head. She breathes shallow, rapid breaths and listens.

It seems she heard the same noise days ago. She doesn't remember when. Maybe it was at night. She listens to a shovel, someone plunging a shovel into the dirt behind the house. She shifts her position on the mattress, and her ankles and wrists throb as if someone is beating them and her shoulders burn. She is hot and thirsty. She can barely think and probably has a fever. The infections are bad and every tender place burns unbearably, and she can't lower her arms, not unless she stands.

She will die. If he doesn't kill her first, she will die anyway. The house is silent, and she knows the rest of them are gone.

Whatever he did to them, they aren't here anymore.

She knows it now.

"Water," she tries to call out.

Words well up inside her and disintegrate in the air like bubbles. She talks in bubbles. They float up and vanish without a sound in the hot, foul air.

"Please, oh please," and her words go nowhere and she begins to cry.

She sobs and tears fall on the ruined green robe in her lap.
She sobs as if something has happened, something final, like
a destiny she never could have imagined, and she stares at
the dark spots her tears make on her ruined green robe, the
splendid robe she wore when she preached. Beneath it is the
small pink shoe, a left shoe, Keds. She feels the little girl's
pink shoe against her thigh, but her arms are raised and she
can't hold it or hide it better, and her sorrow deepens.

She listens to the digging beyond her window and begins
to smell the stench.

The longer the digging goes on, the worse the stench gets
inside her room, but it is a different stench, a dreadful
stench, the acrid, putrid stench of something dead.

Take me home, she prays to God. *Please take me home.
Show me.*

She manages to get on her knees, to kneel, and the sound
of the digging stops, then starts again, then stops. She sways,
almost falls, willing herself to stand, struggles and falls and
tries again, sobbing, and then she is on her feet and the pain
is so awful, she sees black. She takes a deep breath and the
blackness passes.

Show me, she prays.

The ropes are thin white nylon. One is tied to the coat
hanger bent and twisted around her inflamed, swollen wrists.
When she stands, the rope is slack. When she sits, her arms
are raised over her head. She can't lie down anymore. His
latest cruelty, shortening the rope, forcing her to stand as
much as she can, leaning against the wooden wall until she
can't stay on her feet any longer and she sits and her arms go
straight up. His latest cruelty, making her cut off her hair,
then shortening the rope.

She looks up at the rafter, at the ropes over it, one tied to
the coat hanger that binds her wrists, the other to the coat
hanger bent around her ankles.

Show me. Please God.

The digging stops and the stench blots the light out of the
room and stings her eyes, and she knows what the stench is.

They're gone. She is the only one left.

She looks up at the rope tied to the coat hanger around her wrists. If she stands, the rope is slack enough to loop once around her neck and she smells the stench and knows what it is and she prays again and loops the rope once around her neck and her legs go out from under her.

43

The air is thick and wavy like water and slaps hard, but the V-Rod doesn't wobble or seem stressed as Lucy grips the leather seat with her thighs and pushes the speed up to one hundred and twenty miles an hour. She keeps her head low, her elbows tucked in like a jockey as she tests her latest acquisition around the track.

The morning is bright and unseasonably hot, any vestige of yesterday's storms gone. She eases back the throttle at thirteen thousand nine hundred rpms, satisfied that the Harley with its larger cams, pistons and rear sprocket, and souped-up Engine Control Module can scorch the pavement when needed, but she doesn't want to push her luck for long. At even a hundred and ten, she is going faster than she can see, and that isn't a good habit. Outside her pristinely maintained track are public roads, and at such high speeds, the slightest surface damage or debris can prove deadly.

"What's it doing?" Marino's voice sounds inside her full face helmet.

"What it should," she replies, dropping back to eighty, lightly pushing the handlebars, swerving around small, bright-orange cones.

"Damn it's quiet. Can hardly hear it up here," Marino says from the control tower.

It's supposed to be quiet, she thinks. The V-Rod is a Harley that's quiet, a race bike that looks like a road bike and doesn't draw attention to itself. Leaning back in the seat, she eases her speed to sixty and with her thumb tightens the friction screw to hold the throttle in a loose version of cruise control. She leans into a curve and pulls a forty-caliber Glock pistol out of a holster built into the right thigh of her black ballistic pants.

"Nobody down range," she transmits.
"You're clear."
"Okay. Pop 'em."

From the control tower, Marino watches Lucy sweep around the tight curve at the north end of the mile-long track.

He scans the high earthworks, scans the blue sky, the grassy firing ranges, the road that cuts through the middle of the grounds, then the hangar and runway about half a mile away. He makes sure no personnel, vehicles or aircraft are in the area. When the track is hot, nothing is allowed within a mile of it. Even the airspace is restricted.

He experiences a mixture of emotions when he watches Lucy. Her fearlessness and abundant skills impress him. He loves her and resents her, and a part of him would prefer not to care about her at all. In one important way, she's like her aunt, makes him feel unacceptable to the sort of women he secretly likes but doesn't have the courage to pursue. He watches Lucy speed around the track, maneuvering her new hot-rod bike as if it is part of her and he thinks about Scarpetta on her way to the airport, on her way to see Benton.

"Going hot in five," he says into the mic.

Beyond the glass, Lucy's black figure on the sleek, black bike speeds smoothly, almost silently. Marino detects her right arm move as she holds the pistol close in, her elbow tucked in to her waist so the wind doesn't rip the weapon out of her hand. He watches seconds tick off on the digital clock built into the console and at the count of five presses the button for Zone Two. On the east side of the track, small, round, metal targets pop up and quickly fall back in loud, flat clanks as forty-caliber rounds bite into them. Lucy doesn't miss. She makes it look easy.

"Long range on base," her voice fills his headset.
"Downwind?"
"Roger."

His **footsteps** are loud and excited as he walks quickly down the hallways. He can hear what he feels in the way his booted feet move over the scarred old wood, and he carries the shotgun. He carries the shoebox that holds the airbrush, the red paint and the stencil.

He is prepared.

"Now you'll say you're sorry," he says to the open doorway at the end of the hall. "Now you get what you deserve," he says as he walks quickly and loudly.

He walks into the stench. It is like a wall when he walks through the doorway, worse than out by the pit. Inside the room, the air doesn't stir and the dead stench has nowhere to go and he stares, shocked.

This can't have happened.

How could God let this happen!

He hears God in the hallway and she flows into the doorway, shaking her head at him.

"I prepared!" he yells.

God looks at her, the one hanged who went unpunished and shakes her head. It is Hog's fault, he is stupid, he didn't foresee it, should have made sure it couldn't happen.

She didn't say she was sorry, they all do in the end when the barrel is in their mouth, talk around it, try to, *I'm sorry. Please. I'm sorry.*

God disappears from the doorway, leaves him with his error and the girl's pink sneaker on the stained mattress and he begins to shake inside, shake with a rage so powerful he doesn't know what to do with it.

He screams as he strides across the floor, the filthy floor, sticky and foul with her piss and shit, and he kicks her lifeless, disgusting, naked body as hard as he can. She jerks with each kick. She sways from the rope around her neck, angled up to her left ear, and her tongue protrudes as if she is mocking him, her face bluish deep red as if she is yelling at him. Her weight rests on her knees on the mattress, and her head is bent, as if she is praying to her God, her bound arms straight up, her hands together, as if she is celebrating victory.

Yes! Yes! She sways from her rope, victorious, the little pink shoe next to her.

"Shut up!" he screams.

He kicks and kicks with his big boots until his legs are too tired to kick anymore.

He slams and slams her with the stock of the shotgun until his arms are too tired to slam anymore.

44

Marino waits to activate a series of human-shaped targets that will flip up from behind bushes, a fence and a tree on the base curve, or Dead Man's Curve, as Lucy calls it.

He checks the blaze-orange wind sock center field, verifying that the wind is still out of the east and gusting at maybe five knots. He watches Lucy's right arm holster the Glock and reach back to an oversized leather saddlebag as she glides at a steady speed of sixty miles an hour around the crosswind curve, entering the downwind straightaway.

She smoothly pulls out a nine-millimeter Beretta Cx4 Storm carbine.

"Going hot on five," he says.

Sculpted of a nonreflective black polymer, with the same telescoping bolt used in an Uzi submachine gun, the Storm is a passion of Lucy's. It weighs less than six pounds, has a pistol-grip stock that makes it easy to handle, and ejection can be altered from left to right. So it is nimble and no-nonsense, and when Marino goes active on Zone Three, Lucy rolls in and brass cartridge cases flash in the sun, flying behind her. She kills everything on Dead Man's Curve, kills everything more than once. Marino counts fifteen rounds fired. All targets are down, and she has one round left.

He thinks about the woman named Stevie. He thinks about Lucy meeting her tonight at Deuce. The 617 phone number Stevie gave Lucy belongs to a guy in Concord, Massachusetts, a guy named Doug. He says several days ago he was in a bar in Ptown and lost his cell phone. He says he hasn't cancelled the number yet because some lady apparently found his phone, called one of the numbers in it, ended up talking to one of Doug's friends, who then gave her Doug's home number. She called, said she'd found his cell phone, promised to mail it to him.

So far she hasn't.

It's a slick trick, Marino thinks. If you find or steal a cell phone and promise to send it to the owner, maybe he doesn't get his electronic security identification number deactivated right away and you can use his phone for a while, until the person gets wise. What Marino doesn't quite understand is why Stevie, whoever she is, would go to all the trouble. If her reasoning was to avoid having an account with a cellular company such as Verizon or Sprint, why not just get a pay-as-you-go phone?

Whoever Stevie is, she's trouble. Lucy is living far too close to the edge these days, has been for the better part of a year. She's changed. She's gotten inattentive and indifferent, and at times Marino wonders if she's trying to hurt herself, hurt herself badly.

"Another car has just sped up from behind," he radios her. "You're history."

"I'm reloaded."

"No way." He can't believe it.

Somehow, she has managed to drop out the empty magazine and slide in a new one without him noticing.

She slows the bike to a stop below the control tower. He sets his headphones on the console, and by the time he gets down the wooden stairs, she has her helmet and gloves off and is unzipping her jacket.

"How'd you do that?" he asks.

"I cheated."

"I knew it."

He squints in the sun and wonders where he left his sunglasses, new ones, Ray-Bans. He seems to be misplacing things a lot these days.

"I had an extra magazine here." She pats a pocket.

"Huh. You probably wouldn't in real life. So yeah, you cheated."

"He who survives writes the rules."

"What's your thinking about the Z-Rod, about turning all of them into Z-Rods?" he asks, and he knows what she thinks about it, but he asks anyway, hoping she's changed her mind.

It doesn't make sense to increase the engine some thirteen percent, from an already enhanced 1150cc's to 1318cc's, and an already beefed-up breaking horsepower of 120 to 170, so the bike can rocket from 0 to 140 miles per hour in 9.4 seconds. The more weight the bike loses, the better it will perform, but it would mean replacing the leather seat and rear fender with molded fiberglass and losing the saddlebags, and they can't lose those. He hopes Lucy isn't interested in butchering their new fleet of Special Op bikes. He hopes that for once, what she has is enough.

"Impractical and unnecessary," she surprises him by saying. "A Z-Rod engine only lasts ten thousand miles, so imagine the maintenance headaches, and we strip these things down, it's going to call attention to them. Not to mention how much louder they'll be because of the increased air intake."

"Now what," he says with a huff as his cell phone rings. "Yeah," he answers it gruffly.

He listens for a moment, then ends the call and says "shit" before he tells Lucy, "They're going to start processing the station wagon. Can you get started without me at the Simister house?"

"Don't worry about it. I'll have Lex meet me."

Lucy unclips a two-way radio from her waistband and gets on the air, "Zero-zero-one to the stable."

"What can I do for you, zero-zero-one?"

"Gas up my horse. I'm taking her on the street."

"She need a bigger burr under her saddle?"

"She'll do just fine the way she is."

"Good to hear. Be right there."

"We'll head out to South Beach around nine," Lucy says to Marino. "I'll meet you there."

"Maybe it's better we go together," he says, looking at her, trying to figure out what's in her mind.

He never can, not that mind. If she were any more complicated, he'd need an interpreter.

"We can't run the risk she might see us in the same car," Lucy says, pulling off her ballistic jacket, complaining that the sleeves are like Chinese handcuffs.

"Maybe it's some kind of cult thing," Marino says. "Some cult like a bunch of witches that paint red hands all over themselves. Salem's up there in the same part of the world. All kinds of witches up there."

"Witches are by the coven, not the bunch." Lucy pokes him in the shoulder.

"Maybe she's one of them," he says. "Maybe your new friend is a witch who steals cell phones."

"Maybe I'll just come right out and ask her," Lucy says.

"You should be careful about people. That's the only thing with you, your judgment about who you hook up with. I wish you'd be more careful."

"I guess we share the same dysfunction. Your judgment in that department seems to be almost as good as mine. Aunt Kay says Reba's really nice and you were a dick to her at the Simister scene, by the way."

"The Doc better not have said that. She better not have said nothing."

"She didn't say just that. She also said Reba's smart, new on the job, but smart. Not as dumb as a bag of hammers and all those other clichés you like so much."

"Bullshit."

"She must be the one you were dating for a while," Lucy says.

"Who told you?" Marino blurts out.

"You just did."

45

Lucy has a macroadenoma. Her pituitary gland, which hangs by a threadlike stalk from the hypothalamus at the base of the brain, has a tumor.

The normal pituitary is about the size of a pea. It is referred to as the Master Gland because it transmits signals to the thyroid, the adrenals and ovaries or testes, controlling their production of hormones that dramatically affect metabolism, blood pressure, reproduction and other vital functions. Lucy's tumor measures approximately twelve millimeters, or approximately half an inch, in diameter. It's benign but won't go away on its own. Her symptoms are headaches and an overproduction of prolactin, resulting in unpleasant symptoms that mimic pregnancy. For now, she controls her condition with drug therapy that is supposed to lower prolactin levels and shrink the tumor in size. Her response hasn't been ideal. She hates taking her medication and isn't consistent with it. Eventually, she might have to have surgery.

Scarpetta parks at Signature, the FBO at the Fort Lauderdale airport where Lucy hangars her jet. She gets out and meets the pilots inside as she thinks about Benton, not sure she'll ever forgive him, so sick with hurt and anger that her heart is racing and her hands are shaking.

"There are still a few snow showers up there," Bruce, the pilot in command, says. "We should be in the air about two hours twenty. We have a decent headwind."

"I know you didn't want catering, but we've got a cheese tray," his copilot says. "Do you have baggage?"

"No," she says.

Lucy's pilots don't wear uniforms. They are specially trained agents of her own design, don't drink or smoke or do

any kind of drugs, are very fit and trained in personal protection. They escort Scarpetta out to the tarmac where the Citation X waits like a big, white bird with a belly. It reminds her
of Lucy's belly, of what's happened to her.

Inside the jet, she settles into the large leather seat, and
when the pilots are busy in the cockpit, she calls Benton.

"I'll be there by one, one fifteen," she says to him.

"Please try to understand, Kay. I know what you
must feel."

"We'll talk about it when I get there."

"We never leave things like this," he says.

It's the rule, the old adage. Never let the sun go down on
your wrath, never get into a car or a plane or walk out of the
house when you're angry. If anybody knows how quickly
and randomly tragedy can strike, he and Scarpetta do.

"Fly safe," Benton says to her. "I love you."

Lex and Reba are walking around the outside of the
house as if looking for something. They stop looking when
Lucy makes her conspicuous entrance into Daggie Simister's driveway.

She kills the engine of the V-Rod, takes off her black,
full-face helmet and unzips her black ballistic jacket.

"You look like Darth Vader," Lex says cheerfully.

Lucy's never known anybody so chronically happy. Lex
is a find, and the Academy wasn't about to let her go after
she graduated. She's bright, careful and knows when to get
out of the way.

"What are we looking for out here?" Lucy asks, scanning
the small yard.

"The fruit trees over there," Lex replies. "Not that I'm a
detective. But when we were at the other house where those
people disappeared"—she indicates the pale orange house
on the other side of the waterway—"Dr. Scarpetta said
something about a citrus inspector over here. She said he
was examining trees in the area, maybe in the yard next
door. And you can't see it from here, but some of the trees

over there have these same red stripes." She again points to the pale orange house on the other side of the water.

"Of course, the canker spreads like crazy. If trees are infected here, I suppose a lot of trees in the area might be, too. I'm Reba Wagner, by the way," she says to Lucy. "You've probably heard about me from Pete Marino."

Lucy looks her in the eye. "What might I have heard if he's talked about you?"

"How mentally challenged I am."

"Mentally challenged might stretch his vocabulary to the point of injury. He probably said retarded."

"There you have it."

"Let's go in," Lucy says, heading to the front porch. "Let's see what you missed the first time," she says to Reba, "since you're so mentally challenged."

"She's kidding," Lex says to Reba, picking up the black crime-scene case she parked by the front door. "Before we do anything else"—she directs this to Reba—"I want to verify the house has been sealed since you guys cleared the scene."

"Absolutely. I saw to it personally. All the windows and doors."

"An alarm system?"

"You'd be amazed how many people down here don't have them."

Lucy notices stickers on windows that say H&W Alarm Company and comments, "She was worried, anyway. Probably couldn't afford the real thing but still wanted to scare away bad people."

"Problem is, the bad guys know that trick," Reba replies. "Stickers and signs in the flower beds. Your typical burglar would take one look at this house and figure it probably doesn't have an alarm system. That the person inside probably can't afford it or is too old to bother."

"A lot of elderly people don't bother, it's true," Lucy says. "For one thing, they forget their codes. I'm serious."

Reba opens the door and musty air greets them as if the life inside fled long ago. She reaches in and flips on lights.

"What's anybody done about it so far?" Lex says, looking at the terrazzo floor.

"Nothing except in the bedroom."

"Okay, let's just stand out here a minute and think about this," Lucy says. "We know two things. Her killer somehow got inside the house without breaking down a door. And after he shot her, he somehow left. Also through a door?" she asks Reba.

"I'd say so. She's got all these jalousie windows. No way to climb through them unless you're Gumby."

"Then what we should do is start spraying at this door and work our way back to the bedroom where she was killed," Lucy says. "Then we'll do the same thing at all the other doors. Triangulating."

"That would be this door, the kitchen door and the sliders leading from the dining room to the sunporch and on the sunporch itself," Reba tells them. "Both sets of the sliders were unlocked when Pete got here, so he says."

They put on their disposable clothing. Reba steps inside the foyer, and Lucy and Lex follow. They shut the door.

"We ever find out any other details about the citrus inspector you and Dr. Scarpetta happened to notice around the time this lady was shot?" Lucy asks, and on the job, she never refers to Scarpetta as her aunt.

"I found out a couple things. First, they work in pairs. The person we saw was alone."

"How do you know his partner wasn't out of sight? Maybe in the front yard?" Lucy asks.

"We don't. But all we saw was this one person. And there's no record any inspectors were even supposed to be in this neighborhood. Another thing, he was using one of those pickers, you know, the long pole with a claw or whatever so you can pull down fruit from high up in the tree? From what I've been told, inspectors don't use anything like that."

"What would be the point?" Lucy asks.

"He took it apart, put it in a big black bag."

"I wonder what else was in the bag," Lex says.

"Like a shotgun," Reba says.

"We'll keep an open mind," Lucy says.

"I'd say it's a big fuck-you," Reba adds. "I'm in plain view on the other side of the water. A cop. I'm with Dr. Scarpetta and obviously we're looking around, investigating, and he's right there looking at us, pretending to examine trees."

"Possibly, but we can't be sure," Lucy replies. "Let's keep an open mind," she reminds them again.

Lex crouches on the cool terrazzo floor and opens the crime-scene case. They close all the blinds in the house, then Lucy sets up the tripod, attaches the camera and the cable release, while Lex mixes up the luminol and transfers it to a black pump spray bottle. They photograph the area just inside the front door, then lights out, and they get lucky on their first try.

"Holy smoke," Reba's voice sounds in the dark.

The distinct shape of footprints glow bluish-green as Lex mists the floor and Lucy captures it on film.

"He must have had a hell of a lot of blood on his shoes to leave this much after walking all the way across the house," Reba says.

"Except for one thing," Lucy replies in the dark. "They're heading in the wrong direction. They're coming in instead of leaving."

46

He looks grim but fantastic in a long, black suede coat, his silver hair peeking out of a Red Sox baseball cap. Whenever Scarpetta hasn't seen Benton for a while, she is struck by his refined handsomeness, by his long, lean elegance. She doesn't want to be angry with him. She can't stand it. She feels sick.

"As always, we enjoyed flying with you. Just call when you know exactly when you're leaving," Bruce the pilot says to her, warmly shaking her hand. "Get in touch if you need anything. You've got all my numbers, right?"

"Thanks, Bruce," Scarpetta says.

"Sorry you had to wait," he says to Benton. "A headwind that got more wicked."

Benton isn't the least bit friendly. He doesn't answer him. He watches him walk off.

"Let me guess," Benton says to Scarpetta. "Another triathlete who decided to play cops and robbers. The one thing I hate about flying on her jet. Her musclehead pilots."

"I feel very safe with them."

"Well, I don't."

She buttons her wool coat as they walk out of the FBO.

"I hope he didn't try to chat with you too much, bother you. He strikes me as the type," he says.

"It's nice to see you, too, Benton," she says, walking one step ahead of him.

"I happen to know you don't think it's nice at all."

He picks up his pace, holds the glass front door for her, and the wind rushing in is cold and carries small flakes of snow. The day is dark gray, so dusky that lights in the parking lot have come on.

"She gets these guys, all of them good-looking and ad-

dicted to the gym, and they think they're action heroes,"
he says.

"You made your point. Are you trying to pick a fight before I have a chance?"

"It's important you notice certain things, don't assume
someone's just being friendly. I worry you don't pick up important signals."

"That's ridiculous," she replies, anger sounding in her
voice. "If anything, I pick up too many signals. Although I
obviously missed some pretty important ones this past year.
You want a fight, now you've got it."

They are walking through the snowy parking lot, and the
lamps along the tarmac are blurred by the snow and sound is
muted. Usually, they hold hands. She wonders how he could
have done what he did. Her eyes water. Maybe it is the wind.

"I'm worried who's out there," he says oddly, unlocking
his Porsche, this one a four-wheel-drive SUV.

Benton likes his cars. He and Lucy are into power. The
difference is, Benton knows he's powerful. Lucy doesn't feel
she is.

"Worried in general?" Scarpetta asks, assuming he's still
talking about all the signals she supposedly misses.

"I'm talking about whoever just murdered this lady up
here. NIBIN got a hit on a shotgun shell that appears to have
been fired by the same shotgun used in a homicide in Hollywood two years ago. A convenience-store robbery. The guy
was wearing a mask, killed a kid in the store and then the
manager killed him. Sound familiar?"

He looks over at her as they talk, as they drive away from
the airport.

"I've heard about it," she replies. "Seventeen years old,
armed with nothing but a mop. Anybody have a clue as to
why that shotgun's back in circulation?" she asks as her resentment grows.

"Not yet."

"A lot of shotgun deaths recently," she says, coolly pro-
fessionally.

If he wants to be this way, she can too.

"I wonder what that's about," she adds in a detached sort

of way. "The one used in the Johnny Swift case disappears—now one is used in the Daggie Simister case."

She has to explain to him the Daggie Simister case. He doesn't know about it yet.

"A shotgun that is supposed to be in custody or destroyed is just used again up here," she goes on. "Then we have the Bible in the house of these missing people."

"What Bible and what missing people?"

She has to explain that to him, tell him about the anonymous call from someone who referred to himself as Hog. She has to tell him about the centuries-old Bible inside the house of the women and boys who have vanished, that it was open to the Wisdom of Solomon, that the verse is the same one this man called Hog recited to Marino over the phone.

Therefore unto them, as to children without the use of reason, thou dids't send a judgment to mock them.

"Marked with X's in pencil," she says. "The Bible printed in 1756."

"Unusual they would have one that old."

"There were no other old books like that in the house. According to Detective Wagner. You don't know her. People who worked with them at the church say they've never seen the Bible before."

"Checked it for prints, for DNA?"

"No prints. No DNA."

"Any theories about what might have happened to them?" he asks, as if the sole reason for her racing here on a private jet was to discuss their work.

"Nothing good," and her resentment grows.

He knows almost nothing about what her life has been like of late.

"Evidence of foul play?"

"We've got a lot to do at the labs. They're in overdrive," she says. "I found earprints outside a slider in the master bedroom. Someone had his ear pressed up against the glass."

"Maybe one of the boys."

"It's not," she says, getting angrier. "We got their DNA, or presumably it's their DNA, from clothing, their toothbrushes, a prescription bottle."

"I don't exactly consider earprints good forensic science. There have been a number of wrongful convictions because of earprints."

"Like a polygraph, it's a tool," she almost snaps.

"I'm not arguing with you, Kay."

"DNA from an earprint the same way we get DNA from fingerprints," she says. "We've already run that and it's unknown, doesn't appear to be anybody who lived in the house. Nothing in CODIS. I've asked our friends at DNAPrint Genomics in Sarasota to test for gender and ancestral inference or racial affiliation. Unfortunately, that will take days. I don't really give a damn about matching someone's ear to an earprint."

Benton doesn't say a word.

"Do you have anything to eat in the house? And I need a drink. I don't care if it's the middle of the day. And I need us to talk about something besides work. I didn't fly up here in a snowstorm to talk about work."

"It's not a snowstorm yet," Benton says somberly. "But it will be."

She stares out her window as he drives toward Cambridge.

"I have plenty of food in the house. And whatever you want to drink," he says quietly.

He says something else. She's not sure she heard it correctly. What she thinks she heard can't be right.

"I'm sorry. What did you just say?" she asks, startled.

"If you want out, I'd rather you tell me now."

"If I want out?" She looks at him, incredulous. "Is that all it takes, Benton? We have a major disagreement and should discuss ending our relationship?"

"I'm just giving you the option."

"I don't need you to give me anything."

"I didn't mean you need my permission. I just don't see how it can work if you don't trust me anymore."

"Maybe you're right." She fights back tears, turns her face away from him, looks out at the snow.

"So you're saying you don't trust me anymore."

"What if I had done it to you?"

"I would be very upset," he replies. "But I'd try to understand why. Lucy has a right to her privacy, a legal right. The only reason I know about the tumor is because she told me she was having a problem and wondered if I could arrange for her to be scanned at McLean, if I could make sure nobody knew, could keep it absolutely quiet. She didn't want to make an appointment at some hospital somewhere. You know how she is. Especially these days."

"I used to know how she is."

"Kay." He glances over at her. "She didn't want a record. Nothing's private anymore, not since the Patriot Act."

"Well, I can't argue with that."

"You have to assume your medical records, prescription drugs, bank accounts, shopping habits, everything private about your life might be looked at by the Feds, all in the name of stopping terrorists. Her controversial past career with the FBI and ATF is a realistic concern. She doesn't trust that they won't find out anything they can about her, and she ends up audited by the IRS, on a no-fly list, accused of insider trading, scandalized in the news, God knows what."

"What about you and your not-so-pleasant past with the FBI?"

He shrugs, driving fast. A light snow swirls and seems to barely touch the glass.

"There's not much else they can do to me," he says. "Truth is, I'd probably be a waste of their time. I'm much more worried about who's running around with a shotgun that's supposed to be in the custody of the Hollywood police or destroyed."

"What is Lucy doing about her prescription drugs? If she's so anxious about leaving any sort of paper or electronic trail."

"She should be anxious. She's not delusional. They can get hold of pretty much anything they want—and are. Even if it requires a court order, what do you suppose happens in reality if the FBI wants a court order from a judge who just so happens to have been appointed by the current administration? A judge who worries about the consequences if he doesn't cooperate? Do I need to paint about fifty possible scenarios for you?"

"America used to be a nice place to live."

"We've handled everything we can in-house for Lucy," he says.

He goes on and on about McLean, assures her that Lucy couldn't have come to a better place, that if nothing else, McLean has access to the finest doctors and scientists in the country, in the world. Nothing he says makes her feel better.

They are in Cambridge now, passing the splendid antique mansions of Brattle Street.

"She hasn't had to go through the normal channels for anything, including her meds. There's no record unless somebody makes a mistake or is indiscreet," Benton is saying.

"Nothing's infallible. Lucy can't spend the rest of her life paranoid that people are going to find out she has a brain tumor and is on some type of dopamine agonist to keep it under control. Or that she's had surgery, if it comes to that."

It is hard for her to say it. No matter the statistical fact that surgical extraction of pituitary tumors is almost always successful, there is a chance something can go wrong.

"It's not cancer," Benton says. "If it were, I probably would have told you no matter what she said."

"She's my niece. I raised her like a daughter. It's not your right to decide what constitutes a serious threat to her health."

"You know better than anyone that pituitary tumors aren't uncommon. Studies show that approximately twenty percent of the population has incidental pituitary tumors."

"Depending on who's surveying. Ten percent. Twenty percent. I don't give a damn about statistics."

"I'm sure you've seen them in autopsies. People never even knew they had them—a pituitary tumor isn't why they ended up in your morgue."

"Lucy knows she has it. And the percentages are based on people who had micro—not macro—adenomas and were asymptomatic. Lucy's tumor on her last scan was twelve millimeters, and she's not asymptomatic. She has to take medication to lower her abnormally high levels of prolactin, and she may have to be on the medication the rest of her life unless she has the tumor removed. I know you're well aware of the risks, the very least of which is the surgery won't be successful and the tumor will still be there."

Benton turns into his driveway, points a remote and opens the door of the detached garage, a carriage house in an earlier century. Neither of them talks as he pulls the SUV in next to his other powerful Porsche and shuts the door. They walk to the side entrance of his antique house, a dark-red brick Victorian just off Harvard Square.

"Who is Lucy's doctor?" she asks, stepping inside the kitchen.

"Nobody at the moment."

She stares at him as he takes off his coat and neatly drapes it over a chair.

"She doesn't have a doctor? You can't be serious. What the hell have you people been doing with her up here?" she says, fighting her way out of her coat and angrily throwing it on a chair.

He opens an oak cabinet and lifts out a bottle of single-malt Scotch and two tumblers. He fills them with ice.

"The explanation's not going to make you feel any better," he says. "Her doctor's dead."

The Academy's forensic evidence bay is a hangar with three garage doors that open onto an access road that leads to a second hangar where Lucy keeps helicopters, motorcycles, armored Humvees, speedboats and a hot-air balloon.

Reba knows Lucy has helicopters and motorcycles. Everybody knows that. But Reba isn't so sure she believes what Marino said about the rest of what's supposed to be in that hangar. She's suspicious he was setting her up as a joke, a joke that wouldn't have been funny because it would have made her look stupid if she believed him and went around repeating what he said. He has lied to her plenty. He said he liked her. He said sex with her was the best ever. He said no matter what, they would always be friends. None of it was true.

She met him several months back when she was still in the

motorcycle unit and he showed up one day on the Softail he
rode before he got his tricked-out Deuce. She had just parked
her Road King by the back entrance of the police department
when she heard his loud pipes, and there he was.

Trade ya, he said, swinging his leg over the seat like a
cowboy getting off his horse.

He hitched up his jeans and walked over to inspect her
bike as she was locking it and getting a few items out of
the saddlebags.

I bet you would, she replied.

How many times you dropped that thing?

None.

*Huh. Well there's only two types of riders. Those who've
dropped their bikes and those who will.*

There's a third kind, she said, feeling rather good about
herself in her uniform and tall, black leather boots. *The one
who's dropped it and lies about it.*

Well, that ain't me.

That's not what I hear, she said, and she was teasing him,
flirting a little. *The story I hear is you forgot to put down the
kickstand at the gas pumps.*

Bullshit.

*I also hear you were doing a poker run and forgot to un-
lock your front fork before you headed off to the next bar.*

That's the biggest crock I ever heard.

*How about the time you hit the kill switch instead of your
right turn signal?*

He started laughing and asked her to ride to Miami and
have lunch at Monty Trainer's on the water. They rode quite
a few times after that, once to Key West, flying like birds
along U.S. 1 and crossing the water as if they could walk on
it, the old Flagler railway bridges to the west, a storm-
battered monument to a romantic past when South Florida
was a tropical paradise of Art Deco hotels, Jackie Gleason
and Hemingway—not all at the same time, of course.

All was fine until not even a month ago, right after she
got promoted to the detective division. He started avoiding
sex. He got weird about it. She worried it had to do with her
promotion, worried maybe he didn't find her attractive any-

more. Men had gotten tired of her in the past, why wouldn't it happen again? Their relationship fractured for good when they were having dinner at Hooters—not her favorite restaurant, by the way—and somehow got on the topic of Kay Scarpetta.

Half the guys in the police department got the hots for her, Reba said.

Huh, he said, his face changing.

Just like that, he became somebody else.

I wouldn't know anything about it, he said, and he didn't sound like the Marino she had come to like so much.

You know Bobby? she asked, and she now wishes she had kept her mouth shut.

Marino stirred sugar in his coffee. It was the first time she'd seen him do that. He told her he didn't touch sugar anymore.

The first homicide we worked together, she kept talking, *Dr. Scarpetta was there, and when she was getting ready to transport the body to the morgue, Bobby whispered to me, I might just die if I could have her hands all over me. And I said, Good, you die I'll make sure she saws open your skull to see if you really got a brain in there.*

Marino drank his sweetened coffee, looking at some waitress with big tits bending over to take away his salad bowl.

Bobby was talking about Scarpetta, Reba added, not sure he got it, wishing he would laugh or something, anything other than the hard, distant look on his face, watching tits and asses go by. *It was the first time I met her,* Reba talked on nervously, *and I remember thinking maybe you and her were an item. I sure was glad later on to find out it wasn't true.*

You should work all your cases with Bobby. Marino then made a comment that had nothing to do with what she just said. *Until you know what the hell you're doing, you shouldn't handle any case solo. In fact, you probably should transfer out of the detective division. I don't think you realize what you've gotten yourself into. It's not like what you see on TV.*

Reba looks around the bay and feels self-conscious and

useless. It is late afternoon. Forensic scientists have been at work for hours, the gray station wagon up on a hydraulic lift, the windows cloudy from superglue fumes, the carpets already processed and vacuumed. Something lit up on the mat beneath the driver's seat. Maybe blood.

The forensic scientists are collecting trace evidence from the tires, using paintbrushes to sweep dust and dirt from the tread, brushing it off onto sections of white paper they fold and seal with bright-yellow evidence tape. A minute ago, one of the scientists, a pretty young woman, told Reba they don't use metal evidence cans because when they run the trace through the SEM . . .

The what? Reba asked.

A scanning electron microscope with an energy dispersive x-ray system.

Oh, Reba said, and the pretty scientist went on to explain that if you put trace evidence in metal cans and the scan is positive for iron or aluminum, how do you know it's not microscopic particles from the can?

That was a good point, one that would never have occurred to Reba. Most of what they are doing wouldn't occur to her. She feels inexperienced and stupid. She stands off to one side, thinking about Marino telling her she shouldn't work anything solo, about the way his face looked and the way he sounded when he said it. She looks around at the tow truck, at other hydraulic lifts and tables of photography equipment, Mini-Crime scopes, luminescent powders and brushes, trace-evidence vacuums, Tyvek protective clothing, superglue and crime-scene kits that look like big, black tackle boxes. On the far side of the hangar, there is even a sled and crash dummies, and she hears Marino's voice. She hears it as plain as day in her head.

It's not like what you see on TV.

He had no right to say that.

You should probably transfer out of the detective division.

Then she hears his voice and it's real, and she is startled and turns around.

Marino is walking over to the station wagon, walks right past her, a coffee in hand.

"Anything new?" Marino says to the pretty scientist taping up a folded sheet of paper.

He stares at the wagon on the lift, acting as if Reba is a shadow on the wall, a mirage on the highway, something that's nothing.

"Maybe blood inside," the pretty scientist is saying. "Something that reacted to luminol."

"I go to get coffee and look what I miss. What about prints?"

"We haven't opened her up yet. I was getting ready to, don't want to overcook her."

The pretty scientist has long hair, shiny and a deep brown that reminds Reba of a chestnut horse. She has beautiful skin, perfect skin. What Reba wouldn't give to have skin like that, to undo all her years in the Florida sun. There's no point caring anymore, and wrinkled skin looks even worse when it's pale, so she bakes herself. She still does. She looks at the pretty scientist's smooth skin and youthful body and feels like crying.

The living room has fir floors and paneled mahogany doors, and a marble fireplace ready for a fire. Benton crouches before the hearth and lights a match, and wisps of smoke curl up from fatwood kindling.

"Johnny Swift graduated from Harvard Medical School, did a residency at Mass General, a fellowship in the department of neurology at McLean," he says, getting up and returning to the couch. "A couple years ago, he started a practice at Stanford, but he also opened an office in Miami. We referred Lucy to Johnny because he was well known at McLean, was excellent and was accessible to her. He was her neurologist and I think they became pretty good friends."

"She should have told me." Scarpetta still can't grasp it. "We're investigating his case and she keeps something like that to herself?" She keeps repeating herself. "He may have been murdered and she says nothing?"

"He was a candidate for suicide, Kay. I'm not saying he wasn't murdered, but when he was at Harvard, he started having mood disturbances, became an outpatient at McLean, was diagnosed as bipolar, which was controlled with lithium. As I say, he was well known at McLean."

"You don't have to keep justifying that he was qualified and compassionate and not just a random referral."

"He was more than qualified and certainly wasn't a random referral."

"We're investigating his case, a very suspicious case," she says again. "And Lucy can't be honest enough to tell me the truth. How the hell can she be objective?"

Benton drinks Scotch and stares into the fire, and the shadows from the flames play on his face.

"I'm not sure it's relevant. His death has nothing to do with her, Kay."

"And I'm not sure we know that," she says.

47

Reba watches Marino watching the pretty scientist set her paintbrush on a sheet of clean, white paper and open the wagon's driver's door, his eyes wandering all over her.

He stands very close to the pretty scientist as she removes foil packets of superglue from inside the wagon and drops them into an orange biohazard trash can. They are shoulder to shoulder, bent over, looking inside the front, then the back, one side of the wagon, then the other, saying things to each other that Reba can't hear. The pretty scientist laughs at something he says and Reba feels awful.

"I don't see anything on the glass," he says loudly, straightening up.

"Me either."

He squats and looks again at the inside of the door, the one behind the driver's seat. He takes his time as if noticing something.

"Come here," he says to the pretty scientist as if Reba isn't here.

They are standing so close they couldn't fit a piece of that white paper between them.

"Bingo," Marino says. "The metal part here that inserts into the buckle."

"A partial." The pretty scientist looks. "I see some ridge detail."

They don't find any other prints, partial or otherwise, not even smudges, and Marino wonders out loud if the interior of the car has been wiped down.

He doesn't move out of Reba's way as she tries to get close. It's her case. She has a right to see what they're talking about. It's her case, not his. No matter what he thinks of her or says, she's the detective and it's her damn case.

"Excuse me." She says it with authority she doesn't feel. "How about giving me some room." Then, to the pretty scientist, "What did you find on the carpets?"

"Relatively clean, just a little bit of dirt, kind of the way they look when you shake them out or use a vacuum cleaner that doesn't have good suction. Maybe blood, but we'll have to see."

"Then maybe this station wagon was used and returned to the house." Reba talks boldly, and Marino gets that hard look on his face again, that same hard, distant look he had in Hooters. "And it didn't go through any tollbooths after the people disappeared."

"What are you talking about?" Marino finally looks at her.

"We checked out the SunPass but doesn't necessarily mean much." She has information, too. "There's a lot of roads without tollbooths. Maybe it was driven where there aren't tolls."

"That's a big maybe," he says, not looking at her again.

"Nothing wrong with maybes," she replies.

"See how that goes over in court," he says, and he's not going to look at her. "Using maybes. You say maybe and the defense attorney eats you for lunch."

"Nothing wrong with what-ifs, either," she says. "You know, like what if someone or even more than one person abducted these people in this wagon and then later returned it to the driveway, unlocked and partially on the grass? That would be pretty smart, now wouldn't it? If anyone saw the wagon drive away from the house, they weren't going to think it was abnormal. Wouldn't think it abnormal if they saw it drive back, either. And I bet no one saw anything because it was dark."

"I want the trace analyzed right away and the fingerprint run through AFIS." Marino tries to reassert his dominance by sounding like an even bigger bully.

"Sure thing," the pretty scientist says sarcastically. "I'll be right back with my magic box."

"I'm curious," Reba says to her. "Is it true Lucy's got bulletproof Humvees, speedboats and a hot-air balloon in that other hangar over there?"

The pretty scientist laughs, snatches off her gloves, drops them into the trash. "Where the hell did you hear that?"

"Just some jerk," she says.

At seven thirty that night, all the lights are turned off inside Daggie Simister's house and the porch light is off.

Lucy holds the cable release, ready.

"Go," she says, and Lex begins to mist the front porch with luminol.

They couldn't do it earlier. They had to wait until after dark. Footprints glow and fade again, this time more strongly. Lucy takes pictures, then quits.

"What's wrong?" Lex asks.

"I have a funny feeling," Lucy says. "Let me have the spray bottle."

Lex hands it to her.

"What's the most common false positive we get with luminol?" Lucy asks.

"Bleach."

"Try again."

"Copper."

Lucy starts spraying in wide sweeps over the yard, walking and spraying and the grass glows bluish-green, glowing and fading like an eerie luminescent ocean everywhere the luminol touches. She's never seen anything like it.

"Fungicide is the only thing that makes sense," she says. "Copper sprays. What they use on citrus trees to prevent canker. Course, it doesn't work all that well. Witness her blighted trees with their pretty red stripes painted around them," Lucy says.

"Someone walks across her yard and tracks it into the house," Lex replies. "Someone like a citrus inspector."

"We've got to find out who that was," Lucy says.

48

Marino hates the trendy restaurants of South Beach and never parks his Harley anywhere near the lesser bikes, mostly Japanese crotch rockets, that always line the boardwalk at this hour. He cruises slowly and loudly along Ocean Drive, glad his pipes annoy all the cool customers drinking their flavored martinis and wine at their little candlelit outdoor tables.

He stops inches away from the back bumper of a red Lamborghini, pulls in the clutch and rolls the throttle, giving the engine enough gas to remind everybody he's here. The Lamborghini inches forward and Marino inches forward, almost touching the back bumper, and rolls the throttle again, and the Lamborghini inches ahead and Marino does the same. His Harley roars like a mechanical lion, and a bare arm flies out the Lamborghini's open window and a middle finger with a long, red nail flips up.

He smiles as he gooses the throttle again and threads between cars, stopping beside the Lamborghini, peers in at the olive-skinned woman behind the steel-alloy wheel. She looks maybe twenty, is dressed in a denim vest and shorts and not much else. The woman next to her is homely but makes up for it by wearing what looks like a stretchy black Ace bandage around her breasts, and shorts that barely cover what matters.

"How do you type or do housework with those nails?" Marino asks the driver over the roaring and throbbing of big, powerful engines, and he splays his huge hands like cat claws to make his point about her long, red nails, acrylic extenders or whatever they're called.

Her pretty, snooty face stares up at the light, probably desperate for it to turn green so she can blast away from the redneck in black, and she says, "Get away from my car, motherfucker."

She says it in a heavy Hispanic accent.

"Now that ain't no way for a lady to talk," Marino replies. "You just hurt my feelings."

"Go fuck yourself."

"How about I buy you two babes a drink? After that, we'll go dancing."

"Leave us the fuck alone," the driver says.

"I call police!" the one in the black Ace bandage threatens.

He tips his helmet, the one with the bullet hole decals, and rockets ahead of them as the light turns green. He is around the corner on 14th Street before the Lamborghini is even out of first gear, and parks by a meter in front of Tattoo's By Lou and Scooter City, cuts the engine and dismounts his warrior seat. He locks the bike and crosses the street to the oldest bar in South Beach, the only bar he frequents in these parts, Mac's Club Deuce, or what the local clientele simply call Deuce, not to be confused with his Harley Deuce. A two-Deuce night is what he says when he rides his Deuce to Deuce, a dark hole with a black-and-white checkered floor, a pool table and a neon nude over the bar.

Rosie starts pouring him a Budweiser draft. He doesn't have to ask.

"You expecting company?" She slides the tall, foaming glass across the old oak bar.

"You don't know her. You don't know nobody tonight," he gives her the script.

"Ohhhhh-kay." She measures vodka in a water glass for some old guy sitting by himself on a nearby stool. "I don't know anyone in here, least not the two of you. That's fine. Maybe I don't want to know you."

"Don't break my heart," Marino says. "How 'bout putting some lime in it." He pushes the beer back to her.

"Well aren't we fancy tonight." She drops in a few slices. "That how you like it?"

"It's really good."

"Didn't ask if it was good. Asked if that's how you like it."

As usual, the usual locals ignore them. The usuals are slouched on stools on the other side of the bar, glazed as they stare at a baseball game they're not following on the big TV. He doesn't know their names, but they don't need names. There's the fat guy with the goatee, the really fat woman who's always complaining and her boyfriend, who is a third her size and looks like a ferret with yellow teeth. Marino wonders how the hell they fuck and imagines a jockey-sized cowboy flopping like a fish on a bucking bull. All of them smoke. On a two-Deuce night, Marino usually lights up a few, doesn't think about Dr. Self. Whatever goes on in here stays in here.

He carries his beer with lime to the pool table and picks out a stick from the mismatched collection propped in a corner. He racks the balls and stalks around the table, a cigarette hanging out of his mouth, chalking his stick. He squints at ferret, watching him get up from his stool and carry his beer to the men's room. He always does that, afraid someone will swipe his drink. Marino's eyes take in everything and everyone.

A scrawny, homeless-looking man with a scraggly beard, a ponytail, dark, ill-fitting Goodwill clothes, a filthy Miami Dolphins cap and weird pink-tinted glasses walks unsteadily into the bar and pulls up a chair near the door, stuffs a washcloth into the back pocket of his dark, baggy pants. A kid outside on the sidewalk is shaking a broken parking meter that just ate his money.

Marino smacks two solids into side pockets, squinting through cigarette smoke.

"That's right. You keep knocking your balls in the hole," Rosie calls out to him, pouring another beer. "Where you been anyway?"

She is sexy in a hard-ridden way, a little thing nobody in his right mind dares to mess with, no matter how drunk he is. Marino once saw her break a three-hundred-pounder's wrist with a beer bottle when he wouldn't stop grabbing at her ass.

"Quit waiting on everybody and get over here," Marino says, smacking the eight ball.

It warbles to the center of the green felt and stops.

"Screw it," he mutters, propping his stick against the table, wandering over to the jukebox while Rosie pops open two bottles of Miller Lite and sets them in front of the fat woman and the ferret.

Rosie's always frenetic, like a windshield wiper on high. She dries her hands on the back of her jeans as Marino picks out a few favorites from a mix of the seventies.

"What are you staring at?" he asks the homeless-looking man sitting by the door.

"How about a game?"

"I'm busy," Marino says, not turning around as he makes selections on the jukebox.

"You're not playing anything unless you buy a drink," Rosie tells the homeless-looking man slumped by the door. "And I don't want you hanging around here just for the hell of it. How many times I got to tell you?"

"I thought he might like a game with me." He pulls out his washcloth and nervously starts wringing it.

"I'm going to tell you the same thing I did last time you came in here buying nothing and using the john, get out," Rosie says in his face, her hands on her hips. "You want to stay, you pay."

He slowly gets up from his chair, wringing the washcloth, and stares at Marino, his eyes defeated and tired, but there's something in them.

"I thought you might like to play a game," he says to Marino.

"Out!" Rosie yells at him.

"I'll take care of it," Marino says, walking over to the man. "Come on, I'm seeing you out, pal, before it's too late. You know how she gets."

The man doesn't resist. He doesn't stink half as bad as Marino expected, and he follows him out the door onto the sidewalk, where the idiot kid is still shaking the parking meter.

"It ain't a goddamn apple tree," Marino tells the kid.

"Fuck off."

Marino strides over to him, towers over him, and the kid's eyes get wide.

"What'd you say?" Marino asks, cupping his ear, leaning into him. "Did I hear what I think I did?"

"I put in three quarters."

"Well now, ain't that a pity. I suggest you get in your piece-of-shit car and get your ass out of here before I arrest you for damaging city property," Marino says, even though he really can't arrest anybody anymore.

The homeless-looking man from the bar is walking slowly along the sidewalk, glancing back as if expecting Marino to follow. He says something as the kid starts his Mustang and guns it out of there.

"You talking to me?" Marino asks the homeless-looking man, walking his way.

"He's always doing that," the homeless-looking man says quietly, softly. "Same kid. He never puts a damn nickel in the meters around here and then shakes the hell out of them until they break."

"What do you want."

"Johnny came in here the night before it happened," he says in his ill-fitting clothes, the heels of his shoes cut out.

"Who you talking about."

"You know who. He didn't kill himself, neither. I know who did."

Marino gets a feeling, the same feeling he got when he walked inside Mrs. Simister's house. He spots Lucy a block away, taking her time on the sidewalk, not dressed in her usual baggy black clothes.

"Him and me played pool the night before it happened. He had on splints. They didn't seem to bother him. He played pool just fine."

Marino watches Lucy without making it obvious. Tonight, she fits in. She could be any gay woman who hangs out around here, boyish but good-looking and sexy in expensive jeans, faded and full of holes, and beneath her soft, black leather jacket is a white undershirt that clings to her breasts, and he's always liked her breasts, even if he isn't supposed to notice them.

"I saw him just the one time when he brought this girl in here," the homeless man is saying, looking around as if something makes him edgy, turning his back to the bar. "Think she's somebody you ought to find. That's all I have to say."

"What girl and why should I give a shit?" Marino says, watching Lucy get closer, scanning the area, making sure nobody gets any ideas about her.

"Pretty," the man says. "The kind both men and women look at around here, dressed all sexy. Nobody wanted her around."

"Seems to me nobody wants you around, either. You just got your ass kicked out."

Lucy walks into Deuce without looking, as if Marino and the homeless man are invisible.

"Only reason I didn't get kicked out that night is because Johnny bought me a drink. We played pool while the girl sat by the jukebox, looking around as if she'd never been taken to such a slop hole in her life. Went in the ladies' room a couple times and after that it smelled like weed."

"You make a habit of going into the ladies' room?"

"I heard a woman at the bar talking. This girl, she looked like trouble."

"You got any idea what her name is?"

"Sure don't."

Marino lights a cigarette. "What makes you think she has anything to do with what happened to Johnny?"

"I didn't like her. Nobody did. That's all I know."

"You sure?"

"Yes, sir."

"Don't be telling nobody else about this, you got it?"

"No point in it."

"Point or not, keep your mouth shut. And now you're going to tell me how the hell you knew I was going to be in here tonight, and why the hell you thought you could talk to me."

"That's quite a bike you got." The homeless man looks across the street. "Kind of hard to miss. A lot of people around here know you used to be a homicide detective and

now do private-investigation stuff at some police camp or
something north of here."

"What? Am I the mayor?"

"You're a regular. I've seen you with some of the Harley
guys, been watching for you for weeks, hoping for a chance
to talk to you. I hang out in the area, do the best I can. Not
exactly the high point of my life, but I keep hoping it will
get better."

Marino pulls out his wallet and slips him a fifty-dollar bill.

"You find out more about this girl you saw in here, I'll
make it worth your while," he says. "Where can I reach you?"

"Different place, different night. Like I said, I do the best
I can."

Marino gives him his cell phone number.

Want another one?" Rosie asks as Marino returns to
the bar.

"Better give me an unleaded. You remember right before
Thanksgiving, some good-looking blond doctor coming in
here with a girl? He and that guy you just chased out play
pool that night?"

She looks thoughtful, wiping down the bar, shakes her
head. "A lot of people come in here. That was a long time
ago. How long before Thanksgiving?"

Marino watches the door. It is a few minutes before ten.
"Maybe the night before."

"No, not me. I know this is hard to believe," she says,
"but I got a life, don't work here every damn night. I was out
of here at Thanksgiving. In Atlanta with my son."

"Supposedly there was a girl in here who was trouble,
was in here with the doctor I've told you about. Was with
him the night before he died."

"Got no idea."

"Maybe she came in that night with the doctor when you
was out of town?"

Rosie keeps wiping down the bar. "I don't want a problem in here."

———

Lucy sits by the window, near the jukebox, Marino at another table on the other side of the bar, his earpiece in and plugged into a receiver that looks like a cell phone. He drinks a nonalcoholic beer and smokes.

The locals on the other side aren't paying any attention. They never do. Every time Lucy has been in here with Marino, the same losers are sitting on the same stools, smoking menthol cigarettes and drinking lite beer. The only person they talk to outside their deadbeat little club is Rosie, who once told Lucy that the hugely fat woman and her scrawny boyfriend used to live in a nice Miami neighborhood with a guard gate and everything until he got sent to jail for selling crystal meth to an undercover cop. Now the fat lady has to support him on what she makes as a bank teller. The fat man with the goatee is a cook in a diner Lucy will never visit. He comes here every night, gets drunk and somehow manages to drive himself home.

Lucy and Marino ignore each other. No matter how many times they've been through this routine during various operations, it always feels awkward and invasive. She doesn't like being spied on, even if it's her idea, and no matter the logic in him being here tonight, she resents his presence.

She checks the wireless mic attached to the inside of her leather jacket. She bends over as if tying her shoes so no one in the bar can see her talking. "Nothing so far," she transmits to Marino.

It is three minutes past ten.

She waits. She sips a nonalcoholic beer, her back to Marino, and she waits.

She glances at her watch. It is eight minutes past ten.

The door opens and two men walk in.

Two more minutes pass and she transmits to Marino, "Something's wrong. I'm going out to look. Stay here."

Lucy walks through the Art Deco district along Ocean Drive, looking for Stevie in the crowd.

The later it gets, the louder and drunker the patrons of South Beach become, and the street is so crowded with people cruising and looking for parking, traffic barely moves. It's irrational to look for Stevie. She didn't show up. She's probably a million miles from here. But Lucy looks.

She thinks of Stevie claiming to have followed her footprints in the snow, follow them to the Hummer parked behind the Anchor Inn. She wonders how she could have accepted what Stevie said, not really questioned it. While Lucy's footprints would have been obvious just outside the cottage, they would have gotten mixed in with other footprints along the sidewalk. It's not as if Lucy was the only person in Ptown that morning. She thinks of the cell phone that belongs to a man named Doug, of the red handprints, of Johnny, and is sickened by how careless she has been, how myopic and self-destructive.

Stevie probably never intended to meet Lucy at Deuce, just teased her, toyed with her the same way she did at Lorraine's that night. Nothing is Stevie's first time. She's an expert in her games, her bizarre, sick games.

"You see her anywhere?" Marino's voice sounds in her ear.

"I'm turning around," she says. "Stay where you are."

She cuts over on 11th Street, then heads north on Washington Avenue past the courthouse as a white Chevy Blazer with dark, tinted windows drives past. She walks quickly, uneasily, suddenly not so brave, mindful of the pistol in her ankle holster and breathing hard.

49

Another winter storm covers Cambridge, and Benton can barely make out the houses across the street. Snow falls steeply and thickly, and he watches the whitening of the world around him.

"I can put on more coffee, if you'd like," Scarpetta says as she walks into the living room.

"I've had enough," he says, his back to her.

"So have I," she says.

He hears her sit on the hearth, set a coffee mug on it. He feels her eyes on him and turns around, looking at her, not sure what to say. Her hair is wet and she has thrown on a black silk robe and is naked beneath it, and the satiny fabric caresses her body and reveals the deep hollow between her breasts because of the way she sits sideways on the hearth, bending into herself, her strong arms around her knees, her skin unblemished and smooth for her age. Firelight touches her short, blond hair and extremely handsome face, and fire and sunlight love her hair and her face the same way he does. He loves her, all of her, but right now he doesn't know what to say. He doesn't know how to fix it.

Last night she said she was leaving him. She would have packed her suitcase if she'd had one, but she never brings a suitcase. She has belongings here. This is her home, too, and all morning he has listened for the sound of drawers and closet doors, for the sound of her moving out and never coming back.

"You can't drive," he says. "I guess you're stuck."

Bare trees are delicate pencil strokes against luminous whiteness, and there isn't a moving car in sight.

"I know how you feel and what you want," he says, "but you aren't going anywhere today. Nobody is. Some of the streets in Cambridge don't always get plowed right away. This is one of them."

"You have four-wheel drive," she says, staring down at her hands in her lap.

"We're expecting two feet of snow. Even if I could get you to the airport, your plane's not going anywhere. Not today."

"You should eat something."

"I'm not hungry."

"How about an omelet with Vermont cheddar? You need to eat. You'll feel better."

She watches him from the hearth, her chin resting on her hand. Her robe is tied tightly around her waist and she is sculpted in glossy black silk, and he desires her just as much as he always did. He desired her the first time they met some fifteen years ago. Both of them were chiefs. His fiefdom was the FBI's Behavioral Science Unit, hers the Virginia medical examiner's system. They were working an especially heinous case, and she walked into the conference room. He can still see the way she looked the first time he saw her, in a long, white lab coat with pens in the pockets over a pearl-gray pin-striped suit, a pile of case files in her arms. He was intrigued by her hands, strong and capable but elegant.

He realizes she is staring at him.

"Who were you on the phone with a little earlier?" he asks. "I heard you talking to someone."

She's called her lawyer, he thinks. She's called Lucy. She's called someone to say she's leaving him and means it this time.

"I called Dr. Self," she says. "Tried her, left her a message."

He is perplexed and shows it.

"I'm sure you remember her," she says. "Or maybe you listen to her on the radio," she adds wryly.

"Please."

"Millions of people do."

"Why would you call her?" he asks.

She tells him about David Luck and his prescription. She tells him that Dr. Self wasn't the least bit helpful the first time she called.

"No surprise. She's a crackpot, an egomaniac. She lives up to her name. Self."

"Actually, she was well within her right. I don't have jurisdiction. Nobody's dead, as far as we know. Dr. Self doesn't have to respond to any medical examiner at this point, and I'm not so sure I'd call her a crackpot."

"How about a psychiatric whore? Have you listened to her lately?"

"Then you do listen to her."

"Next time, invite a real psychiatrist to speak at the Academy, not some radio jackass."

"It wasn't my idea, and I made it clear I was against it. But the buck stops with Lucy."

"That's ridiculous. Lucy can't stand people like her."

"I believe it was Joe's suggestion to invite Dr. Self as a guest lecturer, his first big coup when he started his fellowship. Getting a celebrity lined up for the summer session. That and getting on her show, a repeat guest. In fact, they've talked about the Academy on the air, which I'm not happy about."

"Idiot. They deserve each other."

"Lucy wasn't paying attention. Never, of course, attended the lectures. She didn't care what Joe did. There's a lot she doesn't seem to care about anymore. What are we going to do."

She isn't talking about Lucy now.

"I don't know."

"You're a psychologist. You should know. You deal with dysfunctions and misery every day."

"I'm miserable this morning," he says. "You're right about that. I suppose if I were your psychologist, I might suggest that you're venting your pain and anger on me because you can't vent it on Lucy. You can't get angry with someone who has a brain tumor."

Scarpetta opens the screen and places another split log on the fire, and sparks fly and wood pops.

"She's made me angry most of her life," she confesses. "There's never been anyone who tries my patience the way she does."

"Lucy's an only child raised by a borderline personality disorder," Benton says. "A hypersexual narcissist. Your sister. Add to the equation, Lucy is unusually gifted. She doesn't think like other people. She's gay. And all that equals someone who learned a long time ago to be self-contained."

"Someone supremely selfish, you mean."

"Insults to our psyche can make us selfish. She was afraid if you knew about the tumor you'd treat her differently, and that would play right into her secret fear. If you know, then somehow it becomes real."

She stares out the window behind him as if transfixed by the snow. Already it is at least eight inches deep, and cars parked along the street are beginning to look like snowdrifts, and even the neighborhood children are staying in.

"Thank goodness I went to the store," Benton comments.

"On that subject, let me see what I can throw together for lunch. We should have a nice lunch. We should try to have a good day."

"You ever had a body that was painted?" he asks.

"Mine or somebody else?"

He smiles a little. "Decidedly not yours. There is nothing dead about your body. This case up here. The red handprints on her body. I'm wondering if it was done while she was alive or after she was killed. Wish there was a way to tell."

She looks at him for a long moment, the fire moving behind her and sounding like the wind.

"If he did it while she was alive, we're dealing with a very different sort of predator. How terrifying and humiliating would that be?" he says. "To be restrained . . ."

"Do we know she was restrained?"

"There are some marks around her wrists and ankles. Reddish areas that the medical examiner lists as possible contusions."

"Possible?"

"As opposed to postmortem artifact," Benton says. "Especially since the body was exposed to the cold. That's what she says."

"She?"

"The chief here."

"Left over from the Boston ME office's not-so-glorious past," Scarpetta says. "Too bad. She single-handedly has pretty much ruined the place."

"I'd appreciate it if you'd look over the report. I have it on a disk. I want to know what you think of the bodypainting, of everything. It's really important for me to know if he did it when she was alive or dead. Too bad we couldn't scan her brain and replay what happened."

She treats it like a serious comment. "That's a nightmare I'm not sure you want. Not even you would want to see that. Assuming it was possible."

"Basil would like me to see it."

"Yes, dear Basil," she says, not at all happy about Basil Jenrette's intrusion into Benton's life.

"Theoretically," he says, "would you want to see it? Would you want to see the replay if it were possible?"

"Even if there were a way to replay a person's final moments," she replies from the hearth, "I'm not sure how reliable it would be. I suspect the brain has the remarkable capacity to process events in a way that ensures the least amount of trauma and pain."

"Some people disassociate, I suspect," he says as her cell phone rings.

It's Marino.

"Call extension two forty-three," he says. "Now."

50

Extension 243 is the fingerprints lab. It is also a favorite forum for Academy staff, a place to gather and talk about evidence that requires more than one type of forensic analysis.

Fingerprints are no longer just fingerprints. They can be a source of DNA, not just the DNA of whoever left them but the DNA of the victim the perpetrator touched. They can be a source of drug residues or a material that was on the person's hands, perhaps ink or paint, that requires analysis by such lofty instruments as the gas chromatograph or the infrared spectrophotometer or the Fourier transform infrared microscope. In the old days, a piece of evidence usually walked onstage alone. Now, with the sophistication and sensitivity of scientific instruments and processes, a solo becomes a string quartet or a symphony. The problem remains what to collect first. Testing for one thing can eradicate another. So scientists get together, usually in Matthew's lab. They debate and decide what should be done and who goes first.

When Matthew received the latex gloves from Daggie Simister's scene, he was faced with a plethora of possibilities, none of them foolproof. He could put on cotton examination gloves, and on top of those wear the inside-out latex gloves. By using his own hands to fill out otherwise-limp latex, he makes it easier to lift and photograph latent prints. But in doing so, he runs the risk of ruining any possibility of fuming prints with superglue or looking for them with an alternate light source and luminescent powders or processing them with chemicals such as ninhydrin or diazafluoren. One process can interfere with another, and once the damage is done, there is no going back.

It is half past eight, and the inside of his small lab right now looks like a mini staff conference, with Matthew, Marino, Joe Amos and three scientists gathered around a large transparent plastic box, the glue tank. Inside it are two inside-out latex gloves, one bloody, hanging from clips. Small holes have been cut into the bloody glove. Other areas of the latex, inside and out, were swabbed for DNA in such a way as not to disturb any possible prints. Then Matthew had to decide door number one, door number two, door number three, as he likes to describe a deliberation that involves just as much instinct, experience and luck as good science. He chose to place the gloves, a foil pack of superglue and a dish of warm water inside the tank.

What that produced was one visible print, a left thumbprint preserved in hard, whitish glue. He lifted it with black gel lifter, then photographed it.

"The gang's all here," he is saying to Scarpetta over speakerphone. "Who wants to start?" he asks the people assembled around the examination table. "Randy?"

DNA scientist Randy is an odd little man with a big nose and a lazy eye. Matthew has never liked him much, and is reminded why the instant Randy starts to talk.

"Well what I was given were three potential sources of DNA," Randy says in his typically pedantic way. "Two gloves and two earprints."

"That's four," Scarpetta's voice enters the room.

"Yes sir, I meant four. The hope, of course, was to get DNA from the outside of the one glove, and primarily that meant from the dried blood, and perhaps DNA from the inside of both gloves. I already got DNA from the earprints," he reminds everybody, "which I managed to swab nondestructively by avoiding what might be considered individual variations or potentially characteristic features such as the inferior extension of the anthelix. As you know, we ran that profile in CODIS and came back empty-handed, but what we just found out is the DNA from the earprint matches the DNA inside one of the gloves."

"Just one?" Scarpetta's voice asks.

"The bloody one. I didn't get anything off the other glove. I'm not sure it was ever worn."

"That's peculiar," Scarpetta's puzzled voice says.

"Of course, Matthew assisted because I'm not really up on ear anatomy, and prints of any type are his department more than mine," Randy adds, as if it matters. "As I've just pointed out, we got the DNA from the earprints, specifically from the areas of the helix and the lobe. And it's obviously from the same person who was wearing one of the gloves, so I suppose you could conjecture that whoever pressed their ear against the glass at the house where those people disappeared was the same individual who murdered Daggie Simister. Or at least was wearing at least one latex glove at her crime scene."

"How many times did you sharpen your damn pencil while you did all that?" Marino whispers.

"What's that?"

"Wouldn't want you to leave out even one fascinating little detail," Marino says quietly, so Scarpetta can't hear. "I bet you count the cracks in the sidewalk and set your timer when you have sex."

"Randy, please continue," Scarpetta says. "And nothing in CODIS. That's a shame."

He goes on in his long-winded, convoluted way to confirm yet again that a search of the Combined DNA Index system database known as CODIS was unsuccessful. Whoever left the DNA isn't in the database, possibly suggesting that the person has never been arrested.

"It also came up empty-handed with DNA from blood found in that beach shop in Las Olas. But some of those samples aren't blood," Randy says to the black telephone on the counter. "I don't know what it is. Something that caused a false positive. Lucy mentioned the possibility it might be copper. She thinks what might be reacting to luminol is the fungicide that's used down here to prevent the canker. You know, copper sprays."

"Based on?" Joe asks, and he's another staff member Matthew can't stand.

"There was a lot of copper at the Simister scene, inside and out."

"Which samples, specifically, were human blood at Beach Bums?" Scarpetta's voice asks.

"The bathroom. Samples from the storage-area floor aren't blood. May be copper. Also the trace from the station wagon. The carpet in the front seat driver's side that reacted to luminol. Also not blood. Another false positive. Again, could be copper."

"Phil? You around?"

"Right here," Phil, the trace evidence examiner, says.

"I'm really sorry about this," Scarpetta's voice then says and she sounds like she means it. "I want the labs in overdrive."

"I thought we already were. About to over-torque, in fact." Joe couldn't keep his mouth shut if he were drowning.

"All biological samples that haven't already been analyzed, I want them analyzed ASAP," Scarpetta's voice says and it's sounding more adamant. "Including any potential sources of DNA taken from the house in Hollywood, the one where the two boys and two women disappeared. Everything in CODIS. We're going to treat everybody as if they're dead."

The scientists, Joe and Marino look at each other. They've never heard Scarpetta say anything quite like that.

"Now that's optimism for you," Joe remarks.

"Phil, how about running the carpet sweepings, the trace from the Simister case and trace from the station wagon—trace from everything—through SEM-EDS," Scarpetta's voice says. "Let's see if in fact it's copper."

"It must be everywhere down here."

"No, it's not," Scarpetta's voice says. "Not everybody uses it. Not everybody has citrus trees. But so far in the cases we're dealing with, that is a common denominator."

"What about the beach shop? I wouldn't think there are citrus trees around there."

"You're right. Good point."

"Then let's just say some of that trace is positive for copper . . ."

"That will be significant," Scarpetta's voice says. "We have to ask why. Who tracked it into the storeroom. Who tracked it into the station wagon and now we're going to have to go back to the house where the people disappeared, look for copper in there, too. Anything interesting about the red paint-like substance we found on the floor, the chunks of concrete we brought in?"

"Henna pigment, definitely not what you see in topcoats, wall paints," Phil replies.

"What about temporary tattoo or bodypaints?"

"Certainly could be, but if it's alcohol-based, we wouldn't detect that. The ethanol or isopropanol would have evaporated by now."

"Interesting it would be back there, and appears to have been there for a while. Someone keep Lucy up on what we're talking about. Where is she?"

"Don't know," Marino says.

"We need the DNA of Florrie Quincy and her daughter, Helen," Scarpetta's voice then says. "See if it's their blood in the beach shop. Beach Bums."

"Single-donor blood in the bathroom," Randy says. "Definitely not the blood of two people, and if there were, we could certainly tell if the two people were related. For instance, mother and daughter."

"I'll get on it," Phil says. "I mean the SEM part."

"Just how many cases are there?" Joe says. "And are you assuming they're all connected? Is that why we're supposed to treat everybody as if they're dead?"

"I'm not assuming everything's connected," Scarpetta's voice answers. "But I'm worried it might be."

"Like I was saying about the Simister case, no dice with CODIS," Randy resumes, "but the DNA from the *inside* of the bloody latex glove is different from the DNA of the blood on the *outside* of it. Which isn't surprising. The inside would have skin cells that were shed by the wearer. The blood on the outside would be from someone else, at least that's what you might suppose," he explains, and Matthew wonders how the man can be married.

Who could live with him? Who could stand it?

"Is the blood Daggie Simister's?" Scarpetta bluntly asks.

Like everybody else, she logically would suspect that the bloody glove found at the scene of Daggie Simister's homicide would, no doubt, be covered with her blood.

"Well, actually, the blood from the carpet is."

"He means the carpet by the window where we think she might have been hit on the head," Joe says.

"I'm talking about the blood on the glove. Is it Daggie Simister's?" Scarpetta's voice asks, and it is beginning to sound strained.

"No sir."

Randy says "no sir" to everyone, regardless of the person's gender.

"That's definitely not her blood on that glove, which is curious," Randy tediously explains. "Now, you would expect it to be her blood."

Oh God. Here he goes again, Matthew thinks.

"Here are these latex gloves at the crime scene, and the blood's on the outside of one but not on the inside."

"Why would blood be on the inside?" Marino scowls at him.

"It's not."

"I know it's not, but why would it be?"

"Well, for instance, if the perpetrator injured himself somehow, bled inside the glove, perhaps cut himself while he was wearing gloves. I've seen it before in stabbings. The perpetrator has on gloves, nicks himself and gets his blood inside a glove, which clearly didn't happen in this case. Which brings me to the important question. If the blood is the killer's in the Simister case, why would it be all over the outside of a glove? And why is that DNA different from the DNA I got from inside that same glove?"

"I think we're clear on the question," Matthew says, because he can stand Randy's supercilious sidewinding monologue maybe one minute longer.

After a minute, Matthew will have to walk out of the lab, pretend he has to visit the men's room, run an errand, eat poison.

"The outside of the glove is where you'd expect blood to be if the perpetrator touched something bloody or someone bloody," Randy says.

They all know the answer, but Scarpetta doesn't. Randy's

building up to the crescendo, playing it out, and no one can steal his thunder. DNA is his department.

"Randy?" Scarpetta's voice sounds.

It's the voice she uses when Randy is confusing and annoying everyone, including her.

"Do we know whose blood it is on that glove?" she asks him.

"Yes sir we do. Well, almost. It's either Johnny Swift's or his brother, Laurel. They're identical twins," he finally says it. "So their DNA's the same."

"You still there?" Matthew asks Scarpetta after a long silence.

Then Marino comments, "I just don't see how it could be Laurel's blood. He's not the one whose blood was all over the living room when his brother's head was blown off."

"Well, I for one am totally baffled," Mary, the toxicologist, joins in. "Johnny Swift got shot way back in November, so how does his blood suddenly show up some ten weeks later in a case that doesn't appear to be related?"

"How does his blood show up at the Daggie Simister murder scene at all?" Scarpetta's voice fills the room.

"It's certainly within the realm of possibility that the gloves were planted," Joe says.

"Maybe you should state the damn obvious," Marino snipes at him. "And what's obvious is whoever blew that poor old lady's head off is telling us he had something to do with Johnny Swift's death. Someone's fucking with us."

"He'd had recent surgery . . ."

"Bullshit," Marino snaps. "No way the damn gloves came from some carpal tunnel surgery. Jesus Christ. You're looking for unicorns when there's horses everywhere."

"What?"

"I think the damn message is pretty damn clear," Marino says again, pacing the lab, talking loudly, his face bright red. "Whoever killed her is saying he also killed Johnny Swift. And the gloves are to fuck with us."

"We can't assume it's not Laurel's blood," Scarpetta's voice says.

"If it is, that certainly might explain things," Randy says.

"It don't explain shit. If Laurel killed Mrs. Simister, why the hell would he leave his DNA in the sink?" Marino retorts.

"Maybe it's Johnny Swift's blood, then."

"Shut up, Randy. You're curling my hair."

"You don't have any hair, Pete," Randy says seriously.

"You want to tell me how the hell we're going to figure out whether it's Laurel or Johnny, since their DNA's supposedly the same?" Marino exclaims. "This is so fucked up it isn't even funny."

He looks accusingly at Randy, then at Matthew, then back at Randy. "You sure you didn't get something mixed up when you did your tests?"

He never cares who hears him when he impeaches a person's credibility or is just plain nasty.

"Like maybe one or the other of you got swabs mixed up or something," Marino says.

"No sir. Absolutely not," Randy replies. "Matthew received the samples and I did the extractions and analyses and ran them in CODIS. There was no break in the chain of evidence, and Johnny Swift's DNA is in the database, because everybody who's autopsied these days goes in there, meaning Johnny Swift's DNA was entered into CODIS last November. I believe I'm right about that? You still there?" he asks Scarpetta.

"I'm still here . . ." she starts to say.

"The policy as of last year is to enter all cases, whether it's suicide, accident, homicide or even a natural death," Joe pontificates, interrupting her as usual. "Just because someone's a victim or his death is unrelated to crime doesn't mean he might not have been involved in criminal activity at some point in his life. I'm assuming we're sure the Swift brothers are identical twins."

"Look alike, talk alike, dress alike, fuck alike," Marino whispers to him.

"Marino?" Scarpetta's voice resumes its presence. "Did the police submit a sample of Laurel Swift's DNA at the time of his brother's death?"

"Nope. No reason to."

"Not even for exclusionary purposes?" Joe asks.

"Excluded from what? DNA wasn't relevant," Marino says to him. "Laurel's DNA would be all over that house. He lives there."

"It would be good if we could test Laurel's DNA," Scarpetta's voice says. "Matthew? Did you use any chemicals on the bloody glove, the one from Daggie Simister's scene? Anything that might cause a problem if we want to do further testing?"

"Superglue," Matthew says. "And by the way, I ran the one print I got. Nothing. Nothing in AFIS. Couldn't match it up with the partial from the seat belt in the station wagon. Wasn't enough minutiae."

"Mary? I want you to get samples of the blood on that glove."

"Superglue shouldn't have made a difference since it reacts to the amino acids in skin oils, sweat, and not blood," Joe feels compelled to explain. "We should be all right."

"I'll be glad to get her a sample," Matthew says to the black telephone. "There's plenty of bloody latex left."

"Marino?" Scarpetta's voice says. "I want you to go to the ME's office and get Johnny Swift's case file."

"I can do it," Joe quickly says.

"Marino?" she reiterates. "Inside the file should be his DNA cards. We always make more than one."

"You touch that case file, your teeth will end up in the back of your head," Marino whispers to Joe.

"You can place one of the cards inside an evidence envelope and receipt it to Mary," Scarpetta's voice is saying. "And Mary? Take a sample of the blood from that card and a sample from the glove."

"I'm not sure I'm following you," Mary says, and Matthew doesn't blame her.

He can't imagine what a toxicologist might be able to do with a drop of dried blood from a DNA card and an equally small amount of dried blood from a glove.

"Maybe you mean Randy," Mary suggests. "Are you talking about more DNA testing?"

"No," she says. "I want you to check for lithium."

———

Scarpetta rinses a whole young chicken in the sink. Her Treo is in her pocket, the earpiece in her ear.

"Because his blood wouldn't have been screened for it at the time," she is saying to Marino over the phone. "If he was still taking lithium, apparently his brother never bothered telling the police."

"They should have found a prescription bottle at the scene," Marino replies. "What's that noise?"

"I'm opening cans of chicken broth. Too bad you're not here. I don't know why they didn't find any lithium," she says, emptying the cans into a copper pot. "But it's possible his brother collected any prescription bottles so the police wouldn't find them."

"Why? It's not like it's cocaine or something."

"Johnny Swift was a prominent neurologist. He might not have wanted people to know he had a psychiatric disorder."

"I sure as hell wouldn't want someone with mood swings screwing with my brain, now that you mention it."

She chops onions. "In reality, his bipolar disorder probably had no effect at all on his skills as a physician, but there are plenty of ignorant people in the world. Again, it's possible Laurel didn't want the police or anybody else to know about his brother's problem."

"That doesn't make sense. If what he said is true, he ran from the house right after he found the body. Doesn't sound to me like he wandered around collecting pill bottles."

"I guess you're going to have to ask him."

"As soon as we get the lithium results. Rather go in when I know what's what. And right now we've got a bigger problem," he says.

"I'm not sure how our problems could get much bigger," she says, cutting up the chicken.

"It's about the shotgun shell," Marino says. "The one NIBIN got a hit on up there in the Walden Pond case."

I **didn't** want to say anything about it in front of everybody else," Marino explains over the phone. "Someone on the inside, has to be. No other explanation."

He sits at his office desk, the door shut and locked.

"Here's what happened," he goes on. "I didn't want to say anything in front of everybody else," he repeats himself, "but earlier this morning I had a little chat with a buddy of mine at Hollywood PD who's in charge of the evidence room. So he checked the computer. It took all of five minutes for him to access the info on the shotgun used in that convenience-store robbery-homicide from two years back. And guess where the shotgun's supposed to be, Doc. Are you sitting down?"

"Sitting down has never helped," she says. "Tell me."

"In our own fucking reference collection."

"At the Academy? Our reference firearms collection at the Academy?"

"Hollywood PD donated it to us about a year ago when they gave us a bunch of other guns they no longer needed. Remember?"

"Have you actually walked into the firearms lab to make sure it isn't there?"

"It's not going to be. We know it was just used to kill some lady up there where you are."

"Go check right now," she says. "Call me back."

51

Hog waits in line.

He stands behind a fat lady wearing a loud, pink suit. He holds his boots in one hand, and a tote bag, driver's license and boarding pass in the other. He moves ahead and places his boots and coat in a plastic tub.

He places the tub and his bag on the black belt, and they move away from him. He stands in the two white foot-prints, both stocking feet exactly on the white footprints on the carpet, and an airport security officer nods for him to pass through the x-ray scanner, and he does and nothing beeps, and he shows the officer his boarding pass, grabs his boots and jacket out of the tray, grabs his bag. He begins walking to gate twenty-one. Nobody pays any attention to him.

He still smells the rotting bodies. He can't seem to get the stench out of his nose. Maybe it's an olfactory hallucination. He's had them before. Sometimes he smells the cologne, the Old Spice cologne that he smelled when he did the bad thing on the mattress and was sent away where there were old brick houses, where it was snowing and cold, where he's going now. It is snowing, not much, but some. He checked the weather before he took a taxi to the airport. He didn't want to leave his Blazer in long-term parking. That costs real money, and it wouldn't be good if someone looked inside the back of it. He hasn't cleaned it up very well.

In his bag are a few things, not much. All he needs is a change of clothing, a few toiletries, different boots that fit better. He won't need his old boots much longer. They are a biological hazard, and the thought amuses him. Now that he thinks about it as the boots walk toward the gate, maybe he should save the boots in perpetuity. They have quite a history, have walked in places as if he owned them, taken people away as if he owned them, have returned to places and climbed up on things to spy, walked right in, brazenly, the boots carrying him from room to room from place to place, doing what God says. Punishing. Confusing people. The shotgun. The glove. To show them.

God has an IQ of a hundred and fifty.

His boots carried him right into the house, and he had the hood on before they even knew what was happening. Stupid religious freaks. Stupid little orphans. Stupid little orphan walking into the pharmacy, Mom Number One holding his hand so he could get his prescription filled. Lunatic. Hog hates lunatics, fucking religious freaks, hates little boys, little girls, hates Old Spice. Marino wears Old Spice, the big, dumb cop. Hog hates Dr. Self, should have put her on the mattress, had fun with the ropes, gotten her good after what she did.

Hog ran out of time. God isn't happy.

There wasn't time to punish the worst offender of all.

You'll have to go back, God said. *This time with Basil.*

Hog's boots walk toward the gate, carry him to Basil. They'll have their good times again, just like those times in the old days after Hog did the bad thing, was sent away, then sent back, then met Basil in a bar.

He was never afraid of Basil, not the least bit put off by him from the first moment they found themselves sitting next to each other, drinking tequila. They had several together, and there was something about him. Hog could tell.

He said, *You're different.*

I'm a cop, Basil said.

This was in South Beach, where Hog often cruised and hung out, looking for sex, looking for drugs.

You're not just a cop, Hog said to him. *I can tell.*

Oh, really?

I can tell. I know about people.

How about I take you somewhere, and Hog had a sense that Basil had figured him out, too. *I've got something you can do for me,* Basil said to Hog.

Why should I do anything for you?

Because you'll like it.

Later that night, Hog was in Basil's car, not his police car but a white Ford LTD that looked just like an unmarked police car but wasn't. It was his personal car. They weren't in Miami, and he couldn't possibly drive a marked car with Dade County on it. Someone might remember seeing it. Hog was a little disappointed. He loves police cars, loves sirens and lights. All those lights lit up and flashing remind him of The Christmas Shop.

No way they'll ever think twice if you talk to them, Basil said that first night they met, after they'd been riding around awhile, smoking crack.

Why me? Hog asked, and he wasn't the least bit afraid.

Common sense would dictate that he should have been. Basil kills whomever he pleases, always has. He could have killed Hog. Easily.

God told Hog what to do. That's what kept Hog safe.

Basil spotted the girl. It turned out later she was only eighteen. She was getting cash at an ATM, her car nearby, the engine running. Stupid. Never get cash after dark, especially if you are a young girl, a pretty one, all alone in shorts and a tight T-shirt. If you're a young girl, a pretty one, bad things happen.

Give me your knife and your gun, Hog told Basil.

Hog tucked the gun in his waistband and cut his thumb with the knife. He smeared blood on his face and climbed over the seat, lying down in back. Basil rolled up to the ATM and got out of the car. He opened the back door, checking on Hog, looking appropriately distressed.

It will be all right, he said to Hog. To the girl he said, *Please help us. My friend's been hurt. Where's the nearest hospital?*

Oh my God. We should call nine-one-one, and she frantically dug her cell phone out of her bag and Basil shoved her hard into the backseat, and then Hog had the gun in her face.

They drove off.

Shit, Basil said. *You're good,* he said, and he was high, laughing. *Guess we'd better figure out where we're going.*

Please don't hurt me, the girl was crying, and Hog felt something as he sat back there, holding the gun on her while she cried and begged. He felt like having sex.

Shut up, Basil told her. *It won't do any good. Guess we'd better find somewhere. Maybe the park. No, they patrol it.*

I know somewhere, Hog said. *Nobody will ever find us. It's perfect. We can take our time, all the time in the world,* and he was aroused. He wanted sex, wanted it something awful.

He directed Basil to the house, the house that is falling apart with no electricity or running water, and a mattress and dirty magazines in the back room. It was Hog who figured out how to tie them up so they couldn't sit without their arms straight up.

Stick 'em up!

Like in cartoons.

Stick 'em up!

Like in campy Westerns.

Basil said Hog was brilliant, the most brilliant person he'd ever met, and after a few times of taking women there and keeping them until they smelled too bad, got too infected or just got too used up, Hog told Basil about The Christmas Shop.

Have you ever seen it?

No.

Can't miss it. Right on the beach on A1A. The lady's rich.

Hog explained that on Saturdays, it's always just her and her daughter in there. Hardly anybody goes in there. Who buys Christmas stuff at the beach in July?

No shit.

He wasn't supposed to do it in there.

Then before Hog knew what was happening, Basil had

her in the back, raping, cutting, blood everywhere, while Hog watched and calculated how they were going to get away with it.

The lumberjack by the door was five feet tall, hand-carved. He carried a real ax, an antique one, a curved wooden handle and shiny steel blade, half of it painted blood red. It was Hog who thought of it.

About an hour later, Hog carried out the trash bags, made sure no one was around. He put them in the trunk of Basil's car. No one saw them.

We were lucky, Hog told Basil when they were back at their secret place, the old house, digging a pit. *Don't do that again.*

A month later, he did something again, tried to get two women at once. Hog wasn't with him. Basil forced them into the car, then the damn thing broke down. Basil never told anybody about Hog. He protected Hog. Now it's Hog's turn.

They're doing a study up there, Hog wrote to him. *The prison knows about it and has been asked for volunteers. It would be good for you. You could do something constructive.*

It was a pleasant, innocuous letter. No prison official thought twice about it. Basil got word to the warden that he wanted to volunteer for a study they were doing in Massachusetts, that he wanted to do something to pay for his sins, that if the doctors could learn something about what's wrong with people like him, maybe it would make a difference. Whether or not the warden fell for Basil's manipulations is a matter of speculation. But this past December, Basil was transferred to Butler State Hospital.

All because of Hog. God's Hand.

Since then, their communications have had to be more ingenious. God showed Hog how to tell Basil anything he wants. God has an IQ of a hundred and fifty.

Hog finds a seat at gate twenty-one. He sits as far away from everybody as he can, waiting for the nine a.m. flight. It's on time. He'll land at noon. He unzips his bag and pulls out a letter Basil wrote to him more than a month ago.

I got the fishing magazines. Many thanks. I always learn a lot from the articles. Basil Jenrette.

P.S. They are going to put me in that damn tube again—Thursday, February 17. But they promise it will be quick. "In at 5 and out at 5:15 p.m." Promises, promises.

52

The snow has stopped and chicken broth simmers. Scarpetta measures two cups of Italian Arborio rice and opens a bottle of dry white wine.

"Can you come down?" She steps closer to the doorway, calling up to Benton.

"Can you come up here, please?" his voice returns from the office at the top of the back stairs.

She melts butter in a copper saucepan and begins to brown the chicken. She pours the rice into the chicken broth. Her cell phone rings. It's Benton.

"This is ridiculous," she says, looking at the stairs that lead up to his second-floor office. "Can't you please come down? I'm cooking. Things are going to hell in Florida. I need to talk to you."

She spoons a little broth on the browning chicken.

"And I really need you to take a look at this," he answers.

How odd it is to hear his voice upstairs and over the phone at the same time.

"This is ridiculous," she says again.

"Let me ask you something," his voice says over the phone and from upstairs, as if there are two identical voices speaking. "Why would she have splinters between her shoulder blades? Why would anybody?"

"Wood splinters?"

"A scraped area of skin that has splinters embedded in it. On her back, between her shoulder blades. And I wonder if you can tell if it happened before or after death."

"If she were dragged across a wooden floor or perhaps beaten with something wooden. There could be a number of reasons, I suppose." She pushes the browning chicken around with a fork.

"If she were dragged and got splinters that way, wouldn't she have them elsewhere on her body? Assuming she was nude when she was dragged across some old splintery floor."

"Not necessarily."

"I wish you'd come upstairs."

"Any defense injuries?"

"Why don't you come up?"

"As soon as lunch is under control. Sexual assault?"

"No evidence of it, but it's certainly sexually motivated. I'm not hungry at the moment."

She stirs the rice some more and sets the spoon on a folded paper towel.

"Any other possible source of DNA?" she asks.

"Such as?"

"I don't know. Maybe she bit off his nose or a finger or something and it was recovered from her stomach."

"Seriously."

"Saliva, hair, his blood," she says. "I hope they swabbed the hell out of her and checked like crazy."

"Why don't we talk about this up here."

Scarpetta takes off her apron and walks toward the stairs as she talks on the phone, thinking how silly it is to be in the same house and communicate by phone.

"I'm hanging up," she says at the top of the stairs, looking at him.

He is sitting in his black leather chair and their eyes meet.

"Glad you didn't walk in a second ago," he says. "I was just talking on the phone with this incredibly beautiful woman."

"Good thing you weren't in the kitchen to hear who I was talking to."

She rolls a chair close to him and looks at a photograph on his computer screen, looks at the dead woman facedown on an autopsy table, looks at the red-painted handprints on her body.

"Maybe painted with a stencil, possibly airbrushed," she says.

Benton enlarges the area of skin between the shoulder blades, and she studies the raw abrasion.

"To answer one of your questions," she says, "yes, it's possible to tell if an abrasion embedded with splinters might have occurred before or after death. It depends on whether there is tissue response. I don't guess we have histology."

"If there are slides, I wouldn't know," Benton replies.

"Does Thrush have access to a SEM-EDS, a scanning electron microscope with an energy dispersive x-ray system?"

"The state police labs have everything."

"What I'd like to suggest is he get a sample of the alleged splinters, magnify them one hundred times up to five hundred times and see what they look like. And it would be a good idea to also check for copper."

Benton looks at her, shrugs. "Why?"

"It's possible we're finding it all over the place. Even in the storage area of the former Christmas shop. Possibly from copper sprays."

"The Quincy family was in the landscaping business. I would assume a lot of commercial citrus growers use copper sprays. Maybe the family tracked it into the back of The Christmas Shop."

"And possibly bodypaint in there, too—in the storage area where we found blood."

Benton falls silent, something else coming to him.

"A common denominator in Basil's murders," he says. "All of the victims, at least the ones whose bodies were recovered, had copper. The trace had copper in it, also citrus pollen, which didn't mean much. There's citrus pollen all over the place in Florida. Nobody thought about copper sprays. Maybe he took them someplace where copper sprays were used, someplace with citrus trees."

He looks out the window at the gray sky as a snowplow works loudly on his street.

"What time do you need to head out?" Scarpetta clicks on a photograph of the abraded area on the dead woman's back.

"Not until late afternoon. Basil's coming in at five."

"Wonderful. See how inflamed it is just in that one discrete area?" She points it out. "An area where there's been a removal of the epithelial layer of the skin by rubbing against some sort of rough surface. And if you zoom in"— she does—"you can see that before she was cleaned up, there's serosanguineous fluid on the surface of the abrasion. See it?"

"Okay. What looks like a little bit of scabbing. But not the entire area."

"If an abrasion is deep enough, you get leakage of fluid from the vessels. And you're right, the entire area isn't scabbing, which makes me suspect that the abraded area is actually several scrape abrasions of differing age, injuries caused by repeated contact with a rough surface."

"That's strange. I'm trying to imagine it."

"I wish I had the histology. Polymorphonuclear white cells would indicate the injury is maybe four to six hours old. As for the brownish-reddish scabs, you generally start seeing those in a minimum of eight hours. She lived for at least a little while after she got this injury, these scrapes."

She studies more photographs, studies them closely. She makes notes on a legal pad.

She says, "If you look at photographs thirteen through eighteen, you'll see, just barely, areas of what looks like localized red swelling on the backs of her legs and buttocks. What they look like to me are insect bites that have begun to heal. And if you go back to the picture of the abrasion, there's some localized swelling and barely visible petechial hemorrhaging, which can be associated with spider bites.

"If I'm right, microscopically you should see a congestion of blood vessels and an infiltration of white blood cells, mainly eosinophils, depending on her response. It's not very accurate, but we could look for tryptase levels, too, in the event she had an anaphylactic response. But I would be surprised. Certainly she didn't die of anaphylactic shock from an insect bite. I wish I had the damn histology. Could be more in there than splinters. Urticating hairs. Spiders— tarantulas, specifically—flick them, part of their defense system. Ev and Kristin's church is next door to a pet store that sells tarantulas."

"Itching?" Benton asks.

"If she got flicked, she would have itched like hell," Scarpetta says. "She might have rubbed up against something, scratching herself raw."

53

She suffered.

"Wherever he kept her, she suffered from bites that were painful and itchy and awful," Scarpetta says.

"Mosquitoes?" Benton suggests.

"Just one? Just one bad bite between her shoulder blades? There are no other similar abrasions with inflammation anywhere else on her body, except on her elbows and knees," she goes on. "Mild abrasions, scrapes, such as you might expect if someone were kneeling or propping herself up by her elbows on a rough surface. But those abraded areas don't look anything like this."

She again points out the inflamed area between the shoulder blades.

"It's my theory she was kneeling when he shot her," Benton says. "Based on the blood pattern on her slacks. Could you get abrasions on your knees if you had pants on when you were kneeling?"

"Sure."

"Then he killed her first, then undressed her. That tells a different story, now doesn't it. If he really wanted to sexually humiliate and terrorize, he would have made her undress, made her kneel nude, then put the shotgun barrel in her mouth and pulled the trigger."

"What about the shotgun shell in her rectum."

"Could be anger. Could be he wanted us to find it and link it to the case in Florida."

"You're suggesting her murder might have been impulsive, perhaps anger-driven. Yet you're also suggesting a significant element of premeditation, of game playing, as if he wanted us to link her case to that robbery-homicide." Scarpetta looks at him.

"It all means something, at least to him. Welcome to the world of violent sociopaths."

"Well, one thing is clear," she says. "For a while, at least, she was held hostage some place where there was insect activity. Possibly fire ants, maybe spiders, and your normal hotel room or house isn't likely to have an infestation of fire ants or spiders, not around here. Not this time of year."

"Except tarantulas. Usually they're pets, unrelated to the climate," Benton says.

"She was abducted from someplace else. Where exactly was the body found?" she then asks. "Right at Walden Pond?"

"About fifty feet off a path that isn't used much this time of year but certainly is used some. A family hiking near the pond found her. Their black Lab ran off into the woods and started barking."

"What a horrible thing to happen upon when you're minding your own business at Walden Pond."

She scans the autopsy report on the screen.

"She wasn't out there long, her body dumped after dark," she says. "If what I'm reading here is accurate. The after-dark part makes sense. And maybe he put her where he did, off the path and not in clear view, because he wasn't taking any chance of being seen. If anybody happened to show up—although not likely after dark—he's out of sight in the woods with her. And this business"— she points at the hooded face and what looks like a diaper—"you could do this in minutes if you'd premeditated it, already cut the eyeholes into the panties, if the body was already nude and so on. It all makes me suspect he's familiar with the area."

"It makes sense he is."

"Are you hungry or do you intend to obsess up here all day?"

"What did you make? Then I'll decide."

"Risotto alla Sbirraglia. Also known as chicken risotto."

"Sbirraglia?" He takes her hand. "That some exotic breed of Venetian chicken?"

"Supposedly from the word *sbirri,* which is pejorative for the police. A little humor on a day that hasn't been funny."

"I don't understand what the police have to do with a chicken dish."

"Supposedly when the Austrians occupied Venice, the police were quite fond of this particular dish, if my culinary sources are to be believed. And I was thinking of a bottle of Soave or a fuller-bodied Piave Pinot Bianco. You have both in your cellar, and as the Venetians say, 'He who drinks well sleeps well, and he who sleeps well thinks no evil, does no evil and goes to heaven,' or something like that."

"I'm afraid there's not a wine on earth that will stop me from thinking about evil," Benton says. "And I don't believe in heaven. Only hell."

54

On the ground floor of the Academy's spacious stucco headquarters, the red light is on outside the firearms lab, and from the hallway, Marino hears the dull thud of gunfire. He walks in, not one to care if a range is hot, as long as it's Vince who's doing the shooting.

Vince withdraws a small pistol from the port of the horizontal stainless-steel bullet-recovery tank, which weighs five tons when filled with water, explaining why his lab is located where it is.

"You been out flying already?" Marino asks, climbing up the aluminum checker steps to the shooting platform.

Vince is dressed in a black flight suit and ankle-high black leather boots. When he isn't lost in his world of tool marks and guns, he's one of Lucy's helicopter pilots. As is true of a number of her staff, his appearance is inconsistent with what he does. Vince is sixty-five, flew Black Hawks in Vietnam, then went to work for ATF. He has short legs and a barrel chest, and a gray ponytail that he says he hasn't cut in ten years.

"You say something?" Vince asks, removing his hearing-protector headset and shooting glasses.

"It's a wonder you can hear a damn thing anymore."

"Not as good as I used to. When I get home, I'm stone-deaf, according to my wife."

Marino recognizes the pistol Vince is test-firing, the Black Widow with rosewood grips that was found beneath Daggie Simister's bed.

"A sweet little .22," Vince says. "Thought it couldn't hurt to add it to the database."

"Doesn't look to me like it's ever been fired."

"Wouldn't surprise me. Can't tell you how many people

have guns for home protection and don't remember they've got them or can't remember where they put it or even know if it's missing."

"We've got a problem with something missing," Marino says.

Vince opens a box of ammunition and begins pushing .22 cartridges into the cylinder.

"Want to try it?" he says. "Kind of a strange thing for an old woman's self-protection. Bet somebody gave it to her. I usually recommend something more user-friendly, like a Lady Smith .38 or a pit bull. I understand it was under the bed, out of reach."

"Who told you that?" Marino says, getting the same feeling he's been getting a lot lately.

"Dr. Amos."

"He wasn't at the scene. What the hell does he know?"

"Not half as much as he thinks. He's in here all the time, drives me insane. I hope Dr. Scarpetta doesn't intend to hire him after he finishes his fellowship. She does, I might just go to work at Wal-Mart. Here."

He offers Marino the pistol.

"No thanks. The only thing I feel like shooting right now is him."

"What do you mean, something's missing."

"We've got a shotgun missing from the reference collection, Vince."

"Not possible," he says, shaking his head.

They climb down from the platform, and Vince sets the pistol on top of an evidence table that is covered with other tagged firearms, boxes of ammunition, an array of targets with test powder patterns to determine distance and a shattered window of tempered automobile glass.

"Mossberg 835 Ulti-Mag pump," Marino says. "Used in a robbery-homicide down here two years ago. The case was exceptionally cleared when the guy behind the counter blew the suspect away."

"Weird you would mention that," he says, perplexed. "Dr. Amos called me not five minutes ago and asked if he could come down and check something on the computer."

Vince moves to a counter arranged with comparison microscopes, a digital trigger-pull gauge and a computer. He taps the keyboard with his index finger, brings up a menu and selects reference collection. He enters the shotgun in question.

"I said no, as a matter of fact he couldn't. I was doing some test-fires and he couldn't come in. I asked what he wanted to check and he said never mind."

"I don't know how he could be onto this," Marino says. "How could he know about this? A buddy of mine at the Hollywood PD knows, he'd never say a word. Only other people I've told are the Doc and now you."

"Camo stock, twenty-four-inch barrel, tritium ghost ring sights," Vince reads. "You're right. Used in a homicide. Suspect dead. A donation from Hollywood police, March of last year." He glances up at Marino. "As I recall, it was one of ten or twelve firearms they were clearing out of their inventory, their usual generous selves. Providing we give them free training and consultation, beer and door prizes. Let's see." He scrolls down the screen. "According to this, it's only been checked out twice since we got it. Once by me last April eighth—on the remote-firing platform to make sure there was nothing wrong with it."

"Son of a bitch," Marino says, reading over his shoulder.

"And Dr. Amos checked it out the second time this last June twenty-eighth at three fifteen in the afternoon."

"What for?"

"Maybe test-firing it in ordnance gelatin. Last summer was when Dr. Scarpetta started giving him cooking lessons. He's in and out of here so much, unfortunately, it's hard for me to remember. Says here he used it June twenty-eighth and returned it to the collection that same day, at five fifteen. And if I look up that date on the computer, there's the entry. What that means is I did get it out of the vault and put it back."

"Then how come it's out on the street and killing people?"

"Unless this record is somehow wrong," Vince considers, frowning.

"Maybe that's why he wanted to check the computer. Son

of a bitch. Who maintains the log? You or the user? Anybody touch this computer besides you?"

"Electronically, I do. You make your request in writing in the book over there"—Vince indicates a spiral ledger book by the phone—"then you sign it out and sign it back in, all in your own handwriting and initialed. After the fact, I enter the information in the computer to verify that you used the gun and it was returned to the vault. Guess you've never played with guns up here."

"I'm not a firearms examiner. I let you do that. Damn son of a bitch."

"In the request, you write in what type of firearm you want and when you'd like to reserve the range or the water tank. I can show you."

He retrieves the ledger and opens it to the last page filled in.

"Here's Dr. Amos again," he says. "Ordnance gelatin test-fires with a Taurus PT-145 two weeks ago. At least this time he bothered to log it. He was in here the other day and didn't."

"How did he get into the vault?"

"He brought his own pistol. He collects guns, is a real yahoo."

"Can you tell when the entry for the Mossberg was entered into the computer?" Marino asks. "You know, like when you look at a file and can see the time and date when it was saved last? What I'm wondering is if there's some way Joe might have altered the computer after the fact, entered the shotgun to make it look like you gave it to him and then returned it to the vault."

"It's just a word-processing file called Log. So I'm going to close it now without saving it, take a look at the last time stamp." He looks hard at it, shocked. "Says here it was last saved twenty-three minutes ago. I can't believe it!"

"This thing not password-protected?"

"Of course it is. I'm the only person who can get into it. Except, of course, Lucy. So I wonder why Dr. Amos called and said he wanted to come down and check the computer. If he somehow altered the computer log, why bother to call me?"

"That's an easy one. If you opened the file for him and you saved it when you closed it, then that would explain the new date and time."

"Then he's pretty damn smart."

"We'll see how smart he is."

"This is very upsetting. If he did that, he's got my password."

"Is it written down anywhere?"

"No. I'm very careful."

"Who besides you has access to the vault combination? I'm going to get him this time. One way or other."

"Lucy. She can get into anything. Come on. Let's look."

The vault is a fireproof room with a steel door that requires a code to unlock it. Inside are file drawers housing thousands of known bullet and cartridge case specimens, and in racks and hanging on pegboards are hundreds of rifles, shotguns and handguns, all tagged with accession numbers.

"Quite a candy store," Marino says, looking around.

"You've never been in here?"

"I'm not a gun freak. I've had some bad experiences with them."

"Like what?"

"Like having to use them."

Vince scans racks of shoulder firearms, picks up each shotgun and checks the tag. He does it twice. He and Marino move from rack to rack, checking for the Mossberg. It isn't inside the vault.

Scarpetta points out the livor mortis pattern, a reddish-purple discoloration caused by noncirculating blood settling due to gravity. Pale areas or blanching of the dead woman's right cheek, breasts, belly, thighs and the inside of her forearms were caused by those areas of her body pressing against some firm surface, perhaps a floor.

"She was facedown for some time," Scarpetta is saying. "Hours at least, her head turned to the left, which is why there's blanching of the right cheek—it would have been against the floor or whatever flat surface she was on."

She pulls up another photograph on the computer screen, this one showing the dead woman facedown on the autopsy table after she was washed, her body and hair wet, the red handprints bright and intact, obviously waterproof. She goes back to a photograph she just looked at, back and forth through a number of them, trying to piece together the artifacts of this woman's death.

"So, after he killed her," Benton says, "maybe he turned her facedown to paint the handprints on her back, worked on her for hours. Her blood settled and lividity began to form, and that's why we have this pattern."

"I have another scenario in mind," Scarpetta says. "He painted her face-up first, then turned her over and worked on her back, and this was the position he left her in. Certainly he didn't do all this outside in the cold dark. Someplace where there was no risk anyone would hear the shotgun blast or see him trying to get the body into a vehicle. In fact, maybe he did all this in the vehicle he transported her in, a van, an SUV, a truck. Shot her, painted her, transported her."

"One-stop shopping."

"Well, that would have reduced the risk, wouldn't it. Abduct her, drive her to a remote area, and kill her inside the vehicle—as long as it's a vehicle with sufficient room in back—then dump the body," she says, clicking through more photographs, stopping on one she's already looked at.

She sees it differently this time, the photograph of the woman's brain, what's left of it, on a cutting board. The tough, fibrous membrane that lines the inside of the cranium, the dura mater, is supposed to be creamy white. In this photograph, it is stained a yellowish-orange, and she envisions the two sisters, Ev and Kristin, with their hiking sticks, squinting in the sun, the photograph on the dresser in their bedroom. She recalls the somewhat jaundiced complexion of one of them and clicks back to the autopsy report, checks on what it says about the dead woman's sclera, the whites of her eyes. They're normal.

She recalls the raw vegetables, the nineteen bags of carrots in the refrigerator at Ev and Kristin's house, and thinks of the white linen pants the dead woman was wearing like a diaper, clothing consistent with a warm climate.

Benton is looking curiously at her.

"Xanthochromia of the skin," Scarpetta says. "A yellow discoloration that doesn't affect the sclera. Possibly caused by carotenemia. We may know who she is."

55

Dr. Bronson is in his office, moving a slide around on the stage of his compound microscope. Marino knocks on the open door.

Dr. Bronson is smart and competent, always neat in a starchy white lab coat. He's been a decent chief. But he can't dislodge himself from the past. The way things were done is how he still does them, and that would include how he evaluates other people. Marino doubts Dr. Bronson bothers with background checks or any other sort of intense scrutiny that should be standard practice in today's world.

He knocks again, this time louder, and Dr. Bronson looks up from the microscope.

"Do come in," he says, smiling. "To what do I owe this pleasure?"

He is a man of the old world, polite and charming, with a perfectly bald head and vague, gray eyes. A briarwood pipe is cold in the ashtray on his neatly arranged desk, and the faint aroma of aromatic tobacco always lingers.

"Least down here in the sunny south they still let you smoke indoors," Marino says, pulling a chair close.

"Well, I shouldn't," Dr. Bronson says. "My wife keeps telling me I'm going to get cancer of the throat or tongue. I tell her if I do, at least I won't complain much on my way out."

Marino remembers he didn't shut the door. He gets up, shuts it and sits back down.

"If they cut my tongue or vocal cords out, then I guess I won't be griping much," Dr. Bronson says as if Marino didn't get the joke.

"I need a couple of things," Marino says. "First, we'd like to run a sample of Johnny Swift's DNA. Dr. Scarpetta says there should be several DNA cards in his case file."

"She ought to take my place, you know. I wouldn't mind if she was the one who took my place," he says, and the way he says it makes Marino realize that Dr. Bronson probably knows all too well what people think.

Everyone wants him to retire. They wanted him to retire years ago.

"I built this place, you know," he goes on. "Can't just let any Tom, Dick or Harry come in and muck up everything. Not fair to the public. Certainly not fair to my staff." He picks up the phone and presses a button. "Polly? How about pulling the Johnny Swift case for me and bringing it in. We'll need all the appropriate paperwork." He listens, then, "Because we need to receipt a DNA card to Pete. They're going to do something with it over at the labs."

He hangs up, takes off his glasses and cleans them with a handkerchief.

"So, am I to assume there's some new development?" he asks.

"It's beginning to look that way," Marino replies. "When it's a certainty, you'll be the first to know. But put it like this, some things have come up that make it pretty damn likely Johnny Swift was murdered."

"Happy to change the manner if you can show that. Never was all that comfortable about the case. But I have to go with the evidence and there just hasn't been anything significant in the investigation to make me sure about anything. Mostly, I've suspected suicide."

"Except for the shotgun missing from the scene," Marino can't help but remind him.

"You know, a lot of strange things happen, Pete. Can't tell you how many times I show up and find the family's completely mucked up the scene to protect the dignity of their loved one. Especially in autoerotic asphyxiations. I get there and there's not a pornographic magazine or bondage accouterment in sight. Same with suicides. Families don't want anyone to know or want to collect the insurance money, so they hide the gun or knife. They do all kinds of things."

"We need to talk about Joe Amos," Marino says.

"A disappointment," he says, his normally pleasant expression fading. "Truth is, I'm sorry I recommended him for your fine institution. I'm especially sorry because Kay deserves a heck of a lot better than the likes of that arrogant little bastard."

"That's what I'm getting at. Based on what? You recommended him because of what?"

"His impressive education and references. He has quite a pedigree."

"Where's his file? You still have it? The original?"

"I sure do. I kept the original. A copy went to Kay."

"When you went over this fancy education and references, did you check them out to make sure they were authentic?" Marino hates to ask him. "People can fake a lot of things these days. Especially because of computer graphics, the Internet, you name it. That's one reason identity theft's becoming such a problem."

Dr. Bronson rolls his chair to a filing cabinet and opens a drawer. He walks his fingers through neatly labeled files and pulls out one with Joe Amos's name on it. He hands it to Marino.

"Help yourself," he says.

"Mind if I sit here for a minute?"

"I don't know what's taking Polly so long," Dr. Bronson says, rolling his chair back to the microscope. "You take all the time you want, Pete. I'll just get back to my slides. A sad one. Poor woman found in the swimming pool." He adjusts the focus, his head bent over the eyepiece. "Her ten-year-old little girl found her. Question's whether she drowned or had some other fatal event like a myocardial infarct. She was bulimic."

Marino looks through letters that medical-school department heads and other pathologists wrote on Joe Amos's behalf. He skims through a résumé that is five pages long.

"Dr. Bronson? Did you ever call any of these people?" Marino asks.

"About what." He doesn't look up. "No old scarring of her heart. Course, if she had an infarct and survived for hours, I'm not going to see anything. I asked if she might have purged earlier. That can really muck up your electrolytes."

"About Joe," Marino says. "To make sure these big-shot doctors really know him."

"Of course they know him. They wrote me all those letters."

Marino holds a letter up to the light. He notices a watermark that looks like a crown with a sword through it. He holds up each of the other letters. They all have the same watermark. The letterheads are convincing, but since they aren't engraved or embossed, they could have been scanned or reproduced with some sort of graphic software package. He picks a letter supposedly generated by the chief of pathology at Johns Hopkins and tries the number. A receptionist answers.

"He's out of town," she tells him.

"I'm calling about Dr. Joe Amos," Marino says.

"Who?"

He explains. He asks her if she could check her files.

"He wrote a letter on Joe Amos's behalf a little over a year ago, on December seventh," Marino tells her. "Says here on the bottom of the letter the person who typed it has the initials LFC."

"There's nobody here with those initials. And I would have been the one who typed anything like that, and those certainly aren't my initials. What is this about?"

"Just a simple case of fraud," Marino says.

56

Lucy rides one of her souped-up V-Rods north on A1A, hitting every red light on her way to Fred Quincy's house.

He runs his Web design business out of his Hollywood home. He isn't expecting her, but she knows he's in, or at least he was when she called half an hour ago to sell him a subscription to *The Miami Herald.* He was polite, far more polite than Lucy would be if some solicitor dared to get her on the phone. His address is two blocks west of the beach, and he must have money. His home is two stories of pale-green stucco and black wrought iron, and the driveway is gated. Lucy stops her bike at an intercom and presses the button.

"May I help you?" a male voice answers.

"Police," Lucy says.

"I didn't call the police."

"I'm here to talk to you about your mother and sister."

"What police department?" the voice sounds suspicious.

"Broward sheriff's."

She slips out her wallet and holds up her bogus credentials, holds the wallet and its badge in front of the closed-circuit video camera. A tone sounds, and the wrought-iron gate begins to slide open. She kicks her bike in gear and bumps over granite pavers, parking in front of a big black door that opens the instant she turns off the engine.

"That's quite a bike," the man she assumes is Fred says.

He is of average height with narrow shoulders and a slender build. His hair is dark blond, his eyes bluish-gray. He is quite handsome in a delicate sort of way.

"Don't think I've ever seen a Harley quite like this," he says, walking around her bike.

"You ride?" she asks.

"Nope. I leave the dangerous stuff to other people."

"You must be Fred." Lucy shakes his hand. "Mind if I come in?"

She follows him across the marble tile foyer into a living room that overlooks a narrow, murky canal.

"What about my mother and Helen? Have you found out something?"

He says it as if he means it the way he should. He isn't just curious or paranoid. Pain fills his eyes, and there is an eagerness, a faint ring of hope.

"Fred," she says. "I'm not with the Broward County Sheriff's Department. I have private investigators and laboratories and we've been asked to help."

"So you misrepresented yourself at my gate," he says, his eyes turning unfriendly. "That wasn't a very nice thing to do. Bet you're the one who called, too, saying you're the *Herald*. To see if I was home."

"Right on both counts."

"And I'm supposed to talk to you?"

"I'm sorry," Lucy says. "It was a lot to explain over an intercom."

"What's happened to make this of interest again? Why now?"

"I'm afraid I need to be the one asking the questions," she says.

Uncle Sam is pointing his finger at YOU and saying I WANT YOUR CITRUS."

Dr. Self pauses dramatically. She looks comfortable and confident in a leather chair on the set of *Talk It Out*. In this segment she has no guests. She doesn't need them. She has a telephone centered on the table next to her chair, and cameras catch her from different angles as she punches buttons and says, "This is Dr. Self. You're on the air."

"So how about that?" she goes on. "Is the USDA stomping on our Fourth Amendment rights?"

It is an easy set-up, and she can't wait to jump right down

the throat of the fool who just called in. She glances at the monitor, satisfied the lighting and angles are catching her favorably.

"They sure are," the fool says over speakerphone.

"What's your name again? Sandy?"

"Yeah, I . . ."

"Stop before you chop, Sandy?"

"Ah, what . . . ?"

"Uncle Sam with an ax? Isn't that the image the public has?"

"We're being screwed. It's a conspiracy."

"So that's how you think of it? Good Old Uncle Sam cutting down all your trees. Chop, chop."

She catches the cameramen, her producer smiling.

"The bastards came into my yard without permission, and next thing I know, all my trees are going to be cut down . . ."

"And you live where, Sandy?"

"Cooper City. I don't blame people for wanting to shoot them or siccing their dogs on . . ."

"Here's the thing about it, Sandy." She leans into the point she's about to make, the cameras zooming in. "You people don't pay attention to the facts. Have you attended meetings? Have you written your legislators? Have you bothered to ask questions point-blank and consider that maybe, just maybe, the explanations offered by the Department of Agriculture might make sense?"

It is her style to take whatever side the other person isn't on. She's known for it.

"Well, the stuff about hurricanes is [bleep]," the fool snaps, and Dr. Self suspected it wouldn't be long before the profanity started.

"It's not *bleep*," she mimics him. "There's nothing *bleep* about it. The fact is"—she faces the camera—"we had four major hurricanes last fall, and it is a fact that citrus canker is a bacterial disease carried by the wind. When we come back, we're going to explore the reality of this dreaded blight and talk it out with a very special guest. Stay with me."

"We're off," a cameraman says.

Dr. Self reaches for her bottle of water. She takes a sip

through a straw so she doesn't smear her lipstick and waits for the makeup person to touch up her forehead and nose, impatient when the makeup person is slow getting to her, impatient when the makeup person is slow to hurry up and finish.

"All right. Okay. That's enough," Dr. Self holds up a hand, shooing off the makeup person. "This is going well," she says to her producer.

"I think in the next segment, we need to really focus on the psychology. That's why people tune in to you, Marilyn. It's not the politics, it's their problems with their girlfriends, bosses, mothers, fathers."

"I don't need coaching."

"I didn't mean . . ."

"Listen, what makes my shows unique is the blend of current affairs and our emotional responses."

"Absolutely."

"Three, two, one."

"And we're back." Dr. Self smiles into the camera.

57

Marino stands beneath a palm tree outside the Academy, watching Reba walk off to her unmarked Crown Victoria. He notes the defiance in her step, tries to determine if it's genuine or if she's putting on an act. He wonders if she sees him standing under the palm tree, smoking.

She called him a jerk. He's been called that a lot, but he never thought she would say it.

She unlocks her car, then seems to change her mind about getting in. She doesn't look in his direction, but he has a feeling she knows he's standing there in the shadow of the palm tree, his Treo in hand, the earpiece in his ear, a cigarette going. She shouldn't have said what she did. She has no right to talk about Scarpetta. The Effexor ruined things. If he wasn't depressed before, he was after that, then that comment about Scarpetta, about all these cops having the hots for her.

The Effexor was a blight. Dr. Self has no right to put him on a drug that ruined his sex life. She has no right to talk about Scarpetta all the time, as if Scarpetta is the most important person in Marino's life. Reba had to remind him. She said what she did to remind him he couldn't have sex, remind him of men who can and want it with Scarpetta. Marino hasn't taken the Effexor for several weeks, and his problem is getting better except he is depressed.

Reba pops the trunk, walks around to the back of the car and opens it.

Marino wonders what she's doing. He decides he may as well find out and be decent enough to let her know he can't arrest anyone and could probably use her help. He can threaten people all he wants, but he can't legally arrest anybody. It's the only thing he misses about policing. Reba grabs what looks like a bag of laundry out of the trunk and throws it into the backseat as if she's pissed off.

"Got a body in there?" Marino asks, casually walking up to her, flicking his cigarette butt into the grass.

"Ever heard of using a trash can?"

She slams shut the door, barely looking at him.

"What's in the bag?"

"I've got to go to the cleaners. Haven't had time in a week, not that it's any of your business," she says, hiding behind a pair of dark glasses. "Don't treat me like shit anymore, at least not in front of other people. You want to be a jerk, at least be discreet about it."

He looks back at his palm tree as if it's his favorite spot, looks at the stucco building against the bright blue sky, trying to think how to put it.

"Well, you were disrespectful," he says.

She looks at him in shock. "Me? What are you talking about? Are you crazy? Last I remember, we had a nice ride and you dragged me to Hooters, never asked if that's where I wanted to go, by the way. Why you'd take a woman to an ass-and-tits place like that beats the hell out of me. Talk about disrespectful? Are you kidding? Making me sit there while you ogle all the tartlets jiggling past."

"I wasn't."

"Were too."

"I sure wasn't," he says, sliding out the pack of cigarettes.

"You're smoking too much."

"I wasn't staring at nothing. I was minding my own business drinking my coffee, then out of the blue you started in on all this crap about the Doc and I'll be damned if I have to listen to such disrespectful bullshit."

She's jealous, he thinks, pleased. She said what she did because she thought he was staring at the waitresses in Hooters, and maybe he was. To make a point.

"I've worked with her a million years and don't let anybody talk about her like that and I'm not going to start now," he goes on, lighting up, squinting in the sun, noticing a group of students dressed in field clothes walking past on the road, heading to the SUVs in the parking lot, probably head-

ing off to the Hollywood Police Training Facility for a
demonstration by the Bomb Disposal Team.

Seems like they were scheduled for that today, to play
with Eddie the RemoteTec robot, watch it move on its tractor
belts, sounding like a crab crawling down the trailer's aluminum ramp, connected to a fiber-optic cable, showing off,
and Bunky the bomb dog showing off, and firefighters in
their big trucks showing off, and guys in their bomb-and-
search suits showing off with dynamite and det cord and dis-
rupters, maybe blowing up a car.

Marino misses it. He's tired of being left out.

"I'm sorry," Reba says, "I didn't mean to say anything
disrespectful about her. All I was saying was some of the
guys I work with—"

"I need you to arrest somebody," he cuts her off, looking
at his watch, not interested in hearing her repeat what she
told him at Hooters, not interested in perhaps having to face
that some of it was him.

Most of it was him.

The Effexor. Reba would have found out sooner rather
than later. The damn stuff ruined him.

"In maybe half an hour. If you can put off going to the
Laundromat," he is saying.

"The dry cleaner's, jerk," she says with hostility that's not
at all convincing.

She still likes him.

"I've got my own washer and dryer," she says. "I don't
live in a trailer."

Marino tries Lucy on the cell phone as he says to Reba,
"I've got an idea. Not sure it will work, but maybe we'll
get lucky."

Lucy answers and tells him she can't talk.

"It's important," Marino says, looking at Reba, remembering their weekend in Key West when he wasn't on Effexor. "Just give me two minutes."

He can hear Lucy talking to someone, saying she's got to
take the call and will be right back. A man's voice says no
problem. Marino can hear Lucy walking. He looks at Reba
and remembers getting drunk on Captain Morgan rum in the

Paradise Lounge at the Holiday Inn and watching the sunsets and sitting up late at night in the hot tub when he wasn't on Effexor.

"You there?" Lucy is asking him.

"Is it possible for me to have a three-way conference call with two cell phones, one landline and only two people?" he asks.

"This some kind of Mensa test question?"

"What I want is to make it look like I'm on my phone in my office talking to you, but what I'm really doing is talking to you on my cell phone. Hello? Are you there?"

"Are you suggesting someone may be monitoring your phone calls from a multiline phone that's connected to the PBX system?"

"From the damn phone on my desk," he says, looking at Reba looking at him, trying to see if she's impressed.

"That's what I meant. Who?" Lucy says.

"I intend to find out but I'm pretty sure I know."

"No one could do that without the system admin's password. And that would be me."

"I think someone's got it. It would explain a lot of things. Is it possible to do what I said?" he asks her again. "Can I call you on my office phone, then conference in on my cell phone, then leave my office phone line open so it seems I'm in there talking but I'm not?"

"Yes, we can," she says. "But not right this minute."

Dr. Self presses a flashing button on the phone.

"Our next caller—well, he's been on hold for several minutes now, and he has an unusual nickname. Hog? I apologize. You still with us?"

"Yes, ma'am," a soft-spoken voice enters the studio.

"You're on the air," she says. "Now, Hog? Why don't you tell us about your nickname first. I'm sure everybody's curious."

"It's what I'm called."

Silence, and Dr. Self fills it instantly. There can be no dead time on the air.

"Well, Hog it is. Now, you called in with a startling story. You're in the lawn-care business. And you were in a certain neighborhood and noticed citrus canker in someone's yard . . . ?"

"No. It's not quite like that."

Dr. Self feels a pinch of irritation. Hog's not following the script. When he called late Tuesday afternoon and she pretended to be someone other than herself, he distinctly said he had discovered canker in an old woman's yard in Hollywood, just one orange tree, and now every citrus tree in her yard and all her neighbors' yards has to be cut down, and when he mentioned the problem to the owner of that particular infected tree, the old woman, she threatened to kill herself if Hog reported the canker to the Department of Agriculture. She threatened to shoot herself with her dead husband's shotgun.

The old woman's husband had planted the trees when they first got married. He's dead and the trees are all she has left, the only living thing left. To cut down her trees is to destroy a precious part of her life that nobody has any business touching.

"Eradicating those trees is to cause her to at last accept her loss." Dr. Self is explaining all this to her audience. "And in doing so, she doesn't see anything left worth living for. She wants to die. That's quite a dilemma to find yourself in, isn't it, Hog? Playing God," she says to the speakerphone.

"I don't play God. I do what God says. It's not an act."

Dr. Self is confused but carries on. "What a choice for you to make. Did you follow the government's rules or follow your heart?"

"I painted red stripes on them," he says. "Now she's dead. You were next. But there isn't time."

58

They sit in the kitchen at a table before a window that overlooks the narrow, murky canal.

"When the police got involved," Fred Quincy is saying, "they did ask for a few things that might have their DNA. Hairbrush, toothbrush, I forget what else. I never heard anything about what they did with the stuff."

"They probably never analyzed it," Lucy says, thinking about what she and Marino just talked about. "Possibly it's still in their evidence room. We can ask them about it, but I'd rather not wait."

The suggestion that someone may have gained access to her system's administrative password is incredible. It's sickening. Marino must be mistaken. She can't stop thinking about it.

"Obviously, the case isn't a priority for them. They've always believed they just ran off. There was no sign of violence," Fred says. "They said there should have been a sign of a struggle, or someone should have seen something. It was the middle of the morning, and there were people around. And Mom's SUV was missing."

"I was told her car was there. An Audi."

"It definitely wasn't. And she didn't have an Audi. I did. Someone must have seen my car when I got there later, looking for them. Mom had a Chevy Blazer. She used it to haul things around. You know, people get things so twisted. I went to the shop after trying to call all day. My mom's purse and Blazer were gone, and there was no sign of her or my sister."

"Any sign they had ever been inside the shop?"

"Nothing was on. The closed sign was out."

"Anything missing?"

"Not that I could tell. Certainly nothing obvious. Nothing in the cash drawer, but that didn't necessarily mean anything. If she left money in it overnight, it wasn't much. Something must have come up if you suddenly need their DNA."

"I'll let you know," Lucy says. "We may have a lead."

"You can't tell me?"

"I promise I'll let you know. What was your first thought when you went looking for them, drove to the shop?"

"Truth? I thought maybe they'd never gone there at all, had just driven off somewhere over the rainbow."

"Why do you put it like that?"

"There had been a lot of problems. Financial ups and downs. Personal problems. Dad had this extremely successful landscaping business."

"In Palm Beach."

"That's where it was headquartered. But he had greenhouses and tree farms in other locations, including around here. Then, in the mid-eighties, he got wiped out by citrus canker. Every damn one of his citrus trees had to be destroyed, and he had to let go of almost all of his employees and came very close to declaring bankruptcy. That was hard on Mom. He got back on his feet and was more successful then, and that was hard on Mom, too. You know, I'm not sure I should be telling you all this."

"Fred, I'm trying to help. I can't do it if you don't talk to me."

"Let me start with when Helen was twelve," he says. "I was beginning my freshman year in college. I'm older, obviously. Helen went to live with my dad's brother and his wife for about six months."

"Why?"

"It was sad, such a pretty, talented girl. Got into Harvard when she was only sixteen, lasted not even a semester, had a meltdown and came home."

"When?"

"That would have been the fall before she and Mom disappeared. She only lasted until November—at Harvard."

"Eight months before she and your mother disappeared?"

"Yes. Helen was dealt a really lousy genetic hand."

He pauses as if trying to decide whether he should go on, then, "All right. My mom wasn't the most stable person. You might have already figured that out, her Christmas obsession. Craziness, more craziness, on and off for as long as I can remember. But it got really bad when Helen was twelve. Mom was doing some pretty irrational things."

"Was she seeing a local psychiatrist?"

"Whatever money could buy. That celebrity one. She lived in Palm Beach back then. Dr. Self. She recommended hospitalization. That's the real reason she sent Helen off to live with my aunt and uncle. Mom was in the hospital, and Dad was really busy and not inclined to take care of a twelve-year-old kid all by himself. Mom came home. Then Helen did and neither of them were, well, normal."

"Did Helen go to a psychiatrist?"

"Not at that time," Fred says. "She was just strange. Not unstable like Mom but strange. She did well in school, really well, then went off to Harvard and crashed and burned, was found in the lobby of some funeral home up there, didn't know who she was. As if things weren't bad enough, Dad died. Mom went into a real downhill spiral, would go places on the weekends, not tell me where she was, freaking me out. It was awful."

"So the police figured she was unstable and into disappearing acts, and maybe ran off with Helen?"

"I wondered it myself. I still wonder if my mom and sister are out there somewhere."

"How did your dad die?"

"Fell off a ladder in the rare-book library. The house in Palm Beach was three stories, everything marble and stone tiles."

"He home alone when it happened?"

"Helen found him on the first-floor landing."

"She was the only one in the house at the time?"

"A boyfriend, maybe. Don't know who."

"When was this?"

"A couple months before she and Mom disappeared. Helen was seventeen then, precocious. Well, truthfully, after she came home from Harvard, she was completely out of control. I've always wondered if it was a reaction to my dad, my uncle, the people on my dad's side of the family. Extremely religious and serious, Jesus this, Jesus that, big in their churches. Deacons, Sunday-school teachers, always trying to *witness* to people."

"You ever meet any of Helen's boyfriends?"

"No. She ran around, would disappear for days. Just trouble. I didn't come home if I didn't have to. Mom's Christmas obsession is such a joke. It was never Christmas in our house. It was always pretty damn awful."

He gets up from the table. "Mind if I have a beer?"

"Help yourself."

He picks out a Michelob, twists off the cap. He shuts the refrigerator door and sits back down.

"Was your sister ever hospitalized?" Lucy asks.

"Same place Mom was. For a month right after she dropped out of Harvard. Club McLean, I called it. The good ole family genes."

"McLean in Massachusetts?"

"Yup. You ever take notes? I don't know how you can remember all this."

Lucy fingers the pen she's holding, the small recorder turned on and invisible in her pocket.

"We need your mom's and sister's DNA," she says.

"I don't have any idea how we're going to get it now. Unless the police still have that stuff."

"Yours will work. Think of it as family-tree DNA," Lucy says.

59

Scarpetta looks out the window at the cold, white street. It is almost three, and she has been on the phone most of the day.

"What kind of screening do you have? You must have some system in place for controlling who makes it on the air," she says.

"Of course. One of the producers talks to the person, makes sure he isn't crazy."

It seems an odd choice of words for a psychiatrist.

"In this case, I'd already had a conversation with the man, the lawn-service man. It's a long story." Dr. Self is talking fast.

"He said his name was Hog when you talked to him the first time?"

"I didn't think anything about it. A lot of people have wacky nicknames. I just need to know. Did some elderly lady suddenly turn up dead, a suicide? You would know, wouldn't you? He threatened to kill me."

"I'm afraid a lot of elderly ladies turn up dead on a regular basis," Scarpetta replies evasively. "Can you give me a few more details? What exactly did he say?"

Dr. Self recounts the story of the blighted citrus trees in the old woman's yard, of her grief over the loss of her husband, of her threat to kill herself with her dead husband's shotgun if the lawn-service man—Hog—had her trees destroyed. Benton walks into the living room with two coffees, and Scarpetta puts Dr. Self on speakerphone.

"Then he threatened to kill me," Dr. Self says again. "Or said he was going to but changed his mind."

"I've got someone with me who needs to hear this," Scarpetta says, and she introduces Benton. "Tell him what you just told me."

Benton sits on the couch as Dr. Self replies that she doesn't understand why a forensic psychologist in Massachusetts would have any interest in a suicide that may or may not have happened in Florida. But he might have a valid opinion about a threat on her life, and she would love to have him on her show sometime. What sort of person would threaten her like that? Is she in danger?

"Does your studio keep track of the call-ins through caller ID?" Benton asks. "Are the numbers stored, even temporarily?"

"I would think so."

"I'd like you to find that out right away," he says. "Let's see if we can determine where he was calling from."

"I do know we don't accept unidentified calls. You have to disable the caller ID block, because once I had this insane woman threaten to kill me on the air. It's not the first time it's happened. Her call came in as unidentified. No more."

"Then you're obviously capturing the numbers of whoever is calling in," Benton says. "What I'd like is a printout of the numbers of everybody who called in during the show earlier this afternoon. What about when you talked to this lawn man the first time? You mentioned you had a phone conversation with him. When was that, and was the call local? Did you capture the number in a log?"

"Late Tuesday afternoon. I don't have caller ID. I have an unlisted, unpublished number and don't need it."

"Did he identify himself?"

"As Hog."

"He called your house?"

"My private office. I see patients in the office behind my house. It's really a guesthouse-slash-pool house."

"How might he have gotten the number?"

"I have no idea, now that you mention it. Of course, my colleagues, anybody I do business with, my patients have it."

"Any possibility this man might be one of your patients?"

"I didn't recognize his voice. I can't think of anybody I see who might have been him. There's something more going on here." She gets pushy. "I think I have a right to know if there's something more about this than meets the eye. In the first place, you haven't confirmed whether there's an old woman who committed suicide with a shotgun because of her blighted citrus trees."

"Nothing quite like that." It is Scarpetta who speaks. "But there is a very recent case that sounds similar to what you just described, an elderly woman whose trees were marked for eradication. A shotgun death."

"My God. Did it happen after six p.m. this past Tuesday?"

"Probably before that," Scarpetta says, fairly certain she knows why Dr. Self is asking.

"That's a relief. Then she was already dead by the time the lawn man, Hog, called me. He called maybe five, ten minutes after six and asked to be on my show, told the story about the old woman threatening to kill herself. So she must have already done it. I wouldn't want to think her death had something to do with him wanting to be on my show."

Benton gives Scarpetta a look that says, *What a narcissistic, insensitive bitch,* and says to the speakerphone, "Right now we're trying to figure out a lot of other things, Dr. Self. And it would be helpful if you could give us a little more information about David Luck. You prescribed Ritalin to him."

"Are you now saying something horrible's happened to him, too? I know he's missing. Is there something new?"

"There's reason to be greatly concerned." Scarpetta repeats what she's said in the past. "We have reason to be very concerned about him, his brother and the two sisters they lived with. How long have you been seeing David as a patient?"

"Since last summer. I think he first came to see me last July. It might have been late June. Both parents had been killed in an accident and he was acting out a lot, doing poorly in school. He and his brother were homeschooled."

"You saw him how often?" Benton asks.

"Usually once a week."

"Who brought him to his appointments?"

"Sometimes Kristin. Sometimes Ev. Now and then they both brought him, and on occasion I would meet with the three of them."

"How was David referred to you?" It is Scarpetta who asks. "How did he end up in your care?"

"Well, it's rather poignant. Kristin was a call-in. Apparently, she listens to my show a lot and decided maybe she could get hold of me that way. She called in to my radio show and said she was taking care of a South African boy who had just lost both his parents and he needed help, et cetera et cetera. It was quite a heartbreaking story, and I agreed on the air to see him. You would be amazed at the mail I got from my listeners after that. I still get mail, people wanting to know how the little South African orphan is doing."

"Do you have a tape of the show you're talking about?" Benton asks. "An audio clip?"

"We have tapes of everything."

"How quickly could you get me that audio clip, and one from your television show earlier today? I'm afraid we're snowed in up here—at the moment, anyway. We're doing what we can remotely but are somewhat limited."

"Yes, I hear you've had quite the storm up there. Hope you don't lose power," she says, as if they've just spent the past half-hour having a pleasant conversation. "I can call my producer right now, and he can get it to you by e-mail. I'm sure he'll want to talk with you about being on my show sometime."

"And the phone numbers of the callers," Benton reminds her.

"Dr. Self?" Scarpetta says, looking out the window with dismay.

It is starting to snow again.

"What about Tony? David's brother?"

"They fought a lot."

"Did you see Tony, too?"

"I never met him," she says.

"You said you know both Ev and Kristin. Did one of them have an eating disorder?"

"I wasn't treating either one of them. They weren't my patients."

"I should think you could tell by looking at them. One of them was on a steady diet of carrots."

"Based on her appearance, Kristin," she replies.

Scarpetta looks at Benton. She had the Academy's DNA lab contact Detective Thrush the instant she discovered the yellowish dura mater. DNA from the dead woman up here has been matched to DNA from yellowish stains on a blouse Scarpetta removed from Kristin's and Ev's house. The body in the Boston morgue most likely is Kristin, and Scarpetta has no intention of relaying this information to Dr. Self, who might very well talk about it on the air.

Benton gets up from the couch to put another log on the fire as Scarpetta gets off the phone. She watches the snow. It falls fast in the light of the lamps at Benton's front gate.

"No more coffee," Benton says. "My nerves have had it."

"Does it do anything besides snow up here?"

"The main streets are probably already clear. They're amazingly fast up here. I don't think the boys have anything to do with this."

"They have something to do with it," she says, moving in front of the fire, sitting on the hearth. "They're gone. It appears Kristin's dead. Probably all of them are."

60

Marino calls Joe while Reba sits quietly nearby, engrossed in hell scenes.

"I've got a few things to go over with you," Marino tells Joe. "There's a problem."

"What kind of problem?" he says cautiously.

"You need to hear about it from me. I've got to return a few calls in my office, take care of a few things. Where you going to be during the next hour?"

"Room one twelve."

"You there now?"

"Walking that way."

"Let me guess," Marino says. "Working on another hell scene you stole from me?"

"If that's what you want to talk to me about . . ."

"It's not," Marino says. "It's a whole lot worse than that."

"You're really something," Reba says to Marino, placing the file of hell scenes back on his desk. "They're really good. They're brilliant, Pete."

"We're going to do this in five, give him time to get into his office," and now he has Lucy on the phone. "Lay it on me, what do I do?"

"You're going to hang up, so am I, then hit the conference button on your desk phone and dial my cell phone. When I answer, hit conference again and dial your cell phone. Then you can either put your desk phone on hold to keep the line open or just leave it off the hook. If someone's monitoring our call, he's going to assume you're in your office."

Marino waits a few minutes, then does what she said. He and Reba walk out of the building while he and Lucy talk to each other on their cell phones. They have a real conversation while he hopes like hell that Joe is listening in. He and

Lucy are lucky so far. The reception is good. She sounds as if she's in the next room.

They chat about the new motorcycles. They chat about all sorts of things as Marino and Reba walk.

The Last Stand motel is a modified double-wide trailer that has been divided into three rooms that are used for mock crime scenes. Each section has a separate door with a number on it. Room 112 is in the middle. Marino notes that the curtain is drawn over the front window, and he can hear the air conditioner running. He tries the door and it's locked, and he kicks it hard with his big, Harley-booted foot and the cheap door flies open and slams against the wall. Joe is sitting at the desk, the receiver to his ear, a tape recorder hooked up to the phone, his face shocked, then terrified. Marino and Reba look at him.

"Know why they call this the Last Stand motel?" Marino asks, walking over to Joe, grabbing him out of the chair as if he weighs nothing. "Because you're as dead as Colonel Custer."

"Let me go!" Joe yells.

His feet are off the floor. Marino is holding him up by his armpits, their faces inches apart. Marino shoves him against a wall.

"Let me go! You're hurting me!"

Marino drops him. He sits down hard on the floor.

"You know why she's here?" He indicates Reba. "To arrest your sorry ass."

"I didn't do anything!"

"Falsifying records, grand larceny, maybe homicide since you obviously stole a gun that was used out of state to blow a lady's head off. Oh, and add fraud," Marino adds to the list, not caring if any of it's valid.

"I didn't! I don't know what you're talking about!"

"Quit yelling. I'm not deaf. See, Detective Wagner here's a witness, right?"

She nods, her face hard. Marino's never seen her look so scary.

"You see me lay a finger on him?" he asks her.

"Absolutely not," she says.

Joe is so scared, he might wet himself.

"You want to tell us why you stole that shotgun and who you gave it to or sold it to?" Marino pulls up the desk chair, turns it around, sits on it backward, his huge arms resting on the back. "Or maybe you blew the lady's head off. Maybe you're living out hell scenes, only I didn't write that one. You must have stole it from someone else."

"What lady? I didn't kill anybody. I didn't steal a shotgun. What shotgun?"

"The one you checked out last June twenty-eighth at three-fifteen in the afternoon. That one that belongs to the computer record you just updated, falsifying that record, too."

Joe's mouth is open, his eyes wide.

Marino reaches into his back pocket, pulls out a piece of paper, unfolds it and hands it to him. It's a photocopy of the ledger page showing when Joe signed out the Mossberg shotgun and supposedly returned it.

Joe stares at the photocopy, his hands shaking.

He says, "I swear to God I didn't take it. I remember what happened. I was doing more research with ordnance gelatin and maybe test-fired it once. Then I left to do something in the lab kitchen, I think it was to check on some more blocks I'd just made, the ones we were using to simulate passengers in an airplane crash. Remember when Lucy used that big helicopter to drop an airplane fuselage out of the sky so the students could . . . ?"

"Get to the point!"

"When I came back, the shotgun was gone. I assumed Vince locked it back up in the vault. It was late in the day. He probably locked it up because he was about to go home. I remember feeling pissed about it because I wanted to fire it a couple more times."

"No wonder you have to steal my hell scenes," Marino says. "You've got no imagination. Try again."

"I'm telling the truth."

"You want her to haul you off in handcuffs?" Marino says, jerking his thumb toward Reba.

"You can't prove I did anything."

"I can prove you've committed fraud," Marino says. "You

want to talk about all those letters of reference you faked so the Doc would hire you as a fellow?"

For an instant, he's speechless. Then he begins to regain his composure. He gets that smart-ass look on his face again.

"Prove it," he says.

"Every one of those letters is on the same water-marked paper."

"Doesn't prove a thing."

Joe gets to his feet and rubs his lower back.

"I'm going to sue you," he says.

"Good. Then I may as well hurt you worse," Marino replies, rubbing his fist. "Maybe I'll break your neck. You haven't seen me touch him, have you, Detective Wagner."

"Absolutely not," she says. Then,"If you didn't take the shotgun, who did? Was anybody else with you in the firearms lab that afternoon?"

He thinks for a minute and something shows in his eyes.

"No," he says.

61

Twenty-four hours a day, guards inside the control room monitor inmates who are considered suicide risks.

They watch Basil Jenrette. They watch him sleep, shower, eat. They watch him use the steel toilet. They watch him turn his back to the closed-circuit camera and relieve his sexual tension beneath the sheets of his narrow steel bed.

He imagines them laughing at him. He imagines what they say inside the control room as they watch him on the monitors. They make fun of him to the other guards. He can tell by the smirks on their faces when they bring him his meals or let him out so he can exercise or make a phone call. Sometimes they make comments. Sometimes they show up outside his cell just as he is relieving his sexual tension, and they imitate the noise and laugh and bang on the door.

Basil sits on his bed, looking up at the camera mounted high on the opposite wall. He flips through this month's copy of *Field & Stream* as he thinks back to the first time he met with Benton Wesley and made the mistake of answering one of his questions honestly.

Do you ever think about hurting yourself or others?

I've already hurt others so I guess that means I think about it, Basil said.

What thoughts do you have, Basil? Can you describe what you envision when you think about hurting other people and yourself?

I think of doing what I used to. Seeing a woman and getting the urge. Getting her into my police car and pulling out my gun and maybe my badge and telling her I'm arresting her, and if she resists arrest, so much as touches the door, I'll have no choice but to shoot her. They all cooperated.

None of them resisted you.

Just the last two. Because of car trouble. It's so stupid.

The others, before the last two, did they believe you were the police and you were arresting them?

They believed I was a cop. But they knew what was happening. I wanted them to know. I'd get hard. I'd show them I was hard, make them put their hand on it. They were going to die. It's so stupid.

What's stupid, Basil?

So stupid. I've said it a thousand times. You've heard me say it, right? Wouldn't you rather I shoot you right then in my car or get you off somewhere so I can take my time with you? Why would you let me get you to some secret place and tie you up?

Tell me how you would tie them up, Basil. Always the same way?

Yeah. I have a really cool method. It's absolutely unique. I invented it when I started making my arrests.

By arrests you mean abducting and assaulting women.

When I first started, yeah.

Basil smiles as he sits on his bed, remembering the thrill of twisting wire coat hangers around their ankles and wrists and threading rope through them so he could string them up.

They were my puppets, he explained to Dr. Wesley during that first interview, wondering what it would take to get a reaction out of him.

No matter what Basil said, Dr. Wesley kept his steady gaze, listening, not letting anything he felt register on his face. Maybe he didn't feel anything. Maybe he's like Basil.

See, in this place I had, there were exposed rafters where the ceiling had come down, especially in this one room in the back. I would throw the ropes over the rafters, and I could tighten or loosen them however I wanted, give them a long leash or a short one.

And they never resisted, even when they realized what was in store for them when you got them into this building? What was it? A house?

I don't remember.

*Did they resist, Basil? Seems as if it might have been dif-
ficult to restrain them in such an elaborate fashion while
you're still holding them at gunpoint.*

I've always had this fantasy of having someone watch.
Basil didn't answer the question. *Then having sex after it
was over. Having sex for hours with the body right there on
the same mattress.*

Sex with the dead body or sex with another person?

*I was never into that. That's not for me. I like to hear
them. I mean, it had to hurt like hell. Sometimes their shoulders got dislocated. Then I'd give them enough slack to use
the bathroom. That was the part I didn't like. Emptying
the bucket.*

What about their eyes, Basil?

Well, let's see. No pun intended.

Dr. Wesley didn't laugh, and that annoyed Basil a little.

*I'd let them dance around at the end of their rope, no pun
intended. Don't you ever smile? I mean, come on, some of
this is funny.*

*I'm listening to you, Basil. I'm listening to every word
you say.*

That was good, at least. And he was. Dr. Wesley was listening and thought every word was important and fascinating, thought Basil was the most interesting, original person
he had ever interviewed.

As soon as I was going to have sex with them, he continued, *that's when I'd do their eyes. You know, if I'd been
born with a decent-sized dick, none of this would have
been necessary.*

They were conscious when you blinded them.

*If I could have given them some gas and knocked them out
while I was performing the surgery, I would have. I didn't particularly like them screaming and jerking all over the place.
But I couldn't have sex with them until they were blind. I explained it to them. I'd say, I'm really sorry I got to do this to
you, okay? I'll be as quick as I can. It's going to hurt a little.*

*Isn't that funny? It's going to hurt a little. Every time
somebody says that to me, I know it's going to hurt like a
bitch. Then I'd tell them I was going to untie them so we*

*could have sex. I said if they tried to get away or do anything
stupid, I was going to do even worse things to them than I already did. That's it. We had sex.*

How long would this go on?

You mean the sex?

*How long did you keep them alive and have sex
with them?*

*Depended. If I liked having sex with them, sometimes I'd
keep them around for days. I think the longest time was ten
days. But that didn't turn out to be a good thing because she
got infected real bad and it was disgusting.*

*Did you do anything else to them? Anything besides
blinding them and having sex?*

I experimented. Some.

Did you ever engage in torture?

I'd say stabbing somebody's eyes out . . . well, Basil
replied, and now he wishes he hadn't said it.

It opened a whole new line of questioning. Dr. Wesley
started in on knowing right from wrong and comprehending
the suffering Basil was causing another human being, that if
he knew something was torture, then he was cognizant of
what he was doing at the time he was doing it and also upon
reflection. That's not exactly the way he said it, but that's
what he was getting at. Just the same old song and dance he
heard in Gainesville when the shrinks were trying to figure
out if he was competent to stand trial. He never should have
let them know he was. That was stupid, too. A forensic psychiatric hospital is a five-star hotel compared to prison, especially if you're on death row, sitting around in your tiny,
claustrophobic cell feeling like Bozo the clown in your blue-
and-white-striped pants and orange T-shirt.

Basil gets up from his steel bed and stretches. He pretends he's not interested in the camera high up on the wall.
He never should have admitted that sometimes he fantasized
about killing himself, that his preferred way would be to cut
his wrists and watch himself bleed, drip, drip, drip, watch
the puddle form on the floor, because it would remind him of
his former pleasant preoccupations with how many women?

He's lost count. It might have been eight. He told Dr. Wesley eight. Or was it ten?

He stretches some more. He uses the steel toilet and returns to the bed. He opens the most recent *Field & Stream*, looks at page 52, at what's supposed to be a column about a hunter's first .22 rifle and happy memories of rabbit and possum hunting, of fishing in Missouri.

This page 52 isn't the real one. The real page 52 was torn out and scanned into a computer. Then, in an identical font and identical format, a letter was embedded into the magazine's text. The scanned page 52 was carefully reinserted into the magazine, a little glue used, and what looks like a chatty column on hunting and fishing is a clandestine communication intended for Basil.

The guards don't care about inmates getting fishing magazines. They aren't likely to even flip through them, not boring magazines that are completely devoid of sex and violence.

Basil gets under the covers, turning on his left side diagonally on the bed, his back to the camera, just like he always does when he needs to relieve his sexual tension. He reaches under the thin mattress and pulls out strips of white cotton from two pairs of white boxer shorts that he has been ripping up all week.

Under the sheets, he begins a tear with his teeth, then rips. Each strip gets tightly tied to what has become a six-foot-long knotted rope. He has enough fabric left for two more strips. He tears with his teeth and rips. He breathes heavily and rocks himself a little as if relieving his sexual tension, and he rips and he ties a strip to the rope, and then he ties on the last one.

62

Inside the Academy's computer center, Lucy sits before three large video screens, reading e-mails as she restores them to the server.

What she and Marino have discovered so far is that before he began his fellowship, Joe Amos was communicating with a television producer who claimed to be interested in developing yet another forensic show for one of the cable networks. For his input, Joe was promised five thousand dollars per episode, assuming the shows ever make it on the air. Apparently, Joe started getting brilliant ideas in late January, about the time Lucy got sick while testing new avionics in one of her helicopters, fled to the ladies' room and forgot her Treo. At first he was subtle about it, plagiarizing hell scenes. Then he became blatant, outright stealing them as he went into databases to his heart's content.

Lucy restores another e-mail, this one dated February 10, a year ago. It is from last summer's intern, Jan Hamilton, who got the needle stick and threatened to sue the Academy.

Dear Dr. Amos,

I heard you on Dr. Self's radio show the other night and was fascinated by what you had to say about the National Forensic Academy. Sounds like an amazing place, and by the way, congratulations on being awarded a fellowship. That's incredibly impressive. I wonder if you could help me get an internship there for the summer. I am studying nuclear biology and genetics at Harvard and want to be a forensic scientist, specializing in DNA.

```
I'm attaching a file that has my photograph and
other personal information.
Jan Hamilton.

P.S. The best way to reach me is at this address.
My Harvard account is firewall-protected, and I
can't use it unless I'm on campus.
```

"Shit," Marino says. "Holy shit," he says.

Lucy restores more e-mails, opens dozens of them, e-mails that become increasingly personal, then romantic, then lewd exchanges between Joe and Jan that continued during her internship at the Academy, leading up to an e-mail he sent her early this past July when he suggested she try a little creativity with a hell scene that was scheduled to take place at the Body Farm. He arranged for her to stop by his office for hypodermic needles and *whatever else you might feel like getting stuck with.*

Lucy has never seen the film of the hell scene that went so wrong. She has never seen films of any hell scenes. Until now, she wasn't interested.

"What's it called?" she says, getting frantic.

"Body Farm," Marino says.

She finds the video file and opens it.

They watch students walking around the dead body of one of the most obese men Lucy has ever seen. He is on the ground, fully clothed in a cheap, gray suit, probably what he had on when he dropped from sudden cardiac arrest. He is beginning to decompose. Maggots teem over his face.

The camera angle shifts to a pretty young woman digging in the dead man's coat pocket, turning toward the camera, withdrawing her hand, yelling—yelling that she's been stuck through her glove.

Stevie.

Lucy tries to reach Benton. He doesn't answer. She tries her aunt and can't get hold of her. She tries the neuroimaging lab, and Dr. Susan Lane answers the phone. She tells Lucy that both Benton and Scarpetta should be here any minute, are scheduled to be with a patient, with Basil Jenrette.

"I'm e-mailing a video clip to you," Lucy says. "About three years ago, you scanned a young female patient named Helen Quincy. I'm wondering if it might be the same person in the video clip."

"Lucy, I'm not supposed to."

"I know, I know. Please. It's really important."

Wonk ... wonk ... wonk ... wonk ...

Dr. Lane has Kenny Jumper in the magnet. She is in the middle of his structural MRI, and the lab is full of the usual racket.

"Can you go into the database?" Dr. Lane asks her research assistant. "See if we might have scanned a patient named Helen Quincy. Possibly three years ago? Josh, keep going," she says to the MRI tech. "Can you stand it without me for a minute?"

"I'll try." He smiles.

Beth, the research assistant, is typing on the keyboard of a computer on the back counter. It doesn't take her long to find Helen Quincy. Dr. Lane has Lucy on the phone.

"Do you have a photograph of her?" Lucy asks.

WOP WOP WOP WOP. The sound of the gradients acquiring images reminds Dr. Lane of the sonar in a submarine.

"Only of her brain. We don't photograph patients."

"Have you looked at the video clip I just e-mailed to you? Maybe it will mean something."

Lucy sounds frustrated, disappointed.

TAP-TAP-TAP-TAP-TAP ...

"Hold on. But I don't know what you think I can do with it," Dr. Lane says.

"Maybe you remember her when she was there? You were working there three years ago. You or someone scanned her. Johnny Swift was doing a fellowship there at the same time. May have seen her, too. Reviewed her scans."

Dr. Lane isn't sure she understands.

"Maybe you scanned her," Lucy persists. "Maybe you

saw her three years ago, might remember her if you saw a picture . . ."

Dr. Lane wouldn't remember. She's seen so many patients, and three years is a long time.

"Hold on," she says again.

BAWN . . . BAWN . . . BAWN . . . BAWN . . .

She moves to a computer terminal and goes into her e-mail without sitting down. She opens the file of the video clip and plays it several times, watches a pretty young woman with dark blond hair and dark eyes looking up from the dead body of an enormously fat man whose face is covered with maggots.

"Good Lord," Dr. Lane says.

The pretty young woman in the video clip looks around, right into the camera, her eyes looking right at Dr. Lane, and the pretty young woman digs her gloved hand in the pocket of the fat, dead man's gray jacket. There the clip stops, and Dr. Lane plays it again, realizing something.

She looks through the Plexiglas at Kenny Jumper and can barely see his head at the other end of the magnet. He is small and slender in baggy, dark clothes, ill-fitting boots, sort of homeless-looking but delicately handsome with dark-blond hair pulled back in a ponytail. His eyes are dark, and Dr. Lane's realization gets stronger. He looks so much like the girl in the photograph, they could be brother and sister, maybe twins.

"Josh?" Dr. Lane says. "Can you do your favorite little trick with SSD?"

"On him?"

"Yes. Right now," she says tensely. "Beth, give him the CD of the Helen Quincy case. Right now," she says.

63

Benton finds it a little curious that a taxicab is parked outside the neuroimaging lab. It is a blue SUV taxi, and no one is inside it. Maybe it is the taxi that was supposed to pick up Kenny Jumper at the Alpha & Omega Funeral Home, but why is the taxi parked here, and where is the driver? Near the taxi is the white prison van that transported Basil here for his five o'clock interview. He's not doing well. He says he's feeling very suicidal and wants to quit the study.

"We have so much invested in him," Benton says to Scarpetta as they walk inside the lab. "You have no idea how bad it is when these people drop out. Especially him. Dammit. Maybe you can be a good influence on him."

"I'm not even going to comment," she says.

Two prison guards stand outside the small room where Benton will talk to Basil, try to talk him out of quitting PREDATOR, talk him out of killing himself. The room is part of the MRI suite, the same room Benton has used before when he talks to Basil. Scarpetta is reminded that the guards aren't armed.

She and Benton walk into the interview room. Basil is sitting at the small table. He isn't restrained, not even with plastic flex-cuffs. She likes PREDATOR even less and she didn't think that was possible.

"This is Dr. Scarpetta," Benton says to Basil. "She's part of the research study team. Do you mind if she sits in?"

"That would be nice," Basil says.

His eyes seem to spin. They are eerie. They seem to spin as they look at her.

"So tell me what's going on with you," Benton says as he and Scarpetta sit down at the table.

"You two are close," Basil says, looking at her. "I don't blame you," he says to Benton. "I tried to drown myself in the toilet and you know what's funny about that? They didn't even notice. Isn't that something. They have this camera spying on me all the time and when I try to kill myself no one sees it."

He is wearing jeans, tennis shoes and a white shirt. He doesn't have a belt. He has no jewelry. He isn't at all what Scarpetta imagined. She thought he would be bigger. He is small and insignificant-looking, slightly built, thinning blond hair, not ugly, just insignificant. She supposes that when he approached his victims, they probably felt the way she does, at least at first. He was nothing, just some nobody with a bland smile. The only thing about him that stands out are his eyes. Right now, they are strange and un-settling.

"Might I ask you a question?" Basil says to her.

"Go ahead." She isn't particularly nice to him.

"If I met you on the street and told you to get into my car or I would shoot you, what would you do?"

"Let you shoot me," she says. "I wouldn't get into your car."

Basil looks at Benton and shoots his finger at him as if it's a gun. "Bingo," he says. "She's a keeper. What time is it?"

There is no clock in the room.

"Eleven minutes after five," Benton says. "We need to talk about why you feel like killing yourself, Basil."

Two minutes later, Dr. Lane has the Surface Shading Display of Helen Quincy on the computer screen. Next to it is the Surface Shading Display of the so-called normal who is in the magnet.

Kenny Jumper.

Not a minute ago, he asked over the intercom what time it

was. Then, not a minute later, he started getting restless, complaining.

BWONK-BWONK-BWONK . . . in the MRI suite as Josh rotates Kenny Jumper's pale, hairless, eyeless head. It ends raggedly just below the jaw, as if he has been decapitated, because of the signal ending, because of the coil. Josh rotates the image some more on one screen, tries to duplicate the exact position of Helen Quincy's hairless, eyeless, decapitated-looking image on another screen.

"Oh boy," he says.

"I think I need to get out," Kenny's voice sounds over the intercom. "What time is it now?"

"Oh boy," Josh says to Dr. Lane as he rotates the image some more, looking from one screen to the other.

"I have to get out."

"A little more that way," Dr. Lane is saying, looking from one screen to the other, back and forth between the pale, eyeless, hairless heads.

"I need to get out!"

"That's it," Dr. Lane says. "Oh, my."

"Whoa!" Josh says.

Basil is getting increasingly restless, glancing at the closed door. Again, he asks what time it is.

"Five seventeen," Benton says. "You supposed to be somewhere?" he adds ironically.

Where would Basil be? In his cell, no place good. He's lucky to be here. He doesn't deserve it.

Basil pulls something out of his sleeve. At first Scarpetta can't tell what it is and doesn't understand what is happening, but then he is out of his chair and around to her side of the table and the thing is around her neck. Long and white and thin and around her neck.

"You try one fucking thing and I tighten it like this!" Basil says.

She is aware of Benton standing up and yelling at him. She feels her pulse pounding. Then the door opens. Then

Basil is pulling her outside the room and her pulse is pounding and she has her hands around her neck and he has the long, white thing tight around her neck and is pulling her and Benton is shouting and the guards are shouting.

64

Three years ago at McLean, Helen Quincy was diagnosed with dissociative identity disorder.

She may not have fifteen or twenty separate and autonomous alter personalities, maybe just three or four or eight. Benton continues explaining a disorder that is caused by a person splitting with his or her primary personality.

"An adaptive response to overwhelming trauma," Benton says as he and Scarpetta drive west toward the Everglades. "Ninety-seven percent of people diagnosed with it were sexually or physically abused or both, and women are nine times more likely to suffer DID than men," he says as the sun turns the windshield white and Scarpetta squints in the glare, despite her sunglasses.

Far ahead, Lucy's helicopter hovers over an abandoned citrus orchard, a parcel of real estate still owned by the Quincy family—Helen's uncle, specifically. Adger Quincy. Canker struck the orchard some twenty years ago, and all the grapefruit trees were cut down and burned. Since then, the orchard has sat, overgrown, with its falling-down house, an investment, an eventual housing development. Adger Quincy is still alive, a slight man, rather unimpressive in appearance, extremely religious—a Bible-banger, as Marino puts it.

Adger denies that anything unusual happened when Helen was twelve and went to live with him and his wife while Florrie was hospitalized at McLean. Adger says, as a matter of fact, he was quite attentive to the misguided, uncontrollable young girl *who needed to be saved* when she lived with them.

I did what I could, did the best I could, he said when Marino taped yesterday's interview with him.

How did she know about your old orchard, your old house? was one of the questions Marino asked him.

Adger wasn't inclined to talk about it much, but he did say that now and then he drove twelve-year-old Helen to the old, abandoned orchard so he could *check on things.*

What things?

To make sure it wasn't being vandalized or anything.

What was there to vandalize? Ten acres of burned-down trees and weeds and a falling-down house?

There's not a thing wrong with checking on things. And I would pray with her. Talk to her about the Lord.

"The fact that he said it that way," Benton comments as he drives and Lucy's helicopter seems to float down like a feather, about to land, far off over the abandoned orchard that Adger still owns, "indicates he knows he did something wrong."

"The monster," Scarpetta says.

"We'll probably never know exactly what he and perhaps others did to her," Benton says, subdued as he drives, his jaw set in a hard way.

He's angry. He's upset by what he suspects.

"But this much is obvious," he goes on. "Her various entities, her alters, were her adaptive response to unbearable trauma when there was no one to turn to, the same sort of thing you find in some survivors of concentration camps."

"The monster."

"A very sick man. Now a very sick young woman."

"He shouldn't get away with it."

"I'm afraid he already has."

"I hope he goes to hell," Scarpetta says.

"He's probably already in it."

"Why must you defend him?" She looks over at him and absently rubs her neck.

It is bruised. It is still tender, and every time she touches it, she remembers Basil grabbing her with a homemade white-cloth ligature, briefly occluding the vessels that supply blood, and therefore oxygen, to the brain. She passed out. She is fine. She wouldn't be if the guards hadn't gotten Basil off her as quickly as they did.

He and Helen are safely tucked away at Butler. Basil is no longer Benton's PREDATOR dream subject. Basil won't be visiting McLean anymore.

"I'm not defending him. I'm trying to explain it," Benton says.

He slows down on South 27 near an exit that leads to a CITGO truck stop. He turns right onto a narrow dirt road and stops the car. A rusting chain stretches across the dirt road, and there are a lot of tire tracks. Benton gets out and unhooks the thick, rusting chain. It clanks when he tosses it to one side. He drives through, stops, gets out again, and puts the chain back the way it was. The press, the curious, don't know what's going on out here yet. Not that a rusting chain will stop the unwelcome and uninvited. But it can't hurt.

"Some people say once you've seen a case or two of DID, you've seen them all," he says. "I happen to disagree, but for something so incredibly complicated and bizarre, the symptoms are remarkably consistent. A dramatic transformation when one alter becomes another, each dominant, each determining behavior. Facial changes, changes in posture, gait, mannerisms, even dramatic alterations of pitch, voice, speech. A disorder often associated with demon possession."

"Do you think Helen's alters—Jan, Stevie, whoever paraded as a citrus inspector and shot people to death and God knows who else she is—are aware of each other?"

"When she was at McLean, she denied she was a multiple, even when staff repeatedly witnessed her transforming into alters right in front of them. She suffered auditory and visual hallucinations. On occasion, one alter talked to another right in front of the clinician. Then she was Helen Quincy again, sitting politely, sweetly, in her chair, acting like the psychiatrist was the crazy one for believing she had multiple personalities."

"I wonder if Helen ever emerges anymore," Scarpetta says.

"When she and Basil killed her mother, she changed her identity to Jan Hamilton. That was utilitarian, not an alter,

Kay. Don't even think about Jan as a personality, if you understand what I'm saying. It was just a phony ID that Helen,
Stevie, Hog and who-knows-what hid behind."

Dust billows up as they bump over the overgrown dirt
road, a dilapidated house in the distance, weeds and
brush everywhere.

"I suspect that, figuratively speaking, Helen Quincy
stopped existing when she was twelve," Scarpetta says.

Lucy's helicopter has settled in a small clearing, the
blades still turning as she shuts down the engine. Parked
near the house are a removal-service van, three marked police cruisers, two Academy SUVs and Reba's Ford LTD.

The Sea Breeze Resort is too far inland to catch a breeze
from the sea, and it isn't a resort. There isn't even a swimming pool. According to the man at the desk inside the dingy
front office with its rattling air conditioner and plastic
plants, long-term rentals get special discounts.

He says Jan Hamilton kept odd hours, disappearing for
days, especially of late, and at times she dressed strangely.
Sexy one minute, sort of in drag the next.

My motto? Live and let live, the man at the desk said
when Marino tracked Jan here.

It wasn't hard. After she crawled out of the magnet and
the guards had Basil on the floor and it was all over, she cow-
ered in a corner and started to cry. She wasn't Kenny Jumper
anymore, had never heard of him, denied having any idea
what anybody was talking about, including knowing Basil,
including why she was on the floor inside the MRI suite at
McLean Hospital in Belmont, Massachusetts. She was very
polite and cooperative with Benton, gave him her address,
said she worked as a part-time bartender in South Beach, a
restaurant called Rumors owned by a very nice man named
Laurel Swift.

Marino crouches before the open closet. It doesn't have a
door, just a rod for hanging clothes. On the soiled carpet are
stacks of clothing, neatly folded. He goes through them with

gloved hands, sweat dripping in his eyes, the window-unit air conditioner not doing a very good job.

"One long black coat with a hood," he says to Gus, one of Lucy's Special Ops agents. "Sounds familiar."

He hands the folded coat to Gus, who places it inside a brown paper bag, writes the date and item and where it was found. There are dozens of brown paper bags by now, all sealed with evidence tape. Basically, they are packing up Jan's entire room. Marino wrote the search warrant from hell: *Put everything in it and the kitchen sink,* in his words.

His big, gloved hands sort through more clothing, shabby, baggy men's clothing, a pair of shoes with the heels cut out, a Miami Dolphins cap, a white shirt with Department of Agriculture on the back, that's all, not the full name of the Florida Department of Agriculture and Consumer Services, just Department of Agriculture, the block printing hand-done with what Marino guesses was a Sharpie.

"How could you not know he was really a she?" Gus asks him, sealing another bag.

"You weren't there."

"I'll take your word for it," Gus says, holding out his hand, waiting for the next thing, a pair of black panty hose.

Gus is armed and dressed in fatigues, because that is how Lucy's Special Ops agents always dress, even if it is unnecessary, and on an eighty-five-degree day when the suspect, a twenty-year-old girl, is safely locked up in a state hospital in Massachusetts, it probably wasn't necessary to deploy four Special Ops agents to the Sea Breeze Resort. But that was what Lucy wanted. That was what her agents wanted. No matter how detailed Marino has been in his explanation of what Benton relayed to him about Helen's different personalities or alters, as Benton calls them, the agents don't quite believe there aren't other dangerous people running around, that maybe Helen has accomplices—like Basil Jenrette, they point out—who are real.

Two of her agents are going through a computer on a desk by a window that looks out over the parking lot. There is also a scanner, a color printer, packages of magazine-grade paper and half a dozen fishing magazines.

Planks on the front porch are warped, some of them rotted, others missing, exposing the sandy soil beneath the one-story paint-peeled frame house not far from the Everglades.

It is quiet, save for the distant traffic that sounds like gusting wind, and the scraping and stabbing of shovels. Death pollutes the air and in the heat of the late afternoon seems to shimmer darkly in waves that get worse the closer one gets to the pits. The agents, the police and scientists have found four of them. Based on soil disturbances and discoloration, there are more.

Scarpetta and Benton are in the foyer just inside the door, where there is a fish tank and a large, dead spider curled up on a rock. Leaning against a wall is a Mossberg twelve-gauge shotgun and five boxes of cartridges. Scarpetta and Benton watch two men, sweating in suits and ties and blue nitrile gloves, push a stretcher bearing the pouched remains of Ev Christian, wheels clattering. They stop at the wide-open door.

"When you get her to the morgue," Scarpetta says to them, "I'm going to need you to come right back."

"We figured that. I believe it's the worst thing I've ever seen," one attendant says to her.

"You got your work cut out for you," says the other.

They fold up the legs with loud clacks and carry the stretcher bearing Ev Christian toward the dark-blue van.

"How's this going to end up in court?" one of the attendants thinks to ask from the bottom of the steps. "I mean, if this lady's a suicide, how do you charge someone with murder if it's a suicide?"

"We'll see you shortly," Scarpetta says.

The men hesitate, then move on, and she watches Lucy appear from the back of the house. She has on protective clothing and dark glasses but has taken off her face mask and gloves. She trots toward the helicopter, the one where she left her Treo not long after Joe Amos began his fellowship.

"There's really nothing to say she didn't do it," Scarpetta

says to Benton as she opens packets of disposable protective clothing—a set for her, a set for him—and by *she,* Scarpetta means Helen Quincy.

"Nothing to say she did, either. They're right." Benton stares at the stretcher and its grim cargo as the attendants clack open the aluminum legs again so they can open the back of the van. "A suicide that's a homicide, the perpetrator DID. The lawyers will have a field day."

The stretcher lists on the sandy, weed-choked soil, and Scarpetta worries it might fall over. It's happened before, a pouched body lands on the ground, very inappropriate, very disrespectful. She is getting more anxious by the moment.

"The autopsy will probably show she is a death by hanging," she says, looking out at the bright, hot afternoon and the activity in it, watching Lucy get something out of the back of the helicopter, an ice chest.

The same helicopter where she left her Treo, an act of forgetfulness that in many ways started everything and led everybody here to this hellhole, this plague pit.

"That's probably all it will show in terms of what killed her," Scarpetta is saying. "But the rest of it is a different story."

The rest of it is Ev's pain and suffering, her naked, bloated body tethered by ropes looped over a rafter, one of them looped around her neck. She is covered by insect bites and rashes, her wrists and ankles with fulminating infections. When Scarpetta palpated her head, she felt bits of fractured bone move beneath her fingers, the woman's face pulverized, her scalp lacerated, contusions all over her, reddish abraded areas inflicted at or around the time of death. Scarpetta suspects that Jan or Stevie or Hog, or whoever she was when she tortured Ev inside this house, kicked Ev's body severely and repeatedly after discovering she had hanged herself. On Ev's lower back, belly and buttocks are faint impressions in the shape of a shoe or boot.

Reba comes around from the side of the house and carefully climbs the rotting steps and picks her way across the porch. She is bright white in her disposable clothing and pushes up her face mask. She's carrying a brown paper bag, neatly folded at the top.

"There's some black plastic trash bags," she says. "In a separate grave, a shallow one. And a couple Christmas ornaments inside. Broken but it looks like Snoopy in a Santa cap and maybe Little Red Riding Hood."

"That's how many bodies?" Benton says, and he has gone into his mode.

When death, even the most vile death, is in his face, he doesn't flinch. He appears rational and calm. He almost appears not to care, as if the Snoopy and Little Red Riding Hood ornaments are just more information to file away.

He might be rational but he isn't calm. Scarpetta saw the way he was in the car just a few hours ago and more recently inside this house when they began to realize far more clearly the nature of the original crime, the one that happened when Helen Quincy was twelve. In the kitchen is a rusting refrigerator, and in it are Yoo-hoo chocolate drinks, Nehi grape and orange sodas and a carton of chocolate milk with expiration dates that go back eight years, when Helen was twelve and forced to stay with her aunt and uncle. There are dozens of pornographic magazines from that same period of time, suggesting that the devoutly religious Sunday-school teacher, Adger, quite likely brought his young niece out here not once. But often.

"Well, the two boys," Reba is saying, her face mask moving on her chin when she talks. "Looks to me like their heads are bashed in. But that's not my department," she says to Scarpetta. "Then some commingled remains. Nude it looks to me, but there's clothes in there, too. Not on them but in the pits, like maybe they dumped some of their victims in there and then just tossed in their clothing."

"Obviously, he killed more than he said," Benton says as Reba opens the paper bag. "Posed some, buried some."

She holds open the bag so Scarpetta and Benton can see the snorkel and dirty pink Keds sneaker, a girl's size, inside it.

"Matches the shoe up there on the mattress," Reba says.

"Found this one in a hole we assumed was going to have more bodies. Nothing in it but this." She indicates the snorkel, the pink shoe. "Lucy found it. I got not a clue."

"I'm afraid I probably do," Scarpetta says, lifting out the snorkel and the little girl's shoe with her gloved hands, imagining twelve-year-old Helen in that hole as dirt is being shoveled in, a snorkel her only means of air as her uncle tortured her.

"Shutting children in trunks, chaining them in basements, burying them with nothing but a hose leading to the surface," Scarpetta says as Reba looks at her.

"No wonder she's all these people," Benton says, not so stoic now. "Fucking bastard."

Reba turns away, stares off, swallowing. She gets hold of herself as she folds the top of the brown paper bag, slowly, neatly.

"Well," she says, clearing her throat. "We got cold drinks. We haven't touched anything. Didn't open the trash bags in the pit with the Snoopy ornament, but by the feel and smell of them, there's body parts in there. One of them has a tear and you can see what looks to me like matted red hair—that kind of dyed henna red color? An arm and a sleeve. I think this one's dressed. The rest sure aren't. Diet Cokes, Gatorade and water. I'm taking orders. Or if you want something else, we can send someone. Well, maybe not."

She looks toward the back of the house, toward the pits. She keeps swallowing and blinking, her lower lip trembling.

"I don't think any of us are exactly socially acceptable right now," she adds, clearing her throat again. "Probably shouldn't be walking into a 7-Eleven smelling like this. I just don't see how . . . if he did that, we got to get him. They should do to him the same damn thing he did to her! Bury him alive only don't give him a goddamn snorkel to breathe! Cut his fucking balls off!"

"Let's get suited up," Scarpetta says quietly, to Benton.

They unfold disposable white coveralls, start putting them on.

"No way we can prove it," Reba says. "No damn way."

"Don't be so sure of that," Scarpetta says, handing Benton shoe covers. "He left an awful lot in there, never thinking we'd come looking."

They cover their hair with caps and go down the warped old steps, pulling on gloves, covering their faces with the face masks.